THE CRUSADER'S HANDFAST

A Medieval Romance

Claire Delacroix

Books by Claire Delacroix

Time Travel Romances
ONCE UPON A KISS
THE LAST HIGHLANDER
THE MOONSTONE
LOVE POTION #9

Medieval Romances
ROMANCE OF THE ROSE
HONEYED LIES
UNICORN BRIDE
THE SORCERESS
ROARKE'S FOLLY
PEARL BEYOND PRICE
THE MAGICIAN'S QUEST
UNICORN VENGEANCE
MY LADY'S CHAMPION
ENCHANTED
MY LADY'S DESIRE

The Bride Quest
THE PRINCESS
THE DAMSEL
THE HEIRESS
THE COUNTESS
THE BEAUTY
THE TEMPTRESS

The Rogues of Ravensmuir
THE ROGUE
THE SCOUNDREL
THE WARRIOR

The Jewels of Kinfairlie
THE BEAUTY BRIDE
THE ROSE RED BRIDE
THE SNOW WHITE BRIDE
The Ballad of Rosamunde

The True Love Brides
THE RENEGADE'S HEART
THE HIGHLANDER'S CURSE
THE FROST MAIDEN'S KISS

THE WARRIOR'S PRIZE

The Brides of Inverfyre
THE MERCENARY'S BRIDE
THE RUNAWAY BRIDE

The Champions of St. Euphemia
THE CRUSADER'S BRIDE
THE CRUSADER'S HEART
THE CRUSADER'S KISS
THE CRUSADER'S VOW
THE CRUSADER'S HANDFAST

Rogues & Angels
ONE KNIGHT ENCHANTED
ONE KNIGHT'S RETURN

The Brides of North Barrows
SOMETHING WICKED THIS WAY COMES
A DUKE BY ANY OTHER NAME

Short Stories and Novellas
An Elegy for Melusine
BEGUILED

Dear Reader;

One of the fun things about writing the *Champions of Saint Euphemia* series has been following the entangled threads of the story. Each character has witnessed different elements of the adventure and knows different things, and I've enjoyed pulling all those perspectives together. It soon became clear, though, that there were some story elements that were missing from all of the books, and that those were likely scenes you'd want to see. What actually happens when Gaston and Ysmaine arrive at his inherited holding? What has Millard done and how is all resolved?

More importantly, whose story would include these details? Ysmaine and Gaston had already found their happily-ever-after before their arrival at Gaston's inherited estate. The option of an extended epilogue didn't appeal to me. I had thought Bartholomew might witness events there, but he was itching to get back to the estate he should have inherited to set all to rights. (Plus, it was high time he met Anna.) Who would show us this side of the story?

I watch movies when I'm trying to solve plot riddles, and invariably they're movies I've seen many times before. I watch and knit and my thoughts wander a bit, in search of solutions. I was watching *Gosford Park*, which I enjoy because the servants know so much about their employers, yet their employers for the most part are oblivious to this, when the penny dropped. Servants are secret-keepers! Who knows more about Valeroy and local gossip than Ysmaine? Her maid Radegunde, of course. In the first scene I wrote from her point of view in this new project, I learned that Radegunde was very interested in Duncan, the man-at-arms in service to Fergus.

That's when I realized this series would have a fifth book. **The Crusader's Handfast** begins in Paris, after the reliquary has been safely delivered to the Paris Temple, and features the romance of Radegunde and Duncan. Their story involves the revelation of secrets, and the resolution of hidden conflicts. I like that these two ensure the futures of their respective employers from behind the scenes, and I also like that Radegunde's cheerfulness is so restorative for Duncan. In a way, their resilience and pragmatism makes them two of a kind, but their fates are not entirely their own. Are they star-crossed lovers? Or will the course of love run true?

The Crusader's Handfast was originally published in monthly installments but the entire story is now available in a single volume. You can either read it after the other four books, or after **The Crusader's Bride** and **The Crusader's Heart**.

As always, please follow my blog or subscribe to my monthly newsletter, **Knights & Rogues**, to keep up to date on all the news about my medieval romances. The newsletter contains advance notice of most sales on my books, as well as chances to win audiobooks, cover reveals, and updated news of releases.

Thank you for reading my books! I hope you enjoy Duncan and Radegunde's story!

All my best
Claire
http://delacroix.net

The Crusader's Handfast

MONDAY, AUGUST 24, 1187

Feast Day of Saint Ouen and Saint Bartholomew

Claire Delacroix

CHAPTER ONE

Paris

adegunde leaned back against the wooden door to her lady's chamber, listening to the laughter from within the room. Lady Ysmaine's merriment was followed by the rumble of her lord husband's chuckle, and the combination made Radegunde smile.

She was fiercely glad that her lady had found happiness after all the trials she had endured. Widowed twice yet still a maiden, Ysmaine had embarked upon a pilgrimage to Jerusalem with Radegunde by her side, only to be robbed by the men hired to defend her. The two women had been left impoverished. Such was the lady's will that they had continued to the Holy City. Though it had been an arduous journey, they had arrived there after a year of hardship.

Radegunde had to believe that the pilgrimage had achieved its objective, for Lady Ysmaine had been lifted from her knees in the Church of the Holy Sepulchre by Gaston, a Templar knight who left the military order to return to France and claim his inherited holding. Radegunde had liked the knight from the outset, for he saw Lady Ysmaine's merit even when she was at her lowest spirits and dressed in rags. He had been kind, and though Radegunde had been vexed with his refusal to consult with his wife on their journey west, all had come right in the end. It was clear to Radegunde on this night that the pair shared an affectionate match, and one that could only grow more ardent over the years to come.

While she was happy for her lady, there could be no more stark contrast with her own life than this. Radegunde had no man and no prospect of true love. Worse, almost two years of adventure had made her former life pale in comparison. While Lady Ysmaine embarked upon the life she had been raised to expect and did so with enthusiasm, Radegunde had little enthusiasm for her inevitable fate.

She knew her duty was to escort her lady to her new abode and that there she would undoubtedly be wed to some alemaker or other peasant perceived by her lord to be a good man. Radegunde had no doubt that Lord Gaston would take a man's measure correctly, but the remainder of her life would be spent within miles of her birthplace. Instead of adventure and travel, her life would become monotonous, as it had been before the Lady Ysmaine had resolved to visit Jerusalem. Radegunde doubted that love was in her future, merely duty and perhaps, comfort.

This left her discontent.

Radegunde supposed that Châmont-sur-Maine was slightly different from Valeroy, but not enough to satisfy her. She could return to her family home instead of continuing to serve Ysmaine, but that had even less appeal. In Valeroy, she would be at the command of her mother and brothers, and her destiny would not be much different than with Lady Ysmaine.

She would not be in command of her own future, either way. Once a comfortable life wedded to a good man would have pleased her well.

Now Radegunde yearned for more. Far more. She might have died several times over on their pilgrimage, which only increased her resolve to savor each and every moment of her life, however long it might be. She wished to journey afar, even though she had fallen so ill in Jerusalem. She wished to dance and fall in love with a man similarly discontent with a routine life. She also wished to find that joy abed her lady seemed to enjoy with her husband, or even shout with pleasure as the courtesan Christina had done in Venice. She wished to awaken each day, alive to the promise of new experience.

On this night, Radegunde felt particularly restless. It had been a day to remember, to be sure. She had aided in saving the sacred reliquary of Saint Euphemia! In the last moment, the prize had nigh been snatched away. She had ridden with all speed through the streets of Paris, entrusted with the priceless treasure herself, to see their party's goal achieved. She had ridden like the wind, fast by the side of the Templar Wulfe on his enormous destrier as he shouted for the road to clear. It had been more thrilling than any deed she had ever done, a feat fit for inclusion in a jongleur's tale.

Then she had been allowed to kiss the reliquary during the mass at the Paris Temple.

To retire contentedly now was impossible. Indeed, her lord and lady celebrated triumph in a most intimate way. Radegunde did not wish to quietly sleep outside their door. Not on this night! She yearned for revels and celebration.

A stolen kiss.

Dancing!

Some reckless deed committed in the company of an alluring man.

She closed her eyes, knowing precisely which man she would choose. Aye, the knight Fergus had a stalwart companion, one Duncan MacDonald, a warrior whose blade swung true and who was well wrought. Duncan missed little, and his eyes oft gleamed with humor. Radegunde liked how he smiled, how there was a little silver at his temples, how he kept his counsel and seemed always to anticipate those matters which surprised others.

There was a man accustomed to adventure, and one who would make an excellent companion when facing any such peril.

Sadly, he appeared to be smitten with Christina, the courtesan who had joined their party in Venice but had abandoned them earlier in Paris. Lady Ysmaine was convinced that Christina and the Templar Wulfe must be safely together this night.

Radegunde had not been able to discern Duncan's reaction to that before the party had separated. Fergus had accepted accommodation in the Paris Temple with his squires and Duncan, while Lord Gaston had taken a room at an inn for himself, his lady, his squire, Bartholomew, and Radegunde.

Would she see Duncan again? Radegunde supposed not and was disappointed by the realization. Fergus rode home to Scotland for his own nuptials, and surely Duncan would remain with him.

Indeed, Radegunde did not have to wait for her life to become dull again. It already had.

Still, she could not and would not sit alone.

Bartholomew was in the stables of the inn along with the steeds. Perhaps he would talk with her. Perhaps he would tell her more of Châmont-sur-Maine.

And its alemakers.

Radegunde wrinkled her nose, knowing a compromise when she heard it. Although Bartholomew was more taciturn than most of the men, he was better company than none at all.

The hour was not so late, although it was dark. Radegunde had smelled winter in the coolness of the evening air. Even though they stayed at an inn and Paris was said to be filled with vice, she had her small eating knife and was not afraid to defend herself. She pulled the knife from her belt and descended the shadowed stairs warily, though she doubted that many were awake. The inn catered to travelers and she knew well enough that after a day's ride and a hot meal, a warm pallet could be most enticing.

Radegunde was on the last flight of stairs, when she realized that someone was yet awake in the darkened kitchen. The doorway to that room was at the base of the stairs and to the right. There was a door opposite the stairs and she knew that portal led to the small courtyard between the inn and its stables.

She gripped the hilt of her knife, watchful, but proceeded at the same steady pace. There was little to be gained by letting whoever it was know that she was aware of his or her presence. After all, there was no light in the kitchen. It seemed whoever lurked there did not wish to be discovered.

Radegunde's heart skipped a little when she reached the second-to-last stair. Could she hear the breath of another? Was she being watched?

She supposed she was having the adventure she desired.

Radegunde descended the last steps boldly and reached for the door handle with her free hand. She managed only to lift the latch before she heard movement. A man seized her from behind even as she tried to spin in his grasp and shout.

She managed to emit only a small sound before he clapped a meaty hand over her mouth to silence her. He locked his other arm around her, trapping her arms against her side. When she writhed in his grip, he lifted her bodily from the floor. To her dismay, he was much larger and stronger than she.

And she could feel his erection against her buttocks.

Aye, she knew his intent well enough, but he would not find her to be easy prey. Radegunde deliberately shuddered, as if terrified, and let herself go limp. Let him think himself triumphant.

He did.

"Good fortune is mine this night," he whispered into her ear, his tone gloating. "For the finest prize fairly steps into my grasp." He chuckled even as his grip loosened slightly. Radegunde hoped he would become even more careless. She felt his fingers caress her cheek. "Perhaps our thoughts are as one. Perhaps you came to seek me out."

Radegunde stifled her revulsion. He smelled dirty and there was ale on his breath. She guessed that he was the man who had watched her from the shadows of the stables when their party arrived, for she had not liked the look of him even then.

"You need not fear that you will be sleepless once we have savored each other," he promised and made to haul her toward the kitchen.

But Radegunde had heard sufficient of his plans.

She bit his hand in the same moment that she drove her heel upward and into his groin. She stabbed backward with the knife and though it was small, she buried it into his torso hard enough that he howled in pain. He loosed his grip as he stumbled back into the kitchen. Radegunde twisted the knife before she spun out of his grasp.

"Bitch!" he cried, evidently shocked that she might spurn his charms.

Radegunde hauled open the door to the courtyard. Before she could step through it, her attacker roared and lunged after her. She spun to face him and lifted her knife again, more than ready to mar his face for so abusing her. Instead, she was seized from behind again. Someone grabbed a fistful of her kirtle and flung her bodily into the courtyard.

It was Duncan!

Radegunde nearly shouted in her delight. There was no other man she would have been more gladdened to see. Aye, there was something about Duncan, about his level green gaze, that sent a thrill through Radegunde and doubly so in this situation.

Duncan punched the astonished offender in the face, and Radegunde was most pleased to see blood spurt from that man's nose. He leaped toward Duncan with outrage in his eyes, but Duncan nimbly kicked the man's feet out from beneath him. The assailant fell heavily to the ground, hitting his head hard on the stone threshold. By the time he opened his eyes, Duncan was sitting upon his chest, a blade at his throat.

He was as quick as she had believed, and as unafraid to do what had to be done.

Radegunde decided she owed Duncan a kiss for his gallantry on this night.

If not more.

"Step aside," her attacker snarled. "The wench is mine. I saw her first."

Duncan laughed. "You should wish it to be so. This lass has been *mine* these three months, since first I glimpsed her in Outremer."

Radegunde's lips parted in shock and her heart skipped with delight. Truly? Their thoughts were as one?

Before she could hope overmuch, Duncan cast her a quick glance that might have been conspiratorial. Aye, she saw his argument. A man like this would never believe that a woman had any right to be unmolested much less to choose her lover. He would only abandon her if he believed she was already claimed by another.

Radegunde said naught.

For the moment.

Her heart skipped a beat at just the possibility of there being truth in Duncan's words.

"She came to meet me," the villain insisted.

"She came to meet *me*," Duncan corrected. "As arranged."

The man's eyes had widened at Duncan's words, but they widened yet more when Duncan cut a fine line across his throat.

"I would advise you not to touch what is mine," Duncan murmured as he moved the knife with infinite slowness. His blade must have been sharp. The wound was not deep yet it bled readily, leaving a line of red drops across the assailant's flesh.

It was clear that the lout had lost all his courage for he begged incoherently for mercy.

"If you so much as look at her again, you will taste my blade truly," Duncan vowed, danger in his tone. The other man nodded slightly, then Duncan stood. He looked down at the fallen villain, who caught his breath and glared at Radegunde.

Duncan kicked him in the groin again, then heaved him back into the kitchen and slammed the door behind him.

Radegunde wanted to cheer. That fiend would molest no other woman this night. Duncan strode to Radegunde, his eyes glinting with such satisfaction that her heart thundered. He wiped the blade of his knife upon his tabard, put it into the scabbard and offered his hand to her.

"Well met, lass," he said in loud voice. "I am glad that you came to me this night."

"As am I," Radegunde agreed, though she did not speak for the benefit of the fallen man. She placed Duncan's hand upon her waist and closed the distance between them, seeing surprise light his eyes. "I thank you for your aid," she whispered, then stretched to her toes and kissed him full on the lips.

This night, she would have her every desire.

It would have to suffice for the rest of her days and nights.

This night, she would have Duncan MacDonald.

Radegunde tasted Duncan's surprise and wished she possessed

the skill of the courtesan Christina to entice a man. Enthusiasm would have to suffice. She locked her hands in Duncan's hair, leaned against him and slanted her mouth over his.

When he froze, she feared that he would deny her touch and step away. She feared that he truly desired only Christina and that her charms were insufficient. But then he made a sound in his throat not unlike a growl of satisfaction, caught her close, and kissed her deeply. Radegunde's heart thundered with pleasure.

Duncan's kiss was fine, more splendid even than she had hoped, which was saying a great deal indeed.

Duncan had not lied to Radegunde.

Indeed, he had confessed more to her than had been his intention.

Oh, he *had* noted her at first sight at the Temple in Jerusalem, even when she was wan and thin. She had been ill beyond belief when their party had departed, and he had been concerned for her welfare. One so sickened should sleep abed, not ride across Palestine at full gallop. He had been skeptical that she would recover at all. But Radegunde and her lady Ysmaine had been determined not to slow the party, and Duncan had been impressed by the resilience of both.

It was clear that Radegunde was of a healthy disposition, for she had regained her color and her strength with remarkable speed. When the sparkle had reappeared in her dark eyes, he had been hard-pressed to hide his interest in the comely maid with her lively manner. She seemed a person who could find the joy in every circumstance, and he found her cheerfulness most beguiling.

It was his wont to see the shadow, after all, though he had not always been so inclined. He knew the reason for the change in his own manner well enough, and any thought of Gwyneth was sufficient reminder of how little he had to offer one such as Radegunde.

Duncan had no right to encourage any maiden's affections, or imply that his future was other than he knew it to be. Fergus would not have cared if Duncan wed again, but Duncan knew that no woman deserved a half measure.

Certainly not Radegunde.

But now she assaulted him with a kiss that addled his wits. Desire unfurled within him, filling him with a need he had not felt in years. She was so soft and welcoming, so vital, that he could have lost himself readily in her embrace.

It did not help that Duncan was so relieved to have arrived in timely fashion.

That she felt similarly had to be the impetus behind her kiss and he knew it well, but the salute became incendiary.

Indeed, it had been long since Duncan had been impetuous yet he could not find fault with the change. Radegunde's fingers were in his hair, her full breasts crushed against his chest and her lips were soft and sweet. He knew immediately that she had never kissed a man thus before, but she learned quickly, mimicking him with such ardor that she set his blood afire. He found himself gathering her closer, lifting her against himself, feasting upon her mouth—and wanting more than he had any right to take. It would have been far too easy to carry her to the stables and introduce her to the pleasures a man and woman could conjure together—and Duncan had no doubt that a night with Radegunde would be a marvel.

Yet at the same time, he felt protective of her innocence. She did not know the fire she kindled and he would not take advantage of that.

Duncan caught Radegunde's shoulders in his hands and broke their kiss with reluctance, putting distance between them. Even that did not diminish his ardor, for she looked both disheveled and enticing. It was her evident pleasure that tightened all within him. Her lips were ruddy and swollen, her eyes dancing with merriment, and Duncan knew he had never seen a more irresistible woman.

"What are you doing abroad?" he demanded, speaking sternly that she might be recalled to decorum. "You should be safely abed in your lady's chamber."

Radegunde grimaced, her expression unrepentant. Indeed, her gaze clung to his lips, and she licked her own once quickly in a way that did little to diminish Duncan's desire for her. "They are coupling, and nigh as noisy about it as Wulfe and Christina were in

11

Venice. On this night, I cannot meekly retire and listen to that."

Duncan fought a smile, for he could sympathize with her view. Again, though, he endeavored to speak of more practical matters than her fiery kiss. "You did well on this day," he said. "The reliquary would not have been saved without the efforts of you and your lady."

She smiled, then eyed him with an appreciation that made his heart skip a beat. "I enjoyed the adventure greatly." Radegunde's smile warmed as she surveyed him. "Though I would not mind having a similar reward as the one my lady savors this night."

Duncan stepped back, knowing he was already tempted to offer her as much. He could not believe she had spoken so boldly, but then, he had noted before that Radegunde was forthright. Indeed, that trait was part of what he admired about her. There was no guile with this maid: she spoke as she thought and he was a man enamored of honesty.

Honesty he would have, though he was certain it would dampen his reaction to her. "And so you came to seek Bartholomew?" Duncan's tone was dour, for it pricked his pride that this comely maiden must be seeking the affections of a man younger than himself. Her inevitable confession would aid his resolve, though.

But Radegunde laughed. "I did, but not for such a merry celebration as that. He was the sole person I could imagine might be nearby, and such was my mood that even his company would be better than naught at all."

Duncan was surprised by her words and her tone. "You are not intrigued with him?" He would have imagined that Radegunde would have been smitten with Gaston's squire, a handsome young man and one not even a decade her senior. It would have been natural for there to be attraction between they two, and perhaps fitting for them to make a match.

Evidently Radegunde did not see the matter the same way. "Oh, he is like my brothers," she said with disdain. "I have no doubt that he imagines he knows what is best for all the women around him. And what has he seen of the world to so instruct me? Nay, I will have a man who is seasoned in the ways of the world, one better suited to teach me much." Her smile was knowing and sent new heat through Duncan.

She meant him.

Radegunde flicked a glance to the stables, then leaned closer to confide in a mischievous whisper. "Plus, I am not certain that Bartholomew even likes women."

"What is this?" Had she been older or a man, Duncan would have been certain of her meaning. As it was, he found himself wondering how much of the world Radegunde knew.

"He is always talking to Laurent." She referred to the squire Fergus had taken on in Jerusalem. Duncan knew well enough that Laurent was truly a Saracen girl, who had sought to escape a marriage arranged by her family, but it seemed that Radegunde was unaware of that. She shook her head, her disdain clear. "Not only does he favor boys, but he likes filthy ones."

"You cannot be certain of his taste," Duncan countered with care.

"Nay?" She granted him a challenging glance. "Then why did Bartholomew blacken Kerr's eye when Kerr taunted Laurent that he was as small and weak as a girl?" She shrugged, not seeing the secret in her observation. "Only twice have I seen him stirred to anger, once over Kerr's comments and once over my lady's suggestion that she prepare a healing salve for her lord husband." She wrinkled her nose. "There was a silversmith with such appetites at Valeroy."

"There are few women Bartholomew might defend," Duncan noted. "For the Temple does not welcome women within its walls, and he has served there with Gaston for many years."

"Then I would expect him to be *fascinated* with women, not to regard us with suspicion." She shook her head. "Nay, it is boys for him." Her eyes sparkled with mischief. "Perhaps that silversmith is yet at Valeroy. I could introduce them."

Duncan chose not to note that the younger man might have learned a suspicion of women at the Temple, as well. He could not begin to think of a reply to her suggestion of an introduction so spoke of Bartholomew and Gaston instead, for he was certain there was naught between the two men save respect. "I understand that Gaston has raised him as a man might raise his own son. It is a good measure of his nature that he is loyal to that knight, and such loyalty could explain his doubts as to your lady's intentions. She did use a poison in her salve."

"True enough." Radegunde smiled at him. "Dare I hope that you came to this inn in search of me?" she teased, clearly enamored of the notion. Duncan found himself smiling, for it was a welcome change to flirt with a pretty maid. "I thought you intended to remain at the Temple with Fergus."

Duncan sighed in mock forbearance, and she was clearly amused by him. "Years living under the austerity of the Rule has proven to be my fill. I thought to find a thick pallet here, and some comfort. I am glad I came to the kitchen in search of a morsel to eat."

Radegunde delight was clear. She placed her hands on Duncan's chest and managed to appear both sweet and coy. His heart leaped at her proximity, though he compelled himself to keep from touching her. "What if I would offer you a morsel?" she whispered and Duncan was tempted as he had never been tempted before.

CHAPTER TWO

ou have already given too much," Duncan said gruffly, when he would have preferred to have taken all Radegunde offered—and more. He gripped her hands, lifting them away. Though he was tempted, he knew what was his to take—and what was not. "You cannot surrender more. It is not yours to give."

It was the wrong argument, he saw as much immediately, for her full lips tightened. "Then whose is it to give?" Radegunde flung out a hand in her frustration. "Shall I leave it to my mother to decide which oaf from the village shall take me as his own? Or is it Gaston's right to give me to a man in his holding, as one might give a loaf of bread or a brood of chickens?"

"You know it is Gaston's right, though assuredly he will consult with his lady wife." Duncan spoke mildly, but Radegunde's eyes flashed with alluring fire. He found himself fascinated by her reaction.

She caught his shirt in two fistfuls and leaned closer, her lips dangerously close to his own. He could not find it within himself to put her aside again, but simply stared down into her eyes.

"What if I do not want this fate?" she whispered. "What if I do not want to return to the life I knew before our pilgrimage?"

"You will be safe at Châmont-sur-Maine…"

"Aye, for I will never travel farther than Valeroy, where I was raised, for the rest of my life." Radegunde's dislike of that fact was clear. "I thought *you* might understand, Duncan. I do not wish to keep a home for some alemaker and bear his children, tending them and a garden and my lady until I die. I wish to see other places…"

"Lady Ysmaine may embark upon a pilgrimage again, or Gaston may need to visit other holdings."

Radegunde's eyes flashed. "I want to *live*, Duncan. I want to savor every day and feel all that can be felt, and see all of Christendom! I would even like to see the lands of the Saracens."

"You have been to Jerusalem," he felt compelled to note.

"I mean their lands beyond, where Prester John is said to voyage." Her eyes lit. "Where there are dragons!" She met his gaze, her expression rueful. "But none of that will happen."

He could not bear her disappointment, though he suspected that she was right. What power this maiden had over him, for he yearned to offer her the life she desired, though he knew that was folly.

He reminded himself that she might have been his daughter.

His niece or his cousin.

He was too old for Radegunde, and he had little to grant to her. Yet his reaction to her was far from paternal.

It had been a long time since he had wished to be younger.

It had been longer yet since he had yearned to offer more than was his to give.

"You must hope for the best, lass," Duncan suggested with false cheer, though he did not believe the future would differ from her prediction.

"Nay." Radegunde shook her head with resolve. "Within the week, I will be returned to the life I knew before our pilgrimage, and surely I will be trapped there for all my days and nights. I cannot change that, and I know it well. But I would fill the time between here and Châmont-sur-Maine with adventure and romance, in the hope that the memories will be sufficient to sustain me."

Duncan was intrigued by her determination to make change where she could. There was a mix of whimsy and practicality in her choice that he found enchanting. "What will you do?"

"First, I will dance," Radegunde said with resolve. "I will celebrate our triumph this day by dancing this night."

"Here?" Duncan gestured to the courtyard, thinking it far from a celebratory setting.

"Nay!" She turned shining eyes upon him. "We passed a fête on our way through the city."

"A celebration of the feast days of Saint Bartholomew and Saint Ouen." Duncan well recalled the crowd before the cathedral of Notre Dame.

"Will you take me to it? Will you dance with me, Duncan?" Without awaiting his reply, she continued in a rush. "I have no doubt that my lord and lady will linger here for a day or two, for they are most intent upon conceiving a son. I could sit outside their door and wait upon them, or I could claim this time as my own. Lady Ysmaine would understand that I need one more taste of the world before I become dull and dutiful."

Duncan could not imagine that Radegunde could ever become dull or fully dutiful.

"Not there," he said. "Such festivities are too dangerous."

"Is that not part of their appeal?"

The reckless edge to her tone fed his protectiveness anew. "I will not see you saved from one assailant only to fall prey to another."

Radegunde considered him, clearly disappointed in his response. "Perhaps I shall go and dance alone, if you will not take me."

"You have more sense than that, lass," Duncan chided. "In a city filled with whores, you should not walk the streets alone."

"Perhaps *you* should not walk the streets alone," she teased. He glowered at her, fighting his urge to return her smile, but his manner had no visible effect upon her mood. "I will dance this night, Duncan, and I would prefer to dance with you."

"Will that be the sum of your celebration?"

"Nay, I would seduce you afterward." She grinned. "Or perhaps you will seduce me." Again, she placed a hand upon his chest and leaned closer. "Would you rather forgo the dance?" she whispered wickedly. "I would surrender to you, Duncan. Indeed, I would learn what it is that made Christina shout with such vigor, and I wager you are a man who knows."

The suggestion so aroused Duncan that he felt less coherent than was his wont. "Your alemaker..." he began to protest, for he believed he should.

"May need instruction or encouragement." Radegunde was dismissive. "Show me what I might well be missing, Duncan."

"But..."

"No one will know. I will not tell, and I will feign innocence on the night in question."

"Radegunde!"

She laughed at his surprise. "My groom will not be innocent. What is sauce for the goose should be sauce for the gander."

Duncan turned away. "I will not do as much. No man of honor would..."

"Then take me to dance, Duncan. I beg it of you."

Duncan should have denied her and he knew it, but when Radegunde eyed him as if he were the finest man in all of Christendom, he could not deny her such a simple request.

After all, it seemed a reasonable compromise and was a far more prudent choice than ravishing her abed—though that notion did have an unholy appeal. He could also understand her urge to celebrate her part in their victory this day. The aftermath of success was a time for jubilation, not for a meek retirement to bed.

Aye, he had come to the inn because he felt a similar restlessness.

Dancing might be the best solution.

"You shall tell no one," Duncan insisted gruffly, but she laughed with such delight that he found himself smiling instead of being stern. "You shall do as I instruct you, lest there be more trouble, and we will only go to the local tavern..." he continued but Radegunde flung herself into his arms and kissed him to silence again.

4

Zounds, but the woman learned the art of seduction with astonishing speed. Her enthusiasm was nigh overwhelming, and Duncan found it beyond difficult to hold on to his senses and put distance between them again.

"I thank you, Duncan," she declared when she had made his blood sing. "I will never forget this, I promise you."

"There will be naught to recall if you do not follow instruction. I must ensure that you return hale to your mistress, and this is a city filled with vice."

"Aye, Duncan."

She was biddable now that she had won her way, so pleased that he could not forget the temptation of her other offer. The sooner they were in a tavern and surrounded by strangers, the better. Duncan led her to stables to tell Bartholomew of their plans. He had to ensure that the younger man would admit them to the courtyard upon their return, and Bartholomew readily agreed to do as much.

When they left the inn, Radegunde brimming with anticipation beside him, Duncan knew that he would never forget this night either.

Much less the maid who made him feel impulsive once again.

One night!

Duncan's hand was rough and warm around Radegunde's own and her heart was racing with delight. She had convinced him! And though he was protective of her, there was much in his kiss that made her hope she might persuade him to do more than dance with her.

Aye, she had not abandoned her other hope. To be seduced by Duncan would be a marvel indeed, she was certain of it, and a deed well worth the sacrifice of her maidenhead. Would she manage to convince him? She certainly meant to try.

Radegunde was glad she still wore her lady's old boots, for the streets were muddy enough to recall her mother's comments upon the mire of Paris. The small path outside the inn was dirt, and she was glad when they reached the wider avenue that led to the Temple. It was in the midst of being paved with stones and was much cleaner for that.

Her kirtle was faded after their journey to the east, and she reasoned she would not appear to be a rich target. Still, Duncan shed his cloak and cast it over her shoulders before they reached the wider street, perhaps to ensure that she did not offer temptation to another man. She inhaled deeply, for the cloak carried the welcome scent of his skin, and felt that she embarked on a forbidden adventure.

He still wore his mail hauberk and the dark tabard he had worn since she had met him. It bore no insignia, though the scabbards on his belt told all that anyone needed to know. His gloves were shoved into his belt, and he also wore boots. He strode back toward the Temple with purpose, and Radegunde was glad to be tall enough to be able to match his pace.

"The street of the jongleurs is ahead," he told her. "I noticed that there was a tavern on the corner and heard music playing."

Radegunde knew she had to make each moment in Duncan's company count. She wanted to know all about him, for she knew she would think about him—and this night—always.

"Tell me a secret, Duncan," she invited and he glanced her way with obvious surprise.

"A secret?"

Radegunde knew well enough that Duncan was not quick with confessions, and that he liked to keep whatever he knew to himself. "Aye, something only you know," she insisted. "Share it with me."

Duncan shook his head. "There are few things known by only one person, lass. I wonder whether there truly are any at all."

Radegunde doubted that was the case, when the person in question was Duncan, but she recognized the futility of pressing him. "Then confide in me something *few* people know."

He pursed his lips, considering this. "Will this be a fair exchange?"

"Of course. Naught less will do."

Duncan nodded and she wondered what he would admit. "You are wrong that Bartholomew prefers boys." He raised a finger when she would have argued. "Because Laurent is truly a girl named Leila."

Radegunde laughed aloud, and she saw immediately that her companion was pleased to have surprised her. "Truly?" At Duncan's nod, she laughed again. "Am I the last to know that secret?"

His smile was quick. "You are not the first, to be sure."

"When did you know?"

He shrugged. "In Jerusalem, before she joined our party."

Radegunde was fascinated. "Why did she join our party? She looks as if she might be Saracen."

"She is, by my understanding. A marriage had been arranged for her, and she did not wish to wed the man in question. She begged Bartholomew to let her accompany the party. He said he could not, but my lord Fergus overheard and intervened."

Radegunde exhaled in astonishment. She had never heard Duncan utter so many words in succession, and she marveled at her own ability to draw secrets from him.

Yet she could not fail to note that he did not share his own secret.

She realized that Duncan awaited her reaction. "I wish I had known. I should have talked to her more."

"I think she is wary of friendship."

"Her French is very good."

"Aye, by my understanding, she has aided Bartholomew at the stables of the Jerusalem Temple for some time. She is said to have a gift with horses."

"And does she?"

He slanted her a look. "Aye, she does. I was much impressed with her insight when we bought that palfrey in Venice. I know something of steeds myself, but she espied a weakness in the one I favored, and a weakness that might have cost us dearly."

Radegunde was intrigued. "How so?"

Duncan explained. "The steed would not have been able to make that run to the pass at such speed. If we had been compelled to abandon it, the coin would have been lost and the other steeds more heavily burdened."

"Which would have slowed our pace even more."

He eyed her anew. "You are smiling. What is amusing in this tale?"

"Naught. I simply admire that you would take counsel from a girl."

"I will take counsel from any soul who knows more of a matter than I do."

"And I admire that, as well." Radegunde gave his fingers a squeeze, liking how he caught his breath. She eased closer, ensuring that her breast was pressed against his arm, and noted the glitter in his eyes. Aye, Duncan was as aware of her as she was of him, and Radegunde found new promise in her hope of adventure beyond a night of dancing in Paris. "When did you first see the treasure?" she asked.

"Is that not another secret?"

"Nay, for I know you must have looked upon it."

He granted her a skeptical glance but she smiled and he complied with her request. "In Jerusalem, of course. I looked before we departed, when we were waiting upon Gaston."

"Because you were curious?"

Duncan's expression was quelling. "Because I will know why I risk my life, the better to resolve how vigorous my defense of any such entrusted baggage will be."

Radegunde nodded agreement. "I looked in Venice for the same reason, when we traded the bundles."

"That was clever," Duncan acknowledged. "None knew you had done it."

"I know!" She laughed up at him. "Not even you, the most observant of all the company."

"Not even me," he acknowledged ruefully.

Radegunde bit her lip, for she guessed the reason for that. Duncan had been openly interested in Christina, the courtesan, and she had joined their party at nigh the same time that Radegunde and Ysmaine had taken the reliquary. She was not certain whether she should mention as much, for she feared the conversation would falter.

But Duncan continued. "And disguising the reliquary as your lady's ripened belly was even more clever." He shook his head.

"Truly, we should have entrusted the parcel to you both from the outset."

Radegunde smiled at his praise. "But now it is safe, and the adventure is over."

"The quest is fulfilled," Duncan corrected quietly. "The adventure continues so long as you draw breath."

Radegunde chose not to argue about that. "Do you think Christina is safe?"

Duncan considered this. "I believe that Wulfe would do all in his power to ensure as much, and he is a formidable fighter."

It was not an absolute answer, but Radegunde supposed there could not be one. Emboldened by Duncan speaking so much to her, she dared to ask what she truly wished to know. "I thought you admired her most of all. Was that why you missed my exchange of the parcel?"

He spared her a hot glance, then hid his thoughts again. "And when am I to have a secret in exchange?" he asked lightly.

Radegunde was not truly surprised that he changed the subject. "It shall have to be a short one, as we are nigh there."

"You could owe me a boon."

Radegunde stretched up to whisper in his ear, endeavoring to be as bold as a courtesan. "If I owe you a boon, Duncan MacDonald, it will not be merely a secret."

Again, his gaze brightened. "A secret will suffice," he insisted, but his voice was more husky than it had been. She watched him swallow and noted how his gaze swept over her. She dared to hope she might succeed in tempting him.

Still she shook a playful finger at him. "Better, I will confide a secret about myself, rather than hiding behind the confidences of others."

"Indeed?" Duncan seemed to be biting back a smile.

Radegunde knew precisely how to surprise him. "Aye, and here it is. My lord Gaston is the first man I have seen fully naked."

Duncan blinked in his surprise, then looked down at her.

Radegunde felt her lips quirk. "And he has very fine…legs."

Duncan coughed, though she knew he did as much to disguise his laughter. "And what would you know about a man having fine

9

legs?"

"Oh, my mother admires men with fine legs, or so she has always insisted. At Valeroy, there are Scottish mercenaries in the employ of the lord. They wear lengths of plaid wool wrapped around their hips with one end cast over the shoulder, as well as boots and jerkins. They oft have long hair and beards, but it is their legs my mother professes to find most alluring. I confess that her affection has passed to me."

Duncan chuckled a little at this. "And your father?"

"He had fine legs, as well, according to my mother. She says she let him bed her to be able to twine her legs with his at night."

Duncan coughed again. "And what does your father say of this?"

Radegunde winced, for this wound was one that did not readily heal. "He is dead," she said flatly, wishing she were more adept at changing the subject.

Duncan turned to consider her, then, sympathy in his eyes. She knew that he had discerned the heat in her reaction. "I am sorry, Radegunde."

As much as she welcomed his compassion, Radegunde did not wish to dwell upon this loss. "I thank you, but it does not matter," she said quickly. "I have four brothers and we had no need of another man in our abode."

Duncan frowned, and she wondered whether her words had been too harsh.

There was an awkward silence between them. Radegunde feared that her confession had destroyed the amiability of their evening thus far. Indeed, she should have studied the arts of Christina more closely, for she made an uncommon muddle of this conversation!

To her relief, she had a sudden thought and turned upon Duncan. "But wait. You are a Scotsman, are you not?"

"Aye, I am, and some would say a mercenary as well." He spoke with undisguised pride.

Radegunde propped a hand upon her hip. "Then where is your plaid?"

"In my baggage. I thought it prudent to look more as other

men when we journeyed south. There are those who dislike my kinsmen."

Radegunde feigned disappointment. "I suppose it is too much, then, to hope that I might have a glimpse of your legs."

Duncan chuckled. "To determine whether they are sufficiently fine or not? You are a bold lass, to be sure," he charged but his tone was teasing. "I should not encourage you in such thinking, lest your mother have words for me."

"You will never meet her."

"Is she dead?"

Radegunde shook her head.

"Then you might be surprised, lass."

Before she could ask what he meant, Duncan drew her into the crowd gathered outside the tavern that had been their destination. Music spilled into the street along with laughter and she heard the pounding feet of the dancers inside. Her own feet itched. "Now, what shall it be? A cup of wine? A juggler's feat? Or a minstrel's tale?"

"A dance," Radegunde said firmly. "And then perhaps a cup of wine."

"One cup of wine is all you will have."

"You need not fear for my becoming drunk," Radegunde chided. "It will surely be thinned beyond belief."

"There is that," he muttered.

She considered the merrymakers on either side, her excitement rising as they entered the tavern. More than one man gave her a thorough perusal, and Radegunde's hand dropped to her knife again. She was prepared to defend her honor.

But Duncan locked his arm around her and drew her against his side in an embrace that appeared affectionate. Radegunde found it thrilling. "Remember that I have claimed you for this night," he murmured and his words made her blood heat. "It will be safer thus."

"Aye," Radegunde agreed and granted him a warm smile. His choice might ensure that she had her other wish this night. Indeed, that might be the reason for his suggestion. Could their thoughts be as one? Radegunde dared to hope as much.

11

She spun in his arms and noted his surprise with a smile. "The illusion must be well maintained," she murmured, then kissed his throat. She could feel his pulse leap beneath her lips.

"Temptress," Duncan whispered, his voice deliciously husky. "You know not what you do."

"On the contrary, I am the daughter of a wise woman," Radegunde retorted. "I know *precisely* what I do, Duncan." She pulled back to consider him. "The sole remaining question is what will *you* do?" She brushed her lips across his once more and was gratified to feel him catch his breath.

Then he slanted his mouth over hers, his kiss so demanding and possessive that it offered all the adventure Radegunde could want.

And more.

When he lifted his head, the company hollered and stamped in their approval. Radegunde saw only the green glitter of Duncan's eyes and felt the hard wall of his chest against her breasts. His arm was locked around her waist and he smiled down at her. "I have told you already, lass," he murmured for her ears alone. "I will dance with you, and no more."

Radegunde smiled, not nearly convinced that dancing would be the sum of all they did this night.

TUESDAY, AUGUST 25, 1187

*Feast Day of Saint Ebba
and of the martyr
Saint Eusebius of Rome*

Claire Delacroix

CHAPTER THREE

t was unlike Duncan to forget himself, just as it was unlike him to simply enjoy an evening with a pretty woman. The years in Palestine had been filled with challenge, hard labor, and the company of men much like himself. He saw only now that the burden of watching over Fergus had been heavier than he had realized.

How long had it been since he danced and sang? How long had it been since he flirted with a maiden as lively as Radegunde? On this night, Duncan felt free and unfettered, and the change was most welcome.

A part of that was certainly the influence of his joyous companion. Radegunde had a zest for life that made him more merry than was his wont, and her beauty was of the kind he appreciated best. Her loveliness came from a good heart, and a nature that gave her a welcome vitality. She was no fool, though, for he saw that she took note of every man with a dangerous gleam in his eye and was always aware of those immediately around her. Her hand dropped oft to her knife, and he knew she could defend herself if need be.

Indeed, she might have defeated the oaf from the kitchen, even if he had not happened upon their battle.

It was a novelty indeed to meet a woman who could fend for herself. Lady Ysmaine was stronger than most would guess, but Duncan guessed that a large factor in that noblewoman's survival had been the advice of her pragmatic maid.

A maid whose dark eyes twinkled so enticingly in her pleasure that Duncan wished to see her smile for all her days and nights.

They danced to the fiddler's tune, danced until their feet hurt and they had to stop to catch their breath. Radegunde was as exuberant as he might have expected and an excellent partner.

He gave more consideration than he knew he should to her impulsive offer. Aye, she was sweetly curved and danced like a fiend, so filled with vigor that he knew a night in her bed would be most satisfying.

Indeed, there would likely be no slumber at all.

They sang along with the minstrels who led familiar songs—although Duncan was not surprised that Radegunde had a fine rich voice, he was surprised that she knew the words to some of the more vulgar ditties. She laughed at his reaction, which meant he had unwittingly revealed his thoughts, her mischievous enjoyment of that tempting him to share yet more.

They had wine, at Duncan's expense, and he granted her a penny to tip a juggler whose feats made her eyes round with delight. He bought her a meat pie, hot from a baker's wagon, when they finally left the tavern and she insisted upon sharing it with him as they walked back to the inn.

The sky was indigo and the stars were bright overhead. Shutters were locked against the night at every abode they passed, and the music of the tavern faded steadily behind them. Great Paris might have been their own at this hour. Once the meat pie was gone and the crumbs brushed away, Radegunde put her hand in his own once more, as if it belonged nowhere else, and Duncan knew a welcome satisfaction.

He felt lighter and younger—although he knew the weight of his burdens would return to his shoulders soon enough. It was beyond restorative, though, to have a reprieve.

There was another detail they had in common. Ahead lay duty

and responsibility for him as well as for Radegunde. He would journey home to Scotland with his knight, witness the marriage of Fergus and Isobel, perhaps welcome the routine of employment as a man-at-arms at Killairic. Though Duncan had yearned for home all these years abroad, his future prospects seemed somewhat bleak after this night.

Because he would be alone. It was his choice, of course, for he knew he had naught to offer to a woman such as Radegunde, but in this moment, he found it a less appealing option than once he had.

She filled his mind with tempting possibilities.

Possibilities Duncan knew could not come to be. He must ensure that she had no expectations of him, beyond a night of dancing and a kiss or two. Her future was yet before her, and he would not be the one to taint it.

"Did you not enjoy yourself?" Radegunde asked, and he realized she had been watching him closely. "I pray I did not compel you to surrender your rest for no gain."

Duncan did not have to force his smile. "It was a fine evening, even if you do know songs I would not have expected you to sing."

Radegunde laughed. Duncan had hoped she would do as much and the sound made him smile.

"I *knew* you were surprised." She leaned against his side in a most companionable and enticing way. "Indeed, Duncan, I wish I had known how very gratifying it is to surprise you. I should have started to do so much sooner." She shook her head. "I have wasted weeks when I could have been tormenting you."

"You are a mischievous wench," he accused.

Her smile was impish. "I do so try."

"Did you injure yourself?" When she did not reply, he gestured to her foot. "You are limping." He feared he had not watched her keenly enough.

Radegunde shrugged. "I have never danced so much in one night. Perhaps I danced too much, but I will never regret it." She smiled up at him. "It was wondrous, Duncan, and I thank you for taking me."

17

He could do naught but look down at her, snared as he was by her charm. "You are welcome," he acknowledged and meant it. "Though I am not certain I truly had a choice."

She laughed again as they turned down the lane that led to the inn. "But I was right. It was a fitting end to both the day and the journey."

Duncan deliberately did not mention her earlier suggestion of another way to end this day. "And so you are prepared to continue home to your duties?"

"Far from that! But it will be as it must be." Radegunde sobered as the gate to the inn appeared ahead, and her voice softened. Though he knew she must be disappointed that their revels had ended, her next words surprised him. "I suppose there is little point in tormenting you, since you are resolved to be a man of honor this night."

Duncan considered her. "I am surprised that you surrender your quest as readily as this."

Radegunde smiled up at him. "Is that meant to encourage me?"

"Nay, for there can be naught more between us, but I did not expect you to be so readily convinced."

Radegunde surveyed the quiet alley. "But as this is likely to be the last time I see you, the matter shall rest there." Again, she cast him a playful smile. "Will you later regret the missed opportunity, Duncan?"

He had not considered the parting of their paths until this moment and found that he shared her reaction.

He regretted his choice already, but he had to think of her future.

"You may be right. This may be farewell," Duncan said, knowing that his answer was vague. There had been talk at the Temple before he left, and he was uncertain what Fergus and the Grand Master might have decided in his absence.

Radegunde, of course, did not fail to note that he was not definite. She turned that bright gaze upon him. "You think it might not be."

"It is possible that Gaston will bring his lady to Fergus' nuptials in Scotland."

Radegunde shook her head. "Not if she conceives his child, and they do pursue that goal most ardently."

"You think him protective?"

"I know he is protective of his wife, as all men of merit are. My lady will be hard-pressed to leave her chamber once she confesses that she is with child, and I doubt that day is far away." Radegunde straightened and resolve lit her eyes. "In all likelihood, I shall have a fair battle to ensure that she is permitted to leave her bed."

Duncan smiled at her ferocity. "I wager it is Gaston who will have the battle, for he will have to contend with you."

Radegunde smiled. "He will!"

"You do not fear him?"

She scoffed. "Of course not! There is a man whose heart is true, and one who will never raise a hand against a woman. I could be most impertinent and he would do no more than glower at me in disapproval." She smiled. "Particularly if my intent is to ensure his lady wife's welfare."

"You think him smitten then?" Duncan asked, wondering whether they had come to the same conclusion about the perfection of the match.

"I think no two souls could be better suited to each other." Radegunde spoke without a doubt.

"Then you will remain in Lady Ysmaine's service."

"I suspect so. She is good to me, kinder than most from what I hear. I have no means of comparison for she is the only lady I have ever served."

Duncan endeavored to find good in the situation. "Perhaps she will see you wed to a good man."

Radegunde wrinkled her nose. "Do not spoil such this evening, Duncan," she chided. "You might as well serve me a cup of vinegar after a sumptuous meal."

"I do apologize."

"You need not. I know it is folly for me to wish to wed for love and yearn for adventure, but I would forget that for a little longer, if you please."

"Lady Ysmaine may let you choose your spouse."

"She might." Radegunde changed the subject with a

deliberation Duncan did not fail to note. "I hope my lady bears many sons, and the first one quickly."

Duncan could not entirely forget his own past. "I hope there is a good midwife to be found when the moment comes," he murmured with heat.

To his surprise, Radegunde made no particular note of his comment. He had seen that she was perceptive, and he thought in hindsight that there had been too much regret in his tone, but she waved away his concern.

"There is naught to fear. My mother will come to Lady Ysmaine. I am certain of it."

"Your mother is a midwife?"

"Aye, and the finest to be found," Radegunde insisted proudly. "She brought Lady Ysmaine and all her sisters into the world, as well as most of the village of Valeroy." Her voice dropped. "She always wished to teach me, and I suppose that now she will."

"You do not sound very enthused."

"It is a great responsibility to usher children into the world, for a babe's arrival is an event that does not always proceed as planned," Radegunde said, her manner more solemn than he had ever seen her. Duncan could only agree, though he was intrigued that she shared his view. She flicked him a look and he knew his earlier comment had not escaped her notice. "As I believe you know."

Duncan averted his gaze and frowned. He felt exposed, even as he had the strange urge to confide in his companion.

Radegunde continued softly. "There is a great trust between mother and midwife, but it must be balanced with the truth to ensure the greater kindness."

"How so?"

"To explain as much, I would have to confess another secret to you," she replied, her tone teasing. "Though not one of my own."

"Perhaps another wager would be timely," Duncan found himself suggesting. "Another exchange of secrets."

"But this one must redress the balance," Radegunde insisted, that challenge back in her eyes. "I told a secret of myself, and you of another. This time, I will tell a secret of another, and you will confess one of yourself."

Duncan balked.

She shook a finger at him, so undaunted that he knew she had anticipated his reaction. "I see you will not take my terms, Duncan, so we shall have no wager."

Duncan felt unsettled, for his feelings were so mixed. On the one hand, he would have welcomed the opportunity to share his secrets with one so sympathetic as Radegunde. On the other, he was accustomed to keeping his own counsel, and worse, he feared she would make much of the import of such a confidence.

He did not wish to encourage any notions she might have.

But he did not wish to part from her as yet.

Radegunde raised a hand to rap on the portal. "No wager and no seduction," she said, then gave a heartfelt sigh. "At least I have had my dance."

Duncan could not resist the urge to respond. "And what if I did take your wager?"

Radegunde's smile was all he could have hoped for. "Which one?"

"The tale, of course."

"Of course!" She poked his arm and shook her head, evidently not so displeased as that. "Then I shall welcome your confidence," she said before she leaned close. "And you may be sure that I shall never share it with another."

It was as if she read his deepest fears, and did so readily. She stood but a step away from him, her back against the gate to the inn, and her cheeks flushed. He dropped his gaze to her mouth, wondering whether she would read the particular thought that consumed him in this moment, and saw her lips curve knowingly. Sure enough, her eyes were sparkling anew.

"Do you take my other wager, as well, Duncan?" she whispered. "Or must I convince you of that offer's merit?"

"I would take a kiss and no more."

"Why not more? Do you not find me alluring?"

"Most alluring," he confessed. "But I would not cast a shadow on your future."

"I knew you to be a man of honor," she whispered, then eased closer. "But consider this, Duncan. I am the daughter of a wise woman. You will not taint me with pleasure, for none will ever know what we have done." Her voice fell lower yet. "Except me, and I will savor the memory forevermore."

This time, she looked to his lips. Duncan was enticed, for he knew their thoughts were as one. A kiss and no more, but he would make it a kiss to recall. A kiss to warm his nights and fuel her dreams. A kiss with which she could challenge her alemaker to do better, and a kiss which would haunt him forever.

He cupped her nape in his hand, his cheek looking fair and soft against his rough hand. He speared his fingers into her hair and felt her braid slip loose. Radegunde smiled up at him, so confident and trusting that his chest clenched.

Zounds, but what would he have given to have been unscarred in this moment?

Duncan bent and brushed his mouth once across Radegunde's, tasting her breath and savoring her sweetness, then he claimed her lips, lifting her against him and slanting his mouth over hers. If he could have possessed her with a kiss, he would have done it with this one, and he made no attempt to disguise his interest. If Duncan had thought that Radegunde might be frightened by his passion, he had erred indeed.

For the lady rose to her toes, locked her arms around his neck, and returned his salute with vigor.

Duncan's kisses grew more intoxicating each time. Indeed, Radegunde was convinced that she could feast upon them and naught else, so intense was the pleasure he granted. Each kiss might have been a taste of heaven.

Radegunde wanted only more. She arched against him and opened her mouth to him, inviting him to partake of all she had to offer. She heard him groan. She felt his knee slide between her thighs and his grip tighten upon her...

Then she heard the bolt sliding on the far side of the gate.

She jumped at the sound, and Duncan stood back, easing her to his side.

"I thought you meant to knock," Bartholomew complained. He

sounded both sleepy and grumpy. He opened the portal and gave them both a thorough perusal as they entered the courtyard. Radegunde felt color rise in her cheeks but Bartholomew showed no interest in her reaction.

Duncan might be right about Laurent, but she was not convinced that he was right about Bartholomew.

"I did mean to knock, but you were quicker than me," Duncan said.

"Quicker? I heard you outside the portal for so long that I thought you had forgotten how to knock," Bartholomew complained. "Any living soul would show more haste!"

Radegunde realized that the squire had not guessed what they were doing. He was not observant, to be sure! Duncan closed the portal behind them and shot the bolt home. All was quiet in the courtyard.

"I have not slept as yet," Bartholomew replied, then yawned mightily. He shoved a hand through his hair, leaving it standing on end, and eyed them with evident exhaustion. "I thought it best that some soul stand vigil. Perhaps you might do as much now."

Without waiting for Duncan to do more than nod, Bartholomew returned to the far end of the stables. Radegunde heard him settling into the hay, and but moments later, he began to snore softly.

Radegunde considered the portal to the inn and thought of the man who had assaulted her before. "I will stay with you," she said to Duncan.

"We will keep only one of your wagers," he insisted.

"Fair enough," she agreed, not wanting to risk another assault by that brute in the kitchen.

Again Duncan took her hand, but this time, he escorted her to the opposite end of the stables from Bartholomew. The hay was thick and sweet, and the spot he chose had a good vantage of the portals. He lifted his cloak from her shoulders and spread it over the straw, making a place for them to sit together. His cloak was thick enough to keep the hay from prickling. Radegunde sat down and Duncan gathered it over her shoulders.

Did he meant to sit apart from her?

"We had best sit close," she informed him. "Lest any hear your secret."

"Lest Bartholomew be awakened anew," Duncan agreed. He sat down beside her, the weight of his arm over her shoulders and the heat of his thigh against her own. Radegunde tugged the ends of the cloak over them both and nestled closer. "Temptress," he murmured again, but she smiled up at him.

"I may well fall asleep, and I would be warm."

His bright gaze clung to hers and she could scarce draw a breath at his intense manner. "I will ensure you are so, lass. You need not fear otherwise."

She dared to rest her cheek upon his chest, but the pose was less comfortable than might have been ideal. Duncan lifted her and turned her so that she sat in his lap, then wrapped both his arms and the cloak around her. Radegunde smiled up at him contentedly. "I like this well, sir." She rolled her buttocks against him. "As, I believe, do you."

He spared her a grim glance. "Tell your secret," he growled and she laughed at his gruff manner.

"It is the secret of another, as I mentioned earlier."

"It is a tale of trust between mother and midwife," Duncan reminded her.

"Indeed it is. My mother, as I said, brought Lady Ysmaine and all her siblings into the world. She was but sixteen summers of age when Lady Richildis bore Lady Ysmaine, and much concerned that she would be responsible for Lord Amaury's first babe. My mother said that Lord Amaury was most anxious for a son."

"As many men are, the better to ensure the suzerainty of their holding for the future."

"Aye, it is an inclination founded in good sense, but my mother was uncertain what to expect of him when the babe was born a girl." Radegunde heaved a sigh. "He is a good man, though, Lord Amaury. She said there was but a glimmer of disappointment before he took his daughter, but in but the blink of an eye, he had lost his heart in truth." Radegunde looked up to find Duncan smiling.

"I like this tale well. It is difficult to dislike a man so readily smitten with an infant, be it boy or girl."

"Aye, it implies a goodness in his nature. Lord Amaury is both gentle and strong."

"A fine balance in a man."

"Indeed, and one that makes his villeins love him. So it was that my mother so admired Lord Amaury that she wished he should have the son he desired. Evidently, Lady Richildis wished for this, as well, for she ripened again with all speed."

"Yet she bore another daughter, by the telling."

"Indeed she did. And my mother said the regret was just a measure longer in Lord Amaury's eyes before he lost his heart anew."

"Something must have changed for this to be a tale of trust," Duncan guessed.

"It was the third child. Lady Richildis was sickly with this babe and spent much time in her bed. My mother said she carried the child differently, as well, and though she did not remark upon it aloud, she knew that both she and the couple hoped this was a sign that Lady Richildis carried a boy."

"One hears such speculation."

"For there is merit in it. There had not been much time between the pregnancies, and my mother did not like that. She feared Lady Richildis was not yet recovered from Jehanne's arrival. When the lady was so ill, my mother feared the worst."

"I am sure she said naught of it to Lord Amaury."

"Naught but to insist that Lady Richildis sleep so much as she desired. The lord took to pacing the floor. There was little festivity in the hall that Eastertide, for the lady had taken to her bed. Despite all efforts to ensure the babe grew to full size, it came too soon. My mother was summoned to Lady Richildis in the middle of the night, by her telling, when the wind was wicked. She reached the keep to find the lady screaming in pain, and the blood flowing too fast. It seemed that the labor had begun quickly, that it was sharp and fierce, that naught could come aright. Lord Amaury was fearful, though my mother said naught to feed his fears, for he was a man of keen wit."

"Was it breech?" Duncan asked and Radegunde smiled at him,

pleased that he had understood.

"Aye. And though my mother turned the child and cleared the cord, even in her haste, she had intervened too late. The babe was dead when it emerged into the world and she knew by its condition that it had been so before the labor began. The lady's child had died in the womb, which was why it came too soon."

Duncan waited, his gaze upon her, and Radegunde knew he had guessed the truth of what her mother had done.

Better, she knew he did not blame her mother for her choice.

Radegunde continued, much encouraged by Duncan's expression. "My mother saw immediately that the babe was a boy. Lady Richildis did not fare well in that moment, and Lord Amaury was much distressed with his wife's condition. My mother feared that knowing the dead babe was the son he desired would be too much for the lord."

"She hid the truth," Duncan said, no surprise in his tone.

"She swaddled him quickly, so quickly that no other saw the truth, called him a girl and entrusted him to a maid. Then she tended to the lady. It took until the dawn to ensure that the lady would survive, and still she was much weakened."

"And the lord?"

"Lord Amaury wept and he prayed, and never left his wife's side. When Lady Richildis finally slept at ease, my mother took the infant from the chamber. She washed and prepared the babe for burial herself. She weighed the merit of telling them the truth, but still she feared that the lady might not recover if such a disappointment was added to her heart."

"She was protective of them, when they were at their weakest. It is not a bad impulse."

"By the time it was clear that Lady Richildis would recover, my mother thought the truth would be cruel. She believed, too, that they might yet have a son."

"And the child was buried without them knowing its sex?"

Radegunde nodded. "They had but a glimpse of the child's face before his coffin was sealed forever." She swallowed, her tears welling at this last detail. "They named him Elena."

Duncan nodded. "She thought she chose the greater good."

Radegunde nodded, blinking back her tears. She could never hear of a dead babe without weeping.

"But there never was a son?" he guessed.

She shook her head, her tears falling that these good people had been denied the one thing they most desired. "Four more daughters, the last after my mother had counseled Lady Richildis to halt, lest her own life be lost. Only the one pregnancy of the seven was so difficult."

"Because only the one was a boy?"

She shrugged. "Perhaps. My mother told them that it might have been the illness of the child at root."

"And when was this?" Duncan surveyed Radegunde, his expression inscrutable.

"Just after I was born. The youngest sister, Constantia, was born when I was ten. Hers was the first birth at which I aided my mother."

Duncan touched a finger to her cheek and lifted away a tear. "And yet you weep for a child you never saw, for a couple who have many blessings to their hand."

"Because they are good, and I like them well. There is a lesson in this, Duncan, that even those who appear to have every advantage can be lacking one thing they most desire."

His gaze was intent, so piercing that she thought he could see her very thoughts. His voice was low, and she knew this query to be of import to him. "So, you have your mother's example. Would you so lie for another?"

Radegunde took a deep breath. "For years, I thought not. It is a lie, after all, and a breach of the trust between them. For years, I thought my mother had chosen wrong." She bit her lip. "But now I see Lord Gaston, wed but weeks to my lady, and I understand how he would be similarly torn. I had not understood how vehemently a lord might desire a son, even as he loved his wife. I understand that it might break his heart to lose both in one night." Radegunde swallowed. "I see now that should I fear such an outcome, I might well deceive the husband as well."

"It would scarce be better to lose wife and daughter," Duncan said, a curious note in his voice. Radegunde studied him, marveling that he was so affected by her tale. He, after all, had never met the lord and lady.

"But when a man so desires a son to secure all he has gained to his hand and to protect the future, I understand that the loss would be greater."

Duncan bent and kissed her brow gently. She felt a tear fall upon her cheek and wondered who had shed it. "Your heart is kind, lass," he murmured, his words husky. "Let no one tell you otherwise." Then he lifted her and settled her in the straw, tucking the cloak around her securely. "Sleep, Radegunde. Sleep, for dawn and duty are not so far away."

"But you?"

"Will stand guard. You need not fear for your safety."

To her disappointment, he moved to sit at the edge of the stables, his back to her and his gaze fixed upon the courtyard. Something had changed in his manner with her tale, though she could not name the reason why. Then was a tension in his shoulders and a new distance between them.

Was he disappointed that she saw merit in her mother's choice?

"Am I wrong?" Radegunde asked softly. "Would the loss be greater?"

"The loss of either wife or babe might have ruined him. The loss of both, regardless of the child's gender, might have shattered his heart forever," Duncan replied, his words so softly uttered that Radegunde scarce heard them.

He might have been a stranger to her, and not just because his back was turned to her. Radegunde suspected that her tale had reminded him of some incident he would have preferred to forget. Had Duncan witnessed the death of a child in his liege lord's home? The demise of a woman in childbirth? The prospect of that terrified Radegunde, for she knew it was not so uncommon and also that there was little the midwife could do when all went awry. She might have asked for his part of the wager, but Duncan's stiff posture kept her silent.

She had pressed him too far this night.

Radegunde nestled into his cloak and inhaled deeply of his scent. She would not regret what they had done this night, nor the time in his company. Indeed, on the morrow, she would do whatever was necessary to make amends.

In the comparative peace of the stables, though, and with Duncan watching over her like a guardian angel, Radegunde could not keep her eyes open.

It was but moments before she was asleep.

Duncan was not surprised that Gwyneth haunted him that night.

He did not sleep, for he knew the power she had over his dreams. Even so, he saw her silhouette in the shadows of the courtyard. He heard the sound of her step in the street beyond the gates. He was certain he discerned her laughter as the servants began their day in the kitchen, and he closed his eyes against the cry of a cock at an adjacent property.

Gwyneth and her chickens.

Zounds, but he could see her chasing them, her bare feet pale against the ground. He could hear the hens scolding as she claimed their eggs, and tears pricked at his eyes as he recalled the way she used to reassure the birds that all would be well. He could smell the sea and feel the wind and his throat was tight with the memory of her wrapped around him, her breath in his ear.

It had been twenty years and still the pain could nigh rip him in half.

He waited until the fetching Radegunde slept behind him, the deep even sound of her breathing telling the truth of her exhaustion. Then Duncan reached into the bottom of his purse and withdrew the small silken bag that Gwyneth herself had fashioned out of scraps from her lady's kirtle. He carefully removed the braid of red gold hair, as radiant as copper in the sun, squeezed it between his fingers, and touched its softness to his lips.

There could be no other, no matter how merry a lass she might be. There could be no other, though she might cast sunlight into his heart anew.

He would not so despoil the memory of his beloved, who had given her all for his love.

Such was not the deed of a man of honor, and Duncan

MacDonald knew it well.

CHAPTER FOUR

aston awakened on the first morning after their arrival in Paris with a powerful sense of well-being. Not only had his party safely delivered the treasure to the Temple in Paris, but his new wife had been key to their success. He knew he had been a knave to distrust Ysmaine at all, and even more of a cur to have kept from confiding in her, but he had spent the night trying to atone for his errors. He had been accustomed to relying on no one, but Gaston could already see the benefit to be derived from a partnership such as the one Ysmaine advocated.

He watched her sleep for long moments, appreciating both her beauty and her keen wits, feeling beyond blessed that she was truly his wife. Her wrist had been broken in the battle with Everard, but he had summoned an apothecary who had bound it and been confident it would heal well, so long as the lady did not use it. Gaston meant to ensure that. As much as he would have liked to have lingered abed, or awakened Ysmaine with pleasure, duty called again.

Gaston arose with newfound purpose, endeavoring not to disturb his wife's well-earned rest. He failed in that, for Ysmaine stirred as soon as he left the warmth of their bed, her lashes fluttering. "Where do you go, sir?" she murmured, even as she smiled in invitation.

"I must ensure that Wulfe did return safely to the Temple," he murmured and tucked her beneath the blankets.

Ysmaine arched a brow. "Surely Wulfe can fend for himself?"

"I have no doubt that he can, but I would like to be certain."

"Tell me that your loyalty to the order is not still stronger than your loyalty to me, sir," she teased.

Gaston smiled, for he heard the concern beneath her jest. "Nay, it is not. I fear I abandoned him, though, and hope all was resolved to advantage."

Ysmaine eyed him. "Your quest is complete, Gaston."

"It is. I would simply confirm that all is as it should be. One walk to the Temple will be the last of it. I vow this to you."

She looked skeptical.

"Sleep," Gaston urged. "You have earned your leisure and then some."

Ysmaine might have complied, but sat up suddenly, her gaze flying to the door. "I forgot about Radegunde!" she said, one hand rising to her lips in horror. "I hope no ill befell her in the corridor."

Gaston had forgotten the maid as well. He was dressed by this point and strode to the portal. He unlocked it and was dismayed to discover that no maid was sleeping on the pallet there. "Perhaps she slept in the stables," he said, gesturing to Ysmaine to remain abed.

She did not, but came to his side in her chemise, her hair falling loose over her shoulders. "She might have sought out Bartholomew to ensure her welfare. Oh, Gaston, how could I have been so thoughtless?" she said, even as she looked herself and gripped his arm. She smelled of the sweetness of sleep, and her own beguiling scent. Gaston had the urge to sweep his wife into his arms and return to bed, leaving both knight and maid to themselves.

"I believe I did my best to distract you, lady mine," Gaston said, and was rewarded with her quick smile. "Do not fear. This inn is reputed to be a good one. That is why I chose it. Perhaps she has gone for hot water already, for she is most dutiful."

Ysmaine winced. "But still, Gaston. I should never forgive myself if she paid a price for my oversight."

He kissed her brow before he left the chamber. "Which is only proof that we are not so different in our objectives as that. You fear for Radegunde and I for Wulfe."

Ysmaine's smile was rueful. "Nay, not so different as that. Tell me when you find her, please."

He nodded agreement. "Bolt the door behind me."

Gaston descended the stairs only after he heard the latch drop. The servants were stirring in the kitchen and one was just entering the courtyard from the street, burdened with loaves of fresh bread. The smell made his belly growl. To his relief, Duncan sat before the stables, his gaze watchful. Behind him, in the hay, swathed in Duncan's cloak, Gaston spied a woman who slept. He knew her identity, for the dark tangle of Radegunde's hair spilled from the hood.

He smiled openly at the warrior in his relief. "I fear my lady forgot her maid's comfort last night. I thank you for seeing she was not accosted in this place."

Duncan nodded his head in acknowledgment. "She was, but my arrival was timely."

Gaston was startled. "Was she injured?"

Duncan shook his head. "She is a doughty lass. I do not doubt she could have defended her virtue in my absence, but I was glad to be of aid all the same."

Though Duncan was seldom cavalier, he seemed uncommonly grim this morn and looked as if he had not slept at all. Gaston might have thanked him again, but the warrior coughed and stood, sparing a glance at the maid.

Radegunde stirred then, perhaps because of the sound of their voices. When she spied Gaston, she stumbled hastily to her feet, curtseying before him. Color stained her cheeks in awareness of her disarray, and her gaze flicked repeatedly to Duncan.

That man studiously ignored her, and that seemed to puzzle the maid.

"Good morning, sir," Radegunde said to Gaston. "Is my lady

awake?"

"Aye, and most concerned for you. I must apologize to you, Radegunde, for my part in your being abandoned outside the chamber."

She smiled. "I am glad that you and my lady have such a fine match, sir. That is what is of import."

"I would argue that your safety and comfort is also of concern. I vow to you that the situation will not be repeated."

"I thank you, sir." Radegunde flushed more deeply, her gaze landing upon Duncan yet again. Still that man did not acknowledge her, but Gaston noted that he stood a little more stiffly.

What had happened between this pair the night before?

He supposed it was not a tale he had a right to know.

Radegunde curtseyed to him again, but this time she lifted her chin high when she straightened. "If you will excuse me, my lord, I will see to my lady."

"Of course." Gaston watched Duncan take a profound interest in his boots, one that ensured there was no chance his gaze might collide with that of Radegunde.

She removed the cloak, swinging it from her shoulders, then offered it to Duncan. "I thank you," she said, and it seemed to Gaston that there was a challenge in her tone.

If so, Duncan did not take it. He murmured some polite reply and accepted the cloak without looking at her.

Radegunde waited, staring pointedly at the older man, and the air seemed to crackle between them. Gaston wondered who had declined the attentions of the other.

Then Radegunde strode away, her chin in the air and her eyes flashing with an annoyance that answered Gaston's unspoken question. Only when she had carried a pail of water up the stairs with her usual cheerful energy did Duncan look after her.

There was a yearning in his expression that Gaston found intriguing.

Still, whatever had passed between them was done, and none of his concern. Gaston turned his thoughts to more pressing matters.

Indeed, the presence of Duncan gave him an idea.

"I return to the Temple this morn," he informed the other man.

"To verify that Wulfe returned safely and that Christina was found. Will you go with me?"

"Aye." Duncan donned his cloak, his expression inscrutable. "I need to discover my lord Fergus' plans for our journey north."

Gaston sought out Bartholomew in the stables and exchanged a few words with the squire, ensuring he would watch over the two women, then departed with Duncan, intent upon seeing many of his responsibilities laid to rest this day.

He needed to know more of what had happened at his home estate while he had been gone. No doubt Ysmaine's father would have some tidings, but while in Paris, and with Duncan's assistance, Gaston would see if there was yet more to be learned.

How much had Gaston guessed?

Duncan felt awkward that the knight had discovered Radegunde sleeping in his cloak, just as he was irked that the happy couple had forgotten the maid in their pleasure. He wanted to charge Gaston to ensure that Radegunde was not left so undefended again, even as he understood how readily a man could forget himself when welcomed abed. He wanted to explain that he had left the maid untouched, but considered that he would have doubted any such tale from another man.

The urge to explain such a situation would make it sound like a falsehood.

He trudged beside Gaston, tired and disgruntled, aching anew from the loss of Gwyneth, regretting that the only honorable course was to deny Radegunde and her allure.

The two men made their way back to the larger road from the courtyard of the inn without exchanging another word. The city was beginning to bustle already, many carrying fresh bread, others disposing of buckets of slops, still more harnessing horses or leading carts into the center of the city for their daily trade.

Gaston cleared his throat once they were on the larger road. "I wonder if you might do a favor for me this day, Duncan, should your obligations to Fergus permit as much."

"Me?" Duncan was surprised by this request. "You would not ask it of Bartholomew?"

"I would leave him to stand guard over my lady wife and her maid," Gaston said, which was a reassuring notion. "If Wulfe is not returned to the Temple, I intend to follow the trail we took yesterday and seek him out. Perhaps he has been injured or is in need of aid. I would not leave my wife and her maid undefended in the inn, not given what occurred last night."

"I doubt the Templar has need of your assistance, sir. Wulfe is most fierce in battle."

Gaston grimaced. "I should not have left him to continue the fight alone. Everard might have had allies."

"Your duty was to your lady wife, sir, and she was injured. You should not blame yourself." Duncan cleared his throat. "Either Wulfe continues to pursue his quarry, or he has succeeded but sees little reason to return and tell you all of his success."

"But he should return to the Temple and make a report. He is beholden to the order, after all."

Duncan pursed his lips, recalling all too well the passion between Wulfe and Christina. He also recalled the knight's defiance of the Grand Master of the Paris Temple and was not certain Wulfe would return to be reprimanded and disciplined, not if any other choice were available to him.

Gaston, of course, would not have been swerved from his obligation, however distasteful he might find it to be. They were different men, to be sure.

Duncan thought it tactless to suggest that a knight sworn to the order might choose to linger with a courtesan instead of report for discipline.

"He might have chosen to return to Outremer with all haste instead," Duncan suggested. "He was most determined to aid in the defense of the Holy City."

"Perhaps." Gaston frowned. "Still, I would like to be certain of his welfare."

Duncan nodded. "He might be at the Temple this morn, sir."

"He might be, and if so, my curiosity will be satisfied."

"But if he is not, you would have me accompany you to learn more." Duncan thought it prudent to travel in pairs in this city. "If my lord Fergus can spare me this day, I should be glad to do as much."

Gaston shook his head. "Nay, Duncan, you mistake my meaning."

"Do I, sir?"

"I would have you seek information for me, if you please, independent of whether I seek out Wulfe or not."

Duncan did not understand and was certain that was clear from his expression.

Gaston gestured back to the heart of the city. "There used to be a tavern near the Palais Royale where mercenaries exchanged tidings of barons offering employment. I remember it from years past and we did ride by it again yesterday. If that tavern is not the one where such tales are shared, they will know of the current favorite. Your countrymen are highly favored here for their valor in battle, so none will think twice of you enquiring after employ."

Duncan frowned, wondering whether Gaston knew some detail he did not. "But I am not seeking employ, sir," he said with care, hoping it were true.

"Nay, but I wish to confirm whether one Millard de Saint-Roux is seeking to hire mercenaries." Gaston's eyes twinkled. "You might feign to be other than you are, Duncan."

Duncan smiled in understanding. "And you would have me listen for his name. I understand."

"Even suggest it as a rumor, if need be."

"Who is this nobleman, sir?"

"My niece's husband. The missive informing me of my brother's death included also the tidings of her nuptials."

This Millard might have hoped that Gaston would not return from Outremer to claim Châmont-sur-Maine, the better that he could claim it for himself. Or he might be making preparations for a confrontation, should the legal heir return. Gaston's inquisitiveness made good sense to Duncan.

"Such a coincidence," he mused.

"Perhaps." Gaston shrugged, then cast a glance at Duncan that did not hint at the same indifference as his gesture. Indeed, his voice hardened. "Or perhaps not."

"Do you know this knight, sir?" Duncan asked, guessing that

his companion's reaction was rooted in past experience.

"I knew him many years ago, when we trained for our spurs," Gaston admitted. "We were not good friends—that possibility was eliminated by the animosity between our fathers—but I was not truly surprised that he never embarked upon crusade."

"What matter stood between your fathers?"

"I do not know. My father and I were not close. He lavished attention upon his eldest son and heir, as was fitting."

Duncan did not think it was particularly fitting for a father to favor one son over another, but his own had done as much and he knew it was common. He declined to express an opinion. "Perhaps they simply disliked each other."

Gaston met Duncan's gaze steadily. "Or perhaps there was more to the tale than that. They were both mercenaries, Duncan, I know this much."

"And you would know more before you reach Châmont-sur-Maine."

"In truth, I would know more before I reach Valeroy. I mean to seek the counsel of Ysmaine's father, for his holding is not so far from the one that comes to my hand."

"And more tidings will grant a more complete tale," Duncan said with a nod.

Gaston frowned. "Matters were seldom simple when I was a boy, though I did not know all of what transpired," he confided. "Châmont-sur-Maine stands just to the north of Angers, with one foot in Anjou and the other in Brittany. My father was granted custody of it by Geoffrey of Anjou, as a reward for loyal service, and with the expectation that he would defend the frontier for the Angevins." Gaston met Duncan's gaze. "There were times when he believed it of greater import to ally with Breton lords, with a view to the end result. I must steer my way with care, as he did before me. I would know whatever you can learn of recent events along the Breton March."

Duncan nodded again. It did not hurt that aiding Gaston in this would ensure that he was far away from Radegunde for the day. He realized that Gaston awaited his response. "I should be glad to do as much, sir, provided that my lord Fergus can spare my services."

On top of the vexation of Duncan's manner this morn, the future Radegunde dreaded was closer than she might have hoped. Indeed, she had only just brought hot water for her lady to bathe when she learned the truth.

Though the day before she had feared her future mightily, it was the last matter weighing upon her thoughts this morn. She was consumed with questions about Duncan. Why had he been so indifferent this morn? They might have been strangers, and their fine night of dancing forgotten—never mind those fiery kisses. Was it so difficult to believe that she knew her own mind? All she desired was a night of affection, no more and no less, and Radegunde found it annoying that she had evidently chosen the one man disinclined to fulfill her wish.

A man of honor, just as he had said.

She supposed that meant her scheme had little hope of success. Her ankle ached, but she ignored it, striving not to limp at all. Surely the dancing was worth a little pain.

As disappointed as she was with Duncan, Radegunde had duties to perform. Her first step into her mistress's chamber had her composing a list of tasks to see completed this day. Doubtless Lady Ysmaine would wish to go to church and must be suitably attired. Her garb was dirty from their long ride, and it would require all of Radegunde's skills to see all put aright with speed. The lady's bandaged wrist should be checked and her boots would need a polish...

"Radegunde!" the lady declared at the sight of her. Radegunde noted that her mistress's hair was unbound and in need of a good combing. Her injured wrist would make it difficult for Lady Ysmaine to perform many feats herself, though she often combed her own hair. "I do apologize for last night. I should have welcomed you into the chamber after my lord husband had his pleasure." Lady Ysmaine blushed in a most comely way. "But in truth, I would not have summoned you much sooner than this."

"I understand, my lady," Radegunde poured hot water into a bowl for her mistress. The steam rose as she fetched the sponge that her lady favored from the saddlebags. They had a fine piece of soap, too, given to her lady as a tribute and gift by that merchant Joscelin. Doubtless he meant to entice her future trade, but it was a fine tactic. The soap was fine and smelled of roses, with petals pressed into it. If she had possessed a single coin of her own, Radegunde would have bought a piece herself to give to her mother before they had left Provins and Joscelin behind.

As it was, she would tell her mother of it.

There was no clean chemise for her mistress this day, for they had been riding with all speed from the Saint Bernard Pass. Had Radegunde been granted access to the chamber last night, she might have washed one, but for this day, Lady Ysmaine would have to wear the one that was the least soiled.

Radegunde would wash the remaining chemises and hang them in the sunshine of the courtyard this morning. Though the sun was not as warm as it had been, still they would dry by the evening. The kirtle her lady had favored for riding these past days was in need of a good shake, and there was a seam in want of a stitch or two. Belt buckles should be polished and stockings mended, the fur brushed out on her lady's hood, and the chamber itself had to be swept. She would fetch fresh bread for Lady Ysmaine as soon as that lady was dressed, and take instruction while her mistress broke her fast.

She might wish for warm milk, as well. Radegunde worked with purpose, anticipating her lady's requests even as she sorted clothes and put matters to rights. She opened the shutters to admit the sunlight once her lady had donned the cleaner chemise, and stirred the last of the coals in the brazier so Lady Ysmaine could warm herself while Radegunde braided her hair.

"Where did you sleep, Radegunde?"

"In the stables, my lady. I thought it wiser to be near Bartholomew."

"And that is good sense," the lady said with approval. She glanced up. "And did you do more than sleep with Bartholomew?"

"My lady?" Radegunde did not have to feign her surprise.

"He is a finely wrought young man," Ysmaine said, no censure in her tone. "And Gaston means to dub him a knight. There is some suggestion that he means to return to the holding where he was born, but I wonder whether he simply seeks a better reason to remain in Gaston's service." She smiled. "A wife might be the reason he needs."

Yet another soul who wanted to twine her path with Bartholomew's! "I barely spoke to Bartholomew, my lady, for he was desirous of his sleep."

"And were you disappointed?"

"Nay, my lady." Not by Bartholomew, at least.

The lady twisted on the stool to study Radegunde. "You do not find him alluring?"

"He reminds me of my brothers, my lady. More a boy than a man." She squared her shoulders and declared her inclination. "If and when I wed, it will be to a man in truth."

The glint in her lady's eye made Radegunde wonder how much choice she would have.

"I understand, Radegunde. Do you wish to remain in my service, or would you remain at Valeroy with your mother?"

"I have no desire to remain at Valeroy, my lady."

"Excellent. Then I shall find you a *man* at Châmont-sur-Maine." Lady Ysmaine beamed. "I shall have to find another candidate who is a little older then. I would have you pleased with your husband."

"I thank you, my lady."

"Indeed, I would not have you miss the wonder I shared with my lord husband last night, Radegunde. Truly I am content this morn."

"Because there is affection between you," Radegunde dared to say. "That is why I would wed for love, my lady."

"For love?" Lady Ysmaine laughed aloud. "No one weds for love, Radegunde, not even in the tales of the troubadours! Matches should be wrought of good sense, and then love will grow between husband and wife." She stood, as content with her scheme as Radegunde was not. "I shall find you a man, older than Bartholomew, of fitting station and good temperament, a man with a trade who can provide for your welfare, and one wrought finely enough that you will be glad to bear his sons. Fear not!"

"But my lady…"

"Radegunde, if you had a spouse and joined him abed each night, I should not have to fear for your welfare at night. It makes good sense for you to wed sooner rather than later." Lady Ysmaine smiled as her kirtle was laced. "You need not imagine that I shall make a poor choice for you. I have a good eye for a husband."

Radegunde could not return her lady's smile. "Aye, my lady."

"You are concerned," Lady Ysmaine said, her manner thoughtful. "You wish to approve the choice, then?"

"Aye, if not make it."

"Do not be foolish, Radegunde." The lady was dismissive of this notion. "But I will cede this: I shall say naught when I find a suitable man. I will suggest him to you first, and if you do not find the prospect of a match with him tempting, we shall continue to seek another. Is that a fair compromise?"

It was far more than Ysmaine was obliged to surrender to her, and Radegunde recognized as much—even though she also knew it was far less than she desired. "I thank you, my lady."

The lady watched her with care. "Is there a man you already favor?" she asked softly.

A part of Radegunde was tempted to declare Duncan's name, but she knew it would be futile. Not only did he answer to lord Fergus, but he had made his lack of intention clear. "There is no one, my lady," she said.

"Indeed? You seem distracted this morn."

"I but think of all that must be done, my lady. Do you mean to visit churches in this city?"

"I do!" Lady Ysmaine's face lit with pleasure. "I would return to Notre Dame to pray for Christina and Wulfe, and I would visit Saint Julien-le-Pauvre. Gaston says it is most fine, and that he will accompany me. On this day, he has errands and would have me remain close to the inn. I thought to give alms at Les Innocents, if Bartholomew can be spared to escort me there."

"Then you will have need of the other kirtle," Radegunde said. "And your cloak so that you are not chilled. The better stockings…"

"And my boots, Radegunde. The streets of this city demand no less."

"Will you have bread this morn, my lady? It is fresh."

"Aye, and if there is honey or milk that would be most welcome."

"Or both?"

Lady Ysmaine smiled. "Or both. I thank you, Radegunde."

Radegunde halted outside the portal to braid her hair and brush the last of the straw from her kirtle. Dread closed a cold hand around her heart, for the future she would avoid already drew near.

Worse, there was little she could do to halt its progress. She would be wedded by the Yule, to be sure.

And not to Duncan MacDonald, which was the most disappointing detail of all. Radegunde lifted her chin and squared her shoulders. If he did not desire her, and it appeared he did not, then that was Duncan's loss.

Wulfe had not appeared at the Temple so Gaston was resolved to retrace the other knight's steps. Duncan would walk with him as far as the island, then their ways would part. Gaston sent a squire to fetch his destrier for him from the inn while Duncan changed his clothing.

In a way, Duncan looked forward to the sound of his countrymen, if not the rough company of mercenaries. A sip of ale would not do him injury either.

It also felt good to don familiar garb again.

Duncan belted his plaid around his waist, smiling a little that he had carried it all the way to Outremer and back again. He laced his boiled leather jerkin over his chemise, eyeing the mail hauberk that he would not be sad to put aside forever. It was weighty, but it had saved his sorry hide more than once. He grimaced and donned it anew, beckoning to Hamish to lace the back of it for him.

"It will mark your chemise," the squire said and Duncan nodded at the truth of that.

"But in this burg, I would not be without it," he acknowledged. In a tavern of mercenaries, he might be glad of its burden.

He heard a footstep and turned to find Fergus leaning at the end of the stall.

That knight smiled. "So close to home as that?" he teased, and

Duncan imagined that the younger man's accent grew stronger with every day's ride north.

"Close enough. Have you need of me this day?"

Fergus shook his head. "The Grand Master has sent a summons that I join him in his chamber for the midday meal."

"Why?"

Fergus' eyes glinted. "Perhaps he feels hospitable. Certainly, I welcome his invitation."

"For otherwise you should eat with the brethren in the refectory and be condemned to silence for the meal," Duncan concluded. "Tell me that I am not the sole one ready to be home."

"You are not and you know it well," Fergus replied with fervor. His expression softened and Duncan knew the knight thought of his betrothed. He stifled the urge to wince, for he did not share Fergus' admiration of the fair Isobel. Indeed, Duncan knew that Fergus' father shared his own doubts of the maiden's heart and those doubts had contributed to the older man's decision to send Fergus abroad for military service.

On the one hand, Duncan hoped the truth of Isobel's nature had revealed itself these past years. On the other, he did not wish to see Fergus disappointed. His affection for Isobel was resolute and any wound to his heart would be a lasting one.

Would it not be worse for him to wed a woman unworthy of him?

Duncan also dreaded the sharing of the tidings of Kerr's death at Killairic. That squire had been a relation of Isobel, a member of their company at her request, though he doubted she would recall that detail when his death was known. She was the manner of woman, he suspected, who blamed others for the results of her own choices. Duncan hoped that he was not required to tell her of the boy's fate.

"When do we depart then?" Duncan asked gruffly, well aware that the stable in the Temple must be filled with listening ears.

"As soon as the Grand Master releases me." Fergus straightened with obvious enthusiasm. "It might be this very day."

"That might be why you are summoned to his board, my lord," Hamish suggested.

"And this might be my last day to see the fabled city of Paris," Duncan said heartily. "I shall return by the evening meal, to be sure."

"Will you not take another with you?" Fergus asked.

"I can fend for myself, lad," Duncan scoffed, hoping the knight did not assign either of the boys to accompany him. He did not want to be obliged to protect them in a tavern as disreputable as he feared his destination might be.

"I would go with you," Hamish offered.

Duncan ruffled his hair. "You must ensure that our lord Fergus looks his best for this midday meal. Have you polished his boots as yet? Ensured his chemise is clean and the hilt of his blade polished?"

Hamish's eyes rounded and he dove into the stall to begin those very duties.

"Use care," Fergus advised Duncan softly.

Duncan held the other man's gaze, wondering how much he saw. The lad had been born to the caul, but if Fergus had the Sight, he hid his ability well.

"And you," he murmured in reply, taking the warning at face value. "For I will not be here to guard your back."

The younger man nodded, his expression so solemn that Duncan had to wonder what he expected to happen in that session.

His own task was clear this day, to be sure.

Duncan cast the end of the plaid over his shoulder and strode out of the stables to meet Gaston. The knight sat upon his dappled destrier, waiting upon him. Duncan knew that the knight would not make much faster progress on the horse than he on foot, given the congestion in these streets.

Aye, the crowds and the stench combined were sufficient to make a man yearn for home.

CHAPTER FIVE

aston had been right about the tavern. It was filled with rough men, whose language was rougher yet. The stench of well-aged sweat was powerful and scarce tempered by the smell of roast meat and spilled ale. The air was so smoky and redolent of the fire that tears rose to Duncan's eyes as soon as he crossed the threshold. Once within, it was impossible to tell whether it was day or night in the street beyond—save when some soul opened the portal.

Ale flowed, coins clattered on the high table where it was poured, and crockery cups were put down empty at a regular rate. The rushes on the floor were dirty and doubtless filled with vermin, though the other men did not seem to care. They sang lewd ditties, shouted in recognition of found comrades, stamped their feet, and played at dice with unrivaled zeal. It was warm in the tavern, and there was something comforting about the familiarity of so many Scots' voices, and the sight of so much plaid.

The fire, though, should have smelled of peat.

Duncan could not help but imagine that Radegunde's mother would be challenged to find the finest pair of legs in the establishment. He ordered a cup of ale, greeted the man beside him in Gaelic, and showed himself to be one of them with astonishing speed.

The tidings flowed fast and thick. His new friend was taller even than Duncan and burly, his hair as red as a flame and his beard full. He might have been a bear for his size, and his laughter was as hearty as his appetite for both ale and gossip.

When Duncan said that he sought employ, the man cast an arm around his shoulders and guided him around the tavern, making introductions. He spoke of Duncan as if they were lost kin found.

All the while, Duncan gathered news, uncertain what would be of use to Gaston. The queen of France had retired to her chamber in the Palais Royale, fairly bursting with child. Speculation was rampant as to the babe's gender, for the king had need of a son, and bets aplenty were made in the tavern. The queen was of an age with the Lady Ysmaine, though the men wagered upon her survival, as well as her prospects of bearing more children, their gender, and numbers. Duncan could only assume that some of his fellow countrymen meant to remain in France for years or they would never see the outcome of those wagers.

There were few reports of the losses in Outremer, and Duncan was intrigued by the accuracy of some tales and the wild fabrication of others. He could have set them straight about the nature of Saladin and the numbers of men lost at Hattin, but preferred to disguise his recent return from Palestine.

Indeed, he had come to the tavern to listen.

There was doubt that the treaty made the previous June between Philip Augustus and Henry II in Berry would hold, even though the territories of Issoudun and Fréteval had been ceded to Philip. What the French king truly desired was the surrender of the duchy of Brittany, and Duncan's ears pricked over these tidings for their route lay in that direction.

The duchy had come to Geoffrey II, son of Henry II, through forcible marriage to the heiress Constance of Brittany. The crowns of England and France insisted that each alone held suzerainty over Brittany—although the Bretons themselves were known to dispute both claims—and both kings had wished the duchy under their control. Upon Constance's delivery of Geoffrey's son the previous winter, the duchy of Brittany had been settled upon the infant by Henry II. Philip had invaded Berry in protest, and also in alliance with Henry's other sons Richard and John.

When Duncan heard that, he could believe the truce would be a fragile one. It seemed that Gaston's skill as a diplomat would be welcome in assuming his inherited holding.

There was considerable head-shaking over the demise of Geoffrey II. Duncan recalled that the older sons of Henry II, both Henry the young king and Geoffrey, had been much involved in tournaments and had expended considerable coin in their pursuit. He knew that Henry the young king had died after turning to actual warfare and fighting against his brother Richard and his father in the Limousin. Duncan was shocked to learn that Geoffrey had died the year before after having been trampled in a tournament. It was a foolish way to die, in his opinion, feigning war when there were battles of merit to be waged.

But real war was not so fetchingly arrayed as the battles of tournament.

Yet there was more. Geoffrey had died in Paris of his injuries and had been publically mourned by Philip Augustus.

The king of France and opponent of Henry II, Geoffrey's own father.

"A tournament," scoffed one man. "An excuse, more like."

Duncan tried to disguise his interest. Did Châmont-sur-Maine not have one foot in Anjou and one in Brittany? Gaston would need to know as much as possible about this situation.

"Indeed," agreed another. "The tournament was to hide the negotiation of another alliance between Philip and Henry's sons, and one that doubtless would not suit Henry well."

"They are a fractious lot, to be sure."

"Ungrateful brats."

"It is the fault of the king himself. All those sons raised to warfare, and not a one of them given the authority he desires."

"The sole authority they each desire is their father's own."

Perhaps naturally, the mercenaries were much taken with the prospect of more war. They had little interest in the suggestion that the French king might lead a crusade after the defeat at Hattin. They had more fascination with the question of what rivalries might be revived in France with the departure of the king and—undoubtedly—some of his more powerful barons. Opportunity, it was agreed, would be ripe for an escalation of hostilities between Philip and Henry, particularly as Henry's two surviving sons seemed to be allied with the French king. Speculation abounded as to which barons would remain behind and which would attack what territories. Duncan's head fairly spun with the rapid flow of names and holdings, for he was less familiar with the nobility of France than this company.

When asked, Duncan told his comrade that he had only just left the employ of a baron in the low countries, but was vague about the location.

His neighbor nudged him. "Is there labor in the low countries?"

"Not so much as a man might hope," Duncan said grimly. He shook his head and echoed a concern common to mercenaries. "And there is trouble in ensuring one is paid in a timely manner."

There was much commiseration over this issue, which plagued a great many of the men present. They spoke then of which lords and barons paid promptly and heads were shaken over the repute of the Angevins.

"There are those who were never paid their due for serving the young king on that last foray. It has been years!"

Heads were shaken over this shameless exploitation of mercenaries, and much said about the inclinations of both Henry and his sons.

"What of those barons near Paris?" Duncan ventured to ask. "Will they defy Philip, if he rides to crusade?"

"If the king journeys to Outremer, there are those who might eye his demesne."

"Angevins!" crowed one man. "Prepared to seize any opportunity!"

"They will have time," insisted another. "He could not be gone less than two years."

"I heard Philip meant to enclose the city of Paris, with a wall."

"Turrets and towers," agreed another. "All wrought of stone."

"He feels the breath of the Angevins on his neck."

"He will have little coin left when that is done."

"Insist that you are paid now, then!"

"And spend what you have while you can!" There was laughter at that and much buying of ale. Stakes were raised in the games of dice, and Duncan recalled well enough what it was like to be uncertain of awakening on the morrow. There was a hunger in this company and he knew it was born of a need to make the most of every moment.

All here knew full well that there might not be another such night for them again. He spied injuries when he looked more closely, missing fingers and patches covering lost eyes, scars and wounds and the wages of war that none discussed so openly as the coin. Most of these men would die comparatively young, and most would die in violence.

He felt a sudden and profound relief that he was not of their profession. All he had to do was see Fergus safely home to pay his debt to that knight's father, then he could live out his days in peace.

And solitude. The prospect was not so appealing as it should have been, and he quaffed his ale, then ordered another. The tidings of warfare put him in mind of all he had left behind and he wondered whether all was as fractious in his birthplace as once it had been.

Not that it was his concern any longer.

The fact remained that Duncan had yet to learn what Gaston wished to know and turned to his companion.

"But such a wall cannot be built overnight, even with the will of a king," he said in a peevish tone, as if protesting the turn of the conversation. "I would find labor this very week, and close by, if it could be managed."

Discussion ensued about various dukes and barons, but Duncan did not hear the name of Millard de Saint-Roux. He was trying to decide how he might slide the name innocuously into the conversation, when his burly companion leaned closer.

"You might ride west," that man confided softly in Gaelic. "Toward Brittany."

"Aye?"

The man spared a glance at the others, who had begun to argue over a game of dice and did not appear to be listening. "I have heard tell that there is a baron seeking doughty warriors, the better to defend his holding against some knight he believes will make a claim against him."

"Who is right?"

"Whoever wins their first confrontation," replied his new friend with the pragmatism of a mercenary. "For I do not doubt that only one of them will walk away." He dropped his voice again. "It is rumored that the challenge comes from one with much experience in battles."

"And the baron? Is he well experienced in battle?"

Again, his companion grinned. "I think not, or he would not have need of hired blades."

"And does he pay?"

The red-haired man winced. "That is the consideration. There are those who do not trust him, but few who know of him. The holding seems to have been at peace for a long while, despite its neighbors."

"Despite?"

The man grinned. "It is on the Breton March, standing vigil on the frontier between Anjou and Brittany. You may be sure that there is much interest in the man who would hold that seal in his hand forever.

Duncan avoided that topic. "If it has been at peace, one would expect it to be prosperous, then."

"Possibly."

"Do you go?"

The other man winced again. "I do not like the smell of it, to be sure. The tale seems to miss a detail or two, which might be pertinent."

"Perhaps that the knight returned is the legitimate baron?"

The red-haired man smiled. "There are those who would not care, so long as they are paid. I am glad to have some ability to wait for a better opportunity." He drained his cup. "I have to wonder who is favored by Henry and who by Philip." He shook his head.

"If you go, friend, be wary about the arrangements."

Duncan pretended to consider this counsel as he finished his ale. "My inclination is to suspect that a man who might try to steal a holding might also decline to pay the wages due."

"You have learned to be wary in the low countries!"

"It is one thing to be cheated once. It is quite another to allow oneself to be cheated again."

"Aye, I see we think as one, my friend." The other man's manner turned more amiable. "Tell me where you are from. I might well know your people or know of them."

"An isle so small it makes Orkney look like Paris," Duncan lied and his companion laughed heartily. He lifted a finger. "But tell me first the name of this baron, lest I forget to ask you later. I would be wary. You said it was west of Paris?"

"Aye. The holding is Châmont-sur-Maine," said his companion with authority. "The baron is Millard de Saint-Roux."

Duncan repeated the name, as if he would commit it to memory. In truth, he did not have to do any such thing. He grimaced. "Yet on the far side of the territory of Anjou. I am not certain I wish to ride through those holdings in these days."

"There is that, to be sure," his comrade agreed. "Now, tell me of this isle."

Duncan fabricated a tale, knowing he had unearthed the very tidings that Gaston had sought. He had to leave, but not too quickly, the better to tell Gaston of all he had learned. He had another cup of ale, to disguise the timing of his departure, then there was a cheer as the whores burst into the tavern and began to slide through the crowd, seeking some employ of their own.

They were lushly curved, bold in their caresses with welcome in their smiles. Not a one of them was foul to look upon and their prices astonished Duncan. But then, this city was filled to bursting with their kind and likely quite competitive. One eyed him, her dark eyes glimmering with sensual intent, yet Duncan was surprised to find no interest within himself. She seemed to take that as a challenge, for she targeted him, draping herself over his shoulder and kissing his cheek. Her breasts rubbed against him, doubtless by design, and her fingers were in his hair.

Duncan extricated himself with an effort. He had been reminded of his future in the company of these men who could not rely upon having one. When he had returned to Scotland, Duncan knew there was but one deed left undone that might haunt him.

It would not be the refusal of this whore's charms.

Nay, it would be the failure to claim one last kiss from the beguiling Radegunde. He drained his cup, wished his companion well, and left the tavern intent upon gathering that very token.

After all, he had to tell Gaston what he had learned and doubtless would see Radegunde at the inn.

There could be no mistaking the identity of the new arrival. Aye, he was a Scot, but in a tavern full of Scots, still there was something about this one that caught the eye. He had a stance that reminded Murdoch of Domnall. A decisiveness in his movements. An expectation of authority.

The blood of kings would out.

When this man turned, there could be no mistake. The set of his eyes, the line of his mouth, even the tilt of his chin, all were reminiscent of his father.

Murdoch had finally found Domnall's missing son, after his long hunt.

Domnall would be pleased. He had not approved of the disappearance of his middle son, even though he did not approve of that son's choices. It was no longer sufficient to disown Duncan and guarantee that Duncan never had a crumb from his father's table. In these times, Domnall would ensure that his youngest, Guthred, was left with clear title, so had dispatched Murdoch to see Duncan dead.

Murdoch had followed Duncan south and then west, the intermittent trail leading him finally to Killairic. He had reached that keep a mere six months before, long after the laird's son had departed for Jerusalem, Duncan as his defender, but not so long before their anticipated return. Murdoch could have waited at Killairic, but the old man—laird and father of Fergus—had asked too many questions. Murdoch preferred to avoid suspicion.

Murdoch could have lingered in London, but he had no confidence that the party would journey that way. Paris was the place to await Duncan's return. Murdoch thought the city a necessary stop upon their route north, and Scots were easily found in this burg. Also, being in Paris offered the advantage of completing his assignment before his prey set foot upon Scottish soil.

Scots died in France, in astonishing numbers, after all. What was one more?

There could be no whisper of his crime associated with either Domnall or Guthred, not if they were to make a successful bid for the Scottish throne.

Murdoch appeared to be so drunken that he dozed, but all the while, he listened avidly to Duncan's conversation with the other mercenaries.

Why did Duncan ask after employ as a mercenary? He could have served his father well in that capacity, but had declined to do as much. Did he leave the service of Fergus of Killairic? If so, why?

Perhaps it would be wise for Murdoch to learn a little more before he struck the fatal blow.

When Duncan left, Murdoch finished his ale, pulled up the hood of his cloak and followed his intended victim. They had never met, but Duncan was reputed to be wily.

And Murdoch did not intend to fail.

Lady Ysmaine and her husband were sharing the evening meal in their chamber and darkness was falling. Radegunde had cleaned and washed and folded, and still bustled about the chamber while they dined.

She could not help but overhear their conversation and knew they were aware of that as well. The pair had discussed Gaston's failed effort to find any tidings of Wulfe or Christina, and Radegunde knew they were concerned for both. It seemed futile to her to chase after the knight at this point, for there was no telling his direction, and indeed, she had to imagine that Wulfe would have returned to the Temple for aid if he had believed himself in need of it. To her, the implication was clear that Wulfe had succeeded, yet saw no reason to deliver word of it to his former companions. He was evidently the manner of man well accustomed to completing his missions alone.

Radegunde would have wagered that Everard was dead, that Wulfe and Christina celebrated their reunion with gusto, and that they had no desire to be found or disturbed. Only then would Wulfe arrive at the Temple to be disciplined by the Grand Master for his defiance. She could not blame him for delaying that moment.

No one asked for her counsel, though. Instead, her lady asked her husband to consider who might make Radegunde a fine husband.

God in heaven. She might well be wed before they even reached Châmont-sur-Maine!

To Radegunde's relief, Gaston had not been home in years, so he did not know much of his villeins. He, too, suggested Bartholomew, but at least her lady dissuaded him of that notion. The lady Ysmaine then began to speculate upon the eligible men who had been at Valeroy before her departure.

"If I may be so bold, my lady," Radegunde dared to interject. "There is not a one of them who would tempt me."

"Too young," the lady said, smiling at her husband. "Radegunde would prefer a *man* to take her hand in his."

Gaston appeared to be amused by this notion, but merely sipped his wine.

"Radegunde, you cannot hope for love at first glimpse, as advocated in the troubadour's tales," Ysmaine chided.

"Even they do not advise a marriage be made upon such a whim," Gaston noted.

Ysmaine nodded and repeated her conviction. "A good match is founded upon good sense."

The lord put his hand over that of his lady. "And provides good soil for affection to grow," he agreed. They eyed each other, clearly much besotted with each other and convinced of the merit of their scheme.

Radegunde could not bear to listen to more of it. She begged to be excused and left them to their discussion. Given their expressions, she had little doubt that their attention soon would turn to more intimate matters than her marital prospects.

She knew they meant well and reminded herself of that with every step she took. She carried the broom she had borrowed back to the kitchen, sparing a glare for the man who had accosted her the night before and still watched her from the far side of the kitchen. She strode to the courtyard to dump out the bucket of dirty water, then paused to rebraid her hair and wipe her face.

She was sore from her efforts of the day, but she was glad to have had honest labor to do. It would not be all bad to rest her ankle, either. She would sleep well this night, to be sure, and she would sleep in the lady's chamber. How long should she wait before rapping at the portal again on this night? She knew the lady would admit her immediately but did not wish to interfere with the pair's desire to conceive a son.

Bartholomew was brushing the steeds and appeared to be deeply in thought. Indeed, she did not wish to encourage assumptions by making conversation with him, but at least his presence kept the cur in the kitchen.

Radegunde inverted the bucket and sat upon it, considering the few stars visible in the sky overhead as she faced the truth. The life she wished to evade was upon her already. She had not left this inn at all during the day, but had been left behind when her lady went to give alms. There had been a lot to do, but Radegunde could not help but yearn to see more of this great city.

Particularly as she might never return.

She wondered whether she would leave the inn at all before they rode to Valeroy, whenever that might be. There, she would be even more confined and doubtless soon wedded. Radegunde felt restless, but there were no sensible alternatives. If she fled her lady's service, she might starve or be injured. She had need of the protection and security that Gaston's household offered.

Still, she could not quell her desire for adventure.

Radegunde supposed she would have to learn to do as much, and the realization made her feel old. She stood and returned to her labor. She shook out her lady's dried chemises and cast them over her arm, then filled the bucket with fresh water and headed for the stairs.

She saw Bartholomew glance toward the gate and his features light in recognition. Radegunde turned, wondering who arrived, only to find Duncan standing in the opening to the street.

Wearing his plaid.

Her mouth went dry as her gaze roved over his legs—which were fine, indeed—then back to the glint of humor in his eyes. He looked so alluring that Radegunde forgot to be annoyed with him, hoping only that he had changed his thinking and returned to be with her this night.

"Is Lord Gaston here?" he asked.

Radegunde had a moment to hope that his reaction earlier this day had been due to Gaston's presence.

But Duncan spoke to Bartholomew, not her. "I have tidings for him," he said by way of explanation and she might not have been standing before him at all. Was he truly so disinterested in her presence?

Bartholomew abandoned brush and steed and brushed off his hands. "Aye, he is in his lady's chamber. I will fetch him for you."

"I would not disturb them," Duncan said.

"They enjoy their meal as yet," Radegunde supplied, hoping to draw his eye. Bartholomew nodded and passed her, taking the stairs several at a time.

Then Duncan's gaze met hers and she saw that glitter of interest in his eyes once more. It was sufficient to make her heart pound.

If he would keep the matter private, that could only be a good sign. Radegunde put down the bucket, then turned to face Duncan fully.

"Are Wulfe and Christina found?"

He shook his head. "Not so far as I know."

"So, these are not the tidings you would bring to Lord Gaston?"

Duncan shook his head again. "I do not think they will return."

"I do not wager that the Templar would think to inform any of his failure or success. He seems most accustomed to relying upon

57

no one."

"He will not fail," Duncan said with conviction. "He will do whatever is necessary to defend Christina."

"How do you know?"

Duncan's eyes twinkled. "He was going to sell his steed in Venice, to buy two lesser ones, so that she had a horse to leave the city."

Radegunde blinked in astonishment. "His destrier?" No knight would surrender his horse willingly.

Duncan nodded even as he smiled at her.

"Then he is besotted indeed!"

"I believe so." Duncan's manner turned thoughtful.

"Is this what you came to tell Lord Gaston? Such tidings might convince him to have less concern for his fellow knight."

"It was not that, but you are right. I should tell him. Affection of such power changes much."

Their gazes clung and Radegunde felt her flesh heat. "And here I hoped you might have returned for me, not to speak to Lord Gaston."

"Perhaps my aim was to do both." Duncan smiled, just a little, but it was sufficient to make her heart skip. "Would you believe me if I said as much?"

Much encouraged, Radegunde took a step closer to him. "You nigh gave me frostbite this morn, sir."

Duncan grimaced. "I did not sleep, but was haunted all the same."

"By dreams?"

"By memories." He looked drawn then, and Radegunde wished she could have eased his concern away.

She dared to guess. "Of what you have done?"

"Of what I have not done." Duncan spoke with resolve, then took a step closer. "And so I will not lose an opportunity." Her heart began to race but he raised a hand. "I still would not take what you offer, but I would have one last kiss, if you would surrender it to me."

"Why?"

"Because I have been reminded that life is uncertain and that a man should live so that he dies without regrets."

"Do you mean to die?"

"No one means to die, lass," Duncan said, his voice so husky that she wondered what those haunting memories had been. Their gazes clung as the light faded even more, and she took another step toward him.

She smiled, making her tone playful, for he was too solemn. "Only a kiss, Duncan?"

"Only a kiss."

"And you with such fine legs," she teased. "My mother will despair of me and my wiles."

"She need not do as much," he replied, his eyes gleaming. Radegunde smiled, intent upon making the most of his concession, and closed the distance between them. She liked how he watched her so intently.

Perhaps she could convince him to do more.

She smiled at the prospect, then suddenly smelled the ale upon him and halted. "You have been drinking!"

"I have been to a tavern, it is true..."

Radegunde leaned close. She smelled smoke and roast meat, then the unmistakable scent of cloyingly sweet perfume.

"Oh! You have been *whoring!*"

Duncan appeared to be startled. "Not precisely," he began to argue.

Radegunde was not prepared to listen to any defense. She was outraged. "This is why you would have just a kiss, for you have given the rest to a whore!" She shook her head. "Nay, you did not *give* it. You paid her to *take* it from you."

He reached out a hand in appeal. "Radegunde, you see more than is the truth..."

"I *smell* the truth," she retorted, retreating quickly. "How dare you return to me and request a kiss after you have lain with a whore? Do not make matters worse by telling a falsehood to me, Duncan MacDonald."

Duncan's eyes flashed. "I tell no falsehood, lass!"

"I say you do. And I say that you are not the manner of man I believed you to be," Radegunde declared, her tone hot. She did not know whether she was more disappointed with herself for misjudging Duncan or him for making such a choice. "I thought you a man of merit, one of honor and principle. You were the one who insisted upon not taking what I offered to you…"

"I did not take what you offered, to be sure, just as on this day, I did not take what *they* offered."

"Liar! You smell like whores, and there is but one way for that to transpire."

Duncan opened his mouth to argue, but Radegunde had heard sufficient. She threw a punch, just as her brother Michel had taught her. Her fist slammed into Duncan's nose and he staggered backward, more shocked than injured. Blood spurted from his nostrils and he gasped, but Radegunde did not care.

She dropped her voice low. "You are a knave and a fool, Duncan MacDonald. You declined what I offered to you out of affection, then bought the same from a whore! I hope she leaves you with a pox, for such a choice deserves no less."

He was holding his nose, and he glared at her over his hand. "I did no such deed."

"Liar," she retorted. "Cur and blackguard."

His eyes flashed. "And this is your tribute to me, for honorably defending your maidenhead?"

"I would choose whether or not to be rid of it."

"And what if you conceived a child?" Duncan demanded hotly. "What then, Radegunde? How will you convince your bridegroom that you are a maiden? What will your life become?" He jabbed a finger through the air at her. "I leave no babes behind me!"

"I would take the risk!"

"I would not!" he roared, more infuriated than ever she had seen him. "Do you think I would be glad to see you in the company of the women in the tavern this day? What if Gaston casts you from his holding? What if you lose your patroness?"

"I will not!"

"You cannot know for certain, and you might learn as much too late."

"You have a poor view of my lord and lady!"

"Who both forgot your safety last night!"

That was true. Radegunde could not defend them against that charge. She and Duncan glared at each other, even as she heard the sound of boots descending the stairs and the murmur of male voices drawing near.

Duncan grimaced, and his eyes were filled with uncommon heat. "I did not lay with a whore this day, lass, but even if I had, it is not so foolish a strategy," he said with quiet insistence. "An interval with a whore is a simple exchange, coin for pleasure, with no lasting bond and no child to recall the deed."

Radegunde shook her head at this paltry excuse. "I expected better of you."

"You need expect *naught* of me, as I made clear."

"I offered all I have to you, with no repercussions, no ties, no coin, because I admired you as a man. You need not fear a repetition of that offer, Duncan." She picked up her bucket so quickly that the water spilled over the lip. "Indeed, sir, you can go to Hell."

With that, she pivoted and marched up the stairs to her lady's chamber, her blood boiling. She stepped past Lord Gaston and Bartholomew, having no doubt both had heard all of the exchange, and did not care in the least.

She would enter her lady's chamber and not leave it again this night.

If that meant she never again saw Duncan MacDonald, Radegunde told herself that was just as well.

Even if she did not believe it.

Claire Delacroix

TUESDAY, SEPTEMBER 1, 1187

*Feast Day of Saint Drithelm
and Saint Giles of Provence*

CHAPTER SIX

uncan had time aplenty to regret his error with Radegunde.

He also had little opportunity to set matters to rights.

Much less apologize.

There were many discussions over the days they remained in Paris, and much debate in private chambers in the Temple. Gaston was prepared to acknowledge the possibility that his niece's husband Millard simply saw Châmont-sur-Maine defended in his choice of hiring mercenaries, and would not assume that those forces would be used to keep him from claiming his legacy. Duncan could see the caution of the former Templar and respected that Gaston's past experience as diplomat and negotiator informed his choices. The resolve in that man's eye, though, proved that he both hoped for the best and prepared for the worst.

Another legacy of Outremer, to be sure.

It was decided that none would seek out Wulfe. At Duncan's urging—and Radegunde's advice—Fergus confided in Grand Master and Gaston both that Wulfe had intended to sell his destrier to ensure that Christina could leave Venice in their company. Both knights were shocked that Wulfe had even considered such a sacrifice and concluded that it revealed much about that man's admiration for Christina, as well as his resolve to defend her. They were all reminded of Wulfe's defiance of the Grand Master, a choice that had seemed impetuous at the time but might be yet another indication of his amorous intent.

It appeared that Wulfe's future was neither in Paris nor with the order.

Given what Duncan had learned in the tavern, Gaston chose not to send word ahead to either Valeroy or Châmont-sur-Maine of the party's pending arrival. The tale was that Ysmaine wished to surprise her family, but Duncan guessed that Gaston wished to keep the tidings of his own return secret for as long as possible.

Finally, Fergus and the Grand Master were wary of assuming that the reliquary was safe without the surety that Everard had been brought to justice. There was much consideration of the best location for it to be secured, for it was the prize of the Templar's hoard.

The Grand Master had no desire to be remembered as the one who had lost the treasure. He knew the mind of the king, as well, and confirmed the rumor Duncan had heard in the tavern: if Jerusalem was lost, the king meant to lead another crusade. In his absence, and the absence of the many knights and barons who would accompany him, how secure would the city of Paris be? The Grand Master also had seen a scheme for the walls that Philip thought to build in the city's defense. The Temple would lie outside their protection, and though he ceded that this was prudent, Duncan saw that the Grand Master expected trouble.

They were all sworn to secrecy as to the true state of affairs in Palestine. The loss at Hattin was known but not its full horror, and the Grand Master would keep the advantage of additional information.

These concerns were debated thoroughly, and all perspectives presented with a thoroughness and attention to nuance that set Duncan's teeth on edge. He would have their plan decided and embark upon it!

Ultimately, it was concluded that Fergus should accompany Gaston to Châmont-sur-Maine, purportedly to witness the dubbing of Bartholomew, but truly to add his support to Gaston's rightful claim of his legacy. The Grand Master assigned six Templar knights to join their company, supposedly a guard of honor for one of their own returning home, but also a provision of power.

The Grand Master also instructed Fergus to take the reliquary secretly with him to Scotland, to secure it and to defend it, and to be prepared to return it at the summons from the Grand Master of the Temple in Paris. It seemed that the squire Laurent would yet have a saddlebag to defend, though Fergus would hide the true prize in Duncan's luggage.

They drank together to the success of all these ventures on their last night in Paris, and Duncan was relieved.

Finally, they would cease talking and ride!

There was thin sunlight on the morning that they finally approached Valeroy, after five long days of riding. The light and the chill in the air were both a reminder of winter's approach and made Duncan consider it likely they would reach Scotland in the snow. The bailey of the inn at Sablé-sur-Sarthe was filled with a merry bustle of activity as boys led horses out of the stables and loaded the baggage. Stallions stamped and palfreys nickered, all of the steeds prepared for the day's ride. They rode out early, for the lady Ysmaine wished to reach her home in time for the midday meal. It was clear to Duncan that a new liveliness had infected the company at the prospect of reaching Valeroy.

He, however, yearned to speak to Radegunde.

The portcullis was lifted at a shout and the gates opened, just as Lady Ysmaine appeared in the bailey at her husband's side. Gaston assisted her to mount, and Duncan knew she would ride at her husband's left hand yet again. Radegunde would ride to the left of her lady as she had done each day. The palfreys with the baggage followed, with the Templar knights and Bartholomew surrounding them. Fergus and Duncan rode at the rear of the party, while the squires mingled with the palfreys burdened with baggage in the middle of the procession.

The rest of the party mounted as the keeper was paid and thanked.

Duncan was well aware of the prize in his own saddlebag, its bulk bumping against the back of his thigh. He had kept his distance from Radegunde this week, hoping her anger would fade, but was increasingly desirous of a moment to speak to her alone. He was encouraged by the single quick glance Radegunde cast his way as she mounted her steed. She was aware of him, to be sure, but did not initiate any conversation.

She left the matter to him, and this day, he would commence their discussion. He told himself that he simply did not wish to part badly, but knew that was only part of the truth.

He owed her a secret, and Duncan would see that debt paid.

He also wanted a kiss.

Curiously, it was Radegunde who had begun to haunt his dreams in these nights since they had argued in Paris. She filled his thoughts with increasing demand. Would she oust Gwyneth forever? Duncan could not believe as much. But it was clear that she had some claim upon his attention, and he would have that kiss.

Radegunde had been granted a new cloak in Paris, or one new to her, and a better pair of boots. The cloak was not as fine as that of her lady but the green hue favored Radegunde's coloring. As usual, her hair was braided and she tugged her hood over it, after that one piercing glance fired in Duncan's direction.

If naught else, he would make her smile this day.

They rode out of the inn's courtyard in pairs, passing through the last of the town and taking the road to Valeroy. The road was sufficiently wide and in such good repair that they could ride two or three abreast. Duncan could see that the territory of Anjou was perhaps a prize worth a battle, for the land was rolling and a pleasing proportion of it was tilled. Mist clung in the valleys at this hour, but the forests were yet verdant. He had an impression of affluence.

Duncan dared to hope that Radegunde's thoughts were as his own when she let her palfrey fall back, ensuring there was a space beside her.

He did not give any other soul a chance to claim that spot. He urged his stallion forward and did not miss Radegunde's quick smile of satisfaction.

"I owe you a secret, lass," he said softly. "And I have not forgotten."

"Nor have I," she replied. "Though as days have passed in silence, I fear to ever collect it."

Duncan smiled. "How else shall I convince you that I am truly a man of honor than with the surrender of a secret?"

"I am surprised you would care," she maintained. "Since there are whores aplenty in this world to provide you with kisses and solace." There was little heat in her words and he was encouraged by that.

"But none to so intrigue me."

"Hmm," she said, her tone skeptical, but to his relief, that twinkle lit her dark eyes again. "Perhaps you only seek another secret from me."

"I think, lass, that between the two of us, we might know the full truth of every member of this company."

Radegunde smiled then, just a little, then glanced at his face and winced. "I am sorry that I struck you. I was vexed."

"I gathered as much."

"How is your nose?"

He touched it with a fingertip. It was still a bit swollen. One side had progressed through a ripe purple to yellowish green, neither being hues he favored. "Tender yet, for you struck it well."

Radegunde smiled outright then, a sight that made his heart skip. "My brother taught me how."

"The older one?"

"Michel." She eyed the road ahead and shrugged. "Indeed, that is one good thing about returning to Valeroy. I shall see my mother and brothers again."

"Only one good thing?"

She wrinkled her nose. "My lord and lady mean to see me wed with haste, Duncan." Her tone was carefully neutral when she continued, as if she feared that couple might overhear her words.

"My lady believes that a match should be wrought of practical considerations, and that only afterward does affection grow."

"For that has been her experience."

"Only once of three marriages," Radegunde pointed out in a whisper. "She would never have loved either of the first two husbands, and those matches were just as advantageous, but she is convinced of her reasoning."

"You might fare well," he felt compelled to say, though he, too, had his doubts.

She seemed to shake herself. "Either way, there is naught to be done about it, other than flee her service and starve in the forest amongst the felons. I will reserve that option for a truly awful prospective spouse." She turned a bright smile upon him then, and he liked that she did not dwell upon matters she could not change. "I will have your secret, Duncan, and I hope it comes with a tale. It will be a long morning in the saddle, to be sure."

"Perhaps not the best place for the confession of a secret then."

Radegunde shook a finger at him. "Particularly as you already agreed to offer one of your own, not one of another."

"Then I shall tell you a tale, and save the secret for a moment when we are alone together. Perhaps this night in Valeroy we might find such a moment."

"Ha!" Radegunde scoffed, those eyes dancing in a challenge. "I will not find myself alone with a man, save a man of honor!"

"Then I must convince you of my merit, it is clear." He surveyed the company, knowing only one tale would do. "Praise be that I have the opportunity to so persuade you."

Radegunde laughed, not nearly so turned against him as she might have him believe.

"So, this is home for you and Lady Ysmaine," he said, well aware that half a dozen souls could readily hear their conversation. "Tell me of it, if you will."

"Gladly," Radegunde agreed, and he liked that she was not one to hold a grudge. "We ride toward the western boundary of Anjou."

"Held by the English King, the Angevin Henry II." Duncan had been shocked to witness how close the holdings of the English king came to the demesne of the French king—on the third day's ride from Paris, they had passed into Anjou. No wonder matters between the pair of kings were so uneasy.

"The very same," Radegunde agreed. "To the east is the demesne of the French monarchy, and the palace of Philip Augustus in Paris." She lifted a hand to point. "To the west, the Breton March, although these lands have been contested and have been sworn to both Paris and Anjou at differing times."

"And the Bretons? Who do they favor?"

Radegunde smiled. "They would prefer to answer to neither, I suspect, but declare their own king as sovereign."

The situation reminded Duncan of Scotland.

"As an example, we will soon pass Chateau-Gontier, a keep of some repute in such matters."

"Indeed? How so?"

"Over a hundred years ago, there was a Breton duke named Conan II. His father died when he was a minor, and his uncle ruled Brittany as regent. Indeed, he kept Conan imprisoned, though the supporters of the true duke saw him freed. Still, his uncle kept the seal. Even when Conan came of age in 1054, his uncle would not surrender the seal to the younger man. It is said he feared to grant Conan any authority, for Conan had a legitimate claim to the duchy of Normandy as well as that of Brittany."

"Do I see the influence of great nobles intent upon securing their advantage?" Duncan asked lightly.

"Perhaps so, for the uncle was allied with William of Normandy, the forebear of the Angevin kings. In 1056, though, Conan gained the upper hand and saw his uncle imprisoned when he forcibly claimed the seal that was his birthright."

"And what had been done to him was done to his uncle."

Radegunde shrugged. "Apparently so. William was not without aspirations of his own."

"To be sure, he invaded England in 1066."

"Aye, and before his departure from Normandy, he warned his neighboring barons not to attack his lands, for he carried the blessing of the pope on his quest."

Duncan chuckled. "I will guess what came of that."

Radegunde's eyes sparkled in a most beguiling way. "Aye, Conan sent word that he would not be dissuaded from claiming what he believed to be his own, and he marched upon Pouancé in William's absence." She lifted a hand and pointed to the west. "It is not so distant. I believe you can see the flag upon the turret."

Duncan squinted and nodded, though he could not discern the color of the banner.

"For as long as can be recalled, Pouancé was a town upon the Breton March, spanning the border, with lands on each side of the division. I have heard it called the door of Brittany."

Like Châmont-sur-Maine, Duncan thought.

"Conan claimed it and then he claimed Segré, riding steadily east, and finally, he took his rest at Château-Gontier, yet further east."

"And so it seemed he made incursions into William's holdings."

A light dawned in Radegunde's eyes. "But William had been warned of Conan's intent, you recall, and by Conan himself."

"Dared, even."

"So there were some unsurprised when Conan was found dead at that keep."

"Dead! Struck in his sleep?"

"Not so forthright as that. It is said he died of poison." Radegunde lifted her gloved hand. "That his leather gloves were treated with poison weeks before." She dragged a finger over her lips to illustrate her point. "Unwittingly, after his conquests, he wiped his mouth, perhaps at the end of the day."

"How clever," Duncan had to acknowledge.

"How wicked," Radegunde corrected. "The trap set and the perpetrator far gone before it is sprung. It was never resolved who might have so prepared the gloves, and indeed, they soon went missing. But Conan was dead, and the holdings he had taken by force were readily reclaimed by William's forces."

"Next you will tell me that Conan's holdings were claimed by William."

Radegunde laughed. "Not so, for the Breton did not care to come beneath any king's thumb. Nay, the duchy of Brittany passed to Conan's sister Hawise, and she chose to wed Hoel, Duke of

Cornouaille. Together, they united all of Brittany, establishing the house of Kernev, which ruled the duchy of Brittany for nigh a hundred years."

"And then?"

"And then you shall laugh, for the heir was named Conan and the stepfather who would deny him his legacy was named Odo."

Duncan arched a brow. "It seems a territory in need of more names."

Radegunde laughed. "It might be so. But much of the rest of the tale remains similar, for there was dissent with Henry II, and Constance, the daughter of Conan, was wed to Geoffrey, the son of Henry." She dropped her voice to a whisper. "And Conan was compelled by Henry to abdicate and make his daughter countess, immediately upon her marriage to Geoffrey."

"Who was titled Duke of Brittany, and who died in Paris, after having been trodden by horses in a tournament, a year ago," Duncan provided.

"He did?"

"Aye, I heard tell of it in Paris. Constance was with child at his death but delivered of a son last March, who is now Duke of Brittany."

"Those are foul tidings," Radegunde mused. "There will be uncertain times ahead."

"Not so uncertain as that. Constance will be wedded again, to be sure, and with haste," Duncan forecast and Radegunde nodded agreement. "Is this tale of poison well known?" he asked, on a more cheerful note, for the woes of their betters were not their concern.

"My mother told me of it, for she found the tale intriguing."

"As a wise woman and midwife."

"Indeed." Radegunde smiled. "And she bade me never wipe my mouth with a gloved hand, though truly, there is no soul who would seek to see me dead."

"Do not even say as much aloud!" Duncan chided, for the notion made him shiver with dread.

"Tell me a tale instead," she invited, and he could not resist the opportunity.

☙☞

Radegunde had been beyond relieved that Duncan finally spoke to her. In four days of riding, she had nigh lost hope that he would ever do as much again.

She clutched the reins of her palfrey and listened to the low rumble of his voice with pleasure. To think of Duncan recounting a story, and doing so for her entertainment, was most gratifying. Before they had reached Paris, she had thought him incapable of uttering two sentences in succession, and now he would tell her an entire tale.

"Once, there was a man," he began and she could not resist the urge to tease him.

"A man of honor, no doubt."

"He thought himself to be one such, to be sure." Duncan feigned a wince. "Though I have heard him called a knave and a fool."

Radegunde laughed, as much because he recalled her words as because he would share some of his own history with her. She was very pleased by this compliment. "We are all fools at some point."

"Indeed. This particular man left all he knew and sought adventure."

"Ah! I like him well already."

They shared a smile. "Perhaps you have something in common with him."

"Perhaps more than he knows." That awareness rose between them again, and Radegunde found her cheeks growing warm. She could not look away from the admiration in Duncan's eyes and wished again for the opportunity to surrender more to him than mere words. She let her gaze drop to his lips and linger there, and he caught his breath in a most satisfying manner.

"This man was careless with his advantage, though."

"Which advantage?"

"The greatest one of all—his life."

"Why?"

"He thought it worthless."

"But why?"

Duncan gave her a sharp look. "That is another tale."

Radegunde resolved in that moment to collect the second story, as well, but she smiled. "And so, he was reckless. What was the outcome of that?"

"He fell into a company of mercenaries, more because he had need of coin to keep himself than of any thirst for violence. And so he fought with them, taking employ where they found it and battling for whichever side paid the most. They had a disregard for the notion of right and wrong, and since he had seen the world to be capricious in its favors, it suited this man to disregard such details, as well. He fought. He earned coin. He ate and drank when he could. He slept and then he rose to do as much again. It was no life for a thinking man, but he had ceased to think."

Radegunde bit her lip, wondering what would drive Duncan to so forget his own nature.

"One day, this company came to a border land, much like this Breton March you tell me about." Duncan gestured to the west. "A place where alliances shifted constantly, and there was always a battle to be found. He fought hard in this locale and was as fortunate as such a man can be, for he earned a goodly measure of coin. It was then that he recalled himself and his own nature, and he began to reconsider the life he had made his own. He thought of remaining in one place and living out his days in peace. As a result, he ceased to carouse with his fellows in the taverns, and carefully saved his coin. He was quiet about it, but in such a company, there are few secrets."

"Perhaps a whore betrayed him," Radegunde dared to suggest.

"Perhaps she did," Duncan acknowledged. "For he was known to take comfort with such women once in a while, to see his needs met."

"Yet leave no bastard behind."

He slanted a glance her way, his expression assessing. "Perhaps so. For I do know that he was assaulted by his fellows one night, when he slumbered deeply, and that he was robbed. When he awakened and tried to defend his coin, he found himself in the midst of a battle again. Despite the disadvantage of numbers, he was not prepared to surrender all that he had earned with his own blade. He fought hard and foolishly, though he had no true chance of success. He knew these men well enough to understand that they would kill for his coin." Duncan paused.

"And was he killed?" Radegunde finally prompted. She thought she knew the answer and was not surprised when Duncan shook his head.

"He was not, but not through any valor of his own. A knight intervened, for he had heard the noise, and he was a fearsome warrior himself. The knight dispatched two of the assailants, then the others scattered. Once he learned that assailants and victim had been comrades, the knight did not allow the villains to flee so readily as that. He hunted down another two and slaughtered them for their faithlessness. Then he returned the stolen coin to the fool."

"The knight saved his life."

"Indeed, he did. And the fool recalled his wits well enough to understand that he was in the debt of the knight. He bowed low and kissed the knight's boots, swearing fealty to him and vowing to serve him well." Duncan swallowed. "And such was the grace of the knight that he decreed the fool would serve him only until the debt was repaid in kind."

"Until the fool saved the knight's life."

"Just so. The years passed and the fool learned much in the knight's abode, and he served him well. He became a warrior and a man of integrity. Never was the knight's life imperiled, though, and the warrior was vexed that he could not repay the debt."

"Did he wish to leave the knight's service?"

Duncan shook his head. "Not particularly. It was simply an outstanding debt, and he liked to see his obligations paid."

"I like him well," Radegunde declared. "That is a sound philosophy. What happened?"

"The knight had a son, one who would inherit all the knight had built as his own. He feared for his son's future, for his holding was upon that treacherous March. So, he instructed his son to serve two years with the Templars in Outremer, the better to learn how to defend himself and his holding. And he bade the warrior to escort the son to Jerusalem and back again, to protect his son in lieu of himself. The warrior knew he would lay down his life, if need be, to repay the debt he owed."

"He understood that the debt had passed from father to son."

"That was how he saw the matter, to be sure."

Radegunde glanced back at Fergus. "And when the son returned home, hale and whole? What happened to the warrior?"

Duncan smiled. "I do not know. I would wager that the knight had another quest for him."

And so it would be until the debt was paid. Radegunde understood that Duncan could not promise any deed in his own future, for it was not his to command. So long as he stood indebted to Fergus' father, he would do as he was bidden.

"I think this warrior sounds to be a man of honor," she said.

Duncan smiled at her with obvious satisfaction. "I am glad to hear it."

She smiled back at him. "I would even venture to spend an interval alone with such a man, for his nature cannot be doubted."

"Even in the evening?" He feigned such surprise that Radegunde laughed aloud.

"Even so, for my confidence is considerable."

Duncan grinned outright. "Then you may find it deserved, lass."

"I should hope as much," she said. "For he owes me a secret still." Duncan chuckled and Radegunde was more impatient to arrive at Valeroy than she had been.

It was not long later that she lifted a hand and pointed out the familiar towers to Duncan. "Valeroy!" she whispered, her heart thumping with delight, and she watched him survey the keep with evident approval.

It was a fine fortress, and she was surprised by the vigor of her pleasure to be home again. Was it because she could show its pleasures to Duncan? Or was it the promise of that evening alone in his company? Radegunde, to be sure, knew many places to find a bit of privacy at Valeroy.

CHAPTER SEVEN

ady Ysmaine dismissed Radegunde nigh as soon as her baggage was carried into the chamber she would share with Lord Gaston. Her own mother, Lady Richildis, was yet arm-in-arm with her oldest daughter, and Lady Ysmaine's younger sisters filled the chamber with their chatter. Already Sibilla and Melissande plucked at the saddlebags, curious as to see their sister's new acquisitions. Juetta and Constantia appeared to be a little awed by Ysmaine's return, or perhaps it was the sight of Gaston arriving in the portal that made them retreat so hastily.

"Go!" Lady Ysmaine said to Radegunde with a smile. "Your mother will be as glad to see you as mine has been."

"And we have aid enough in the unpacking," Lady Richildis said with an indulgent smile. "Truly, Ysmaine, you should have bought more to better occupy us."

"She did not deign to purchase more," Gaston supplied, granting his wife an affectionate smile. "Your daughter is most frugal."

Lady Richildis was clearly pleased by this comment. "The lady of the manor must be careful with coin," she said. "For the treasury cannot always be full."

"Go!" Lady Ysmaine whispered to Radegunde again, her delight enough to make Radegunde believe she would not be missed. She bowed and kissed her lady's hand, then turned to flee down the stairs.

"Do not forget to take a loaf of bread from the kitchens to your mother!" Lady Richildis called from behind her.

Radegunde returned to the portal, glad that the lady had recalled her usual gift. "I thank you, my lady. That is most kind."

"It is a habit and a good one," Lady Richildis said, then waved her fingertips. "Go, while the bread is yet warm."

"Aye, my lady." Radegunde smiled as she hastened away, her heart fluttering with a joy to be home and the promise of Duncan's attention later.

"And do not let me see you here again before midday on the morrow," Lady Ysmaine called.

"A most loyal girl," Lady Richildis declared, and Radegunde heard her words.

"The most loyal companion any woman could have," Lady Ysmaine asserted. "I hope you do not mind if she comes to Châmont-sur-Maine with me."

"You will have no argument from me," Lady Richildis replied, humor in her voice.

Radegunde wondered at that. Did Lady Richildis believe Radegunde's mother would insist she remained at Valeroy?

Radegunde knew it would not be so. She raced down the stairs and through the hall, pausing only for a cursory bow to Lord Amaury, who appeared to be amused by her haste. Then she strode down the corridor to the kitchens. The cook and the baker and the sauce maker were all familiar and exclaimed in greeting at the sight of her. She was hugged and kissed, and only just escaped the immediate recounting of her adventures. "I am bidden to visit my mother with all haste, and Lady Richildis says I should take her a loaf of fresh bread."

"You shall have to speak to the sergeant-at-arms' new warrior," the cook said. His expression was dour but there was a twinkle in his eye.

"What new warrior?"

The sauce maker pursed his lips. "A most commanding young man."

"And one who takes an active interest in defending the treasures of his lord's home," the baker added.

Radegunde was certain she must know this man, but she knew of no knights or warriors.

"Indeed, he takes his responsibilities seriously indeed," the cook agreed.

"Is he not known in these parts?" the baker asked and could not fully halt his smile.

It was clear that they teased her, though Radegunde could not imagine who it might be. "Tell me where to find him and I shall ask," she said. "Though Lady Richildis already gave her command."

The baker chortled just as Radegunde realized someone stood behind her. The cook made a spinning gesture with one finger.

"I shall decide who takes bread from this kitchen," a man said, his voice deeper than she recalled yet most beloved. Radegunde gasped aloud and had but a glimpse of the satisfaction of cook, baker, and sauce maker before she pivoted. All of her brothers shared her coloring, having dark wavy hair and dark eyes, but only Michel was taller than she.

"Michel!" Radegunde hooted at the sight of her older brother, then flung herself into his arms. At twenty summers, he was fully grown and she felt how he had become stronger in her absence. He hugged her tightly and spun her around, kissing her on both cheeks when he set her on her feet again. "Look at you!" she declared, brushing off his tabard. "In the lord's livery and serving in his hall. How can you be taller and look even more valiant than I recall?"

"Look at you," Michel mimicked, brushing her kirtle in turn. "All the way home from Outremer, the dust of Jerusalem itself in your shoes. How can you be thinner and yet more boldly spoken than before?" They grinned at each other, for they had always been close. He touched her cheek with his fingertips. "You look well, Radegunde."

"As do you." She gestured to him again. "How was this contrived?"

"As if it must be a jest or a bit of trickery!" Michel folded his arms across his chest and pretended to glower at her. "I thank you for your confidence, sister."

"But to fight in the lord's army?"

"To be trained in the lord's army," her brother corrected. "Lord Amaury is good to me, indeed."

"I am certain you must deserve his confidence."

"There is the endorsement I expected!"

Radegunde propped a hand on her hip. "And with this good fortune, are you wedded yet?"

"You sound like *Maman*!" He kissed her brow, then took a step back. "*Maman* will have heard of the party's arrival, so you had best arrive at her door soon." Michel raised his brows in mock horror. "I will not answer to her for delaying you."

Radegunde turned to find that the baker had wrapped a fresh loaf of bread in a napkin for her. He held it out and she thanked him as she accepted it, then she walked through the kitchen to the garden. Once out the gate, she broke into a run, each step making her more excited to see her family again.

Perhaps adventure was better appreciated when one could return home at the end of it.

There was a thought to consider.

Mathilde was standing in the garden before her cottage, arms folded across her chest as she surveyed the path to the keep. Radegunde could see at a distance that her mother looked both expectant and not so much older than before.

Especially when she smiled at the glimpse of her daughter returned.

"Radegunde!"

They embraced tightly and Radegunde was surprised to find tears on her mother's cheeks when they pulled back to examine each other. "Did you think I would not return?"

Her mother spoke bluntly, as was her wont. "I feared you might not have a choice."

Radegunde understood, for she knew that her mother oft saw portents of the future. "Did you dream of us?"

Mathilde shuddered. "The first six months after your departure, I had terrible nightmares." She averted her gaze. "After that, it was hard to sleep." She gripped Radegunde's hand tightly. "Come in, child, and tell me all of it. Lord Amaury already sent a gift to us all that we might celebrate your return."

"Lady Richildis sent another, with this fresh bread."

"And it is welcome, indeed. Come!"

Radegunde halted before the threshold, hearing her younger brothers within. "We were robbed by the men Lord Amaury hired to protect us," she confessed, her words falling in a rush. She wanted to admit the worst of it quickly. She let her voice soften, for she knew her mother would find this detail difficult. "Thibaud was killed in our defense, *Maman*."

"I feared as much." Mathilde sighed, then ran a hand over her brow. "I saw his death, over and over again. God in Heaven, but I hoped it was kinder than what I dreamed." To Radegunde's relief, her mother did not seem to expect a reply. Instead, she hugged Radegunde again and her next words were hoarse. "He was a good man, a loyal man who would give his all in service of Lord Amaury. Ah, child, I am selfish, for I feared his all had not been sufficient."

"I have learned much, *Maman*," Radegunde whispered. "No thief will readily surprise me again."

Mathilde considered her daughter again and Radegunde wondered how much her mother saw in her eyes. "You carry more secrets, which means you hold Lady Ysmaine's trust. That is good, for it will ensure your future in her household." She smiled with affection. "Not for you a village life. Nay, my sole daughter would sleep in a nobleman's hall."

"Do not tease me of that again!" Radegunde protested.

"You were but four summers of age when you informed me that you would sleep in a fine hall and eat venison every week once you were grown and wed."

"I do like venison still."

"And I wager you have had little of it these past two years."

"Little indeed."

Her mother smiled and opened the door, and it was only then that Radegunde both smelled the meat and heard what her younger brothers were quibbling about. "Lord Amaury sent a roast haunch of venison."

"He is generous indeed!"

"You brought his daughter home, Radegunde. I am certain his gratitude extends beyond a gift of game." Mathilde smiled. "Though the fare is welcome indeed."

"Radegunde!" Jacques cried, then the three boys assaulted her in a most affectionate greeting. "Look! Fresh bread from the hall."

"Do not eat it as yet," Mathilde advised sternly.

Yves and Ogier crowded around her, demanding the tale of her adventures noisily. How had they all become so tall? Indeed, Jacques at fifteen summers was nigh as tall as Michel though not yet as broad. Yves at ten summers and Ogier at eight were much bigger, though their eyes still danced with mischief. The cottage was much as it had been, clean and neat, though on this day, it was filled with the divine scent of that venison.

"I saw Michel at the keep," Radegunde managed to tell her mother before any words she said were drowned out completely.

"We will talk later, once these ruffians are fed." Her mother smiled at her, her gaze flicking over the boys. "Who has laid the board? I see no napkins. Jacques, cut the bread. Yves, fetch the bowls and spoons, and Ogier, wash those hands."

"Tell us of Outremer, Radegunde," Yves entreated when they were seated at the board and their bowls were full. Radegunde took a bite of venison first, closed her eyes in rapture, then began her tale with their impoverished arrival in Jerusalem. Her mother sat back, her eyes gleaming, to listen, and Radegunde did not doubt that her mother heard both what she did say and what she did not.

There could be no doubt that the young man granted the responsibility of showing Duncan to the space over the stables was related to Radegunde. His hair was as unruly and his eyes as dark as hers, to be sure, but there was a greater resemblance in the merriment of his expression. Duncan saw that this Michel was well trusted in Lord Amaury's house and concluded that her family had long resided on the holding.

"Have you any other requirements for your comfort?" the young man asked politely.

"Nay, this accommodation will suit me well, and I like to be close to the steeds," Duncan acknowledged. "I would ask you merely for some tidings."

"Sir?"

"Call me Duncan, lad."

"Aye, Duncan."

"That is better. The maid who serves Lady Ysmaine and arrived in our party this day. Would she be a relation of yours?"

"Is there a reason you ask, sir?"

Duncan shrugged. "I think I see a resemblance, no more than that."

Michel smiled broadly and there was much in that expression to recall Radegunde. "She is my sister, sir, my sole sister. My mother will be heartily pleased to see her return."

"I have no doubt of that."

Michel sobered. "It is more than a mother's concern, sir."

"Indeed?"

"Indeed. My mother oft dreams of future events, or knows of doings far afield."

Duncan straightened and turned to face the younger man. "Aye?"

"Aye. She had nightmares after Lady Ysmaine's party departed and has been most fearful."

Duncan nodded, well familiar with such powers. "At home, we would say she had the Sight."

"Aye, sir." Michel frowned and corrected himself. "Duncan."

"Their journey, from what I understand, was not an easy one," Duncan said with care. "Although our paths joined only in Jerusalem several months ago."

"The lady left with a party of men to defend her."

"I gather that she was betrayed, as can happen."

Now it was Michel who watched Duncan avidly.

"Doubtless you will be told the fullness of the tale at some point, but I have heard the name Thibaud mentioned by Lady Ysmaine with much grief and regret."

Michel's shoulders sagged. "Odo said that the lady told him as much at the gates. I was hoping he had heard her incorrectly Thibaud was a good man, a man-at-arms in service to Lord Amaury and much trusted."

Duncan nodded and frowned at the floor. There was likely already much speculation in both keep and village. "I fear he surrendered all to defend his lord's daughter."

"He would, sir."

Duncan arched a brow.

"Duncan," Michel corrected, a flush of color rising on his neck. "I thank you for telling me of this. We were all very fond of Thibaud."

"Doubtless there will be a mass sung for him here at Valeroy."

"If not a dozen. Lord Amaury leaves no such matter untended."

Duncan smiled. "Then he is a worthy lord to serve."

"That he is," Michel said with enthusiasm. "Do you mean to join the meal in the hall?"

"Aye, lad, but I would wash first."

"Of course. Let me show you the way." Michel gestured and Duncan followed him, noting the affluence of Valeroy's stables and the power of its defenses. "I wish I could see Radegunde's arrival at our home," the younger man said wistfully. "My mother will be pleased indeed."

"I can imagine as much."

"And Lord Amaury sent venison to our abode, for he knows Radegunde's fondness for the meat."

"A most generous baron." Duncan was well aware that his own anticipation of joining the company for the meal was much diminished. Radegunde would not be present and he found himself wishing that he, too, could witness her return home. "Does your mother live in the village then?" he asked, hoping his curiosity was not notable.

"Aye, she has the last hut on the distant side, the one closest to Lord Amaury's forests," Michel supplied readily.

"That would be of convenience to her," Duncan said and the younger man cast him a puzzled glance. "Radegunde said her mother was both midwife and wise woman. I assume that there are useful plants to be found in the forest."

Relief touched Michel's features. "You speak aright in that." The younger man showed Duncan where he might find all he needed, his manner keeping Duncan from asking more.

He could not help but think that the distant side of the village, near the forest, would leave Radegunde with a long walk upon her return. He doubted she would remain with her mother for the night, for Lady Ysmaine might have need of her service and Radegunde was most loyal.

By the time he reached the hall, Duncan was resolved. He would find this mother's abode when darkness fell and ensure that Radegunde was escorted safely back to the hall.

It would give him the opportunity to pay his debt of a secret to her.

And if that merry lass felt inclined to surrender a kiss to keep him warm this night in exchange, Duncan would have no argument with that.

It was late when Mathilde put a cup of ale before Radegunde, then sat opposite her daughter with a second cup for herself. A single wax candle burned on the board between them and the boys were already snoring in the loft overhead. Night's darkness slipped between the shutters and Radegunde could hear the singing of crickets.

"Winter comes," she said, as her mother always did when the crickets became louder at the end of each summer.

"And the harvest," Mathilde agreed and smiled. "It is a year of bounty and blessing, to be sure." She sipped of the ale. "And so Lady Ysmaine is wedded to a knight formerly in the service of the Templars."

"Aye. Lord Gaston is a fine man," Radegunde said, then bit back a smile in recollection of Duncan's reaction to her mischievous comment. Her mother arched a brow. "With fine legs."

"And how would you know such a thing?"

"I saw him nude in Venice. He was cast into the canal and brought back to the house insensible. My lady stripped him to see him warm and to ensure the wound was treated."

"And was it?"

"He had been struck from behind. We washed the wound and she sat vigil with him."

"She has a good memory, but then her grandmother could have been a wise woman herself, had she not been a nobleman's wife." She lifted her cup of ale, looking over the rim at Radegunde. "And there is one adventure you did not share."

"Is there?"

"You have fallen in love, daughter mine."

Radegunde felt herself flush.

"Is he a good man?"

"I think so." Radegunde smiled. "I shocked him when I told him of Lord Gaston's legs."

Her mother laughed at that. "And what of *his* legs?"

"Most fine."

They laughed together, and Radegunde felt a communion with her mother that was newfound. "Can he fight?"

"Aye, he is quick with a knife when that is warranted."

"And his nature?"

"Noble indeed." Radegunde sighed and fell silent.

Of course, Mathilde saw to the nut of the matter. "Yet you do not bring him to meet me," she said softly. "Does he not see the merit of my sole daughter?"

"He vows to not take more than is his right," she admitted. "And I believe he is yet beholden to his liege lord. He returns to Scotland in his service."

"Ah." Mathilde swirled the ale in her cup, her thoughts disguised from Radegunde. "It says much good of a man, to my thinking, if he is so concerned with honor."

Radegunde nodded reluctant agreement.

Her mother straightened and smiled, changing the subject so they might converse readily again. "And soon you will go with Lady Ysmaine to her new abode, of course. Is it far? You did not tell me the name of her husband's holding."

Radegunde was only too glad to speak of happier matters. "Lord Gaston is to take custody of his inheritance, Châmont-sur-Maine. It is not far at all, *Maman*. Indeed, I believe Lady Ysmaine would hope for you to assist in the arrival of any child she bears..."

"Châmont-sur-Maine?" her mother asked, interrupting her. Her tone was unnaturally sharp.

"Aye." Radegunde was surprised by her mother's reaction. "His older brother Bayard died and he is heir. He left the order of the Templars to assume his title."

Mathilde rose to her feet and paced the width of the cottage.

Radegunde was confused. "Are these bad tidings, *Maman*? Has something gone awry at that holding?"

Mathilde waved a hand and paced more quickly. Though her mother's agitation was clear, Radegunde could not explain it. She knew better than to ask further, though, for her mother was evidently deciding upon how much to confide in her.

It was best to simply wait.

When her mother sat opposite her again, she drained the cup of ale. She met Radegunde's gaze steadily. "This is a matter of secrets, and is a confidence that is not mine to share. You must ask Lady Ysmaine for permission to visit Lord Gaston's mother."

Radegunde blinked. "She spoke to me of her intent to do as much herself."

"When?"

"She has said little of it since. Her wrist was broken in Paris and I believe the wound fatigues her, though she does not complain. I suspect we will ride to Châmont-sur-Maine first..."

"Nay," her mother interrupted. "Someone must learn what Eudaline knows before you depart Valeroy." Mathilde leaned across the board. "Lady Eudaline was Fulk's third wife and bore Gaston to him. When I tended Lady Richildis for the birth of her second child, Jehanne, Fulk had just died." She leaned back, her eyes darting back and forth as she recalled the past. "It was nigh Easter, an early Easter that year, and the wind was bitterly cold. There was much chatter in Lord Amaury's hall, for Châmont-sur-

Maine is close enough for its lord to be considered a neighbor. I thought little of it, for the aged oft die just before the most foul winter turns to spring."

"But it was not so simple as that?"

"I am not certain. There was much agitation. To be sure, my greater concern was with lady and babe, and I did not trouble myself overmuch with distant matters then." She looked at Radegunde and smiled. "You had just been born, on the day after Epiphany, and I had brought you with me, the better to nurse you as required."

"It sounds most busy."

"It was, but it was merely days before Fulk's widow Eudaline retired to a convent."

"Did you know her?"

"I had heard tell of her. A most forthright woman, by all accounts, certainly not one inclined to quiet reflection."

"It seemed unlikely that she would choose the convent, then?"

"One can never account for the choices of widows and noblewomen, but it did seem odd. Then Lord Bayard assumed the lordship and wed, and all thought well of him, so it seemed any suspicion must be groundless."

Suspicion?

Radegunde leaned forward. "Lord Gaston, I believe, was most astonished that his brother died."

Her mother's gaze was level. "Aye. So were many others."

"But how…"

Radegunde's mother interrupted her. "Tell Lady Ysmaine and Lady Richildis that I advise you to seek out Lady Eudaline. Since Lady Ysmaine has been injured, it will be better for her to rest and for you to undertake this errand. I do not know the convent Eudaline chose, or I do not remember, but Lady Richildis will know. Whatever Eudaline knows or suspects, it would be best for Lady Ysmaine to learn of it before she and her new husband arrive at his father's holding."

It was cursedly mysterious, but Mathilde would not elaborate. She insisted again that she could not do as much.

It was only when Radegunde rose from the board to retire that her mother added one more piece of advice. "Take your man with you," Mathilde said with quiet urgency. "No matter what skills you have learned, Radegunde, you may have need of a man who is swift with a knife."

"What do you know?"

Mathilde smiled. "There are brigands in these parts. Any soul traveling alone cannot show too much care."

That was not the fullness of the truth, and Radegunde knew it, just as she recognized that her mother would not explain further.

She would have to visit Eudaline to learn more.

If that woman chose to confide in her.

But first she had to contrive a way for Duncan to accompany her.

She might have kissed her mother and retired, but there was a cry from outside the hut. Something heavy fell to the ground. Her gaze flew to that of Mathilde, who picked up a knife and flung open the door to the hut, her posture fearless.

"Who comes?" she bellowed into the darkness.

Radegunde stood behind her mother, holding the candle high. The light did not penetrate far into the shadows. She could hear distant music from the keep and lights burned brightly from that structure. There were few lanterns alight in the village, for many had gone to the lord's hall to celebrate the return of his daughter.

She narrowed her eyes, thinking she saw a figure duck into the forest but it disappeared so quickly that she was unsure. Then she saw the silhouette of fallen figure on the path, the path that led to her mother's door.

Mathilde made to step out of the cottage.

"It might be a trick, *Maman*," Radegunde counseled, halting her mother with a touch.

She left the candle and took her mother's knife before creeping out of the hut. Mathilde remained on the threshold. Radegunde strained to hear any sound as she crept toward the still figure, but she heard only the barest crackle of fleeing footsteps and the thunder of her heart. She eased closer, wondering whether the person on the path was truly injured or meant to trick her. She lifted her knife as she drew closer.

It was a man, lying on his stomach, his face hidden. In the darkness, it was hard to be certain, but Radegunde feared she recognized his boots and tabard.

"*Maman!*" she cried, even as she eased him to his back with one hand.

It *was* Duncan. He rolled over without resistance and she could see the dark stain on his chemise and jerkin even without a light. Something glimmered on the ground, and she realized that he had drawn his knife, then dropped it.

Because he had been assaulted. To Radegunde's dismay, he had abandoned his hauberk this night, undoubtedly believing Valeroy village to be safe.

"Nay!" she whispered and fell to her knees beside him. Her mother was there in a moment, her expression revealing her concern. She touched the dark stain and lifted her fingers away, and Radegunde saw that they were stained red with blood. Radegunde pressed her fingers to Duncan's throat, and to her relief his pulse still could be felt.

"You know him," Mathilde said, no real question in her voice.

"It seems he is not as quick with a knife as I had believed," Radegunde admitted.

Her mother spared her the barest glance, then unlaced Duncan's jerkin and opened his chemise in search of the wound. It was in his shoulder and looked deep, but her mother ran her fingers over the wound and the tension in her expression eased.

"It may not be as bad as it appears," she murmured and Radegunde hoped it was so. "Let us get him inside." They hefted him together and carried him into the hut. Once there, Radegunde saw his pallor and feared for him anew. Her mother dispatched her with a gesture and Radegunde returned for his blade.

She returned to the hut to find her mother unlacing Duncan's jerkin and pulling him free of it. She tore his chemise to reveal the wound and a small red square fell to the floor. Both women glanced at it, and Radegunde picked it up as her mother examined Duncan's wound.

It was not a square, but a small bag, made with careful stitches and closed with a drawstring. It was wrought of fine silk, silk fit for a queen's kirtle.

Radegunde's curiosity knew no bounds, but she set the treasure aside for the moment. She fetched and carried for her mother, bringing water and herbs and cloth.

When Mathilde finally urged her aside and Duncan appeared to be sleeping, she could not resist. She peeked inside the small red bag and at first thought it was empty. Then she realized there was a long thin thread within it.

Nay, it was three red-gold hairs braided into a fine plait and coiled with care inside the silken bag.

Radegunde's mouth went dry. He carried a lock of hair from a lady.

The silken bag made her conclude the woman in question was a noblewoman.

That Duncan carried this prize so close could only mean it was from a lady he loved. Indeed, it looked like a gift, wrought by the lady for the man who held her own heart, a token and a talisman to bring him home safely.

He said he would not promise what he could not give.

She felt the weight of her mother's gaze upon her and saw Mathilde look from her face to the silken bag and its gossamer contents. A shadow touched Mathilde's expression and she turned her attention back to the wounded man.

She did not have to say a word. Radegunde understood her mother's conclusion and shared it. Duncan was a man of honor in truth, and one who surrendered his secrets with care. She found herself wishing that this one might have remained hidden.

Too late she recalled his promise to confess a secret of his own. Was this the one he had meant to surrender to her? Or was the lock of hair only a part of the tale?

Radegunde could only hope that Duncan had the opportunity to tell her more.

WEDNESDAY, SEPTEMBER 2, 1187

*Feast Day of Saint Margaret
and Saint Antoninus*

CHAPTER EIGHT

uncan awakened with no clear sense of where he was. He was in a hut, by his best guess, laid by the hearth. The fire had burned down to embers that glowed in the shadows and cast a welcome heat. Darkness gathered in the corners and the shutters were closed, so it was night. He smelled venison stew and his shoulder hurt.

He raised a hand to check the wound, but someone caught at his wrist.

"Leave it be," a woman said, her instruction firm for all the softness of her voice. Her grip was strong, and he realized only then that his jerkin was gone, as was his belt and knife. He made to sit up at this but she planted the weight of her hand in the middle of his chest. "You are safe here. Do not make the injury worse."

He settled back with reluctance and surveyed her. The woman's hair had been dark and now was heavily threaded with silver. It was plaited back from her face, which showed the mark of experience. Her gaze was steady, her confidence as familiar as their shape and hue. Given his destination earlier, he guessed her to be Radegunde's mother.

The healer and midwife.

Duncan exhaled, relieved at this. He must be within her hut. Where was Radegunde? A quick glance revealed that she sat behind her mother, more deeply cloaked in shadows, and watched him avidly. She was uncharacteristically silent and he wondered at that.

Duncan was relieved that she had not attempted to return to the hall. The women must have discovered him and brought him inside. He compelled himself to relax, for he was amongst allies.

"Better," Radegunde's mother acknowledged beneath her breath.

Duncan guessed that she was of an age with him. It was an unwelcome reminder of his own folly in encouraging Radegunde's attentions at all. He had been irresponsible to even come in pursuit of that kiss, much less to plan to share a secret. Secrets bound people together and he had no right to forge such a link with Radegunde. To do as much, when she was destined to wed another, could interfere with her happiness.

There was naught like a taste of death to clarify a man's thinking, to be sure. Duncan had been unscathed, by and large, in Outremer. It had been long since he had been assaulted like this, and longer yet since he had feared for his own survival.

But his days were not endless, and his means of earning his way was not without its peril. He should not be tempted to take any more from Radegunde. Another kiss would not mitigate his own desire—it would only tempt him further. He frowned in impatience that he wanted all and despised his own selfishness in this moment.

He must think of Radegunde's future, not his own! That was the course of an honorable man. What if he despoiled her, then was killed, and she was left alone with a bastard child to raise? He would not so sully her future to sate his own desire. It would be reprehensible.

Duncan made to sit up again, despite the warning of the healer. She let him do as he willed, sitting back on her heels to watch him as he leaned against the wall beside the hearth. "You do not stop me this time," he noted and she smiled.

"A man can only be given good counsel. He cannot be

compelled to take it. I am of an age that I no longer cast my words to the wind." She rose to her feet then, and he saw Radegunde more clearly as her mother stepped aside.

His heart sank that his most precious treasure, the red silken bag, was in her hand. There was the reason for her silence.

She desired an answer, to be sure, and he would not be able to deny her request.

Indeed, should he not seize this opportunity to destroy her interest in him, for the greater good?

Duncan scowled anew and tentatively touched the injury on his shoulder. The bleeding had stopped and there was a newly formed scab on the wound. Though he could not see it, he could feel that the skin was not enflamed, at least not as yet. He also felt that his movement had resulted in a new trickle of blood from the corner of the wound.

Radegunde's mother halted before him, offering a wet cloth. He could smell the pungency of herbs and gave her a questioning glance. "I am a healer, Duncan MacDonald," she said with some asperity. "This compress will speed the healing of your injury, as will following my counsel."

He accepted the cloth and pressed it to the wound, wincing at the stab of pain from the pressure. "And I thank you for both. Is the wound clean? How deep?"

"You must have moved in the last moment," she said, then knelt at his side to adjust the position of the compress. He followed her guidance this time, wincing when she pressed harder against the wound. "You *are* sitting up," she noted. Duncan caught his breath and applied the same pressure, for he was not about to lie supine without his knife at hand, regardless of the location.

Her brows lifted and she sat back with a slight smile. "Warriors are all the same," she mused, but there was no censure in her tone. "I am Mathilde."

"Radegunde's mother," he said and she nodded. "She has told me of your skills, and I thank you for your assistance in this." Duncan was well aware that Radegunde listened, the question she wished to ask fairly shining in her eyes.

"You must have heard your assailant and turned," Mathilde

97

speculated.

"I heard something. A step. The snap of a twig. I do not recall precisely, but I sensed the presence of another. I drew my knife and began to turn." Duncan frowned, wishing he had taken more care.

"Your knife was beside you and had no blood upon it." Mathilde offered it, as well as his belt. Duncan checked the weapon, then returned it to his scabbard with one hand. He knew he had to keep pressure on his wound. He eyed the belt, wishing he could don it, and saw Mathilde's fleeting smile.

So, she would not aid him in this task. He could guess well enough that Radegunde would not either.

Until he satisfied her curiosity.

Duncan sighed. "I wish I had inflicted an injury upon him, too."

"Do you know who it was?" Radegunde asked. "Or who it might have been?"

"Nay. I thought this village to be safe." He lifted the cloth and was relieved to see that there was little blood upon it. Mathilde eyed the wound and nodded that he might set the compress aside.

"We have been plagued by brigands these past few years," she said as she rinsed the cloth, and he sensed that she chose her words with care. "The villainy has been worse since Lord Bayard's demise at Châmont-sur-Maine, when the seal passed to his lady wife."

"Even at this distance? I did not think the holding so close as that."

Mathilde nodded grimly. "There are those who note that Angers, and thus Châmont-sur-Maine, which guards its northern flank, are the gateway to Breton. With King Henry resolved to make Breton his possession, there are many in those lands who would see his will defied."

"Many perceive weakness in a woman's stewardship,"

"Aye, and Lady Marie is not so fierce in nature as some noblewomen. I have heard rumors that justice can be bought in her courts." Mathilde's opinion of that was most clear. "And yet more rumors that she is seldom seen. It is good that Lord Gaston is returned from Outremer to claim his holding. A knight of his experience will not tolerate such foolery in his domain." She turned a bright eye upon Duncan. "Why were you abroad so late?"

"I thought of Radegunde returning to the hall alone and meant to escort her."

Radegunde straightened a little, hope in her expression, and he realized his own folly in admitting such a truth.

"So you are not so convinced of the safety of Valeroy as that," her mother noted.

"Perhaps not," Duncan was compelled to acknowledge.

Mathilde folded her arms across her chest. "And what, sir, are your own intentions toward my daughter?" It seemed that she shared a bluntness of manner with her daughter—or that Radegunde had come by that trait honestly.

Duncan took a breath then made the declaration he knew he must. "None," he said with assurance. "I would defend her as a member of our company, no more than that."

Mathilde arched a brow and there was a charged silence in the hut for a moment.

Then Radegunde leaped to her feet, her outrage clear. "None!" she echoed with disdain and it was evident that her silence had come to an end. Even knowing he had chosen rightly did little to keep Duncan from wincing at her reaction.

Mathilde watched them both with open curiosity.

Radegunde crossed the hut with furious steps and cast the red silk bag at him. "I suppose *this* is why." She propped her hands upon her hips and glared down at him.

"You would be right in that, lass." Duncan picked up the bag, fingering it to verify that the contents were yet there. He could feel the coil of the fine plait even through the silk and was relieved to find the token intact. He only realized after he had done so that his concern and maybe even his reverence for that hair would be clear to these two observant women.

He did not doubt that Radegunde had looked within it.

"Who is she?" she demanded. She then pulled up a stool to sit before him, as if she meant to wait however long it took for him to make his confession. Her mother retreated, but Duncan knew

Mathilde listened as well. "You owe me a secret, Duncan," Radegunde continued with resolve when he said naught. "I will have this one." She glared at him. "And I will have it now."

He knew it was a fair request, and might in fact ensure that she lost interest in him.

Was that why he was so reluctant to utter the truth?

"Duncan, tell me," Radegunde entreated.

Duncan kept his gaze fixed on the silk bag. "My wife," he admitted, then flicked an upward glance to discover that Radegunde was not surprised. "It is my wife's hair."

Her anger had faded, to be replaced by a wariness that surprised him. "And you love her," the maiden concluded. "That is why you carry such a talisman. I suppose it is only to be expected that you might have lost your heart to the woman you wedded." She squared her shoulders, as if making best of the news. "What is her name?"

"Gwyneth."

"And she awaits you in Scotland."

This was the moment of decision for Duncan. It would be simple to let Radegunde believe that Gwyneth yet drew breath. He knew she had a firm moral code, and knew she would not try to tempt him to break his marital vow. It would have been the wiser choice, and Duncan knew it well.

But a part of him did not wish to deceive this enticing maiden, much less destroy her interest in him. She alone in all these years had pushed the memory of Gwyneth from his thoughts, after all. That part of him whispered that he had evaded death and should make the most of life, however long it might endure.

"Gwyneth is dead," Duncan confessed, seeing the hope immediately light Radegunde's eyes. "She has been dead these twenty years, and it is only her grave that awaits me in Scotland."

"Dead!" Radegunde whispered and he saw tears of sympathy glitter in her eyes. "Oh Duncan, I am so sorry."

Such compassion she had for others! Her reaction humbled him. "As am I."

"Yet twenty years is a long time," Mathilde noted softly, revealing where Radegunde had learned her talent for naming the truth.

"Aye." Radegunde studied him. "Why do you so honor her memory?"

"Because I loved her," he confessed, holding her clear gaze. "Because she was joyous and beautiful." He swallowed, realizing that Gwyneth's liveliness was a quality that Radegunde shared. He could not be responsible for two such women leaving this earth too soon. "But mostly because her death was my fault."

"Well, then," Mathilde murmured.

Radegunde did not flinch.

Of course, she did not. Duncan should have anticipated her reaction.

"I cannot imagine that you left her undefended," she said, so determined to think well of him that his resolve to treat her with dignity redoubled.

"Nay, I did not. It was not violence that claimed her." He found himself stroking the silken bag with his thumb and knew Radegunde noted his gesture.

She leaned forward and covered his hand with hers. "Will you tell me about her?" Her interest was clear and it tightened Duncan's chest, along with the realization that Radegunde wished to hear the tale so she could absolve him of any responsibility he felt for Gwyneth's demise.

She was wrong, of course, for she did not know the truth, but a warmth spread through him all the same.

"You are not a killer, Duncan," she whispered, confirming his suspicion.

He scoffed. "I earn my way with a blade, lass."

She waved off this protest. "I mean you are not a man of violence. Your trade is not of import in this. There are men who kill because it is a necessary task and there are others who relish the deed. You are not of this second type."

It was true enough that he did not like the killing.

"Tell me of Gwyneth, please," Radegunde asked again. "I should like to know of the woman who claimed your heart so well."

The plea in her voice and in her eyes was an invitation that

Duncan MacDonald could not refuse.

This was the power of Radegunde. She could convince him so readily to abandon what he knew he should do, and worse, he would succumb to her appeal with no regrets.

In this moment, Duncan was powerless to do anything other than fulfill her request.

That did not mean, however, that he had to confess the entirety of the tale.

Radegunde watched Duncan frown at the silken bag. She hoped he gathered his thoughts and found a place to begin, for she was not truly convinced he would share the truth of his past with her so readily.

Perhaps he meant to warn her.

Perhaps he meant to frighten her.

He knew little of her if he believed she could be so easily convinced to abandon any course. Her mother busied herself with stirring the fire. The sky grew lighter and Radegunde's brothers were stirring. She knew her mother began her day and ensured the boys could break their fast, but she was also aware that Mathilde was listening.

Aye, she had seen her mother assess Duncan's legs and noted the way her eyes had gleamed afterward.

Her man. That was what Mathilde had called Duncan, and Radegunde hoped with all her heart that he might become as much. Her mother had, as ever, seen to her heart and Radegunde realized that a single night with Duncan would no longer suffice.

It was inconvenient indeed to desire a man who would keep himself from her.

Because he yet loved his dead wife. Still, Radegunde admired his code of honor and his loyalty to Gwyneth. She did not believe for a moment that he truly was responsible for that woman's demise, and hoped that if she convinced Duncan as much that he might look more favorably upon her.

He cleared his throat. "We met when we were children. Her family lived in the same village as mine. The women in their family kept chickens and sold the eggs, later the meat. Her father was the village baker. The children had the red-gold hair of their father, all of them."

"The same hue as Christina's hair," Radegunde said, feeling the need to draw his attention to the courtesan.

"'Twas more fiery," he said. "As if each wore a corona of flame. They were known to be passionate and her father had a temper, to be sure. He would rage at a man who did not pay for his bread, but once his diatribe had ended, he would calm again and oft give the man bread. Gwyneth's mother said he was like a tempest that spends itself before it does any damage. He used to tease her that his tempest kept her warm at night and she would blush." He met Radegunde's gaze. "There were nine children in their family, and Gwyneth was the very middle child. She did not share her father's temper, but she had his passion, to be sure."

Radegunde swallowed at that. Had his wife been so lusty that only a whore's experienced touch would suffice in her absence?

"'Twas Beltane, the first celebration of the spring and the night before the Maying. I was a man by law, but too young to be one in truth. I had seen only ten and seven summers, as had she. The fires were lit and sent sparks into the clear night sky. It was a potent night, one filled with desire and opportunity and joy. 'Twas the first time we touched, as man and woman do, the first time that we were more than companions. I shall never forget it."

Radegunde wondered whether she had been a fool to ask for this tale. The yearning in Duncan's voice made her own heart ache. "And what is amiss with that?" she managed to whisper.

Duncan granted her a fierce look. "She was pledged to another. I had no right to touch her, and she had no right to surrender to me what she should have kept for him. But impulse steered us both false. We surrendered to temptation and did not even have the wits to disguise what we had done."

Radegunde exchanged a glance with her mother.

"We thought of naught but the pleasure we gave each other and it was a poor master. So it was that morning came, and we were yet together. Even then, we could have hidden our deed, but I was too proud for that. The night had been too much of a marvel for me to pretend that it did not matter. I could not let Gwyneth wed another. I led her to the center of the village and I took her hands in mine in the old way, and I pledged a handfast to her before all who came to witness it."

"An old custom," Mathilde murmured.

Radegunde glanced toward her mother.

"A pledge of a year and a day of fidelity," her mother told her softly. "A commitment that can be abandoned or renewed. Did you pledge to your Gwyneth anew?"

Duncan shook his head and Radegunde felt a spark of hope. "Nay, for she was dead by then," he admitted, extinguishing her hope as soon as it was sparked. "The man to whom she was sworn stepped forward that morn and challenged me, for I had taken what was his due. We fought and it was not a noble duel. We were young and strong and did not care what had to be done in order to win. I defeated him."

"And he ceded?" Mathilde said.

"That day," Duncan acknowledged. "But when Gwyneth rounded with the child we had wrought that Beltane, his fury grew anew. He attacked me when I left the village on an errand for our lord, and we fought in the forest, where none could witness the battle."

"He thought to assail you, unobserved," Radegunde said.

"Perhaps so, but his was the corpse left in the forest." Duncan grimaced. "We had once been friends. I felt the fullness of my error when he moved no more, and I vowed then to change my ways and not be stirred to such a deed again."

He paused then, his throat working, then shook his head. "But it did not matter. I had erred and I was punished for my deed. The laird of the holding absolved me of my crime, for I had defended myself from an attack he decreed to have been unprovoked, but his justice was not sufficient. It was Gwyneth who paid the price of my sin." Duncan lifted his gaze. "She died before we could renew our vows, died in the birthing of the son we had wrought at Beltane." He heaved a sigh. "Her merry laughter was silenced forever because of my unruly desire."

"Surely she had some, as well," Mathilde said.

"I was impetuous. I was impulsive. It was my responsibility to be a man of honor, and I was not. I killed the man who had the right to her, the man who had been my friend, and when the laird granted me forgiveness, the Lord took his own toll." Duncan pursed his lips. "I betrayed them both, and I vowed at her grave that I would never surrender to impulse again."

The hut was silent for a moment, the fire on the hearth crackling.

"And the boy?" Mathilde asked, before Radegunde could do so.

"Dead as well. Born dead, after much labor on her part."

Her own throat was tight and she felt tears slip down her cheeks. "This was why you became a mercenary," Radegunde whispered. "You left home because she died."

"There was no future for me in that place." Duncan studied her for a long moment, as if marveling at her tears. "You weep for those you never knew."

"Because you loved them," she whispered. "And because I always weep for babes who do not draw their first breath. So much lost before it has begun." She turned away and wiped at her own tears, aware that Duncan watched her in silence.

Moments later, he continued his tale. "By the time the year and a day had passed, I was far from home, alone and earning my way with my blade, determined to never be beholden to man or woman again." His tone turned gruff and he looked drawn. "I might have continued that way if my life had not been saved by that knight."

"And then you had no choice but to entwine your life with his," Radegunde said.

The loss of Gwyneth then had been the reason that Duncan had lost hope and wandered in despair, the reason the knight who was Fergus' father had saved him, the reason he owed a boon to that knight and his family. Had Radegunde been of different nature, she might have wept for herself and for Duncan, for the future they would not share because he yet loved his wife.

But it was not her nature to regret what she could not change.

It was her habit to change what she could. Radegunde cleared her throat and wiped her tears, intent upon arguing against Duncan's conviction of his guilt.

"You did not kill her," she insisted.

"Aye, I did."

"Childbirth is a peril all women face, and I doubt that any who greeted a man in admiration or love would call it a risk not worth the taking."

But Duncan shook his head. "You cannot know her thinking, lass."

"I cannot believe that any woman would regret the better part of one year by your side."

His eyes narrowed as he met her gaze. "You cannot know."

"And I do not agree that the impulse and desire was all your own. That does not give credit to Gwyneth and her choices," Radegunde continued. "Perhaps she did not wish to wed the man to whom she was promised. Perhaps seducing you was the sole way to change her own fate."

Duncan appeared to be startled by this.

"She may have glimpsed his truth. I would not have been wedded to a man who chose to solve disputes with violence."

Duncan opened his mouth, frowned, then shut it again. He cast Radegunde a mutinous glance. "You see all as you would choose to view it."

"Is that not your choice as well?" she retorted and heard her mother chuckle. "Tell me this—did she blame you? Did she gnash her teeth in despair at what you had inflicted upon her, or was she happy by your side?" Radegunde heard the challenge in her own voice and noted how Duncan looked away. "What did she say at the last?"

Duncan's lips tightened and his gaze locked with hers. She could fairly feel his determination to convince her. "That she would love me forever, and I vowed that I would do the same."

Radegunde saw that he wanted her to believe that his heart was surrendered and beyond retrieval, buried with the woman who had first laid claim to it. But what manner of woman would expect the man she loved to live alone in her absence? Not one who loved as Radegunde believed people should love.

On impulse, she leaned closer to Duncan.

"And what did Gwyneth say to that?" she asked. "Did she truly wish for you, her beloved, to spend all your days and nights alone?"

Duncan appeared to be discomfited. His lips set and the back of his neck turned ruddy. Aye, he was a fine man, a man who did not utter falsehoods with ease, and she had caught him. "It does not matter what she said," he said gruffly, and Radegunde knew she was right.

"I say it does."

"She was dying, lass! She did not know what she said!"

Radegunde scoffed. "You cannot pick and choose. Either you believe all she said on her deathbed or none of it. You cannot sift through it, and believe the words that suit you best, while discarding the rest."

Mathilde smothered a smile and turned away. Radegunde felt her mother's amusement more than saw it, but she witnessed the sharp glance Duncan cast at her mother.

"Of course, she would insist that I should wed again and be happy. Gwyneth was generous of nature…"

"And so you tried to see yourself killed, and then you lived for twenty years as if you had been killed," Radegunde said, interrupting his protest. "I would wager that your Gwyneth will have words for you when next you meet. Any man of mine who behaved thus would earn a fair scolding from me."

"You do not understand!"

"I *do* understand, Duncan MacDonald." Radegunde swept to her feet and shook a finger at him. "You are afraid. You have loved and you have lost and the pain has left you in fear of loving again. I thought you a bold warrior as well as a man of honor, not one afraid to live his life and savor every moment as if it might be his last. *I* wish to live my life to the fullest and I desire a man to take my hand in his who will be my equal match in that." She shrugged, goading him a little more, for his eyes were as dark as a stormy sky. "I thought that man was you, but it appears I erred."

"Radegunde!" he began furiously, but she strolled to her mother's door, knowing he was not sufficiently hale to follow her.

She pivoted on the threshold to face him. "I challenge you, Duncan, to change my view of you, if I have the matter wrong." Radegunde did not grant him time to reply. She kissed her mother

107

Claire Delacroix

and left the hut, knowing he glared after her, fuming.

Her step was light for she was certain Duncan would take her dare.

Duncan found himself wanting to take Radegunde's challenge with a vigor that surprised him.

Her argument was all too reasonable. He *had* mourned Gwyneth long enough. He had behaved like a man passing through his life instead of savoring it. It would not be unsuitable for him to take another wife, particularly after he fulfilled his duty to Fergus' father. Still, he believed it should not be Radegunde, as alluring as she was, because of the difference in age between them.

The gift Radegunde granted him was an awakening, but it did not change his resolve to deny his desire for her.

Duncan had been able to convince Mathilde to send the two older boys after their sister, although in daylight, he did not imagine there was much risk. Still he would see her safe, and he knew that Mathilde savored his concern for her daughter. He sat in silence by the fire and considered his course.

Why had he been assaulted? By Mathilde's reckoning, some brigand had thought he carried items of value. Telling Radegunde of his past had conjured memories though, and matters left undone, and that made him uneasy.

Did the past stalk him?

Perhaps the fiend had wanted his weapons or any coin. Duncan could not account for the fact that his knife had been left beside him on the ground, for it was a fine blade and of an ilk most men would be glad to possess. His purse was yet full, as well, but perhaps Mathilde and Radegunde had disturbed the thief before he could complete his crime.

Had he simply been in the wrong place at the wrong time? Or had he been targeted? Why? Duncan shook his head, fighting the answer he did not wish to accept, then looked up to realize that Mathilde watched him steadily.

He was discomfited to realize that her gaze was locked upon his face not his wound. Indeed, her expression was resolute and she did not seem to blink. He was not a man who was readily daunted,

108

but something chilled within him to be the focus of this woman's attention. It was more than her being a wise woman, more than her being Radegunde's mother, more even than her having taught Radegunde how to hold secrets close.

He recalled then Michel's confession that his mother had the Sight.

Duncan feared what she might perceive about him.

Or in Radegunde's future.

She poured ale into a pair of cups, pushing one toward him. Duncan had no intention of drinking it. He moved to join her at the board out of courtesy, grimacing a little at the pain when he sat down opposite her. She put the pitcher down between them. "Shall there be honesty between us, Duncan MacDonald?"

"Why should there not be?"

"Indeed." Mathilde seemed to approve of that. "My daughter speaks well of you, of your loyalty to your lord and of your skill with a knife."

"She is a fine lass."

A glint lit in the depths of her dark eyes. "Lass? If you think to dismiss my daughter as a foolish young woman, then you are less observant than I imagine you to be."

"She possesses a welcome merriment."

Mathilde cocked her head, inviting more.

"And is most perceptive."

Duncan felt cornered when Mathilde arched a brow.

"And indeed, is a most fetching maiden."

"Maiden?"

"Maiden." Their gazes held for a long moment.

Then Mathilde sat back and sipped her ale, her gaze assessing. "I thought her sting had more reason than pride." When Duncan shook his head, she set the cup aside. "Perhaps you are not so tempted as I imagined. Perhaps you do not see the fullness of her merit."

"What I see is a woman deserving of far more than I can grant to her," Duncan replied.

"How so?" Mathilde challenged. "Your wife and son are dead by your own admission. Unless you have another?"

109

Duncan shook his head. "Radegunde should be wedded to a man who not only holds her in high regard but surrenders his heart fully to her. She has too joyous a temper to be compelled to satisfy herself with less."

Mathilde inhaled and nodded. "I see. Because your wife died in the birthing of your son, you decline to surrender your affection again."

"It is not mine to surrender!"

"Is it not? If desire was all that drove your choices, you would have had Radegunde by now and been sated. She must be right. You must be afraid."

Duncan's temper flared at that. "She deserves better."

"She desires you."

"She will forget me."

"Because she is young, and so her interest must be a passing whim." Mathilde laughed heartily at the notion, then restored herself with ale, her eyes twinkling. "Let me tell you something of my Radegunde, something you have evidently not learned for yourself. You see her joy and think her simple."

"I do not." Duncan found himself taking a swig of the ale.

"You think her life has been simple, then. You think she has always been blessed, and like so many we have known and served of such good fortune, you fear that she has no resolve."

"I do not understand your point," Duncan protested, though he believed he did.

"The nobles we serve, they have come of age with every advantage. Their lives are comparatively easy, and so, their will is like gossamer. Just as a mere leaf in the wind will shred a fine spider's web, their will can be broken by a single stroke of ill fortune. You think Radegunde's cheerfulness is the result of her never having been tested." Mathilde shook her head. "But nay. Her merry heart was God's gift to her that she might be better able to overcome adversity."

Duncan was intrigued.

"Not for Radegunde the easy conquest." Mathilde saluted Duncan with her cup, evidently including him in that company. "She was born on the coldest night of the winter, in the darkest moment of my own life." She stared into the depths of the cup, lost in memories, and this time, it was Duncan who lifted the pitcher and filled their cups. "She came early, and I was alone. She was small, so small, and she did not cry as babes so often do." Mathilde bit her lip. "I feared for her life, for the first time but not for the last."

Duncan was rapt. He wished to know more of Radegunde.

If not all there was to know.

"I should have learned that night all I needed to know of this child." Mathilde lifted her gaze. "She never cried, not then or any other time. I came to understand that she saw no point to it. To weep was futile. A waste of strength when she had little. She waited with uncommon patience and confidence. She smiled when I lifted her to feed her, smiled with such radiance that the sun itself could not compare. She won with charm what other babes demanded with their cries. In but a month, all in this village would have done any deed for her."

Duncan found himself smiling at this tale. He could well understand that impulse.

Mathilde lifted her brows. "By the time she was a year of age, we were lost in truth."

Duncan chuckled.

Mathilde shook a finger at him. "But here is the meat of the matter, Duncan. Naught was easy for my Radegunde. Not only was she small for her age, not only did she manage to contract every illness ever known, not only did she lie at death's door time and again, but—"

"But she always recovered?"

"Clearly, for she was at this board but moments ago. The key, however, is that she is persistent beyond all. It is her nature to identify what she can change and to set her will upon that quest."

"Her will is formidable."

"You have not seen the half of it. Her foot was not right, from the first. It was turned, so that the weight landed upon the outside of it. It was formed well enough, but twisted. I feared she would never walk well, but Radegunde came honestly by her determination. Her father constructed a harness for that foot, one

111

that compelled her to walk correctly. I know it gave her pain, but he aided her, every night."

Duncan thought of Radegunde limping in Paris and regretted that he had danced so much with her, in his ignorance.

But then, he wagered that she thought it fair exchange for the night of dancing she desired, even if it caused her pain later. His heart tightened with admiration.

And something more.

"What is it?"

"I took her dancing in Paris, at her request, and now know why she limped. I should not have so indulged her."

"I invite you to try to halt her." Mathilde gestured to the space behind her. "She and her father went back and forth across this very hut, night after night. At first, she could not manage three steps, but neither of them surrendered. Cursed stubborn pair," she said with affection. "Soon she made one width, then two, then they were counting dozens each night. By the time she was four, she walked without the harness."

"And never a tear."

"Never a tear." Mathilde smiled. "What purpose would it serve? We knew the foot gave her pain. She knew we could do naught to eliminate the pain. She chose a course to see her circumstance changed."

Duncan lifted his cup to salute the maiden in question, and both he and Mathilde drained their cups. It was only then he realized that something Mathilde had told him did not make sense.

"What?" Mathilde prompted, noting the change of his expression. He had to remember the perceptiveness of this pair.

"You said you were alone when Radegunde was born."

"Aye, her father had left." Mathilde appeared to be fascinated by her cup. Duncan sensed that she told him only part of the truth. "After she was born, he returned, I think to look upon her, but she stole his heart and he stayed."

"She said he was dead."

"Aye?"

"But you have sons, younger than Radegunde."

Mathilde took a breath, her eyes flashing with a familiar fire.

"He did leave again, and then he did return at intervals." She held Duncan's gaze with defiance. "Do you imagine that my children have different fathers? For they do not."

Duncan could believe that, for the resemblance between the siblings was strong, though neither Michel nor Radegunde had Mathilde's green eyes.

"I do not understand," he admitted. "Radegunde spoke as if she scarce knew her father. I understood that he had died without her knowing him at all."

"I know." Mathilde sighed. "And therein lies a tale. By the time I see you next, you will understand much more."

"Not all?" He could not help but jest.

Mathilde smiled. "Only God Himself ever knows *all*, Duncan." She drained her cup and set it aside, her manner indicating to Duncan that he should remain seated. "But God in His wisdom granted Radegunde a merry heart that she could better face the challenges before her. Consider the power of that joy before you decide that she has not the fortitude to be with you."

"There are too many years between us," Duncan protested. "She would spend too long alone after my demise."

Mathilde scoffed. "And who are you to be so certain that you will die first? Did you not survive your wife?"

Duncan winced.

"And what of the babes you would give her? Even if she does survive you, those children will warm her heart and ensure her welfare, for they will be your children."

"But..."

"Make no mistake, Duncan. It shows your merit that this loss has scarred you and that you would hold a vow true. But it should not keep you from opening your heart to another, to welcoming Radegunde, should you desire her as she desires you. My own mother oft said that we were granted life that we might live it well." She arched a brow. "Would your Gwyneth have wanted you to remain always alone? I suspect that Radegunde speaks the truth and that the notion would sadden her."

Duncan could not summon a word, for he knew this was so.

Mathilde smiled fully. "There are no gossamer webs for your

kind, Duncan, just as there are none for Radegunde. She would be a valiant partner, whatever lies ahead for you. You are alive as is she. Make each other happy."

He heard a warning in her tone and considered her. "What does your gift show you of the future?" he asked quietly. "Your son Michel told me that you had dreams of what might be, a gift that I would call the Sight."

Mathilde's manner turned coy. Duncan recognized the evasiveness for what it was: he had oft seen Fergus avoid a question in like manner. She turned the cup in the wet mark on the board, avoiding his gaze. "I cannot speak of it." She swallowed. "It would not be right."

"It has been said that abuse of the Sight means its loss," he said and Mathilde smiled.

"There is more in common in our beliefs than one might expect, given the distances between our countries."

There was that. Duncan recalled Radegunde's tales of the Breton March and its defiant border lords and knew they shared many convictions.

"I will tell you this, Duncan MacDonald," Mathilde said in a voice that made him shiver. "Your past is not so forgotten as you would have it be." She lifted her gaze to his. "And you are yet your father's son."

Duncan caught his breath at this reminder.

Could she truly see what he had left behind? He had abandoned it willingly. Was that not sufficient?

Duncan felt a shadow pass over him. He feared then that the assailant of the previous night had been hunting for him, and was not some brigand in the forest.

"I thank you for your aid and your counsel," he said, his words heartfelt. "Can you tell me what I can I do for you in return?" He fully anticipated that she would insist upon him seeing her daughter happy, but Mathilde surprised him.

"I have told Radegunde that she must seek out Lord Gaston's mother, Lady Eudaline, on behalf of Lady Ysmaine and her husband, and do so before the party journeys to Châmont-sur-Maine. I have told her to entreat Lady Ysmaine to dispatch her to the abbey where Lady Eudaline lives, and to do so without delay."

"Why?"

"It is a matter of secrets, Duncan, and this one is not mine to share. I have only suspicions. Lady Eudaline knows the truth, but I believe Lord Gaston should know more before his return home."

"I see." It was easy for Duncan to recall Gaston's doubts about Millard de Saint-Roux and that man's intentions. Had he come by those doubts from his mother's counsel?

"It could be a matter of his survival," Mathilde added, taking his pause for reluctance.

"Indeed." Duncan frowned. "Lady Ysmaine was injured in Paris..."

"So Radegunde tells me and I will visit her this day to ensure that the bone was set correctly. I will also advise her to rest for several days before riding on."

"Regardless of her condition," Duncan guessed.

Mathilde's smile was fleeting. "Her family will not protest, and then she can send Radegunde on this quest." She sobered. "I would have you accompany Radegunde."

"My path is not mine to choose," Duncan reminded her gently, but Mathilde only smiled.

"You can influence the choice of the knight you accompany, and you know that as well as I do." She leaned closer. "Radegunde will need you. I have dreamed of this, and so I ask it of you."

Duncan's heart skipped. "What did you dream?"

"There was peril, peril you can only conquer together." Mathilde's breath caught and Duncan thought her eyes misted with tears, before she blinked rapidly and shook her head. "And more." She swallowed. "When you meet the wild man of the woods, tell him that I miss him." The corner of her mouth lifted. "He believes otherwise, but I know his fine legs are not marred, and his heart is as true as ever it was."

"There is a wild man in the woods?"

"There are many, but you will recognize this one for what and who he is."

Duncan understood. "He is Radegunde's father," he murmured.

"Cursedly stubborn man," Mathilde said, neither agreeing or

disagreeing.

"I will tell him," he vowed.

"Aye. I know."

Their gazes held for a long moment, and Duncan understood that a trust was being passed to him. He nodded slightly, accepting the burden of ensuring Radegunde's defense, whatever peril her mother saw in the journey ahead.

Mathilde rose and gathered items into a basket. "I would have you rest by the fire this day, even while I go to Lady Ysmaine. Do not be afraid to sleep. You need the rest to be healed quickly, and Ogier will watch over you until the other boys return. Even the brigands in these times are not bold enough to attack in daylight."

Duncan was not so certain of that, though he knew her counsel about his injury to be good. He nodded agreement, determined to remain awake this day and return to the keep with all haste. "Ask Lord Amaury to send a man to guard your cottage," he suggested. "Your home is close to the forest, and I am certain he would ensure your defense."

Mathilde smiled and donned her cloak. Her two older boys returned in that moment, and she assigned them tasks in the hut and garden before taking her leave.

"Finish your labor and I shall tell you a tale of Outremer, lads," he offered and the boys accepted with enthusiasm, completing their chores with all haste.

It was not long before they sat with him before the fire, anticipation lighting their eyes. Duncan found his heart warmed by the simple hospitality of Mathilde's home, and the company of her sons. He thought of Radegunde, a hut much like this one, and sons of their own, and knew he had denied himself the simplest and most satisfying of pleasures, for the memory of Gwyneth.

That was when he knew that he would take Radegunde's challenge.

But under his own terms. There could be no impulse and no fleeting satisfaction. There would be a bond between them, if a lesser one than she might desire.

A man of honor could offer no less.

SATURDAY, SEPTEMBER 5, 1187

Feast Day of Saint Quintin

Claire Delacroix

CHAPTER NINE

Radegunde was in a foul temper.

There was no good cause for it, or so she told herself. The weather was fair. Lady Ysmaine's wrist healed admirably and her mother had pronounced the bone to be setting well. Valeroy's hall was filled with merriment, the many pleasures of the harvest amplified by the return of Lady Ysmaine and the tidings of her good match. There was feasting in the hall each night and she oft saw her brother, Michel. There was conviviality in the kitchens as well, and she appreciated the familiarity of routine at Valeroy.

It was good to be certain of a warm meal each day and a dry pallet each night, to know that the gates were defended and that one was amongst friends and allies. Truly, Radegunde appreciated all of these things more since she had been without them.

Still, she knew she would become restless for adventure again, and already wondered when they would depart for Châmont-sur-Maine.

She was vexed to be sure, and she knew it was because she had not seen Duncan for three days. She had not been idle, but she had caught herself straining for a glance of him, like a lovesick fool, and despised herself for her weakness.

He had not taken her challenge.

It was disappointing beyond belief. Radegunde had been certain she understood him well and had guessed that her dare would provoke him into action.

She could not believe she had been wrong. She had been certain that she would find him at her elbow by the end of that first day. She had been convinced he would ask her to speak with him, if not to join him in the evening for that private moment she had offered. She had thought he might send her a gift, or a word by her brother.

But there was naught.

She might have concluded that Duncan had left, but she heard rumors of his presence yet.

He truly must not desire her, not even for simple pleasure. He saved his all for a dead woman, more fool he, and she was irked with him for so denying them both. Aye, it was noble to mourn his wife and lost son. It was right and good to commit to naught when his future was not his own to command, and yet, and yet, Radegunde yearned for more than the few kisses they had shared.

Worse, she thought she had desired only to share a night with Duncan, simply to know what it was like, but she recognized the truth in her mother's charge. She loved Duncan. It was a fearsome detail to know, for Radegunde suspected that only misery would come of that, if her affection was not mutual.

She felt all a-tangle. It was not like Radegunde to be indecisive or to fret over what she could not change, but she fretted over Duncan. There were times in the course of each day when she wished to see him above all else, to have him tease her or call her lass, to smile at her or kiss her. She tried to glimpse him at the gate or in the stables, in the bailey or in consultation with Fergus. She was convinced in those moments that she could overwhelm his reservations with her touch, convince him to change his mind, perhaps even seduce him outright. It was impossible in those moments to believe that he evaded her.

But in the darkness of the night, when she despised her own weakness in yearning for what she could not have, Radegunde wished him gone forever. She tossed and turned on her pallet, finding it impossible to sleep, the memory of those precious kisses heating her skin. She wanted only that temptation might be removed in those hours, though she feared the finality of that would shatter her heart.

Each morn, she arose even more tired than the day before. It was in those moments that she wished Duncan happy, wherever he might go and whatever the cost to herself. In the morn, she could almost weep for herself and her own folly, but then there was labor to be done.

Was she so powerless to control her own feelings? It seemed that she was, which did little to improve her temper. Radegunde was mightily annoyed with herself. Love was an irksome state, to be sure!

It was on the third morning after the assault upon Duncan that Lord Gaston returned to the chamber that he shared with his wife while Radegunde was yet braiding Lady Ysmaine's hair.

It was still early and the keep was only beginning to bustle to wakefulness. Gaston, though, had risen hours before. He placed a pair of woven baskets on the floor by the door.

"You will go this day to the abbey," he instructed Radegunde. "For the weather is fair and you will be able to return before nightfall."

"Aye, my lord." Radegunde kept her expression calm, but she was glad of the opportunity to leave Valeroy, even for a day.

"And as discussed, you will not reveal that you arrive on my behalf," Lord Gaston reminded her. "Lady Richildis has spoken of her desire to send greetings to her old friend, Eudaline, and you will say that you have arrived on her behalf."

"It is not much of a feint," Ysmaine noted.

"It is possible that those at the abbey have yet to hear of our nuptials," he countered. "They are supposed to be retired from the world."

"That does not mean their servants are, my lord," Radegunde felt compelled to note.

"It is not *that* distant," Ysmaine observed, as she had done before. "A mere three hours ride."

Gaston replied calmly, as was his wont. "That only provides another reason for Radegunde to depart sooner."

"I could have gone yesterday, or even the day before."

"But I would have you defended," the lord insisted. "Such tales I hear of brigands at large that I will not have you ride alone. Duncan is sufficiently hale to accompany you now and Fergus has granted his permission that he do as much."

Radegunde straightened, well aware that her lady watched her. A day's ride with only Duncan for companionship? She was certain she could not bear it—and yet, she desired naught else. Her heart fluttered like a caged bird and she dropped a pin. "Michel could go with me," she suggested, her voice a little higher than normal.

"Duncan is less likely to be recognized," Gaston continued. "And I would have you tell as few as possible from whence you have come. Those who note your passage may think you visitors to Anjou, which would suit me best."

"Then how will Lady Eudaline know I come from you?"

Lord Gaston smiled. "There is a missive of greetings from Lady Richildis, in case the basket is stolen or perused before my mother receives it. The gifts within appear innocuous but they will reveal my hand to my mother." He offered a small roll of vellum, secured with a seal of red wax. "Hide this, Radegunde, and surrender it to my mother only when you are alone and unobserved."

It was of a size that Radegunde could hide it between her breasts and she guessed this was his intention. Lady Ysmaine granted her a nod and stood. "I will aid you in hiding it," she said. "Turn your back upon my lord husband."

Radegunde did as instructed, evading her lady's perceptive gaze.

Gaston continued. "She might well grant you some token in return. See it hidden, as well."

"Aye, my lord."

Lord Gaston hefted the baskets anew. "Duncan awaits you in the stables. I shall see the gifts secured and say they come from Lady Richildis."

"Aye, my lord."

"Are you certain that you wish to take the risk, Radegunde?" Lady Ysmaine asked.

Many had been shaken that Duncan had been attacked so close to Valeroy's keep, and the watch had been doubled on the sentry wall. Two men stood sentry at Mathilde's hut, which reassured Radegunde's concerns for the safety of her mother and brothers greatly. There had been no other incidents, which was a relief to all.

"I could send another, if you preferred not to go," the lady added.

Would Radegunde decline even this opportunity to be with Duncan? Nay, she would not. "But I would go, my lady, and keep your trust. I would follow my mother's instruction and discover what Lady Eudaline knows. It may be of great significance to you."

"If your mother warns of it, it must be so," Lady Ysmaine said, her concern clear. She turned to her husband. "Might we not send a larger party?"

"It would arouse notice and suspicion. I wish to see this accomplished quietly," Gaston reiterated. "Neither Radegunde nor Duncan are compelled to undertake this task."

"Aye, my lady. I wish to go."

Lady Ysmaine was not reassured. "I shall not cease my prayers for your protection until you return to my side."

"I thank you, my lady." Radegunde smiled for her mistress. "But recall that we have been all the way to Outremer and returned."

"Not without incident," Lady Ysmaine reminded her.

"This is but a short journey and will take less than a day. I shall be back before the evening meal."

Lady Ysmaine sighed. "Now that I am safely home, I wish to remain that way. Perhaps I grow timid, Radegunde."

"Never that, my lady."

Gaston cleared his throat and glanced pointedly at the window. The sky was brightening with rapid speed. Radegunde pushed the last pin into Lady Ysmaine's hair and donned her cloak. She already wore her warmest kirtle and the boots she had been given by Lady Ysmaine.

"Godspeed to you, Radegunde," Lord Gaston said when he opened the portal. "Return as swiftly as you can, for I too would know that you are safe."

Radegunde nodded, her heart skipping at the warning in his tone.

"They will have packed a good meal for you in the kitchens," Lady Ysmaine called after her, and Radegunde strode to the portal. "And have a look at Bertrand," her lady added in an undertone. "He is the nephew of the ostler and has expressed a desire to come to Châmont-sur-Maine."

Radegunde spun to find both lord and lady smiling at her.

"He is a good man," Lord Gaston said. "In need of a good wife."

Lady Ysmaine arched a brow. "And a man in truth, Radegunde."

Radegunde's heart clenched. The trap closed, so soon and with surety! "I shall do so, my lady," she said and curtseyed quickly, rebellion rising hot within her.

"I would see you as happy as I am, Radegunde," her lady added.

Though Radegunde knew that to be true, still she felt defiant. She had met Bertrand, a great bear of a man known to be both loyal and kind. Was it better or worse that she would spend most of the day alone with Duncan when such a choice was before her?

Better, she resolved as she reached the hall. For this would be her last adventure, by all reckoning, and Radegunde would make it count.

Duncan's heart soared at his first sight of Radegunde in days. He had deliberately avoided her, knowing he would not be able to speak with her in private, saving his arguments for when they might be alone. Even though he had braced himself for his reaction to her presence, still the view nigh overwhelmed him. She marched into the stables, her fine eyes flashing and her determination clear. There was vigor in her step and her gaze might have set the straw afire with a single glance. His heart thundered even as he drank in the sight of her, even as he desired all she had to surrender to him. 'Twas then he knew that his choice was the right one, for no woman had ever prompted such a reaction from him.

Would Radegunde accept his offer?

There could be no negotiation in this, and he feared that she might have changed her mind about him. That she pointedly ignored him could be construed either as a sign of her awareness or of her displeasure that he would accompany her.

One of the ostlers handed her into her saddle, his expression adoring, but Radegunde cast him only an indifferent smile of thanks. The blaze in her eyes was for him, Duncan realized when she cast him a glance, and he was cursed glad to be singed by that look.

The other man noted the crackle in the air between them, to be sure.

Duncan swung into his saddle, much encouraged, and rode after Radegunde, ensuring his stallion was alongside her palfrey when they had passed through Valeroy's gates. They continued along the road in charged silence, eventually taking a smaller path that wound to the right. It was still large enough for the horses to canter alongside each other, but Duncan imagined that situation would not last.

"You have an admirer," he said, hoping to prompt a response, and earned more than expected.

Radegunde's eyes flashed as she faced him. "Aye, and one I do not desire. The cage closes as surely as the sun rises in the sky. They intend to wed me to him, that Bertrand, for he wishes to pledge to Lord Gaston and become an ostler at Châmont-sur-Maine."

Duncan was shocked that Lady Ysmaine proceeded with such haste, but spoke with temperance all the same. "You could decline the honor."

"On what grounds? He is a good man; he has need of a wife; he is known to be loyal and kind. Indeed, I could do far worse." Radegunde glared at him. "I could love a man who spurned all of my attentions, for example, that he might yearn for the dead."

"You cannot fault me for being true."

"Nay, I cannot!" Radegunde pulled her palfrey to a halt and eyed Duncan with ferocity. "But I have offered my all to you, and you have declined the honor of partaking of my feast."

"You know I will not dishonor you."

"It is not dishonor to seize what can be claimed, to make the most of a morsel, to take pleasure where it can be found or even stolen." She was magnificent in her fury, to be sure. "I expected better of you, Duncan MacDonald. I expected you to be a man who welcomed adventure, who shaped his own future, who claimed passion. I expected you to be a man who, when he found circumstance to be less than his desire, would remake it as he would have it be." She exhaled mightily. "And the worst of it is that even being this vexed with you, knowing your reasons I cannot think less of you." She glared at him anew. "Irksome man."

Duncan smiled. "I have a suggestion for you that I hope you do not find so irksome as that."

Her eyes lit, sending fire through his veins. "Aye?"

"Aye, but you must wait for it, lass." He gestured to the road ahead. "We shall complete our errand first, and then I will have an offer for you."

Radegunde held his gaze, then gave her palfrey her heels. "I think you delight in vexing me," she muttered and Duncan laughed.

"You cannot blame a man for wanting to keep your attention, once he has resolved to win your heart."

She cast a sparkling glance over her shoulder at him. "Have you, truly?"

"I am indeed a man who would try to shape his future, though the barriers are not small. I thank you for reminding me of it." She parted her lips, her pleasure clear, but Duncan indicated the road. "Duty first, lass."

"And pleasure after?"

Duncan only smiled. Radegunde laughed, her merry manner restored, and he found his own mood light as he rode behind her. What a marvel of a woman she was. He admired that she did not hold a grudge, and that her anger, once spent, was dismissed.

Aye, to have her hand in his would suit him well.

Truly, this errand for Gaston could not be completed soon enough.

The lady Eudaline was majestic.

It did not matter that she wore plain garb of a woman devoted to prayer. She was both tall and statuesque, a woman who commanded the attention of all when she entered a room—even such a room as the small unadorned chamber where Radegunde had been bidden to await her.

It must be said that Radegunde was impatient with the task before her, for she wished above all to know what Duncan schemed. He had confessed naught more, and she had not been able to convince him to elaborate on his mysterious comments. He had watched the forest keenly as they rode, so intent upon defending her that she knew herself to be safe. The ride had been uneventful, though they had set a crisp pace, and they had arrived at the abbey in the late morning.

Duncan had been ordered to wait outside the gates of the convent, with the horses. He had carried the baskets over the threshold to the porter, then retreated. The porter had carried the baskets into this room, but only after the abbess had peered into them.

That woman had claimed one of the bottles of wine, as well, granting Radegunde a quelling look when she might have protested.

Perhaps it was a tithe.

The abbey was so quiet that Radegunde found herself agitated. She felt as if she visited a tomb, so silent and cold was the chamber. It was dark, as well, having only one very high window that did not face the sun. She could hear the nuns at prayer and the soft whisper of leather slippers on the stone floors, but the place was devoid of vitality.

Until Lady Eudaline swept into the chamber. She carried a candle, and the scent of beeswax combined with the glow of the flame to make the room seem both warmer and more welcoming. Her manner was imperious and decisive, the flick of her wrist at the abbess who might have remained surprising Radegunde with its dismissiveness. She might have been a queen, and Radegunde marveled that such a woman would have retired from the world for any reason.

The abbess, however, did not fully retreat. She hovered just beyond the portal.

It was clear that Lady Eudaline did not appreciate this.

Radegunde wondered how to address her, for she seemed a high noblewoman yet, not a woman who had abandoned the trappings of the material world. She decided to call her by her secular address, hoping it might please the lady.

Lady Eudaline had her height in common with her son, as well as her vivid blue eyes. Her silent but thorough perusal of Radegunde was also reminiscent of Gaston, and the maid doubted that the lady missed any detail.

She seated herself regally, as if compelled to endure an unwelcome audience, set the candle on a table beside her, then eyed Radegunde coolly. "Should I know you?" she demanded before Radegunde could introduce herself.

She was blunt then, as Lord Gaston was not.

"Perhaps only by association, my lady," Radegunde said, refusing to falter under that sharp gaze. She was well aware that the abbess listened. "My mistress is Lady Richildis de Valeroy…"

"Richildis!" Lady Eudaline eyed the pair of baskets. "What a delight that she recalls me." She beckoned and Radegunde brought one basket to her feet, the one with the letter from Lady Richildis. She unfastened the top, then fetched the other basket. By the time she had placed it by Lady Eudaline's feet, that woman had already claimed the missive. She examined the seal, ensuring it had not been broken, and flicked the barest glance to the portal.

"Sister! You know that correspondence should be read first by me," the abbess protested. "And all the wealth that comes to us individually should be shared with all."

"And I know that there has already been some wine shared," Lady Eudaline retorted. "I see the gap in the basket's contents."

The abbess' lips tightened but she did not move.

"Was anything else claimed for the order?" Lady Eudaline asked Radegunde.

She shook her head. "Nay, my lady."

Lady Eudaline fixed a glare upon her supposed superior. "Take the other bottle of wine then and leave me with my guest."

The abbess, to Radegunde's surprise, did as instructed. It made her wonder how much Lady Eudaline had contributed to the foundation.

When the abbess was gone and the portal closed, Lady Eudaline shook her head. "Well worth the price of her absence, I would say. I cannot abide wine any more at any rate." She flicked a twinkling glance at Radegunde. "Dare I hope that is *eau-de-vie*?"

"It is, my lady."

"And mine to savor." She gestured and Radegunde removed the wineskin that was wedged in the lower realm of the basket, offering it to the lady with a curtsey. "It smells of plums," Lady Eudaline murmured and took an appreciative sniff. She gestured to a shelf on one wall and Radegunde fetched a cup. She poured a small measure for the noblewoman, who indicated that Radegunde should drink of it first.

Radegunde thought she was being hospitable and took a small sip. It seared her throat like liquid fire.

Lady Eudaline eyed her for a long moment, then plucked the cup from her grip. She topped it up and set it aside. She capped the wineskin and considered it for a long moment. "*Richildis* sent me this," she mused, then fixed that sharp gaze upon Radegunde once again. "How curious. From whence does it come?"

"Italy, my lady. I believe from Venice."

Lady Eudaline arched a brow. The wineskin disappeared beneath her skirts and Radegunde was instructed to return the empty cup to its former location. The noblewoman watched intently, her gaze so knowing that Radegunde fairly squirmed, then peered into the basket again. "Dried figs! My favorite." She offered one to Radegunde.

"They are your gift, my lady."

"And there is more to you than meets the eye, girl," the lady countered softly. "Eat a fig." There was no doubting that it was a command.

Radegunde was glad that she knew none of the gift had been tainted, although she was intrigued by the lady's caution. She took a fig, as daintily as she could, and ate it under Lady Eudaline's sharp gaze.

Silence filled the chamber.

Lady Eudaline did not seem to blink.

Radegunde could hear her heart pound in her ears and wondered what she should say or do. The noblewoman simply watched her, as if she endured a test, but Radegunde did not know what it was, much less how to succeed at it.

When Lady Eudaline finally spoke, her words were so softly uttered that Radegunde had to lean closer to hear her. "There is only one person in all of Christendom who would send me these two gifts together, and it is not Richildis de Valeroy." Her stare was as piercing as a hawk on the hunt. "Who are you and why are you here in truth?"

"I am the maid of Lady Ysmaine, the oldest daughter of Lady Richildis of Valeroy, and now the wife of G—"

"No more!" Lady Eudaline held up a hand to silence Radegunde. She glanced to the portal, then leaned closer, her expression avid. "He is at Valeroy yet? He is well?"

Radegunde nodded to both queries. "If you will excuse me, my lady." At Lady Eudaline's nod, Radegunde opened her kirtle to retrieve the small sealed scroll tucked between her breasts. Though she wished to be modest, she did not want the lady to think she was deceptive. Lady Eudaline smiled a little when she saw the scroll, and her gaze brightened when she had opened it.

"No clerk could match his horrific scrawl, to be certain," she murmured and ran a fingertip over the script with obvious affection. "His father did not wish to have him trained for the church, even though he was the younger son." She eyed Radegunde again. "Let me feel your pulse. Does it race?"

Radegunde stretched out her wrist and the older woman locked finger and thumb around it. She counted, then nodded with satisfaction. She unfurled the missive then, and selected a fig herself.

"You thought they were poisoned," Radegunde whispered.

"Much is possible in these times," the lady acknowledged without regret. "You brought both and consumed them willingly enough. If the gifts were poisoned, it was done without your knowledge. Still, it was not out of the question." She smiled. "I am glad they are not, though, for I do like both figs and *eau-de-vie*."

Why did she fear to be poisoned?

What did she know?

Lady Eudaline sipped the *eau-de-vie*, then cast it back. She blinked, evidently surprised by the potency of the contents, then smiled. "And there is a potion for a winter's night."

She then ate a fig and read Lord Gaston's missive more slowly than she had read that of Lady Richildis. When she was done, she rolled it up and held it to the flame of the candle. She ensured that it was burned completely, then blew the ashes across the floor so that they could not be discerned.

Then she eyed Radegunde once more.

"So he is wed." Lady Eudaline murmured, her satisfaction was clear. "And wed well."

"Aye, my lady, I believe as much."

She tapped a fingertip on the arm of the chair. "And so close as Valeroy." Radegunde heard the yearning in the older woman's voice. "He was right to send you. He must go home with all the knowledge I can give him. You must take it, and reveal it to none."

"Aye, my lady." Radegunde thought the lady would confess a tale to her then.

But Lady Eudaline stood and raised her voice. "How kind of Lady Richildis to send such gifts to me in memory of our friendship. I would send a small token to her in your care. Come with me, girl, to my cell. I will then pray for your safe journey home."

She swept from the small chamber then, leaving the baskets on the floor, and Radegunde could only follow behind her. The figs she kept in her hand, however, and Radegunde guessed that the abbess would not have any success in claiming them.

"But, it is not acceptable," the abbess began to protest, appearing in the corridor ahead and stepping into Lady Eudaline's path.

"It is for a moment and no more," the lady argued, and it was clear she would not be stopped. "Do not make such a fuss over a small matter, Adela," she chided and the chastised abbess stepped aside.

Radegunde hastened after Lady Eudaline.

As they strode down a walkway on one side of a cloister, Eudaline spoke quickly and softly. "I arrived as a new bride in 1153, knowing full well that my predecessor, Rohese, had been buried only six months. She and her youngest son had been killed when a boat capsized. Fulk did not believe it an accident. He confessed that he was glad he had taken Bayard with him on that day's ride, for he had chosen to do so in the last moment."

"Bayard?" Did she mean Lord Gaston's older brother?

"His son and heir," Eudaline confirmed. "He was but six years of age and should have been on that boat with his mother and younger brother. They had planned the excursion weeks before and the boy was disappointed to be denied it in the last moment."

"The whim saved his life, though."

"That it did. If only a similar whim had done as much this year."

Radegunde struggled to hide her reaction. The lady believed that Bayard had been killed! "Did Fulk know who did it?"

Eudaline shook her head. "He had suspicions, though. Châmont-sur-Maine had only come to his hand in 1142, by grant of Geoffrey of Anjou, as reward for loyal service. Fulk held it against the assault of Elias II in 1151, and the grant was reaffirmed by King Henry." She granted Radegunde a sharp look as they reached her cell. "But Fulk was not the sole one who desired such a gift from the king's hand. When he died, I left the matter to Bayard, to ensure that my own son was not made prey."

"He might be so now, my lady."

"Indeed," she agreed grimly. Lady Eudaline ducked into the cell, which was small and spare, as well as sufficiently chilly to make Radegunde shiver. Lady Eudaline plucked a small crucifix hung on a lace from the wall, pressed it between her hands briefly, then gave it to Radegunde. "It was Fulk's and his mother's before that. It is wrought of ebony. Hide it. Tell him I hope it brings him all the good fortune he needs."

The token was no sooner secreted in Radegunde's bosom than the lady seized a small book from the bed and spun to return to the chamber where they had met. The abbess was watching from the far end of the cloister, her expression disapproving.

"This will cost me, to be sure," Lady Eudaline muttered, although she sounded as if she looked forward to the confrontation.

"But who did your husband suspect?" Radegunde whispered, trying to look as if she did not speak at all.

"His oldest adversary, of course." Lady Eudaline halted then spun to face Radegunde, bending to kiss her cheeks in succession. "Sebastien," she said when she touched one cheek with her lips. "De Saint-Roux," she said when she touched the other.

But surely that man was dead, if he had been a competitor of Lord Gaston's father?

Lady Eudaline pressed the small book into Radegunde's hands and spoke again for the benefit of the abbess. "I thank you for making this journey to bring me such kind greetings from Lady Richildis. Please thank her for her generosity. This is but a small gift, but I would grant it to her, in gratitude for her kindness." She kissed the book and gave it to Radegunde. "Godspeed to you," she said, sounding much like her son, then pivoted and joined the other women as they filed toward the chapel for mass.

Radegunde felt that she had gained little information for her lord and lady, but there was no opportunity to ask for more. Lady Eudaline was disappearing into the chapel, and the impatience of the abbess was clear.

Perhaps there was some detail hidden in the book.

Radegunde hoped as much. She disguised her glance after Eudaline by admiring the cloister, then curtseyed before the abbess. "Such a place of beauty and tranquility," she said. "I thank you for permitting my lady's errand to be completed."

The abbess studied her. "How strange that Lady Richildis would think of an old friend after so many years. Eudaline has been here for sixteen years and has few visitors."

"If I may be so bold as to say, I believe one's thoughts often turn to the past when battling an illness," Radegunde said, thinking it was not precisely a lie. She had not specified that Lady Richildis was ill.

The abbess straightened in understanding. "We shall pray for her."

"I thank you." Radegunde cast a glance at the sky. "I must make haste back to my lady's side."

"Of course."

Radegunde strode to the door and the porter opened it for her.

"What did you say your name was?" the abbess called and Radegunde's heart leaped for her throat.

"I am Marie, my lady," Radegunde lied, for there were three of such name in service in Valeroy's hall.

"And your companion?"

Radegunde concocted another tale. "A man-at-arms, recently sworn to my lord's service. He was the sole one who could be spared this day." She shrugged. "It is tedious to ride with an escort one cannot understand."

The abbess smiled. "He speaks only the tongue of the Scots, then?"

"Evidently so, my lady. I can make no sense of his words."

"May you be quickly back at Valeroy again, then." The abbess inclined her head, watching, as Radegunde departed.

She was glad indeed to see Duncan yet awaiting her, and had she not feared they were watched, she might have seized his hand and told him all. As it was, she smiled primly and mounted her palfrey, as if they were merely employed in the same household. She did not spare him a glance, but rode on, hearing that he followed.

Radegunde could not wait to be far enough away to talk to Duncan in truth.

Aye, she wanted to look within this book, to be sure.

CHAPTER TEN

t was only midday, and a fine day as well. Duncan waited until the abbey was far behind them, confirmed that there were no signs of pursuit, then urged his steed closer to Radegunde's palfrey.

"Did you speak with her?" he asked quietly.

Radegunde nodded. "She gave me a book, then a crucifix in secret."

Duncan nodded, knowing that Gaston had anticipated his mother would send him some token. "I noted a path, lass," he said. "It winds to the left, just ahead."

"Where does it go?"

"Away from the road, which is all I desire. Let me take the lead. Perhaps we can find a place to share the repast sent with us."

"Only the repast?" she teased, and he spared her a grin.

"Perhaps more than that."

Radegunde slowed her palfrey so Duncan could pass her, and he walked his steed along the narrow path. As he had hoped, it wound steadily away from the path to the abbey and grew smaller as they rode. It was not long until the forest had closed around them and the sound of songbirds had increased. He heard water running. The horses strode onward, until the forest opened into a clearing that could not have suited his purposes better.

It was hidden from the road but open to the sky, and the sun illuminated it. The clearing felt sheltered and warm, the perfect place for his plan. Duncan dismounted, casting the reins over his steed's head and leaving the beast to graze. He then lifted Radegunde from her saddle, holding her captive before him for a long moment. She regarded him with shining eyes.

"I am glad you changed your thinking, Duncan," she whispered.

"And I am glad you provoked me to do so," he countered. "It is the nature of a stubborn man to become set in his path."

She grinned. "What good fortune that I do not mind urging you from it."

"What fortune indeed, lass," he murmured then bent and touched his lips to hers.

Radegunde leaned against him immediately, welcoming his embrace and wrapping her arms around his neck. The heat of their kiss flared, as he had guessed it might, and he was tempted to continue without delay.

But there was an order to matters that must be followed, to ensure that honor was kept. He would not indulge in passion first and make amends later, not this time.

Duncan broke their kiss, then tugged the reins over the head of Radegunde's palfrey. The horses nudged against each other, grazing contentedly as he led Radegunde by the hand to stand in the sunlight.

He turned to face her and met her expectant gaze. "I would accept your challenge, lass, and seize what we might share this day. You speak aright that the future is unknown, and there is little merit in a life shadowed by regret."

She smiled with visible delight, but he put one fingertip over her lush mouth.

"But I will not steal your maidenhead from you, like a thief in the night, and leave you with the burden of that loss. There may be a child, and though you believe that all can be as you desire, I would not see you pay a price for any sweetness there might be between us."

Her smile faded, her expression turning wary.

"And so I would propose to you a handfast, a commitment of but a year and a day."

"Is that not a marriage?"

"It is similar but requires no priest and can be secret between man and woman. It is the nature of such pledges to be renewed if both are willing and able, though after that year and a day, both are free to do as they will."

"So it *is* like a marriage."

"Not quite. It is a vow between man and woman, and one that both can honor or nay. There will be none to enforce it when we are apart, and your lady may not hold it in regard." He held her gaze. "I will honor it, Radegunde, though I will not blame you if you choose to abandon it."

"My word is of greater merit than that!"

"But your lady might compel you to wed another."

Radegunde studied him.

Duncan shook his head. "This is a compromise, Radegunde, for it is a vow that I hold in esteem, but not the one you would desire of me. I cannot offer for your hand for my future is not mine to determine. I will not take your maidenhead and leave you alone with any repercussions. This is a compromise, but it is one offered with honor."

"What if Fergus' father releases you from his service?"

"Then I will ride back to your side more swiftly than any might believe possible."

Radegunde looked pleased with this prospect, and leaned closer. "And do you love me, Duncan MacDonald? Even just a little?"

Duncan hesitated at that. Though he knew that he did, he also guessed that making such a confession might keep Radegunde from forgetting him if he did not return, or making a happy life with another. "I admire you," he said. "I like how you laugh and that you are stubborn and outspoken. I admire how you savor life, and that you believe you can make matters be as you desire." He let his gaze sweep over her and knew that heat lit his eyes. "And I find you more alluring than any woman I have ever known."

If Radegunde was disappointed by this confession, she hid it well. "That is a fair beginning to a match," she said with a smile. "I accept your offer of a handfast. Tell me what we must do."

Duncan felt a profound relief. He took her right hand in his, and her left hand in his, their hands crossing between them as they faced each other. Her expression was expectant.

"And so I vow to you, Radegunde of Valeroy, that I will treat you with honor from this day forth, for a year and a day, that I will hold you in my heart when we are apart and treat you well when we are together."

Radegunde smiled. "And so I vow to you, Duncan MacDonald, that I will treat you with honor from this day forth, for a year and a day, that I will hold you in my heart when we are apart and treat you well when we are together."

Duncan did not recall being so powerfully affected when last he had pledged himself in a handfast, but it seemed on this day as if a fist tightened around his heart. "I will take responsibility for any child of our union, whether our vows are renewed or not," he vowed.

"I will take responsibility for any child of our union, whether our vows are renewed or not," Radegunde echoed.

Duncan gave her hands a slight squeeze. "I will defend you and I will be faithful to you, and do my best to ensure our union fares well."

"I will defend you and I will be faithful to you, and do my best to ensure our union fares well." Radegunde smiled outright, her delight so clear that Duncan could not believe his good fortune.

He bent his head to kiss her and seal their vows, but Radegunde ducked his embrace. Her eyes sparkled, so he knew she did not evade his affections. "We said naught of soundly seducing each other, and with regularity," she said.

"I believe that is implied."

She squared her shoulders. "But I shall add it all the same. I vow, Duncan MacDonald, to surrender myself to you in the pursuit of pleasure, to welcome you abed and acknowledge you as my man with pride, whether we be together or apart."

Duncan smiled. "And I vow, Radegunde of Valeroy, to surrender myself to you in the pursuit of pleasure, to welcome you abed and acknowledge you as my lady with pride, whether we be together or apart."

She flushed at that. "I am no lady."

"You are to me."

"Be warned, sir, that I mean to claim your heart and keep it as my own forever," she jested, her manner merry.

Duncan smiled, rather than confess that she already possessed it. "Come here, lass, and seal our vows," he said gruffly and she laughed.

Then she stretched to her toes and kissed Duncan sweetly. "What changed your view?" she whispered against his mouth, her gaze searching his own.

Duncan smiled and caught her nape in his hand. "You did, with your challenge. You were right."

Radegunde's smile was joyous. "Aye, there is a better start to a match—you declaring that I am right!"

Duncan laughed then kissed her again, ensuring that the embrace was long and lusty. Radegunde met him touch for touch, her breasts crushed against his chest, her tongue dueling with his own. He lifted her against himself and deepened their kiss, loving how passionate and willing she was.

He stepped back with an effort, then unfastened his cloak and cast it upon the ground. "Come here, lass," he said, his voice rough. "Let us celebrate our union as it should be done."

Radegunde cast her own cloak atop his with a flourish. "You wear too much garb," she complained, and though he knew that they would meet leisurely at some point, on this day, he was glad to see that she shared his desire for haste.

"I can be rid of it faster than you," he challenged her and she laughed aloud.

"I take your dare!" Radegunde kicked off her boots and shed her stockings. In a heartbeat, she cast aside her girdle and her kirtle, her dark eyes dancing as she watched his progress.

Duncan shed his own boots and gloves. It took cursed long to unlace his jerkin and she laughed at him, coming to unfasten the lace with her nimble fingers. He stole a kiss for her impatience and she dropped her hands to the buckle of his belt. "I am not in need of such assistance," he growled, loving how merrily she laughed.

Radegunde's hair was unbound and her chemise shed with lightning speed. Even though she paused to tuck what had to be the volume from Lady Eudaline safely beneath her belt and added the crucifix that had been between her breasts, still she was nude far sooner than he. His plaid was yet around his hips and he wore his chemise when she confronted him, toe tapping. He yet wore his chemise, as well.

"Indeed, sir, I think you do not share my enthusiasm for our path."

"Do I not?"

"You linger over your garb, as if I should wait yet longer."

"Some things are better with a wait."

Radegunde propped her hands upon her hips and regarded him with mock disapproval. "Aye? What spoils for the victorious then?" she demanded, her eyes so filled with merriment that he wished that she only ever had cause to smile.

Duncan grinned and shed his belt. He unfurled his plaid, casting it aside, then tugged his chemise over his head. "All I have to give," he purred and Radegunde's delight with the view was more than clear.

"'Tis more than your legs that are fine, Duncan," she teased.

"Aye, I have no complaint with my view, either. Come here, lass."

She laughed when he swung her into his arms and deposited her on the cloaks, then he silenced her with a kiss that he had no intention of ending soon.

It was impossible for Radegunde to fear intimacy when she was with Duncan.

To be sure, this was all new to her, but she trusted him fully.

She had told no lie about him being fine and she liked the differences between his body and her own. He was toned and trim, his body honed like a fine blade for its task. He was tanned as well, the back of his shoulders of the darkest hue of gold. She could see scars on his flesh that were the mark of his trade, but there were fewer of them than she might have expected. They were on his arms, one on his thigh, several on his back. She did not like that the one on his shoulder was so fresh, but he was so hale that she knew he would heal quickly. The hair on his chest was dark and she followed the line of it to his erection, the size of which made her catch her breath.

Duncan cast her a little smile at that, a confident smile that echoed the gleam in his eyes. She knew he found her as alluring as she found him, and that was more heady than the finest aphrodisiac. His kiss was pure pleasure, the feel of his hands upon her bare skin as satisfying as she had expected. It was easy to surrender to sensation and to trust him to guide her on this new adventure.

She loved when he caught her in his arms, then deposited her on the cloaks like a prize he meant to savor.

Radegunde was on her back, Duncan looming over her, the luxurious fur lining of his cloak beneath her. He kissed her with a hunger that echoed her own, his mouth feasting upon hers as his hands roved over her. Radegunde locked her fingers into his hair and pulled him closer, arching her back to rub her breasts against his chest as he followed her to the ground. He kissed her ear, her throat, the underside of her chin and she laughed at the tickle of his whiskers against her flesh.

"What manner of fur is this?" she asked, digging one hand into his cloak.

"Wolf," he admitted, then drew a trail to her nipple with the tip of his tongue. He circled the areole and the cool air made the peak tighten even more, then he closed his mouth over her and suckled gently. Sensation flooded through Radegunde from that point and she found herself clutching at his hair as she gasped in pleasure.

"Why wolf?" she managed to ask.

"Because their pelts are thick and warm," he murmured against her flesh, moving to tease the other nipple the same way. "A lady's bed should be piled high with their pelts, as guarantee of both her warmth and her safety."

"How many?"

"Six to line a cloak. Maybe seven." His teeth grazed her nipple and she caught her breath.

"Did you kill them all?"

Duncan lifted his head and eyed her. There was a gleam of resolve in his gaze. "What do you think?"

"That you stalked them alone and slaughtered them alone, skinned them and wear their pelts as your trophy."

His smile was quick, and she knew he was pleased that she understood him. He captured her lips once more and kissed her deeply, his hand sliding down the length of her. Radegunde felt his fingers slip between her thighs and caught her breath at his sure touch upon her there. She gasped his name, and he whispered a command that she should part her thighs. Radegunde did, only to gasp in wonder at the surety of his caress.

She reached down and touched him, caressing the hard length of him and hearing him catch his breath. He whispered her name with urgency and she smiled, liking the power she had over him. She might have become even bolder, but Duncan moved, making a trail of burning kisses down the length of her until his mouth replaced his fingers.

Radegunde fell back against the fur with a cry. His touch was intimate and beguiling, his tongue and his teeth teasing her as she had never believed was possible. She felt aflame with desire, yet yearned for more and more. Duncan continued when she thought she could bear it no longer, and she cried out when a tide swept through her. She gasped aloud and whispered his name, though he did not cease his assault until she was trembling in the aftermath.

Then he chuckled at the sight of her and braced himself above her once more. "Temptress," he whispered, easing himself between her thighs. Radegunde welcomed him, arching her back as his strength slid inside her. He surrounded her. He filled her. He closed his eyes and leaned his brow upon her shoulder, shaking before he began to move within her.

She was possessed, and happy of it.

Against all expectation, Radegunde felt the storm rise within her again. She held fast to Duncan, her nails digging into his shoulders, her legs wrapped around him to draw him closer, her kiss his to claim. She thought she would be devoured or consumed, but she wanted more and more.

"More," she whispered to him and Duncan's eyes flashed. "All of you, Duncan," she urged. "Claim me fully and make me your own." He caught her nape in his hand and kissed her with fervor, moving so that her own passion rose to a crescendo once more. She might have cried out with pleasure, but he devoured the sound, then roared against her throat in his own release.

He kissed her neck and her ear softly then, and she ran her hands over him in wonder. Radegunde was both hot and shivering, her heart pounding and her skin warm. She felt both sampled and treasured, claimed and content. She held Duncan close and he lowered himself to the cloak beside her, drawing her into his embrace and pulling the cloak over them both.

Radegunde was surrounded by the soft fur, nestled against Duncan's strength. There was nowhere else she would rather be than in Duncan's embrace in this sunlit glade.

"Slower the second time," he vowed, his voice rough.

Radegunde smiled as she dozed, well content.

Duncan supposed they should rise and return to Valeroy.

The sun had moved across the sky as they loved and dozed and loved twice more. Soon it would dip below the highest branches of the trees. The air would chill and he did not wish Radegunde to become cold. Still, he felt as if they had stolen an interval for themselves, away from their responsibilities, and wished to prolong this golden afternoon as much as possible.

Radegunde dozed contently against his shoulder, her softness curled against him and her legs entangled with his. He stroked his fingers through her hair, savoring all they had shared. Her passion had not been a surprise, but it had been a delight.

Of course, he had to escort Fergus all the way home to Killairic, for he had given his word, but such was the marvel of Radegunde that Duncan was giving serious consideration to the merit of breaking his word.

What if he remained with her? Would Fergus understand? Would his father?

She deserved more than the uncertainty of the wife of a man-at-arms, to be sure. That was what had truly held Duncan's tongue. But what if he could offer her more than that?

What if he could claim what once he had spurned? He had not considered his legacy in years, and had not thought it worth the inevitable battle that would be required. With Radegunde's hand as the prize, Duncan wondered.

He frowned then, for the sun sank and they could linger no longer. He kissed her brow and rose from their bed, dressing with impatient gestures.

Radegunde rolled over and stretched, then propped her chin on her hand to watch him. "I suppose we must go."

She misinterpreted the reason for his impatience and he was glad of it, for he had no argument with her.

She had a gift for making him desire more and to choose to strive for it. Did she guess the adventure she would set him upon? She could not.

He cast her a smile. "Indeed, we have hours yet to ride and must make the gates before the evening meal."

Radegunde showed no inclination to move. She stretched like a cat and burrowed deeper into the cloak. "It was wondrous," she said. "Though perhaps you have known more wondrous days abed."

"How so?"

"With courtesans," she replied, no charge in her words. "They know what they do, while I could only enjoy."

Duncan smiled. He crouched down beside her, catching her chin in his hand. "You are wondrous," he corrected. "And all the more wondrous for your enthusiasm and lack of wiles." She smiled before he granted her a lingering kiss. "But you will be chilled if you do not dress. The sun is dipping lower already."

"Will you come to me at night at Valeroy?" Her smile was impish. "Now that I know of this pleasure, I am disinclined to be without it."

Aye, Duncan could agree with that.

"I do not know whether it would be wise." He frowned. "I would like to, but should confer with Fergus."

"He will likely agree, for he knows of your custom. It is my lord Gaston and Lady Ysmaine who might forbid it." Radegunde grimaced and rose to her feet. She tugged her chemise over her head and tied the cord at the neckline. "My lady will not like these tidings, to be sure. She may think I would destroy her plans apurpose."

"Will she think you defiant?"

"I do not know."

Duncan wondered whether the lady might dismiss Radegunde from her employ in such circumstance. Would Radegunde go with him to Scotland then? Or would she not want to leave her mother so far behind?

Again in so many moments, his thoughts turned to Inverness, as they had not in years.

Radegunde granted him a glance. "You fret over some detail. Do you regret what we have done?"

"Never!" Duncan held her gaze until she smiled. "You?"

"Never," she whispered with heat.

Another kiss was necessary then, and yet again, it was a kiss that did not readily end. Duncan put her aside with reluctance, stroking her cheek. "We must return," he reminded her and she nodded agreement. He fastened his belt over his plaid and checked his weapons, then heard the crack of a breaking twig.

Duncan froze. Radegunde stared at him, for she had evidently heard the sound as well. He lifted a finger for silence, though it was not necessary, then drew his knife. Radegunde quickly fastened her girdle and tucked the crucifix away, then bound the book into the purse that hung from her belt.

There was another rustle in the forest and the horses snorted.

Someone pursued them. Duncan seized his cloak and Radegunde grabbed her own. They made as one for the horses, but a shadow lunged through the woods toward them to intervene. Duncan could see only the silhouette of a man and the gleam of an upheld blade.

The assailant lunged through the undergrowth, evidently realizing that he'd been seen and determined to make his attack while he could. The horses spooked and ran, bolting back toward the road.

Radegunde gasped and might have fled after the horses, but Duncan seized her hand and ran in the opposite direction. It was immediately clear that the assailant came after them. Footsteps pounded in pursuit and Duncan urged Radegunde to greater speed.

Who attacked them?

And why?

What had Lady Eudaline told Radegunde—or what was in the book she had surrendered? Too late, Duncan wished they had discussed the visit more, that he might know the tidings sent by the lady as well. Still, he could not regret the sweet hours they had spent together. He raced through the undergrowth, Radegunde's hand fast in his own, then leaped across a stream.

Radegunde gave a little cry as she stumbled. She valiantly tried to match his pace, but Duncan did not waste a moment. He cursed himself for not recalling her weakened foot. Without hesitation, he scooped her up onto his back, as one would play with a child, and ran on.

"Duncan, you cannot carry me!" she protested.

"I can and I will."

"But I am too heavy."

"As light as a feather. Hold fast!" He felt the trickle of blood from his recent injury and cursed that the wound was opened again. Radegunde quickly perceived the reason for his exclamation.

"You bleed anew! Put me down!"

"Press on the wound, lass," he instructed through his teeth. "We shall only survive this together."

"Stubborn man," she chided softly, though she did as instructed. "You could save yourself without me."

"To what point?" Duncan leaped over a fallen log, hearing the other man close behind him.

"You were the one attacked the other night. Perhaps he hunts you."

"Perhaps it is not the same man," he argued. "Perhaps it is but an outcast in the woods."

"There are not so many at Valeroy."

He spared her a glance, knowing he had to say what was obvious to him. "He might have watched us, lass. He may want to sample the feast I have savored."

Radegunde caught her breath and clutched him more tightly.

"I will not leave you behind, lass, upon that you can rely."

She pressed a kiss to the back of his neck and hung on, her forehead against his shoulder. The flat of her hand was pressed against his injury and he could nigh feel her will that they should succeed.

He knew not where he fled, for this forest was unfamiliar to him. It looked the same in every direction, as strange forests will, and he did not know which way to turn. In the moment when he might have feared their fate, Duncan glimpsed the shadow ahead of him in the dappled light of the forest.

Another man?

One who ran ahead of them?

Duncan was not whimsical so he watched for another glimpse. The figure ahead was large, that of a tall and robustly built man. He moved in silence, unlike the assailant behind them, seeming to flit from one shadow to another. But whenever he was in view, he beckoned to Duncan.

Why?

Could he be trusted?

Duncan thought of Mathilde's comment about the wild man of the woods and decided he had naught to lose.

He followed the direction suggested by the shadow ahead, hoping he chose aright.

Duncan ran like a hare. Radegunde held fast to his shoulders, unable to resist the urge to glance back. She caught glimpses of the man who pursued them, but could not discern his features. The light was already fading and the shadows in the forest were becoming darker. Who was he and why did he attack them?

And where did Duncan take them? Even she did not know these forests well, and she had come of age at Valeroy. Duncan took a decisive path, as if he had a destination, and she could only wonder where it might be.

Radegunde hoped it was close. She could feel Duncan's heart racing and the blood seeping from his wound. His breath came more quickly and there was dampness on his skin. She was about to ask him when he emerged abruptly from the shelter of the forest.

She heard falling water in the same moment that Duncan caught his breath and tried to halt. A hand reached out of the shadows and hauled Duncan to one side of the path he had taken.

Another hand clapped over Radegunde's mouth. She smelled forest and earth and a man's perspiration. She and Duncan were held fast by a man who was taller than Duncan, and who had his back to a massive tree.

Just steps ahead of them, the ground dropped away. A river splashed on the left, flowing down to a pool below. The lip of the cliff was hidden by undergrowth and Radegunde gasped that they had so narrowly missed such a fall.

Had the hand not seized Duncan, she and he would have gone over the lip.

Radegunde had a moment to wonder whether they had leaped from fat to fire before the man who had pursued them emerged from the forest, just steps away from them. Unlike Duncan, he raced over the cliff, bellowed in frustration, then fell to the pool.

He wore plaid, much like Duncan, though Radegunde noted that his legs were not nearly so fine.

"And so your past has pursued you, Duncan MacDonald, all the way from Scotland," the tall man said gruffly, then released them both. He pushed Duncan slightly forward, and Radegunde peered down at the pool just as Duncan did. Far below, their assailant came to the surface and glared up at them, shouting a curse. "Look at your enemy and name him!" the tall man insisted.

But Duncan shook his head. "I have never seen him before," he said, but Radegunde heard the consideration in his tone.

"But you know from whence he came," she guessed and Duncan sighed.

"Aye, lass, that I do." He turned to confront the tall man, offering his hand. "I thank you for your intervention."

The man who had aided them was tanned to the hue of dark wood. There was mire on his face and his hair was long and untended. His beard was long and matted, too, his mustache so long that she could scarce see his mouth. His garb was so dirty that Radegunde could never have guessed its original hue, and he had the pelt of some creature belted around his waist. His eyes were dark and his gaze so piercing that she had a sense he was no fool.

He looked at Duncan's hand and she thought she glimpsed the flash of his teeth. "And I thank you for treating my sole daughter with honor," he said, turning that gaze upon Radegunde.

She gasped in astonishment and would have retreated if her foot had not been injured again. "You are mistaken. My father is dead!"

"Your father is an outcast," the man corrected.

"The wild man of the woods," Duncan added, evidently unsurprised. "I have a message for you from Mathilde."

The man gave Duncan a quick glance, then bent before them. "Let me look at that foot, Radegunde," he murmured. "We saw it healed once before, and we can do as much again." And when he looked up at her this time, Radegunde did not see a filthy outcast from the forest. She saw the familiarity of her father's eyes, his gentleness and his compassion, and she was embarrassed to find herself weeping like a child.

CHAPTER ELEVEN

he wild man of the woods carried Radegunde easily, as if she were yet a small child.

He also covered distance with fearsome speed. Duncan was hard-pressed to keep up with Radegunde's father and admired how silently the other man could move through the forest. His ragged garb was such that he blended into the trees, and Duncan feared to fall too far behind him lest he be lost.

Radegunde clutched her father and peered over his shoulder.

Her father followed a path that only he could discern, their route winding downward and taking many twists and turns. Duncan kept up as well as he could, though his boots slipped more than once on the wet plants underfoot. He was panting but dared not slow his path and lose sight of his Radegunde.

Even as he ran, Duncan puzzled over the attacker's identity. Twice he had been attacked in days, and this time, it could have been Radegunde who paid the price. The notion that she could be injured, or worse, because of him was more than sobering.

It was terrifying.

Who had the assailant been? Duncan had not recognized him.

Could Radegunde's father be right, that his past had followed him? Certainly the attacker had worn the plaid, but there were Scottish mercenaries aplenty in France. He had drunk ale with dozens of them in Paris.

But who would have hired a man to attack Duncan? He possessed naught of value himself, and he could not believe that his own history had caught up with him now, after so many years of silence. His father knew he wanted naught of him and should be content to let the matter be.

It had been years, after all.

Duncan felt the blood running from his shoulder wound and trickling over his chest. The wet warmth was a potent reminder of the risk posed by the attacker. Why would any seek to kill him?

Perhaps this concerned Fergus and his father. Perhaps some soul wished to do injury to Fergus and perceived Duncan as an obstacle—rightly so, to Duncan's thinking. He would willingly lay down his life for his patron's son. That was why he had been dispatched to accompany the younger man, after all.

But who? And why? Yet again, Duncan considered his sense that Fergus' regard for his betrothed was not returned in equal strength, but Isobel had only to deny Fergus to see the engagement ended. She did not need to see him killed, and truly, if there had ever been any fondness between them, such an extreme strategy made little sense. Duncan did not like her or trust her, but he did not think her wicked.

Or perhaps it was about the reliquary. Duncan had been entrusted with its burden after their departure from Paris, after all. The notion chilled his heart. Perhaps Everard had evaded Wulfe and survived to seek the treasure again.

Perhaps Wulfe had been injured or killed.

Duncan had to warn Gaston!

Yet he was in the forest, without a horse, chasing the wild man of the woods to a destination unknown. What was more, that man set a killing pace. On a steep slope, Duncan slipped and fell, wincing as he hit the rocky ground hard. He slid on the wet vegetation, then came to a halt, his hands braced against the ground. He was covered in mire.

And he was alone.

The other man had vanished as if he had been gobbled up by the forest. Duncan remained motionless and listened, but could discern no sound. He stood slowly and turned in place, quietly panicking.

Nay! She could not be gone!

"Here!" Radegunde said, her whisper carrying through the shadows. "This way!"

Relief surged through Duncan.

He still could not spy the pair, but he followed the sound of Radegunde's voice, stepping with care. He crossed a shallow stream, noting the sequence of rocks that appeared to be strewn randomly in the water but made a crooked line of stepping stones at precisely the distance of a man's stride. He reached the other bank and confronted dense forest growth and a wall of vines. Their winding course must have led to the bottom of a cliff.

"Here!" Radegunde whispered, and Duncan saw her hand extend through the thick layer of vines. When he approached, he realized that in this one place, the growth was a curtain.

Disguising the opening to a cave.

Radegunde was seated just inside the refuge and greeted him with a smile. Duncan peered into the darkness lit by a beam of sunlight. There must be an opening that wound to the top of the cliff. The silhouette of Radegunde's father appeared, as that man returned to the opening, He carried a length of braided rope.

"I will try to retrieve the horses," he said gruffly, sparing a concerned glance at Radegunde. "You can light a fire safely on the hearth."

Then he was gone.

There was a haste about his departure that might have made Duncan doubt their welcome, had the man not brought them to the cave himself. He and Radegunde exchanged a glance and she took a steadying breath.

"Is it broken?" Duncan crouched before her and checked the bone.

"I hope not." She bit her lip and watched as he gently touched and moved it.

"I think it is but a strain."

"Aye. It does not click and is tender but not as sore as that." She heaved a sigh and made to tear a length of cloth from the hem of her chemise. "If it is bound, it should not swell overmuch."

Duncan smiled.

"And this amuses you?" she demanded in a teasing tone.

"I like that you are pragmatic, my Radegunde. Many a woman would have wept inconsolably, but you simply see the matter resolved as well as you can."

"Which is not well enough. I will not be able to walk for several days, and not until the morrow even with assistance." She spared him a grim glance. "And you are hunted."

"We do not know as much," Duncan demurred, but Radegunde scoffed.

"You would wait until you are dead to be sure of the matter?" She shook her head as she knotted the cloth. "Not I. You are hunted, Duncan, and we must discover why to ensure that your attacker is not successful on his third attempt."

"I would simply dispatch him first."

"And without knowing the cause, open yourself to assault by a replacement." Radegunde shook her head, then shivered. "Nay, we must figure out the truth."

"But first you must be warmed." Duncan surveyed the space. The cave was clearly the abode of her father, and he had mentioned a hearth. Duncan lifted Radegunde and carried her toward that beam of light. The path toward it was uneven and convoluted, dipping down to the roughly circular space. Duncan felt he descended a number of steps to the roughly circular space that was marked in its middle with ash. He looked back but could not clearly see the opening from the forest, not without peering over the highest "step."

The light slanted into the cave from a gap in the rock that extended high above them. The cave was not without some comfort—beyond the welcome one of relief from the elements and being a secret refuge. There was wood for the fire stacked dry against one wall, a metal box with a flint, and bags hanging from makeshift hooks, wrought of sticks jammed into gaps in the stone.

Radegunde explored them while Duncan lit a blaze and he saw her choose one. There was an iron tripod to place over the fire and a sturdy if plain pot. The space was soon warm and filled with golden light. There were pelts piled at one side, and he stacked them to ensure Radegunde's comfort.

"There is a vessel of water," she said. "And the bags contain dried herbs." She held up the one she had chosen. "If you can heat some water, we can have an infusion from this one, which I remember well. It is most restorative."

"And it will be good to have warmth in the belly," Duncan agreed, wanting to ensure her comfort. He found a bowl, which would suffice for them to share this tisane.

He set the water to heat as she instructed, then sat beside her. He might have asked about her ankle, but Radegunde insisted upon seeing his own injury. When she had cleaned it and halted the bleeding to her satisfaction, he realized that she had matters of greater import to discuss.

"Who would desire to kill you?" she demanded quietly.

Duncan chose not to burden her with the tale of his own past, as he thought it irrelevant. "What if my faith that Wulfe would see Everard dispatched was wrong?"

Radegunde caught her breath. "Because you carried the relic from Paris."

"Aye."

"But you do not carry it now."

Duncan shrugged. "He might not know it. He might have seen my leaving Valeroy with you alone as an opportunity."

Radegunde considered this. "But you did not have it when you came to my mother's abode either."

"Perhaps he seeks to ensure it is granted to another, one he could defeat more readily."

Radegunde shook her head. "It is too complicated a scheme. If he wanted the relic, he would attack you while you carried it."

"He could have erred."

She fixed an intent look upon him. "Or there could be another reason, one you decline to share with me."

Duncan smiled. "I did wonder whether it concerned my

protection of Lord Fergus."

"Because eliminating you would make him more vulnerable."
Radegunde considered this. "But who would wish him dead?"

"I cannot say."

"You will not say." She granted him a stern glance. "There is
more to this than you are telling, Duncan MacDonald, and you had
best seize the opportunity to confide in me while still you can."

He claimed her hand and kissed her palm, closing her fingers
over the warm imprint. "I would warn Gaston and confer with
Fergus first."

"Because I am a woman?" she asked, her opinion of that clear.

"Because I would not create concern where none is deserved."

"I say it is well deserved when you have been twice attacked."
Her eyes were flashing with a determination that was rapidly
becoming familiar. "Must I remind you that we are pledged each to
the other now, Duncan?"

"Nay, but I would remind you that our vow makes your
protection my responsibility." She looked unwilling to abandon the
discussion, but the water in the pot was steaming. He rose and
poured some into the bowl, letting her mix the herbs within it. The
scent alone was restorative, being both fruity and sharp.

"You first. You have bled this day," she instructed and it was
clear she would have no argument.

Duncan sipped the hot liquid under her watchful eye and by the
time it had cooled to a good temperature for drinking, she
consented to have some herself. He granted her the bowl and she
sipped with real pleasure.

"I know that you are accustomed to keeping your counsel to
yourself, Duncan," she said finally. "But that undermines the full
power of a match."

"As Gaston discovered when he failed to trust his lady with all
of the truth," he continued, anticipating her argument. "I
understand your meaning, Radegunde, but am uncertain what else
I might confide."

She studied him so intently that he wondered whether he
should tell her of his father. But then he dismissed the notion. It
had been twenty years! They were estranged and the matter was

done. He spared her a glance and her gaze dropped.

"You knew my father lived," she said softly. Duncan heard the implication that he had not confided in her, even without Radegunde saying as much, and knew he had to defend his actions.

"Your mother implied that he lived in the woods, though I had no notion where he might be found. I was not entirely convinced that she was right or that we would see him, so did not wish to raise your hopes."

Radegunde said naught.

Duncan nudged her. "I admit that I am no judge of a man's fine legs, but I could only assume that he aided us because he was the man in question."

Radegunde did not smile at his jest. "You could have told me."

"Your mother might have been wrong," Duncan felt obliged to repeat.

Radegunde smiled at this. "My mother is never wrong. You will learn that in time, to be sure."

"And I think you should do naught this night but rest," Duncan countered.

"If you mean to warn Gaston, you should return to Valeroy without me. I will be safe enough here."

Duncan granted her a fierce glance, for the notion was unthinkable. "I will not!"

Her smile was genuine then and he was relieved to see it.

"You truly thought him dead?" he asked.

Radegunde considered this. "Aye and nay. It was the tale I was told when I was too young to question my mother." She frowned. "I knew that my mother welcomed some man on occasion, of course."

"You have younger brothers."

"Aye, but I never saw him. Not clearly. He came late and left early, and their whispers were not to be overheard."

"You tried?"

Radegunde's smile was quick. "Of course! I have more than my measure of curiosity."

"Did you not notice that your younger brothers strongly resembled you, but not your mother?"

"I suppose, but her green eyes are unusual at Valeroy. Most people have dark hair and dark eyes."

It was true enough. "I am surprised that no helpful neighbor confided the truth in you."

"Perhaps they did not know. Perhaps they did not see him clearly either. My mother's cottage is the last and nigh surrounded by the forest."

"There must have been whispers."

Radegunde laughed a little. "People whispered of it a little, but I think they feared my mother's ire, for they did come to her for healing, and none dared speak to me of it."

"No one would want to be declined when in need."

"And I think they like her, as well." She shrugged, but Duncan could see that she was reconsidering all that she had believed to be true. "It was simply as my life was."

"While I noted immediately that there was great similarity between all of you, though none of you have Mathilde's eyes. I assumed you had the same father and was surprised to learn that he was believed to be so long dead. I suspected a ruse then."

"I suppose we each see what we expect to see."

"Indeed." Duncan shed his cloak and tucked it over her shoulders. "What did Lady Eudaline say to you?"

"Very little, in truth." Radegunde reached into her chemise. "She asked me to give Lord Gaston his father's crucifix, which was that of Fulk's mother before."

Duncan found little remarkable about the token, for he had seen a hundred that were much the same. "It is dark of hue."

"She said it was ebony." She surrendered it to Duncan, who examined it and returned it to her custody. Radegunde then removed the small book he had noted earlier from her purse. "And she granted me this book to give to Lord Gaston."

"Perhaps she believes prayer to be the answer to all woes." Duncan was startled when his companion laughed. "Why are you so amused? It is the thinking of many who retire to religious life."

"Not this lady!" Radegunde spoke with confidence. "She is most pragmatic. She feared I had brought her poisoned gifts and demanded that I both drink of the *eau-de-vie* and eat a fig first, while she watched and waited for my demise."

"How dare she!" Duncan knew his outrage showed.

Radegunde laid a hand on his arm. "I knew there was no poison, Duncan. I was not in peril."

"Still...!" The notion unsettled him, truly.

"She is cautious. She reminds me, to be sure, of Lord Gaston, for she is tall and has those eyes of blue. She stares so steadily and in such silence that she might read one's own thoughts." Radegunde opened the small book and turned the pages slowly.

"Is it a psalter?"

"It is a small Bible," she replied. "See? Here is the Book of John." She squinted and leaned closer to the fire. "How curious. Someone has written in the margins."

"The monks oft add detail in the margins when they illustrate a volume."

"Nay, nay. This was added later, in less formal script, and sideways. Look."

Duncan looked. On the edge of each right page from about halfway through the volume, was a line of script running from bottom to top. It was as if someone had written a letter, with one line on each page.

Had Lady Eudaline shared more tidings than Radegunde had realized?

"Wait! This is what she told me about Fulk!" Radegunde declared, then began to read. "*I arrived as a new bride in 1153—*" she read, then turned the page to continue "*—knowing full well that my predecessor, Rohese—*" Again a page was turned "*—had been buried only six months.*" And so it went, Radegunde reading a phrase, then turning the page to read the next. "*She and her youngest son had been killed when a boat capsized. Fulk did not believe it an accident. He confessed that he was glad he had taken Bayard with him on that day's ride, for he had chosen to do so in the last moment.*"

"Gaston's older brother," Duncan mused.

"This is precisely what she said to me!" Radegunde said with excitement. "Every word here matches hers."

"That cannot be a coincidence."

"Nay, it cannot. This book is of import." Radegunde turned the pages more quickly as she read. "*He was but six years of age and should have been on that boat with his mother and younger brother. They had planned the excursion weeks before and the boy was disappointed to be denied it in the last moment. Fulk had his suspicions as to who might be the guilty party.*"

Duncan watched her, intrigued.

"*Châmont-sur-Maine had only come to Fulk's hand in 1142, by grant of Geoffrey of Anjou, as reward for loyal service. Fulk held it against the assault of Elias II in 1151, and the grant was reaffirmed by King Henry.*" Radegunde separated the next page with some effort.

"The volume looks to have become wet at some point," he noted.

"Aye. And the pages are sealed to each other." She gently rubbed the thin pages between her fingers, coaxing them to separate, and her smile flashed at her success. She read on from the next two pages in succession. "But Fulk was not the sole one who desired such a gift from the king's hand."

The subsequent page was even more difficult to separate from its fellows and Radegunde frowned. "It could not have been water that dampened the book," she said, coming to the same conclusion as Duncan. "How vexing! The pages are most securely adhered to each other in this corner. I do not wish to damage it."

"Perhaps a scribe dipped it in glue."

"Then why would a client have paid for it? Nay, it must have happened later."

Who kept glue, save the scribes who used it to bind books? Duncan could not say.

The fire crackled as Radegunde patiently tried to work the pages apart. Finally she managed to separate the next page. She cast Duncan a triumphant glance when she turned it. "*When he died, I left the matter to Bayard—*" The next page turned more readily "*—to ensure that my own son was not made the prey of—*"

"She went to the convent to protect Gaston," Duncan concluded.

"Aye, that is what I thought when she told me as much." Radegunde nodded, then shook her head that the next page was stuck. "And here she will name the villain, as she did during our discussion."

"She did?"

"Aye. Sebastien de Saint-Roux." Radegunde whispered and Duncan could not say he was completely surprised. "Do you think it written here?"

Duncan leaned closer as she fought to free the page. Radegunde cursed, then raised her hand to her mouth.

"Do not touch your fingers to your mouth!" came a rough command.

Radegunde and Duncan both froze.

Her father appeared at the top of the descent to the rough chamber where they sat. He glowered at Radegunde, looking wilder and more fierce than he had earlier.

Duncan's hand dropped to his blade as he began to rise to his feet.

"The pages are poisoned!" their host declared.

"Poisoned?" Radegunde echoed, knowing that her astonishment showed. Duncan seized the book from her grip and turned it in his grasp, studying the secured corner.

"Poisoned," her father affirmed, crossing the width of the cave with three strides and seizing the volume. He pointed to a bucket of water. "Wash your skin thoroughly and quickly," he commanded and Duncan brought her a measure of water.

Radegunde did as instructed, glad there was a bar of rough soap to use. She flicked a glance over her shoulder, still amazed that her father stood before her. "How do you know?" she demanded.

"That is not of import," he said gruffly.

Radegunde felt her lips tighten. It seemed that she was in the company of two men who did not see fit to confide fully in her. She frowned and scrubbed her hand. Her vexation showed for Duncan bit back a smile.

Her father folded his arms across his chest to consider her, as he had when she had been small. "And why do you read from the book?"

"I would know whether its tale matches that confided in me by Lady Eudaline."

"Does it thus far?"

"Word for word."

"Then you have no need to explore the book's secrets, for you know them already."

"There might be more detail. It implies that the villain is named..."

"But Eudaline already confided in you." Her father shook the small volume at her. "The book is a trap, one prepared by Eudaline for the day that some soul appeared who might be relied upon to deliver it. It was irresponsible of her to grant it to you without a warning."

"But she did not trust me either," Radegunde admitted.

"How do you know this?" Duncan asked, his skepticism clear.

Her father raised his brows. "I *know* Eudaline."

"Should you not call her Lady Eudaline?" Radegunde asked.

Her father avoided her gaze, a hint of yet another hidden truth. "Perhaps. I am not so concerned with convention and etiquette in these days." He spared her a bright glance. "Is it true that you have been to Outremer and back?"

"You change the subject to evade my questions," she accused and he smiled, but did not dispute it.

"Did you retrieve the horses?" Duncan asked.

"Alas, only one. The warhorse was too far ahead of me and fled back toward Valeroy. I would hope he is safe within his stall by now."

"I would be certain," Duncan said, and Radegunde noted the concern in his sidelong glance.

"And Lady Ysmaine will be worried." Radegunde tried to get to her feet, only to have both men halt her. Each put a hand beneath one of her elbows.

"You will not do yourself further injury," her father said. "You should rest."

"I will not allow my lady to fret. We should return with all haste."

"I will carry you to the palfrey, then lead it," Duncan said. Though the prospect of opening his wound again displeased Radegunde, she saw his determination and knew he would not be swayed.

"You must pledge to me that you will rest on the morrow then," she said but he swung her into his arms without reply.

"I will lead you," her father concluded. "Give me the last of that infusion before we depart. It smells most restorative."

"*Maman*'s blend," Radegunde said, a challenge in her voice.

Her father did not take the invitation, merely sipped of the brew with real pleasure.

Did he not love Mathilde? Why had he left her? Why had he returned at intervals? It seemed indecisive, and Radegunde did not think her father possessed that trait. Nor did she imagine that he was one to play with the affections of another.

He set the bowl aside and helped Duncan to kick the fire to ashes. Duncan then lifted Radegunde and they left the cave. Her palfrey was tethered to a tree, ears flicking. Duncan lifted Radegunde to the saddle, and she ran her hands over the beast with relief. Her father was yet silent, though there was much she would ask him.

She took a breath and asked one of her many questions. "How could you let me think you dead?"

Her father granted her a solemn glance. "Would you entrust your safety in the ability of a child to hold her tongue?" he demanded and she had to acknowledge that she would not. "In truth, I thought you might discern the truth when you were older." He claimed the reins and led them through the forest. It was growing darker and the shadows already lengthened. The air felt chilly after the warmth of the cave, and Radegunde drew her cloak closed.

"But you and *Maman* deceived with great success." There was bitterness in her tone and Radegunde did not try to hide it. She was aware that Duncan listened with care as he walked alongside. He kept one hand on the saddle, and she dropped her hand to close over his own.

Her father sobered. "You will tell no others, Radegunde."

"You could confide in me now. Why do you live like this when you could be with us in the hut?"

"Because I could not remain with you, not when I was hunted, for I would not risk the lives of all of you."

"You risked it sometimes, when you returned to *Maman*."
Radegunde had a thought then. Had Duncan's attacker believed
him to be her father? Nay, it could not be. Though both men were
tall and broad of shoulder, her father was larger and more heavily
set.

Meanwhile her father smiled a little. "That is the true peril of
love, for I could not abandon her until she bade me do as much."

Radegunde straightened. "She sent you away?"

"She challenged me to remain or to leave forever. I dared not
risk her life, so I left. I hope it is not forever." He nodded once.
"Tell me of Outremer."

"I did not realize the tale of my journey was known in the
forest."

"I am not without tidings here, Radegunde, and you have been
gone for years."

"But only returned for days."

"Then it is clear that tidings reach me in a timely fashion.
Perhaps the birds told me of it. Will you tell me of your
adventure?"

Radegunde felt her lips set. He was determined to evade her
questions, while drawing out all information from her. The
combination vexed her mightily and made her feel as if she were
still distrusted, like a small child. "Not unless you tell me why you
left us."

To her dismay, her father turned his attention to her
companion, clearly having no intention of doing as much. "Tell
me, Duncan MacDonald, what are your prospects?"

"I am a fighting man," Duncan replied. "Sworn to the service
of the man who saved my life until the favor is returned. By his
command, I escorted his son to Outremer and will see him home
again to Scotland."

"Will you go with him?" Radegunde's father asked her.

"I do not know." She glanced at Duncan. "We have not
discussed it."

"But you are sworn to each other all the same," he mused and
did not seem overly troubled. "Well. Ensure her happiness,
wherever you choose to live, and you will have my blessing."

"It is my intention to do as much, sir." Duncan eyed her father. "Your blessing is welcome but unexpected, sir."

Her father smiled. "There was a time, Duncan MacDonald, when I would have thrashed your hide for taking my daughter's innocence with such a small guarantee in return, but it is your good fortune that I have spent so long in exile. I am no longer so concerned with the judgment of others."

Duncan nodded, but Radegunde straightened.

"Exile?" she echoed, seizing upon that one detail. "So your abandonment of us was at the order of some soul other than *Maman*? What have you done, Papa, to be condemned to live as an outlaw?"

He gave her a glittering look so filled with defiance that she knew he would not confess it to her. He gestured to a parting in the trees just ahead. "And here is the road to Valeroy. I will follow you, remaining hidden in the forest, until you are within sight of the gates. It is possible that your assailant has found his way back, and I would welcome the opportunity to surprise him again."

"But this time, he should not escape," Duncan added. "I have questions for him."

"Which he is unlikely to answer," Radegunde's father noted. "Still he might be convinced to share some detail of import. I will continue to hunt for him and send word if I learn more."

"I thank you, sir." The men shook hands and exchanged compliments, then Radegunde's father came to her stirrup. He took her hand in his, then touched his lips to its back. "Godspeed to you, my Radegunde," he murmured, his gaze so filled with warmth that a lump rose in her throat. "It is a gift to see you grown and beauteous, and so in love." His lips touched her hand again and then he shook Duncan's hand.

"I am bidden by Mathilde to tell you that she misses you," Duncan said and Radegunde saw wariness dawn in her father's eyes.

Had her mother truly sent him away?

Her father said naught in reply, but pivoted and strode into the forest, disappearing so quickly that she might have imagined his presence.

Save for the warm imprint of his salute on her hand. She blinked back her tears and swallowed, then smiled for Duncan. "He likes you," she ventured to say and Duncan smiled.

"He loves you," he countered. "Do not place too much weight on his reticence, Radegunde. I believe he tries to protect you." He kept his hand on the saddle and walked alongside her, his other hand on the hilt of his knife.

It occurred to Radegunde that her father was not the sole one who would ensure her safety.

"We could ride together," she invited, but Duncan shook his head.

"I have been thinking of this. If your father is right, and Lady Eudaline has granted the perfect bait to you, then we should ensure that a trap can be set with success. Such a prize should not be wasted."

Radegunde could only agree. The book had been an expensive trinket to prepare or to sacrifice. "But Sebastien de Saint-Roux is named as the villain and he must be dead, as is Fulk."

"Aye. So, we must discover who has taken the cause."

"What do you suggest?"

"That we feign to be less intimate than we are, until this matter is resolved. I escorted you to the convent, but we did not confide in each other." He gave her a sharp look. "If we were observed by the villain, this would focus his attention upon you, which is why you must surrender the book to Lady Ysmaine with all speed."

"But there can be no villain in Lord Amaury's hall!"

"You have been away, Radegunde. You do not know the alliance of every servant and new arrival in Valeroy."

"Do you not suspect Millard, Sebastien's son and the husband of Gaston's niece?"

Duncan shrugged. "We have need of more evidence than the word of Fulk's widow against Millard's father." He frowned. "Not all sons share their father's sins."

It seemed to Radegunde that Duncan spoke of someone other than Millard. "But what of our handfast?" she asked, seeing the gates of Valeroy ahead.

"It is but the first day of our year and a day, my Radegunde," he said with confidence. "This situation will not last, and then we can be together openly."

"Until you escort Fergus to Scotland," she could not help but note, disliking that he did not argue the matter with her. How could happiness have such short duration? Radegunde felt cheated, even though she knew that Duncan spoke good sense and wished to ensure her safety.

"You are vexed," he noted, even as a cry of greeting rose from the porter. They had been spied.

"I feel as if a most welcome gift has been taken back," she said and he laughed wryly.

"Aye, Radegunde, I share your view in that. Be patient, lass. With both of us urging this matter to its completion, it cannot remain unresolved for long."

"Is that so, Duncan MacDonald?" she asked, choosing to tease him. "Are you so influential in the fate of the world as that?"

He granted her a simmering glance that heated her own blood. "You are mine, lass, for a year and a day, and I will do all in my power to make it a lifetime."

She leaned toward him. "Then prove as much to me, Duncan. Seize every moment we can share together. Let me come to you at night." He opened his mouth to protest, but she dropped a finger across his lips. "I will take the risk, for truly I believe it to be much diminished if I am with you."

He hesitated but Radegunde did not let the matter be. That he was tempted meant she had a chance of success. "Indeed, I believe that you are in need of my protection, sir, and would see you defended."

Duncan's slow smile made her heart flutter, for she knew he would cede to her. "Aye, lass, I see your point. If we are to be together always, the sooner we begin, the better."

"Precisely!" she said with a triumphant smile.

Duncan kissed her hand and gave her fingertips a squeeze. "And here they come. Tell none but your lady of what you have learned."

"Aye, though I will not tell her of my father."

Duncan had time to nod before they were surrounded by

sentries and guards, then welcomed back into the haven of Valeroy. Radegunde found herself looking back, seeking some glimpse of her father in the shadows of the forest. The hair prickled on the back of her neck as if they were watched, but she could discern no sign of his presence.

She heard an owl hoot then, remarkably early for such a bird to be abroad. She smiled to herself, for it had to be her father's call of farewell. He loved them all. He had been badly served, she was certain, and exiled unfairly.

Somehow she would see justice done.

CHAPTER TWELVE

uncan was certain he had never seen such a ruckus. Truly, Radegunde had rightly anticipated the fears that the arrival of the warhorse devoid of rider would create within Valeroy. Lady Ysmaine herself came to the gates, her agitation more than clear. She kissed Radegunde's cheeks and Duncan imagined that the lady—whom he had thought most intrepid—was trembling.

Indeed, the sight gave him greater cause to consider. Would Radegunde leave Châmont-sur-Maine and abandon her mistress? He did not wish to make Radegunde unhappy or to force her to surrender all she held dear, but he knew that he would be unhappy to remain away from Scotland any longer than he had. He missed the cold wind and the wild hills, the solitude that a man could find when he sought it, and the surety of being where he belonged.

Was their handfast doomed to endure only a year and a day?

Duncan hoped it would not be so. He must discuss his concerns with Radegunde at first opportunity. But first, he must confer with Fergus to learn what options he had.

Lady Richildis and Lord Amaury and all of Lady Ysmaine's sisters spilled out of the hall, followed by maids and squires and most of the servants of Valeroy. Radegunde's brother pushed to the fore and lifted his sister from her saddle, proving that Duncan's estimation of the younger man had been correct. There was no chance of speaking with her when she was so surrounded by those who were concerned for her welfare, though he felt her gaze upon him.

He waved to her and led the palfrey to the stables, thinking furiously.

To Duncan's relief, Fergus was standing in the palfrey's empty stall as if awaiting him. He also was glad to see that his own stallion had been brushed down and divested of his trap. The beast gave a whinny at Duncan's arrival, and he patted the destrier's rump as he passed the palfrey's reins to Fergus. They worked in silence for a few moments, seeing to the care of the steed, then began to brush her from opposite sides.

"I feared you lost," Fergus said.

"Did you see as much in a dream?" Duncan had to ask.

The younger man shook his head. "I see a challenge before you, Duncan, one that will demand much of you, but no more than that." Fergus smiled. "It has not disappeared, so this was not the fullness of it. What happened?"

Duncan recounted the details of their journey and the attack, and Fergus frowned at the tidings that a highlander had been responsible.

"I cannot think who would assault me, much less seek me out, all the way from Scotland," Duncan said, even as he once again ignored that single doubt. "Do you think it concerned the prize?"

"But you did not carry it this day, nor did you carry any item that might have disguised it." Fergus shook his head. "It might have been brigands. There are said to be many of them in the vicinity."

"To be attacked twice by brigands, in two different locations, seems bad fortune in a most unlikely measure."

"There is that." Fergus gave Duncan a hard look. "Are you certain there is naught in your past that might have pursued you?"

"Not after twenty years' silence," Duncan said. "Nay, it is far more likely to concern you or your father or our journey."

They worked in silence, neither able to think of any such cause.

"I would consult with you on another matter, as well, my lord," Duncan said when the brushing was complete and Fergus might have returned to the hall.

The younger man leaned against the stall, smiling as he regarded Duncan. "My lord?" he echoed. "This must be a weighty matter indeed."

Duncan cleared his throat. "I have pledged a handfast with the maid Radegunde…"

"These are merry tidings!"

"For the moment, they are. But I am uncertain what I can offer to her. It is clear that we will leave Châmont-sur-Maine to return to Killairic."

Fergus nodded, his smile fading. "I would release you from my service, if you would remain with her here."

Duncan winced. "I pledged to your father that I would escort you to Outremer and home again, and I would not break that vow."

"And truth be told, I would not be without your service on that journey, given all that we will carry." The pair exchanged a significant glance.

"Aye," Duncan said, uncertain whether any might be listening. "You have been generous in acquiring gifts for your betrothed. Another steed or two will be welcome to bear the burden."

Fergus nodded. "I see that we understand each other well. Will she leave Lady Ysmaine's service?"

"I have not spoken to her of it, for I chose to consult with you first."

The knight's eyes began to sparkle. "Yet you have pledged a handfast already and doubtless consummated the match. How impetuous of you, Duncan. I have never known you to be so impulsive." Duncan felt the back of his neck heat that his thoughts had been so readily discerned, but before he could reply, his companion continued. "It must be love, then, and I must do my part to ensure its course runs true. What of this scheme? Encourage your lady's admiration and affection while our paths run the same path, part until we complete our journey home, and then I shall ensure that she is invited to accompany Gaston and Ysmaine to celebrate my nuptials with Isobel. You will be several months apart, but that is little for a heart that is true. I have not seen Isobel for nigh three years! Then Radegunde can see your home and I leave it to you to convince her to remain."

"If your father will cede that I might wed."

Fergus clapped him on the shoulder. "Duncan, when we arrive home, my father will see fit to grant you whatsoever you desire."

"But if I have not returned his favor in saving my life by saving his own..."

"He will dismiss your obligation, for it has been many years that you have served him faithfully. I would wager upon it."

"I will not, until the words pass his lips."

"There! You are cautious again. My old friend is returned." Fergus sobered then. "If we reach Killairic with success, all will be well for both of us. I am confident of it." He arched a brow, his tone teasing. "Now, as to whether you can persuade the lady to choose you over the mistress she has served all her life, that is a challenge only you can win."

Duncan smiled, more than prepared to do just that.

Indeed, he would continue his conquest of Radegunde's heart this very night. He shook hands with Fergus and went to wash before the evening meal, then ensured that the chamber he had been granted would not be shared by any others.

He desired his lady to himself.

Radegunde wished that she and Duncan did not have to part, but there was little choice. They were separated at the gates, the assumption clear that he belonged in the stables and she in the hall. Truly, she came to despise her obligations.

Would he come for her this night?

She could only hope she had convinced him and that others did not persuade him to alter his course. Truth be told, though, Radegunde could not believe that Duncan readily changed his thinking once he had made a choice.

It was part of what she admired about him, to be sure. A resolute man was one a woman could rely upon.

After the bustle of their greeting, Radegunde was assisted by her brother, Michel, to the chamber shared by Lady Ysmaine and Lord Gaston. She was deposited by the fire in the chamber and had to insist yet again that he not summon their mother before the morning. Lady Richildis and several of her daughters hovered in the doorway to listen.

"She would wish to look at your ankle," Michel said.

"It is merely twisted and will be healed fully within a matter of days," Radegunde said yet again. "Recall that Duncan was attacked outside her home just days ago."

"That is why I would have her move to the keep," Michel said. "But she will not. *Maman* is cursed stubborn."

"So you know she will not be deterred from visiting me with all haste when she hears, and that she will not remain at the keep for the night. I would not so imperil her with a lonely walk."

"I could escort her…"

"You know she would not abide it." Radegunde shook her head, aware of the amusement shared by Lady Ysmaine and her husband. "Leave the matter until the morning, Michel, I implore you."

He ceded with such obvious reluctance that Radegunde felt the battle was hard-won.

Finally, all were dismissed save herself, Lady Ysmaine, and Lord Gaston.

"Your mother is not the sole one who is stubborn, it appears," Lord Gaston noted, his tone mild. "But he means well."

"For me if not for my mother. I have sufficient care for such a minor injury. Indeed, it begins to seem too much."

"And so?" Lady Ysmaine asked in the same moment that Radegunde removed the book from her purse.

Radegunde shared the majority of the tale, including the warning from the wild man of the woods about the poisoned pages, while Lord Gaston turned the small volume in his hands.

She did not confide that the wild man of the woods was her father and spared them the detail of visiting his abode. By her telling, a stranger had simply retrieved the palfrey for them, no more and no less.

Lord Gaston frowned at the fire then, clearly considering his course, while his lady ensured Radegunde's comfort and checked the binding on her ankle. Lady Ysmaine asked her about the convent, the journey, and other such details, while Lord Gaston sat in silence.

"My lady, we must argue," he said with such finality that both women looked at him in surprise. "Though we have suspicions aplenty, Sebastien de Saint-Roux is dead. Who has taken his cause, if any? Or do we leap at shadows? We must move with prudence, yet not waste this gift from my mother." He held up the book. "Let us use it to see what can be learned."

"How?" asked Lady Ysmaine.

"Only the villain will find interest in the accusation," Lord Gaston said. "So, we will bait the trap by appearing to be estranged."

"But why?" The lady's confusion showed.

"So that the secret is believed to be solely in your care, and that you are perceived to be undefended." Lord Gaston smiled. "Of course, you will not be."

"My parents will never be convinced of this dispute," Lady Ysmaine replied. "You know that I take the model of their match and insist upon consultation between husband and wife."

"And you have consulted together since Paris," Radegunde noted.

"But it was a hard lesson for me," Lord Gaston said. "And why not? For my father never spoke to my mother as a partner and confidante. He came to her solely for the rendering of the marital debt and expected her to do as bidden."

"Lady Eudaline?" Radegunde could not help but ask in surprise.

Lord Gaston chuckled. "Naught says that my father gained his expectation. My mother gave every appearance of ceding to him, then did as she desired. She made a point of learning as much as possible then influencing the situation when she could. I cannot believe that he was fully in ignorance of her deeds, but such was his manner that he could not soften his stance. He came to marriage repeatedly but reluctantly, desiring only sons." He lifted his brows. "There is no reason that I could not share his belief."

He handed the volume to his wife. "You will hide this in one of your trunks, but ensure that it is not too difficult to find. Radegunde, you will check upon it in the morning and at night. When it disappears, we will be able to narrow the possible suspects."

"And if it does not disappear?" Lady Ysmaine asked.

"Then we shall know ourselves to be safe."

The lady sniffed, displeased with this conclusion. She turned to Radegunde. "You must ensure that word is spread amongst the servants of the gift you retrieved for me from my lord's mother. Do so with discretion, confessing it as a secret to only a few. The tidings will spread and find a ready ear."

Radegunde nodded agreement. "There is this, too." She offered the crucifix.

Lord Gaston's smile was immediate. "I recall this well. I thought it gone." He admired the token, then offered it to his lady wife as well. "If you would wear it, as have the women in my family, I should be most honored, Ysmaine." She donned it and they shared a smile warm enough to put the fire in the brazier to shame.

"Shall I wear it in secret?"

"It might be wise, for the moment."

She nodded and tucked it inside her chemise.

"And so the argument," Lord Gaston continued. "I will take issue with you sending your maid to my mother, insisting that Eudaline and I are estranged. I will call it defiance and deception, and as a result, will be in apparent ignorance about the book and the crucifix."

Lady Ysmaine nodded, a familiar gleam lighting her eye. "And I will be deeply injured by your distrust of me."

"Indeed. How could you be otherwise?" Lord Gaston smiled. "However, I will still come to you to conceive that child."

"Would you not reconcile, though?" Radegunde felt obliged to ask. "It seems a choice that might be challenged then forgiven, particularly if you are together each night."

"Then we must find a means to deepen the dispute," Lady Ysmaine said.

There was a knock at the portal in that moment. Lady Ysmaine wrapped the volume in a napkin and hastened to tuck it into her largest trunk. She ensured that Radegunde noted its location, then closed the trunk and returned to sit by the brazier again.

"Aye?" Lord Gaston said. "Enter."

The portal opened to reveal Duncan, looking determined.

"Is something amiss, Duncan?" Lord Gaston asked.

"Nay, sir. I come for Radegunde, for I would not have her walk to the stables while her ankle is so injured."

Both Lord Gaston and Lady Ysmaine looked at Radegunde with astonishment. "The stables?" Lady Ysmaine repeated in a whisper. There was a sudden twinkle in Lord Gaston's eyes.

Radegunde's cheeks were hot but she kept her chin up. "Duncan and I have pledged a handfast to each other, my lady. I will spend my nights in his protection."

"A handfast!" Lady Ysmaine said, her dismay clear. "But Radegunde, such a pagan promise is no substitute for vows exchanged in a church…"

"And I believe we have found our greater argument," Lord Gaston murmured, interrupting his wife firmly.

"But Gaston!" she protested, only to have him raise a finger for her silence.

"The world is full of differing ways, my lady, yet their variance from our favored ones does not make them wrong."

"But…"

Again her lord husband interrupted her, this time with greater steel in his tone. "Ysmaine, heed me in this."

The lady evidently understood the warning, for she fell silent. She folded her arms across her chest and glared at her spouse in a manner that might have been amusing in other circumstance.

Radegunde did not doubt that her mistress would not be readily swayed from her view, but she smiled at Duncan, wanting him to know that her intention was unchanged.

"I know that you hold Radegunde in affection, my lady," Gaston continued in a low voice. "And rightly so, for she has served you loyally and with honor. And I know that Duncan is a man of honor who will not pledge what he cannot be certain will be. I trust his judgment in this decision and am glad to see Radegunde's pleasure in his arrival here. It bodes well for their future happiness, however they choose to continue."

Lady Ysmaine's eyes flashed. "And you, a former Templar," she uttered.

"And I, a former Templar, who has served in Outremer. I understand as once I did not that there are many solutions to the same dilemma, and that we should not let minor differences blind us to the greater good."

"Minor differences!" the lady's protest erupted. "I should think that you would argue for the rules of the church!"

Gaston smiled. "And so I shall, for most will expect as much."

Lady Ysmaine looked as astonished as Radegunde felt.

"But such words will be solely for those who listen when they should not." Gaston inclined his head to Duncan, who stood silently inside the closed door. "I beg your forgiveness in advance, Duncan. I have no qualms about your choice, but the task of securing my legacy demands some subtlety and subterfuge."

"I understand completely, sir, and thank you for your endorsement."

"Gaston!" Lady Ysmaine began to argue anew, but had no greater success than before.

Her husband strode to stand before her and took her hand in his. "You, my lady, will argue the opposite side from the one you prefer. You will protest that your loyal maid has the right to choose her companion and follow her heart, for she is no heiress, while I will be outraged by such promiscuity in my household and blame you for it."

Lady Ysmaine's mouth worked in silence for a moment, and it was evident that she was shocked. "But how can I argue in favor of such folly?" she whispered.

Lord Gaston lowered his voice. "Because you know, my lady wife, that Duncan is such a valiant and trustworthy warrior. So great is your admiration for him and his merit that you know he will treat Radegunde well."

"But they should wed before a priest..."

"Nay, nay. That is my argument, my lady." Lord Gaston

watched as Lady Ysmaine came to terms with this decision. "The household must believe that you and I are estranged."

Radegunde was not surprised when her lady's eyes lit with fire.

"You shall have your argument, sir," Ysmaine murmured, and Lord Gaston smiled in anticipation. "Do not complain when you receive what you have invited."

"I will not," he declared, his gaze locked with that of his wife.

Indeed, the air in the chamber seemed to simmer.

Radegunde cleared her throat. "Shall I aid you with your kirtle and your hair, my lady?"

"Not on this night, Radegunde," Lady Ysmaine said, raising her voice and letting it harden. "My lord husband and I have matters to discuss in private."

"Aye, my lady."

"Know that I give my blessing to your union, no matter what my husband dares to say about it."

"My lady!" Lord Gaston roared. "This is outrageous!"

"You, sir, have no right to decree the happiness of my sweet maid…"

The pair began a furious dispute that would readily be heard outside of their chamber. Duncan strode across the room and picked up Radegunde. She nestled contentedly against him as they left the room, and Lord Gaston slammed the door behind them with force.

"What madness is this?" Lord Gaston bellowed. "First, you defy me by sending your maid to my mother!"

"It is only right that I send greetings to your mother!" Lady Ysmaine shouted in return.

"Even if she and I are estranged? You should have spoken to me!"

"I do not need your approval for simple courtesy!"

"And now you accept your maid is intimate with a mercenary in the stables each night? Is this simple courtesy, as well?"

"She can make her choice…"

"She will not make such a choice in *my* household…"

And so the battle continued, their words echoing through the hall of Valeroy as Duncan carried Radegunde to his chamber over the stables. "If you laugh aloud, you will ruin their ploy," he murmured and she reached up to kiss him.

"I only smile at the prospect of a night in your bed," she retorted, liking the gleam that lit Duncan's eyes.

"And you do not even know what preparations I have made for your pleasure as yet," he mused, but would not confess one word more. Radegunde teased him lightly, enjoying the glances of the household as they passed, and was glad indeed to have Lord Gaston's blessing.

As well as Duncan's company from this night forward.

Duncan was rewarded by Radegunde's smile when they reached the chamber he had been granted over the stables. He left her on the thick pallet, wrapped in his heavy cloak, and returned but a moment later with a lantern.

Radegunde was sniffing appreciatively. "You have laid a feast," she said with approval. "That was well done. I am hungry indeed after this day."

Duncan removed the cloth that had covered their repast with a flourish. "The cook was persuaded to part with some of the roast venison, when he heard it was for you. There is bread and some confection of eggs, as well as wine."

"Wine!" Radegunde's eyes lit. "You spoil me indeed, sir."

"I treasure you," he corrected gruffly, bringing the meal to her and sitting beside her.

"You do not eat?"

"I dined with my lord Fergus in the hall."

Radegunde paused between bites to consider him. "Did you tell him?"

"Aye, you need not fear his displeasure." He lowered his voice and confided Fergus' plans to her, his voice so quiet that only she could hear.

"So he has not decided when to depart?"

"I believe he will wait for Bartholomew's knighting. Perhaps we will remain for the Yule. I cannot say."

"He has not decided."

Duncan shook his head.

Radegunde put aside the bowl. "I cannot eat so much as this, Duncan," she confessed with a sparkle in her eyes. "You brought me a man's portion."

"I would not see you dissatisfied."

"Half such a quantity will suffice in future, but I do not wish to waste it. It is too good for a hound."

"But not for me." Duncan smiled, then lifted the bowl from her hand and began to eat. He indicated the cup of wine and she sipped, savoring it. It was clear she reflected upon some matter and he was content to wait for her conclusions. When the meal was done and the bowl put aside, she offered the cup to him that he might drink, as well.

"My mother will come in the morning, of this I have no doubt."

"I am certain of it, as well. I am glad you dissuaded Michel from fetching her on this night."

Radegunde frowned a little. "She will bring an herb to me, perhaps several. We must decide if I am to consume them or not."

Duncan did not understand the reason for her doubt. "If it will aid in the repair of your ankle, then of course, you must consume it."

Radegunde was already shaking her head. "Not for my ankle, Duncan." Her hand dropped to her belly, and he realized her meaning.

He was caught then, caught between his memories of the past, between his fears and his desires. Duncan averted his gaze, uncertain what to say. The possibility of Radegunde bearing his child filled his heart with joy. He could well imagine how fine a mother she would make and how a little girl with Radegunde's laughing eyes would steal his heart anew. Yet he could not bear the possibility that he might lose his lady, or worse, both her and the child, and be left alone again so soon after he had found happiness again.

His throat was tight with the realization of his own folly. He should never have claimed her this day. He should never have taken even that one risk. He had been an impetuous fool, an impulsive lover...

"Duncan," Radegunde whispered with heat, her hand on his arm and her breath upon his cheek. He realized then that she had read his thoughts and discerned his dismay. She smiled at him. "I would take this risk willingly. I would delight in bearing your child, in bearing many of them, and I would celebrate our union with joy each and every night until you must depart with Fergus."

"But I cannot leave you alone, expecting a child," he protested. "I cannot risk your welfare."

"If I bear a child, there will be little you can do in the delivery to aid me. My mother is a midwife and wise woman. Her assistance may change the outcome, but this is not your realm of expertise." As ever, Radegunde was practical, but Duncan could not so readily dismiss his agitation.

"I might not be able to return," he argued. He flung out a hand. "Any misfortune could befall our party! I would not leave you alone, undefended and without coin."

Radegunde's expression set with a stubbornness he had come to recognize. "I will never be undefended so long as my mother and brothers draw breath, nor will I be impoverished. I would be blessed to have your child to remember you by."

"It is not sufficient," he said, disgruntled as he did not wish to be.

"This interval may well be all that we are granted, though I believe you will do all in your power to return to me." She straightened with resolve. "I would prefer not to consume the herbs, Duncan. They do not always ensure success at any rate, but I would not hinder whatever may occur between us. I would take the chance."

"You cannot do this!"

"You have not convinced me otherwise." She smiled as if to reassure him. "You cannot forbid it, but I welcome you to persuade me."

Duncan shoved a hand through his hair. "Words are not my weapon of choice," he said, and she laughed a little.

"I know, Duncan, but your feelings are clear."

"Radegunde, I entreat you not to take such a risk."

She seized his hand. "And I entreat you, Duncan, to dare to

hope for good in your life."

He blinked in astonishment.

"You always see the shadow first." She shook a finger at him. "Just this once, look at the light first. Think of a child, Duncan, a babe of our own. Think of the joy that could be ours, if you would simply dare to wish for it."

"There might not be one."

"There might not."

He sighed and surveyed the room, wanting to surrender to her desire yet still constrained by his past. "Might we compromise? Might you agree to take this herb until my departure, then upon my return, we would try for a child?"

She studied him. "You are as fearful for yourself as for me. I did not realize as much."

"I have been attacked twice in days. I feel that Death rides close to me." Duncan seized her hand and kissed it, seeking to convince her. "I could not bear to lose you, my Radegunde. I could not bear to compromise this happiness so lately found." He heaved a sigh and knew the sole way to change her thinking. "If you refuse to take your mother's herb, then we cannot be intimate again, not until I return."

"Oh, you set the price high indeed!" she said lightly. She was not insulted, to his relief, and reached up to soothe the frown from between his brows with her fingertip. "I see the magnitude of your concern now, Duncan, and I would not have you be so distressed."

"I should not have taken so much from you as I did this day." In truth, he did not know how he would resist doing as much again. She was curled against him, soft and warm, her eyes so alight that his pulse raced. It was a marvel that she had such a power over him already, yet he did not wish to be loosed from her spell.

"But it was wondrous," she whispered with an awe he shared. "Do not regret what I cannot."

"And the herb?"

Radegunde smiled. "I will consume it, but only for this interval, and only to see that shadow dispelled from your eyes." She wagged a finger at him. "But make no mistake, Duncan MacDonald, I will have my pleasure abed nightly, and when you return, I will bear you as many sons as I can."

It was a compromise he could not criticize. Indeed, he could not resist her, when she looked up at him with that confident smile, her eyes sparkling with the surety that she held him in thrall.

He had no desire to be otherwise.

"Come here, lass," he growled. "I would keep you warm this night, though there cannot be more before you have that herb."

"I accept your offer gladly, sir." Radegunde granted him a kiss that set his blood afire, and it was long indeed before he put her aside with reluctance. He fetched a bucket of water and put the slops outside the door, smiling at the sight of her in her chemise, with her feet bare and her hair unbound. She combed her long tresses and the light of the lantern touched it with gold. The door had a latch but not a lock and he surveyed the chamber, seeking a way to barricade it. He put their boots behind it, reasoning that the sound of their falling would awaken him.

"Put the cup from the wine atop the boots," Radegunde suggested. "A clatter is more startling than a thud."

"You speak aright in this." He did as much, then shed his hauberk, belt, and chausses, setting his knife beside the pallet. Radegunde watched him, her appreciation of the view most clear, then he extinguished the light and joined her abed.

She burrowed against him as he tucked their cloaks over them. "It has been a day of much adventure, to be sure. I will sleep well this night. Will you?"

"I cannot say."

Radegunde rolled over, as if to study him even in the darkness. "Tell me a secret, Duncan," she invited.

"I have no secrets to tell."

She laughed at that, laughed so heartily that he found himself smiling. "You have more secrets than any dozen men!" she charged. "But I respect your right to hold them close. I will forgo a secret if you tell me something of Gwyneth and your son."

Duncan caught his breath. It seemed unfitting to speak of his wife when another woman lay in his arms.

"You cannot be disloyal to a woman dead these twenty years, Duncan," Radegunde whispered. "And I would know a bit of her, because you loved her." She tapped his chest. "Tell me something happy about her."

He sighed and nodded in concession, casting his thoughts back to those days. "Chickens," he said. "She always kept chickens."

Radegunde chuckled. "My mother always kept chickens. I loved chasing them around the garden."

"She thought them a practical choice."

"Indeed. Eggs, chicks, and finally stew." She wriggled, moving closer to his warmth, and he liked how they were curled together, her buttocks in his lap, her hair tickling his nose. "We could keep chickens."

"We could."

"And a little garden, like that of my mother."

"Indeed." Duncan could see the cottage well, perched in the hills he loved, though he wondered whether Radegunde imagined it near her mother's. He might have asked her, but she spoke again.

"What was his name, Duncan?"

"Domnall. 'Tis Gaelic and my father's name. Gwyneth chose it." He cleared his throat. "In English, it would be Donald."

"A strong name and a family name. I like it well."

"She never knew that he died," he found himself admitting.

Again, Radegunde turned, as if glancing over her shoulder. "You said he was born dead."

"Aye, but neither the midwife nor I told Gwyneth. She was glad it was a boy and told me she was glad I would not be alone. Those were her last words when she knew she was dying."

"And you could not take that relief away from her," Radegunde whispered. He felt the softness of her lips on his cheek, her fingertips on his jaw. "Oh, Duncan, it is no wonder you see the shadow first."

He heard the break in her voice and felt the wetness of her tears, and pulled her closer. "You have cried for this babe already," he murmured to her, the softness of her heart making him feel fiercely protective. "Now it is time for you to see the light."

"Aye, you loved and loved well. There is naught to regret in that."

It was true.

Radegunde's breathing slowed and she fell asleep, the warmth of her doing much to reassure Duncan. He lay awake much longer, listening to the sounds of the stables and the men settling for the night, thinking about her accusation that he looked first at the shadow. It was his training and it had been his experience, but Duncan resolved to change his habit and his view.

It was time.

And it would be a fitting way to please his Radegunde.

SATURDAY, SEPTEMBER 12, 1187

Feast Day of the Seven Sleepers

Claire Delacroix

CHAPTER THIRTEEN

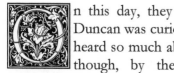n this day, they would arrive at Châmont-sur-Maine. Duncan was curious indeed about the abode, for he had heard so much about it. His anticipation was tempered, though, by the knowledge that their journey to Châmont-sur-Maine brought him one step closer to parting from Radegunde.

She had woven a spell that snared his heart in truth these past days. Each night, he fetched her from her lady's chamber and she came merrily to his bed. Each night, they shared a repast in his chamber and talked of the day. Each day, he strove to see the light first, as she had bidden him. If one of them was required to eat with master or mistress, still their hours were companionable. Duncan usually managed to procure some wine, for Valeroy was affluent and the butler was fond of Radegunde. He oft found that a measure had been set aside for them as a result.

Gaston and Ysmaine retained the outward sign of their dispute, letting all see that there was dissent between them. The book remained untouched in Lady Ysmaine's trunk, for Radegunde checked regularly upon it as instructed. It had not even been moved by her accounting. Duncan could only conclude that the villain had no spies in this hall, or that he or she awaited a chance.

Perhaps matters would be more clear at Gaston's home estate.

The hall of Valeroy had been a whirlwind of activity, for Gaston and Amaury had resolved to ensure Gaston's entry to his father's keep with a display of pageantry. Men and squires from Amaury's holding fell to one knee to pledge themselves to Gaston's service, and all of them were to be garbed in Gaston's colors. Gaston himself would arrive already wearing his inherited insignia, and Ysmaine garbed to match her spouse. The needles flew in the chambers of Lady Richildis and the lanterns burned late with so much embroidery to complete. Gaston would have a banner, as well, and Lord Amaury would accompany him along with a number of warriors and knights.

More guards and sentries had been posted at Valeroy after the second attack upon Duncan, but there had been no more incidents. It seemed the culprits might well have been brigands, and that they were deterred by the increased defenses. Duncan was not the sole one intending to be vigilant when they rode out, and he suspected that Lord Amaury had augmented the number of men who accompanied him. The walls of Valeroy bristled with sentries when the party gathered in the bailey on the morn of their departure.

Of course, they secretly carried the reliquary of Saint Euphemia, as well, and could not risk its theft.

Duncan heard all the plans, yet still he was awed when the company departed from Valeroy. The insignia that Gaston had decided upon was striking in itself. He had chosen a deep sapphire blue, graced by a single golden lion rampant to represent his alliance to the Plantagenet kings, who favored three such lions on their insignia. The background, though, carried the mark of Breton, in the silver symbols of ermine traditionally associated with that county. The insignia showed Gaston to be balancing the concerns of both realms, with perhaps a greater reliance upon Henry II. Duncan thought it perfectly expressed the diplomatic balance the new Lord of Châmont-sur-Maine would be required to strike, time and again.

The garments for both Gaston and his lady had been made of

silken velvet of that hue of blue, and Lady Ysmaine's long cloak was both trimmed and lined with ermine. The ermine spots were embroidered upon the blue with silver thread and a line of golden lions guarded the hem. It was a glorious garment, all the more splendid when she appeared in a silken kirtle worked with blue upon silver. There were lions upon her girdle and embroidered on her red slippers and her golden circlet caught the light.

"The new lord brings home a prize of a bride," murmured one man in the bailey when Gaston lifted Ysmaine to her saddle. Gaston himself looked no less fine, his cloak similar but much shorter, his tabard trimmed with ermine as well. Two squires preceded the party, banners with Gaston's insignia held high before them, followed by Gaston and Ysmaine on his left. Her father, Lord Amaury, rode with them and took the place at his daughter's left hand.

Behind them rode Fergus and the six Templars who journeyed with their party. Behind this group rode Duncan, Radegunde, and Bartholomew, Radegunde granted such a position because she would have to aid her lady with that cloak when she dismounted. Duncan's position was won by the precious burden he carried in his saddlebag. Radegunde had a new kirtle herself, cut also in the blue of Gaston's colors but wrought of wool instead of silk. Though it suited her well, particularly the line of gold around the edges, Duncan could not help but consider that Lady Ysmaine expending coin upon her maid might have implications for the future.

They were followed by the knights who would swear to Gaston and those who accompanied Amaury. Then came the mercenaries and warriors, and squires of great number. Laurent and the other boys who served Fergus, as well as those serving the Templars, were fated to ride in that group. A falconer was in their party, his services and two of his birds a wedding gift from Lady Richildis to her daughter. The birds fluttered their wings, one on that man's fist and the other on the fist of his assistant. At the rear were the carts with baggage and provisions. Four deer had been hunted in Valeroy's forests and sent with the party to ensure that there was meat enough for all once they arrived.

The company streamed long on the road, though they rode closely together at Gaston's dictate. It was a fine sunny day, the air crisp with the promise of winter. Duncan liked the echo of the horses' hooves, the cheers of those in the village of Valeroy as they passed, but liked better when the horses sped to a canter and the miles slipped away with greater speed.

He rode alongside Radegunde, which satisfied him indeed. How soon would Fergus lead them north? He did not wish to think about a departure, not when he had such joy in the moment.

"Did your mother ever surrender more of your father's tale?" he asked, for he knew that mother and daughter had met that morning before the party's departure.

Radegunde sighed. "She insists still that the tale is not hers to share, that he must tell me if he so desires. Indeed, she seems somewhat irked with him."

"There is some matter unresolved between them, it appears."

"Aye."

"And they must find a solution themselves."

Radegunde smiled. "You speak aright, of course, but I am impatient to see them both happy."

"But not your curiosity satisfied?" Duncan teased and she laughed, her eyes dancing with familiar merriment.

"You know me well, already."

"And still he comes to her?" Duncan asked.

"Less oft than before." Radegunde's eyes sparkled that Duncan might misunderstand. "*I will tell you a secret,*" she mouthed. She nodded at Lady Ysmaine and, beneath the shadow of her cloak, she laid a flattened hand across her belly.

Ah, the lady had conceived.

Duncan wished Ysmaine well but hoped that did not mean that she would refuse to release Radegunde from her service.

Or that Radegunde would refuse to leave her.

"You are displeased?" she asked, her gaze fixed upon him.

"I wonder whether you will ride to the wedding, then."

Radegunde's eyes lit with laughter. She counted on her fingers then granted him a pert look. "You can be certain, sir, that I shall procure a nursemaid with all haste come May."

Aye, Duncan could well imagine that Radegunde would see matters resolved to her satisfaction. He was less convinced that Lady Ysmaine would be readily bent to her maid's plans, but said naught.

Radegunde had sobered, either guessing his doubts or thinking of the inevitability of their parting. She considered the silhouette of the keep before them. "Do you know when Fergus will ride north?"

Duncan shook his head. "You will be the first to hear of it when I know." He reached out and took her hand, giving her fingers a squeeze. "Until then, we can only make the most of each day."

"And night," Radegunde added in a wicked whisper that made his heart skip. They shared a smile that heated him to his toes, then a cry rose from the lead of the party.

"Châmont-sur-Maine!"

"Send a runner to announce our arrival," Gaston commanded.

"He sent one yesterday," Radegunde said softly.

"And so he will not be accused of sparing any courtesy to the widow Marie," Duncan replied in an undertone. He knew full well the scheme that Gaston had planned, for both Radegunde and Fergus had told him parts of it in confidence. It seemed that Gaston's experience would serve him well in this arrival and that he thought of every detail. It would be an artful performance, and Duncan could only hope it would succeed.

The keep itself was wrought of stone and old enough to be weathered. It appeared to be an island in the river, which was wide and as smooth as a mirror in this area. Its walls rose from the water and surrounded the tower of the keep. Duncan noted a gate high enough in the walls to avoid flooding, and there was a bridge from it to the shore.

Breton was on the far side of the river, the river being the boundary between the two territories, and he wondered if there was another gate on the far side. He could discern a road approaching the keep on that shore, the twin of the one they rode. The land was fairly flat, which would give those in the keep a long view, and was clearly fertile, judging by the area that had been tilled.

A pennant snapped in the wind above the tower, and to the south, he could see the city of Angers, not half a day's ride away. The curtain wall of Gaston's inheritance bristled with sentries and archers, and it was clear that the holding defended the frontier. On this side, the Norman side, there was a small village, a chapel, and fields of grain being harvested. More than one villein halted to watch the party and several cheered when they evidently identified Gaston, perhaps by his colors.

By the time their group reached the bridge, it was clear that Gaston's arrival was well known and much anticipated. Peasants pressed forward to call a welcome to him and he responded in kind. He had removed his helm and dismounted to walk beside his destrier, pausing to shake the hand of more than one man and clearly recognizing many. Lady Ysmaine had been granted a sack of pennies to distribute and Radegunde helped her to cast them to those who came to greet them. The combination of these favors prompted many smiles amongst the villagers and, again, Duncan admired Gaston's foresight.

Lord Gaston's homecoming would be recalled by these souls as a happy occasion, to be sure. Duncan knew that the knight intended to host a dinner for those from the village, as well. He was generous, but also meant to reassure them as to his intent as lord.

"I thank you for your greeting," Gaston said to the villagers, raising his voice so all could hear. "I would celebrate my return home with my new lady wife, and do so with all of you. You are invited to share in the repast in the great hall three days hence, on the feast day of Saint Euphemia."

The villagers cheered at these tidings, and Gaston mounted his steed once more. Duncan watched the gates of the keep, hoping the welcome from that quarter was as warm.

The portcullis was yet down. Gaston gave no indication of being irked by this, though Duncan knew that he could not have failed to note the gesture. His destrier stepped first onto the end of the bridge and Gaston sat alone, still without his helm, his cloak lifting in the wind. He looked splendid and virile, an armed knight in magnificent garb, astride a fine destrier caparisoned in his colors.

"Good morrow, my lady Marie!" he called. "It is Gaston returned from Outremer, the son of Fulk and the brother of your lord husband, Bayard. I thank you for your summons and request both admission and a welcome home."

The villagers cheered, though Duncan noted that he did not claim his legacy outright.

Gaston continued, as if he had anticipated the silence that followed his words. "I am joined by my wife, Ysmaine of Valeroy, and have the honor of the company of her father, Lord Amaury of Valeroy."

Again the villagers showed their approval.

Gaston reached back for the reins of Lady Ysmaine's steed. He granted a single look to the archers who had escorted them at Lord Amaury's assistance, then began to ride across the bridge. Bartholomew had loaded his own bow and aimed at the archer visible above the gates. Duncan heard a rustle in the company and knew that the other archers had done the same.

Lord Amaury was fast behind the couple, both he and Gaston scanning the high walls. The bridge was wide enough for three warhorses to ride abreast, and doughty indeed. Gaston made a spectacle, though, ensuring that he and his lady were clearly first—and far from undefended.

Duncan knew they had argued about this strategy. Gaston saw it as imperative to appear confident that his claim would be surrendered. Amaury had feared for his daughter's safety. Ysmaine had insisted that her husband's scheme be followed, to the point of threatening not to welcome her father at their abode if he did not cede. The argument had been long, but in the end Gaston had prevailed, not in part because of his lady wife's view.

Duncan watched the walls and hoped Gaston was right.

The portcullis was raised when Gaston reached the middle of the bridge. Radegunde sighed with evident relief, but Duncan was not yet convinced of the good will of those within. He escorted her across the bridge as planned, his knife blade free of its shaft as he watched for any motion.

"God in Heaven but you are wary," she whispered.

"It is a learned habit and you know it well," he replied in an undertone.

"Gaston!" a man cried in apparent pleasure, and Duncan saw that a knight of an age with Gaston had appeared in the open gates. "You are welcome indeed!"

"Lord Gaston is not a guest," Duncan murmured beneath his breath as Radegunde watched avidly. He wondered how Gaston would correct the tone of the exchange.

"I should think so, Millard," Gaston said, his voice low enough that few beyond the lead party could hear him. He halted his steed and put out his hand, his expectation clear as he raised his voice anew. "I would welcome the seal to my inheritance."

The other man smiled. He was handsome, to be sure, and trim, with no shortage of confidence. "Will you not enter the bailey first?"

"I will pass beneath these gates when I know that all within the walls are answerable to me alone." There was a vigor in Gaston's voice that Duncan admired. He was decisive and firm, and Duncan guessed that the other knight had only a whisper of Gaston's experience. Gaston continued when the other knight did not move. "I would have them know it, as well."

Millard hesitated. He considered. Then he smiled and retreated, clapping his hands for a clerk and dispatching him to the hall. The party waited in the autumn sunlight and Duncan did not think the delay overlong.

"He was not prepared for this," Radegunde whispered.

Duncan scoffed. "Nay, for he did not desire to do it."

"You already dislike him."

"I already sense little good of his intentions. I believe Gaston planned aright."

She nodded understanding.

The seal was evidently fetched and it was placed in Gaston's hand by the other knight. Gaston held it high and looked back to the shore. "The seal to Châmont-sur-Maine is in my possession, as my father decreed it should be."

The gathered villagers greeted this with applause.

"And now the ring," Gaston said to Millard. Something gleamed upon the other man's hand, and Duncan realized it was the signet ring for the holding. Millard again hesitated for a moment, then removed it and offered it to Gaston with grace.

As if he would put it on Gaston's finger.

Duncan smiled. Radegunde glanced his way. "He does not bestow the holding," he murmured and she nodded again.

"Nay, not thus," Gaston murmured to Millard. "Understand well that you do not make me lord of this holding, Millard. My father has done as much with his legacy and only the king can grant the holding otherwise. You will simply give the ring to me."

Duncan could feel the force of Gaston's will. He saw Millard suddenly avert his gaze, as if compelled to do Gaston's bidding when he might have wished otherwise. His gaze flicked over the company, now strung along the shore.

Gaston left his saddle and stood before the other man, extending his hand, palm up. It was a command. Millard took a breath, then offered the ring. Gaston shook his head and nodded toward the ground.

This displeased Millard, to be sure. His lips tightened for a moment, then he dropped to his knee. He bowed his head and offered the ring. Gaston put it upon his own hand, then turned, raising his fist so the sunlight glinted off the ring. "The son of Fulk is returned and my legacy is claimed!" he cried.

He could not have seen the resentment cross Millard's features and quickly be disguised. Duncan took that as a warning.

"All hail the new Lord of Châmont-sur-Maine!" Lord Amaury bellowed.

"All hail!" repeated the company and the villagers.

Gaston nodded at Ysmaine's father and they entered the keep on either side of the lady's steed, Gaston yet leading his destrier. Gaston strode into the bailey and dropped the creature's reins, continuing to the doorway to the hall. A boy raced from the back of the company, one liveried in Gaston's colors, and took custody of the steed.

Three steps there were before the portal and Gaston climbed them, then turned to face the company. He looked imperious and regal.

Lord Amaury aided his daughter to dismount. Radegunde slipped from her saddle and hastened forward to straighten the hem of the lady's cloak. Gaston had been particular about how the matter should be done, and Radegunde had confessed to Duncan that she and Ysmaine had been compelled to practice this as he watched. The cloak was spread to its widest measure and more than one breath caught at its magnificence. Lady Ysmaine was escorted to her husband by her father and fell to her knees before Gaston.

She was first to make her obeisance.

All within the bailey watched transfixed as she pledged to serve his will, her voice resonant and filled with resolve. That cloak of blue edged with ermine spread behind her, the silver embroidery shining in the sunlight. When she had kissed his ring for the second time, he lifted her to her feet and held her hand in his as she climbed the steps to take her place at his left. Their hands remained clasped, Gaston holding her hand at his left shoulder.

The import was clear. They would rule together.

Lord Amaury saluted them both and stood on the step below them, the two knights flanking the lady. Millard was the next to make his obeisance, followed by three women who had come out of the chapel. Duncan readily identified the oldest, with her silver hair, to be Marie, Bayard's widow. The other two must be her daughters, the older one who stood with Millard being Azaläis, the younger, much less confident, being Rohese.

The priest was there and he bowed before Gaston, then stood beside him as they faced the company. Each man in Gaston's party dismounted, then went to Gaston, kneeling before him and kissing his ring in obeisance.

They were within the walls of the keep, and Gaston held both the seal to his inheritance and the signet ring.

But Duncan did not believe for a moment that the other man's claim was secured.

There was only one deed worse than a journey, in Radegunde's view, to make for extra labor and that was a move. The move of a nobleman and his wife, even a pair as austere in their possessions as Lady Ysmaine and Lord Gaston, increased the work even more.

To be met with resistance, if not something closer to defiance, was more than Radegunde could tolerate. The solar had to be settled, her lady's possessions unpacked and her bed made with fresh linens, her jewels locked in the treasury and all arranged before Lady Ysmaine finished the ceremony of obeisance with Lord Gaston. Radegunde knew well that her mistress would be tired after such a day and was determined that both Ysmaine and the babe she carried had a chance to rest in peace before the evening meal. Radegunde had no patience for the tardiness of Lady Azalaïs in vacating the solar, for that woman had known well enough when Lord Gaston would arrive.

No less that his claim was the true one.

Worse, the maids in the employ of Lady Azalaïs, her mother, and sister were slow and mutinous. The solar was dirty, the braziers overflowing with ashes and the strewing herbs on the floor so old and dry that they had to be filled with vermin. Lady Azalaïs's trunks had to be moved, and Radegunde did not care where. There was a knot of whispering maids on the stairs, resentful in their sidelong glances as they did naught at all.

Radegunde took command of the noble chamber, casting open the window shutters and then setting any maid she could find to work. They could protest and mutter all they wished: the new and rightful lady of the keep would be served and served well. The old strewing herbs were swept away and burned in the great hall. The braziers were emptied of ashes. The carpets and the mattress were beaten in the bailey, the very walls washed and the floor scrubbed. There was not time to fetch clean herbs from the village, a constraint of the keep's island location, but soon enough, the solar was sufficiently clean to suit Radegunde.

She cast out every piece of furniture save the great pillared bed itself. It was wrought of dark wood and heavily carved, the canopy nigh at the ceiling. It was old, and she had to wonder whether Lord Gaston and his older brothers had been conceived upon it. The mattress was soundly beaten.

She summoned new candles and positioned her lady's trunks.

Lord Gaston's possessions were also brought to the chamber, and Bartholomew helped her to make all as right as the pair would expect. He assisted her in hanging the new velvet drapes for the bed, for she was not tall enough. Lady Richildis had insisted upon supplying them, and they were most fine. The new mattress was placed on top of the existing one, and new linens tucked over it. There were plump pillows and several furs, as well as a coverlet of silken velvet for her lady's pleasure. There were several thick carpets from Valeroy, as well, and Radegunde had them placed by the bed. The braziers were lit so that the chamber was filled with a welcoming glow. She sent a maid to fetch a meal and wine for the lady and lord, then glanced out the window that overlooked the bailey.

Lord Gaston was leading his lady to the great hall.

Radegunde summoned hot water for a bath and was glad they had brought a tub from Valeroy, for there seemed to be confusion about the ability to supply one in this keep. She could not believe there was not one, only that the defiance continued. She closed the shutters to keep the chamber cozy.

The tub was full, the water steaming and the air scented with lavender when the noble couple appeared at the portal.

Lady Ysmaine's relief was more than clear. "Radegunde, you are a prize, to be sure," she said, exhaustion in her voice.

"I have summoned a repast for both of you, my lord."

"I thank you, Radegunde," Lord Gaston said. "But I cannot linger."

"Gaston!" the lady protested, and he kissed her hand.

"The treasury key is not yet mine, Ysmaine," he said and gestured to the portal. "And I will have every key to this lock before I retire for the night."

"You are suspicious, sir."

"I am cautious, lady mine, and will grant my trust when I perceive it to be deserved."

Lady Ysmaine smiled. "Or there is no opportunity left to deceive you."

The pair smiled at each other in perfect understanding.

"I will survey the stables, the hall, and the stores. I believe we should ride to hunt this afternoon, to ensure that there is sufficient fare for the feast two days hence." Gaston pursed his lips. "It might give Millard and me the opportunity to better our understanding."

"Mind you watch his aim," the lady counseled tartly and Gaston smiled.

"I have survived this long by keeping my wits about me, lady mine. Do not fear for my fate now." He kissed her brow. "Partake of the preparations Radegunde has made and even slumber a bit. I will escort you to the board when it is time."

Ysmaine smiled and sat down with a sigh of relief.

Lord Gaston granted Radegunde a glance. "I will send Bartholomew to guard the portal," he said, and she nodded understanding. He strode from the solar then, raising his voice to summon his squire. Radegunde heard him greet Lady Marie on the stairs and forbid her from visiting Ysmaine in the solar, then ushering her back down to the hall.

Lady Ysmaine lifted her circlet and set it aside. "I did not expect it to be so tiring."

"You were concerned, my lady, and fearful of the outcome. That always adds to the effort." Radegunde bustled around her mistress, divesting her of her finery before the bath cooled too much. "And now you may take your relief."

"Indeed. I am most impressed by this chamber. Tell me you did not have too much to do to make it our own."

Radegunde only smiled. Lady Ysmaine had settled into the bath water with a sigh of contentment when there was a discreet tap at the door. There was no screen in the chamber, and Radegunde resolved to find one. Instead, she only opened the door enough to have a glimpse of Bartholomew outside.

He offered her a pair of keys. "It is a beginning," he said, revealing that he held a third.

"It is the trouble with an old lock. There is no telling how many keys might have been cast."

"Indeed. Gaston may send to Paris for a new one."

Radegunde nodded at the wisdom of that. "And does he ride to hunt?"

Bartholomew nodded and took his place by the door. "Lord Amaury and Fergus ride out with them, while Duncan, the Templars, and I remain here."

Radegunde thought that splitting the company made good sense, and she was glad that Duncan remained in the keep. Doubtless he guarded the reliquary himself.

"It seems that Millard welcomed the opportunity to become better acquainted," Bartholomew continued. "Perhaps we misunderstood his greeting."

"Perhaps not."

Bartholomew smiled. "You gain some of Duncan's wariness in the time you spend with him," he teased. Radegunde could not help but smile in return. "But Millard already presented Gaston with a fine gift."

"Indeed?"

"Indeed. Hunting gloves of finest red leather, tooled and embroidered." It was clear that Bartholomew was impressed. "They are magnificent. He said he had them made when he heard that Gaston would return."

"Hunting gloves?" Radegunde echoed. "Did Duncan see this?"

Bartholomew frowned. "Nay. He is in the chapel…"

"Did my lord Gaston don them?"

"He could scarce have done anything else, with the whole company watching!"

Radegunde seized Bartholomew's sleeve. "Guard my lady, I beg of you. I must see Lord Gaston warned!"

"But they have ridden out already," Bartholomew protested as she ran past him. "And warned of what?"

But Radegunde had not a moment to spare. She saw an echo of the past in the present and had to ensure that Lord Gaston did not touch those gloves to his lips.

They might well be poisoned, like those of Conan, the duke who had crossed the Breton March in defiance of the Angevin king and wiped his mouth with his hunting glove at Château-Gontier.

Then died there.

Radegunde did not doubt that others knew the tale as well as her mother—and Lady Eudaline had been most concerned about poison, after all. She ran down the stairs as quickly as she could, hoping against hope that she could reach the hunting party in time.

CHAPTER FOURTEEN

he hunting party was gone.

Of course.

Radegunde could scarcely hear the departing horses as she crossed the bailey. When she reached the gate, they had long since passed over the bridge. She insisted that the guard let her through the gate and peered at the party in the distance. They were too far away to hear her shout and already they coaxed the steeds to a gallop.

They would be out of sight within moments.

She had to wonder whether that was Millard's scheme.

Her heart in her throat, Radegunde spun to seek Duncan. Bartholomew had said he was in the chapel. She did not trouble to hide her haste but ran to the small chapel and burst through its door. Duncan was bent on one knee at the altar, his saddlebag by his side, the priest before him. Several other members of the household were also at prayer. Duncan glanced up at the sound of her arrival.

He took one look and genuflected, then strode toward her. To her relief, he brought his saddlebag. "What is amiss?"

She stretched up to whisper in his ear. "Millard gave fine gloves to Lord Gaston, and he donned them for the hunt this day."

Their gazes clung, and she knew their thoughts were as one.

"I will ride out immediately in pursuit," he said grimly, then passed her the saddlebag. "I do not yet know my accommodation. Will you keep it for me?"

"Of course." Radegunde recognized the weight of the reliquary within the bag and knew her lady's chamber was the best place to see it secured. That Duncan had not yet surrendered it to the priest or his treasury told her much.

Duncan grimaced. "But I do not like that we will be so divided."

"The Templars remain here, and Bartholomew."

He arched a brow. "While my lord Gaston, his wife's father Lord Amaury, Fergus, and myself are outside the gates." He shook his head. "I do not like it, Radegunde, but there is naught for it." He took her hand in his and strode for the stables, calling for his horse to be harnessed anew. The steed had just been brushed and blew out its lips to find the saddle upon its back again.

"You have run farther than this in a day," Duncan reminded the destrier, giving it a hearty pat. It snorted but turned to leave the stables readily enough. He swung into the saddle and Radegunde felt that some of his concern cast a shadow over her own heart. He bent and caught her chin in his hand, giving her a sweet kiss.

Then his gaze searched hers. "Suspect all," he whispered, his eyes dark, and Radegunde nodded.

"Be careful," she whispered, fearing for him.

Duncan smiled to reassure her, then turned the horse to ride out. She held his bag close to her chest and followed him across the bailey. Duncan raised his voice at the gates and the guards let him pass. He urged the steed to a canter on the bridge itself, and she glimpsed the horse galloping along the shore in pursuit of Gaston's party.

"Is aught amiss?" a man asked, and she found one of the Templar knights beside her. It was Enguerrand. His gaze dropped to the saddlebag, then met hers again.

"I hope not," Radegunde replied, keeping her voice low. She urged him aside and spoke quietly, not wanting to be overheard by the ostler or stableboys. "Do you know the tale of Conan, the duke who crossed the Breton March?"

"The one who died at Château-Gontier?" Enguerrand did not lower his voice—vexing man! Radegunde held her finger to her lips but he ignored her. "Of course. My family seat is in Anjou. Further east than this, but the tale was oft told. Why?"

"Did you ever hear about his gloves?" Radegunde whispered.

Enguerrand shook his head. "His gloves?"

"That they were responsible for his demise?"

"Nay, it was his valor and his folly in defying his liege lord, if not the divine vengeance for those who are faithless."

"He was murdered, by the tale I heard," Radegunde said, for it was imperative that the Templars, her lady's sole allies in this keep while her husband was at hunt, should appreciate the peril. The ostler cast them a glance of disinterest and she hoped he was not listening to their words.

"How?"

"By poison applied to his gloves," Radegunde confessed quietly. "A preparation that he would ingest when he wiped his mouth after a hard ride."

Enguerrand's eyes narrowed and finally his voice dropped. "Such a scheme must have been laid far in advance."

"Which makes it worse, not better. Someone anticipated that he would defy his liege lord and planned accordingly."

Enguerrand fixed her with a look. "Who told you of this? And what matter if it is true?"

"My mother told me the tale as a warning."

"Your mother, the wise woman?" His voice boomed again, and Radegunde yearned to strike him.

"Aye."

The Templar's lips tightened. "A wise woman would know best how it might be done. To others, it might seem a tall tale. How much did *you* learn of your mother's arts?"

Radegunde was insulted that his tone filled with suspicion. "Only enough to aid my lady when her time comes, if necessary," she snapped, then whispered anew. "What is of import is that Lord Millard gave Lord Gaston a pair of gloves this day."

"Aye, I saw them." Enguerrand smiled. "They were most fine. A truly thoughtful gift."

"And Lord Gaston is wearing them to hunt."

Enguerrand glanced between Radegunde and the open gate, his frown deepening. "But you cannot be accusing..."

"Can I not?" Radegunde continued in quiet haste. "He did not welcome Lord Gaston's arrival with joy. He loses his stewardship of this holding with Lord Gaston's return."

Enguerrand's gaze flew to the tower, and she saw that he finally understood the peril. "Our party is divided," he murmured. "Duncan rides to warn Gaston and he will be protected by the others if need be. The lady must be defended by those of us who remain." He raised his voice to shout to Yvan, one of the other Templars, then turned a glittering gaze upon Radegunde again. "I sincerely hope that you are wrong," he hissed, his gaze boring into hers. "But if you are right, or if any soul in this keep dies of poison, you had best be prepared for questions, for you alone are the daughter of a wise woman."

Radegunde gasped in outrage at his implication.

The Templar's gaze fell again to the saddlebag before she could correct his thinking. "And you had best surrender that to me."

"I will not," she retorted.

"You are but a maid and that bag..."

Radegunde stepped back and raised her own voice. "Belongs to my man, Duncan MacDonald. I have been entrusted by him with his belongings, and I will keep them with me in my lady's chamber." She saw the Templar's gaze flit over the stableboys who were now listening avidly and watched his lips tighten.

Before he could argue with her, she marched away, holding the saddlebag tightly against her chest. She was aware of a shadow moving beside her when she stepped into the bailey and glanced that way to see that it was Laurent.

Fergus' squire.

Leila, by Duncan's telling. Now that Radegunde knew the truth, she wondered how she had missed it. Disguised as a squire, the Saracen girl had guarded the reliquary from their departure from Jerusalem and Radegunde knew she was trustworthy. Only the fact that she had kept herself mired in dung had kept others from looking too closely.

The smell of her garb was still enough to bring a tear to Radegunde's eye.

"You there," she said crisply. "I would have your aid in ensuring that all is to my lady's satisfaction in her chamber. Come along. I doubt you will be missed."

And Leila might win a fair prize in exchange.

The squire bowed low, then scurried after Radegunde.

In Duncan's absence, she would keep all of her allies close.

Duncan knew he was being followed.

Again.

Ever since the assault in the forest, he had wondered about the Scotsman who had attacked him. The fact remained that Duncan had not recognized him. He had not known his tartan either. Had the man been in the tavern in Paris? If so, Duncan had not noticed him there.

Was the attacker truly a Scotsman, or simply another man garbed as one of his fellow Scots?

Why did the man follow him? Was it because of the reliquary? It was impossible to know whether Wulfe had caught Everard and naught said that Everard did not have an ally either—or had not bought one. That Paris tavern was likely well known as a place to find able men in search of labor that paid well.

And Duncan could believe that there were more than a few who had no scruples.

An assailant seeking the reliquary might have believed it to be in Duncan's possession when he and Radegunde had left the protection of Valeroy's walls. Indeed, it could have been a gift intended for the convent where Gaston's mother lived.

But they had been attacked *after* leaving that place, on their return to Valeroy.

Not to mention the assault outside Mathilde's hut, when he had carried naught at all. Nay, he was himself targeted, and Duncan must deduce the reason why.

Though it was true that Duncan had been entrusted with the

burden of the reliquary, accosting him would simply mean that another in the party carried it. It could not be that.

He had to believe the matter was more personal.

He also believed the man did not intend to do him a mild injury. Nay, his goal was to kill Duncan.

But why?

Either someone needed him dead to see Fergus undefended or Duncan's own past caught up with him. Duncan, to be sure, found both possibilities unlikely, which was why he had refused to discuss the matter with Radegunde. There was no cause to alarm her when he had only speculation to share.

That strategy had made more sense before he heard the sounds of stealthy pursuit.

He galloped his destrier after the hunting party. He had to reach Gaston in time and being with others would also be his own best defense. The party rode toward the shadow of a forest, and by the time Duncan reached its perimeter, the large group had disappeared inside. A wagon was left at the side of the road, doubtless because the path through the forest was too narrow. Whatever horses had drawn it had been taken onward with the party.

Duncan entered the cool of the forest, slowing Caledon's pace. The party was far ahead of him, so far that he could not see them. He halted at a fork in the path beneath the forest's shadow and listened.

Caledon was breathing heavily but still tossing his head, ready to run again. Ahead, to both the left and the right, Duncan could hear dogs bay at intervals and the sound of scrub being trodden. He heard a shout in the same moment that a horse's hooves clattered to silence behind him.

The hair stood on the back of his neck, and he urged Caledon quickly to the right path. He gave the steed his heels, not caring whether he interrupted Lord Gaston's hunt or not. The people of Châmont-sur-Maine would have far more to mourn than an empty trencher two days hence if Duncan did not reach Gaston in time.

Fergus could not shake his sense of pending doom.

He had slept poorly for several nights, haunted by nightmares that he could not recall when he awakened. He knew they were nightmares, though, or portents because he could not shake the cold grip of terror. He had awakened every time with his heart racing, cold sweat on his flesh, the urgent need to flee with all haste.

Who was threatened? How and why? That he had dreamed of danger in the future seemed more curse than blessing when he could not recall any details of his vision. Did he fear for himself? Fergus could not imagine that it was so. He was far from home and from any who might wish to challenge his inheritance or have any other quibble with him.

Did he fear for Duncan? It was true that his companion had been entrusted with the burden of the reliquary, and Fergus did fear that Everard might have eluded Wulfe.

Did he fear for Gaston? This seemed the most likely possibility as the dreams had begun after the decision was made to leave Valeroy for Châmont-sur-Maine. He had noted Millard's reluctance to surrender the seal to Gaston and wondered at the truth behind the gloves that man had given to the new lord of the holding. Had they truly been prepared for Gaston's arrival? Fergus doubted it. They were beautifully made and had been expensive, to be sure. Millard did not strike him as a man who spent coin on those other than himself. Fergus suspected that they had been made for Millard, perhaps to celebrate his own claim of the signet ring for Châmont-sur-Maine, and come to mind when the man had felt obliged to offer some gift to Gaston.

Fergus noted also that Ysmaine's father, Lord Amaury, ensured that he rode between Gaston and Millard at the head of the hunting party. Fergus was not alone in his suspicions. Fergus rode at Gaston's left, wanting to be alert for any threat but fearing his recent sleeplessness would leave him slow to respond.

He was so very tired.

"And so, these are the woods where you most often hunt," Amaury said to Millard. "What do you find here?"

Fergus suddenly saw a boar in his mind's eye. He blinked and scanned the undergrowth on either side but there was no such creature to be seen. He felt unease, for boar were known to be great fighters and as likely to injure the hunter as to be felled themselves.

Was a boar behind his dreams?

"Hares, of course, and pheasants," Millard said. "There are deer aplenty."

"No boar?" Fergus asked without meaning to do so.

"Boar!" Gaston nodded approval. "That is what I should like to take back to the hall. A great boar, five or six summers of age."

"Not a sow, for you will need them in your woods to breed for future hunts," Amaury advised.

"And the male will be bigger," Millard added.

And more fierce. Fergus felt his lips tighten.

"A boar would be ideal," Gaston said. "Think of the quantity of meat! A boar would make for a feast to remember."

And this was his friend's ambition, Fergus understood, to make his return to his family holding cause for celebration for all pledged to his hand. Would Gaston's desire be his undoing? It would not be the first time Fergus had witnessed such a situation, and he had difficulty believing that Gaston had much experience hunting such wily creatures. There were none in Outremer, after all, even if the Templars had hunted.

He feared that Millard also doubted Gaston's experience, for that man showed a suspicious enthusiasm for the notion. Fergus could only recall Millard's tepid greeting of Gaston and wondered whether that man expected Gaston to be wounded in such a hunt.

"You speak aright, Gaston," Millard said warmly. "People would talk of a feast of boar for months to come. I have not seen one in many years, but it was long said that they could be found deeper in the forest. This way."

Millard took the lead, urging his horse along a narrow path that wound away from the wider route. Fergus did not like the look of the path. Gaston seemed untroubled. He turned and shouted to the servants in the party, telling them of his plan, and three hastened forward on foot to scout for a suitable animal. They disappeared into the shadows of the forest within moments, moving silently through the woods. The dogs ran with them, noses to the ground and tails wagging. Millard rode onward, Amaury behind him.

Gaston spared Fergus a smile that spoke of his confidence and followed his wife's father. The entire party fell quiet, moving steadily forward through the undergrowth. They fanned out, each horse picking its own path. Soon Fergus could see only the three knights ahead of him.

A whistle carried high and clear from far ahead, then another.

Followed by the unmistakable grunting of a boar.

"Mine," Gaston murmured. His destrier shouldered past Millard and Amaury, forcing their steeds from the path. Millard, Fergus noted, loaded his crossbow and Amaury drew his sword. Fergus also drew his sword, his sense of unease growing by leaps and bounds, and followed Gaston.

A servant appeared in the greenery ahead, beckoning to Gaston. "There is a clearing ahead, sir, with a rock wall on one side and a stream on the other. Guillaume says we will corner him there."

"Excellent," Gaston agreed, his words a low murmur. He nodded to the servant and followed at a canter, Fergus fast behind. The trees seemed too dense and the shadows too dark for there to be a clearing, and Fergus feared a trick.

Until they suddenly burst forth into a cleared space. As promised, there was a face of rough stone on one side and a stream running past it.

Fergus did not see the boar until they were into the clearing and it charged them.

It roared with fury then, and Gaston's destrier turned in the open space as if he perfectly anticipated Gaston's desire. Gaston struck down low and hard with his blade, even as his steed turned out of the boar's path.

His sword was driven into the boar's shoulder, but the beast never missed a step. Indeed, it tipped its head back and Gaston's destrier shied as the tusk grazed its belly. Gaston tried to pull out the sword but the boar did not halt. He was forced to release the weapon and gain control of the destrier again. The boar turned at the far side of the clearing, its eyes as red as the blood that streamed from its wound.

To Fergus' relief, the rest of the company had claimed safe refuge to watch the battle. Many were on the far side of the river, while still more had climbed the trees and perched in their lower branches. Lord Amaury had guided his steed so that the trees were between it and the clearing, though Millard remained in the clear. He lifted his crossbow, but Lord Amaury seized his elbow.

"It is not your kill," that man declared, and Millard lowered his weapon with obvious reluctance.

Gaston's destrier's nostrils flared and it pranced in place. Fergus knew Fantôme had been valiant in battle and did not spook at the scent of blood, but he feared for the steed against such an opponent.

Fergus had steered his horse to the other side of the clearing—indeed, the creature had needed little encouragement to skirt the boar's path—and watched as the boar prepared to charge again. Its small eyes were fixed upon Gaston, and Fantôme stamped in place. From his vantage point, he could see the other two knights, and the expression on Millard's face convinced him that his doubts about that man's intentions were right.

Of all of them, Gaston seemed the most serene, even though the boar clearly meant to attack him. Gaston patted the destrier's neck and dismounted, seemingly on impulse. He slapped Fantôme's rump and the destrier ran to the cover of the forest where a servant caught its trailing reins.

Gaston pulled his knife and smiled as he faced the boar. He walked slowly toward it, which seemed to confuse the beast.

"Was it your forebear I watched my father kill, all those years ago?" he murmured, as if to taunt the boar. Fergus was reassured that Gaston had at least witnessed a boar hunt. But then, it was Gaston's nature to fully understand his foe before he entered a battle.

The boar heaved and grunted, pawing the ground as it watched Gaston's approach. It was wary. Fergus could almost taste its suspicion. To its thinking, Gaston should have fled. The boar sniffed the air, but Fergus doubted it could smell fear on Gaston.

Indeed, Gaston smiled.

He turned his knife, letting the blade flash in the light, as the company watched rapt. "That one tried to claim a good blade, too, but I am no more ready to relinquish my weapon than my father was."

The boar charged suddenly. The company gasped but Gaston alone did not seem surprised. The knight held his ground and the beast's gaze, as if daring it to attack him. It charged directly at him, but Gaston spun out of the way in the last moment, as graceful as a dancer. He drove his knife into the boar's side as the creature sailed past him, putting all his weight behind the blow. He sank the knife up to the hilt and blood flowed onto his gloves. The boar wailed in pain and twisted so that Gaston could not remove the blade.

Fergus saw him grimace as the hilt slipped from his fingers, the blood doing little to aid his grip. The boar leaped at Gaston again. Its tusk tore Gaston's chausses before the knight spun and kicked at the boar's head. When the beast stumbled, Gaston seized the hilt of his knife and tugged it forcibly out of the wound. The flesh ripped, the wound gaping wide, and Fergus could see the white glimmer of a rib. The boar ducked its head to gore Gaston, but he drove the short blade into the creature's small red eye.

The boar faltered, but Fergus knew it would rise again.

"Say the word and I will finish it!" Millard whispered, lifting his crossbow.

"You will do no such thing," Amaury declared, then seized Millard's weapon.

Meanwhile, Gaston kicked the boar twice more, then reclaimed his dagger. The boar leaped at him, albeit more slowly than before, and Gaston appeared to fall beneath it. Every man gasped, but Gaston struck upward. With a savage gesture, he sliced the boar's gullet open and the boar fell heavily to the ground.

Atop him.

Gaston grunted and shoved the weight of the boar aside. His tabard was marred and there was blood on his fine new gloves, as well as his chausses and boots. He stared at the beast as it bled, then removed both of his blades.

The creature did not stir.

There was silence as all watched and waited, in case the beast should rise again. It would have defied belief, but the vigor of boars was well known. After several moments, Gaston leaned close to the creature, then placed a hand on the beast's chest.

"His other eye is closed," he said. "And his heart beats no more. So falls a mighty king of the forest."

"All hail, Lord Gaston, Baron of Châmont-sur-Maine!" Lord Amaury cried and the cheers of the servants rang through the forest, as Gaston made to wipe the perspiration from his lip.

"Do not touch the glove to your lips!" a man cried and to his astonishment Fergus recognized Duncan's voice. He turned at the sound of a steed racing through the undergrowth and soon enough, Duncan appeared, pushing the rump of Millard's steed aside in his haste to reach Gaston.

Gaston had frozen, the back of his gloved hand a finger-span from his lips.

"It may be poisoned!" Duncan declared. Shock rippled through the company, and yet again, Fergus wondered whether this was responsible for the shadow in his dreams.

"What madness is this?" Millard demanded. "At whose behest do you tell such lies?"

Duncan recovered his composure, undoubtedly because Gaston shed the gloves. "There is a tale in these parts of a knight felled by doing just as you were about to do, sir, for his gloves were laced with poison in anticipation of that gesture."

"What tale?" Millard demanded. He laughed. "Surely you do not make your decisions based upon such tales, Gaston?"

"There is no cost to being prudent," Gaston said, his tone more mild than Fergus' own might have been. "And they are badly soiled at any rate."

"But..." Millard sputtered.

"It was Conan of Breton," Duncan said. "Radegunde's mother Mathilde told her of it. It seems that she regards a gift of gloves to be a bad omen."

Amaury's smile was cool as he tucked Millard's crossbow beneath his arm. "How interesting. I recall the tale of Conan's death, but not the detail of the gloves."

"But it is no more than a tale," Millard protested. "An idle rumor spread by ignorant peasants." He laughed again, though the sound was strained. "You are as cautious as an old woman, for a knight who has battled in Outremer."

"I learned in Outremer to listen well and proceed with care," Gaston said quietly.

"I would take Mathilde's advice on matters of poison," Amaury said, his tone robust. "She has shown much wisdom and given good counsel all the years she has lived at Valeroy."

"But surely this rumor can be proven to be wrong," Millard scoffed. "Surely you will not insult me by spurning my gift?"

Gaston smiled thinly, his eyes dark. Fergus knew he was angry, but Millard evidently did not perceive the signs. Gaston held up the gloves and turned before the company. "A pair of fine gloves for any man so bold as to touch his lips to them first."

There were no volunteers.

Millard's face reddened. "But this is madness," he began, then shook his head. "Gaston, I must admit that the gloves were ordered for my own use. I apologize for any indignity done to you, but I did not prepare them for you as I said earlier." He looked fully discomfited now. "I simply felt on this day that a gift should be made to you, to welcome you home, and only the finest item in my possession would do. If the gloves are poisoned—which I highly doubt—then I was the target, not you." He laughed lightly. "If you would cast aside such fine garb, do not see them destroyed."

"Indeed, I would not endorse such a waste of good craftsmanship." Gaston strolled across the clearing and offered the gloves to Millard. "Perhaps you would like them returned to you," he said smoothly. His gaze was hard and Millard could not hold it. "For I confess I will never don them again."

Millard reached eagerly for the gloves, and Fergus feared that Gaston surrendered the sole opportunity to learn their truth. Millard never claimed them, though, for Lord Amaury plucked them from Gaston's outstretched hand.

"Perhaps you will indulge my curiosity, Gaston," that man said. "I would like to know for certain whether Duncan's charge is true. I would seek the counsel of Mathilde." He tucked the gloves into his own belt, but Fergus could only see the fear in Millard's eyes.

It *was* true, then.

"I see no reason not to have the truth ascertained." Gaston smiled at the company. "In fact, I would gladly learn that my loyal comrade had been mistaken."

"As would I!" Duncan cried and the company cheered. He urged his steed forward. "Did you fell this boar on this day, Lord Gaston?" he asked. "For I have never seen its equal."

"He did," declared Lord Amaury. "And by himself. Such valor is rarely witnessed."

"Such a feast we will enjoy," Fergus contributed and the men in the company cheered.

Their merry mood was restored, though some eyed Millard with concern. Fergus did not doubt that Gaston had been saved with only a moment to spare, and he hoped his dreams would be less dark.

The company jested as the boar was gutted at Gaston's command. The offal would be left for other scavengers in the forest. Several men hastened back to the wagon and returned with a heavy pole and some rope. The boar's ankles were trussed to the pole and its weight hung from it.

Six men hefted its weight to carry it back to the wagon, and Fergus could see that the weight was considerable. They called for a song to aid in their labor and the larger part of the company trudged through the forest to the wagon. The air was turning chilly and it seemed there was little taste for more hunting at this hour.

Indeed, any other prey would be anticlimactic to the taking of the boar.

"Before the feast, perhaps you would be so kind as to hunt some smaller game," Gaston said to Millard and Amaury. "On the morrow, of course, we shall be at worship, and then I shall be occupied in a review of the ledgers, but a variety of fare would be welcome for the feast." Millard's lips tightened again, and Fergus wondered what secrets would be revealed by the ledgers.

"These woods must abound with pheasant and hare," Amaury said with gusto. "We shall fill a wagon with them!"

"Only if my crossbow is returned to me," Millard said sourly.

Amaury offered it to him, after he removed the bolt. He offered that on the flat of his hand, after Millard had slung the weapon from his saddle. The other man accepted it in poor temper.

To Fergus' surprise, Duncan rode alongside Gaston. He doffed his gloves and offered them to Gaston. "They are not so fine as the pair you lost this day, but you are welcome to them for the ride back."

"But surely you will need them as much as I do."

Duncan smiled. "Caledon has run a good deal this day and is not so young as your destriers. I mean to walk him back to the gates."

Gaston spared a glance at the darkening sky, then back to Duncan. "Is he lamed? I would not have you outside of the walls when night falls."

"It will do us both good to have a walk after this day," Duncan said, and Fergus knew his old comrade told only part of the truth.

"I will walk with you," Fergus said but Duncan shook his head.

"Nay, lad," he said, his tone as hard as rock. "This I will do alone."

With that, Fergus guessed why the sense of doom would not leave him. Duncan had been attacked in Valeroy, and the wound had been vicious. Duncan had escaped an assailant in the forests of Valeroy on the journey to visit Eudaline, but the attacker had not been killed. The glint in Duncan's eyes made Fergus wonder whether his companion knew more than he had when last they talked of the matter.

Perhaps he merely guessed that the attacker was close.

Duncan might not have the Sight but his instincts were finely honed.

It was Fergus' impulse to insist upon accompanying Duncan, yet he also knew the warrior well enough to understand that his thinking would not be changed. Duncan's expression was one of grim resolve.

"Be careful," Fergus advised when he walked his horse past his comrade.

"I am always careful, lad," Duncan vowed.

"I see a shadow."

"As do I," Duncan replied grimly. His gaze locked with Fergus' own. "And I tire of it. I will see it dispersed before I sleep again, upon that you may rely."

CHAPTER FIFTEEN

ergus' squire accompanied Radegunde in silence, hesitating outside the solar when Radegunde would have urged her companion inside. Radegunde watched the disguised maiden look at Bartholomew, who stood guard at the door, her uncertainty clear.

"I *know*," Radegunde said so quietly that only they two could hear and felt their surprise. "And if my lady does not, she will soon."

Leila's eyes widened in alarm. "I cannot leave the service of my lord Fergus…"

"And you will not. I thought it best for all of us to be together, with our burden." Radegunde patted the saddlebag then smiled at Leila. "And that you might savor a bath."

The lips of the supposed squire parted, and Radegunde knew that no one who saw this expression of joy could doubt her gender.

She raised her voice and spoke sternly. "You should be strong enough to aid me in moving my lady's trunks, Laurent," she said. "And there is more labor yet to be done after that. There is no cause for you to sit idle in the stables, even if Lord Fergus has ridden to hunt."

"Aye. I will help." The squire bowed, eyes sparkling.

"Indeed, we will be occupied until the evening meal. Do not doubt as much for a moment."

"I am at your service."

Radegunde turned to Bartholomew. "My lady intends to sleep, and I will draw the curtains on the bed so she is untroubled by our activity. Will you ensure that none disturbs her, save her lord husband on his return?"

Bartholomew bowed. "You may rely upon me to do as much."

Radegunde gave a little tap on the door to announce herself and peered around it, to find that Lady Ysmaine had already abandoned the bath. She sat on the bed in the clean chemise that Radegunde had laid out for her, combing her hair. She looked more tired than Radegunde would have preferred, but smiled at her maid. "Is Gaston returned?"

"Not yet, my lady."

"But you left with such haste. I thought something was amiss."

"I had merely forgotten something in the stables, my lady," Radegunde lied. She indicated the saddlebag. Lady Ysmaine appeared to be puzzled, which meant she recognized it.

"I thought Duncan…"

Radegunde interrupted her before too much was said aloud. "My lady, I would beg your indulgence, but the solar should be set fully to rights before my lord Gaston's return."

Lady Ysmaine's gaze flitted over the chamber without understanding. To be sure, Radegunde had already set it to rights. Radegunde urged the squire into the solar, following fast behind her companion and closed the door firmly.

Lady Ysmaine gasped and seized her cloak to cover herself, for her chemise was sheer. "Radegunde!" she began, clearly intending to chide her maid, but Radegunde knew that would only support the ruse.

"I will pull the drapes, my lady. I apologize, for I had need of assistance," she said in a loud voice. She hastened to Lady Ysmaine and whispered. "Laurent is truly Leila, and I thought that she might savor a bath herself."

Claire Delacroix

Lady Ysmaine's eyes began to sparkle, and she covered her mouth with her hand to silence her laughter. "So this is why the bag must be here. Its champions are otherwise occupied."

Radegunde nodded and set the saddlebag against the wall.

Lady Ysmaine smiled at Leila and gestured to the bathwater in silent invitation. It was still steaming and smelled of that rose soap.

Leila stared at the water with such yearning that Radegunde felt sympathy for her. "Should you not be next?" she asked softly of Radegunde.

"I have no time on this day," Radegunde said, which was not strictly true.

"How long have you known?" Lady Ysmaine whispered.

"Since Duncan told me, in Paris."

Leila looked up with alarm. "Did he tell others?"

"Nay, only me." Radegunde felt her lips curve. "And only because I thought your friendship with Bartholomew meant he favored boys over women."

"Hardly that," Leila scoffed, her dark eyes sparkling.

"Yet Gaston thought to wed you to him!" Lady Ysmaine began to laugh. "Oh, Radegunde, no wonder you showed such dismay!"

When their smiles had faded, Leila plucked at her mucky tabard even as she eyed the water.

"Do you not welcome this opportunity?" Radegunde asked.

"Oh, I do," Leila admitted. "But I am not certain I will be able to bear these garments afterward."

"Yet if you abandon them, your secret might be discerned."

"I think it is more a question of abandoning their scent," Lady Ysmaine said. "What provoked you to make such a choice and join our party? Surely it was fraught with risk?"

Leila's lips tightened. "There was less peril in leaving than in remaining. My uncle meant to wed me to a man I knew to be cruel. My betrothed was cunning and hid his true nature from other men. My uncle thought my protests frivolous and would not heed them."

"But you feared him," Radegunde guessed.

The other maiden squared her shoulders. "I would make my own choice, for good or ill, rather than accept a bad one inflicted

220

upon me."

"I can find no fault with that." The women shared a glance of understanding. Leila still did not remove her garb though Radegunde knew she wished for the bath. Perhaps she was shy. "Come, bathe, before the water is cold. I will tend my lady's hair while you take your leisure."

"You are kind, indeed."

Radegunde smiled at Leila, then pulled the drapes around her lady's bed. She lit the coal in the brazier, then retreated to comb Lady Ysmaine's hair, leaving Leila alone.

In mere moments, Radegunde heard the clothing drop to the floor. She heard the water splash as Leila entered the bath. She was drawing the comb through the ends of her lady's hair when Leila sighed with such obvious contentment that both Radegunde and her mistress smiled.

Lady Ysmaine placed her hand over Radegunde's and gave her fingers a squeeze. "You have done well this day," she said, barely mouthing the words, then tried to hide her yawn without success. "I cannot fathom why I feel such fatigue, Radegunde. It was not so long a ride."

"Can you not?" Radegunde murmured and her lady caught her breath.

"My courses," Lady Ysmaine murmured, her eyes lighting. Then she frowned. "But I went months without them en route to Jerusalem."

"But now you are safe and well-fed. Does your belly not feel soft?"

"I thought I ate too well as a wife," Lady Ysmaine admitted with a low laugh.

"You cannot see the change in your breasts as I do. It is early yet, but I think the signs are clear."

"When do you think the babe will arrive?"

"May, my lady, if all goes well."

"May." Lady Ysmaine was evidently filled with delight. "I shall not fear the birth if you are with me. Oh, Radegunde, what should I do without you?"

The heartfelt words startled Radegunde, for though she wished to serve her lady, she wished also to be with Duncan. She frowned as she fastened the braid for her lady, wondering how she and Duncan would contrive a future together.

France or Scotland? Radegunde imagined it would be Scotland, which was well enough, but she would miss her lady. She held her tongue for the moment, for she had no plan to share.

"Dare I tell Gaston?" Lady Ysmaine whispered.

"I should think he would like to know, though matters can yet go awry." Radegunde said then urged her lady to lie back and sleep, which Lady Ysmaine did.

Radegunde cleared her throat, not wanting to surprise Leila. "May I join you?"

"Of course." There was a splash of water again, and Radegunde left the bed, tugging the drape behind herself. She thought to fetch some mending but Leila spoke again. "Would you help me with my hair? It is so mired and tangled."

"Of course!" Radegunde froze in her steps at the sight of Leila. The transformation in her appearance was remarkable. The other woman must have been about her age. She was delicately wrought and so feminine in form that Radegunde was astonished that they had all been so fooled. Leila's skin was golden, of a rich hue beyond that reached by Radegunde's own skin after a summer in the sun. Her hair was dark and gleamed despite her complaints. Radegunde guessed it had been longer, for it fell only to Leila's shoulders and the ends were ragged, as if she had cut it with a knife herself. Leila's eyes were similarly dark and thickly lashed, her lips curved in a smile.

"I cannot believe I was deceived," she admitted when she realized that Leila was aware of her stare.

"I am glad that so many were." Leila indicated Duncan's saddlebag, when Radegunde had left it on the floor. "Is it yet safe?"

Radegunde nodded and came to help with Leila's hair. "Will you tell me of Palestine?" she asked cautiously. "I saw little of it, for I was ill in Jerusalem, but I would know more. Tell me of your home."

"I do not know where to begin."

"Tell me what you love of it." Radegunde smiled. "Tell me what you miss."

Leila sighed and closed her eyes as Radegunde took the comb to her hair. "I miss only my cousin. We were raised as sisters and when I left, she was with child." She hesitated and bit her lip. "I would have liked to have held her babe, just once." And a tear slipped from beneath those dark lashes.

Radegunde's heart clenched. She felt both compassion and respect for this woman who had paid so high a price to have her own choice. She could not imagine losing her family and home forever, to have no chance of seeing them again. Indeed, if Leila's betrothed were a vengeful man, the other woman could not even risk sending word to her cousin of her welfare lest her location be revealed. She realized that even when she had been ill in Jerusalem, even when she had feared to die, the prospect of returning to Valeroy had given her hope and strength. Would she have had the will to survive without that possibility?

"I would have liked to have had a sister," she said lightly instead, working her comb through the dark tresses.

"Do you not have one?"

"Four brothers." At Leila's glance, Radegunde rolled her eyes. "One older and the rest younger than me."

The other woman smiled. "I always wanted to have a brother."

Radegunde guessed that Leila imagined a brother might have defended her choice before her uncle.

"But now I am alone, and I will be missed in the stables." Leila sat up and laid claim to the comb. She tugged it through the last bit of her hair, so clearly putting her concerns behind her that Radegunde sat back. She brought Leila a towel then retreated with her mending as the other woman dried herself, grimaced, then donned her dirty garb once more.

"Your face is radiant," Radegunde noted softly when the squire Laurent was before her once more.

Leila wrinkled her nose and rubbed her filthy sleeve across her face. It left a trail of dirt that disguised her features once again. The smell of dung on her garb was enough to keep much curiosity at bay, to be sure.

Claire Delacroix

When Leila might have left, Radegunde picked up the discarded comb and offered it to her. "Sisters do not have to share blood, but can be bound by confidences," she said quietly, offering the comb. "Will you be my sister?"

Leila's smile fairly lit the room. She stepped forward and took the comb, her eyes sparkling. "I will, Radegunde. I will." They made to embrace but the smell of dung made Radegunde cough.

They parted with a laugh, and smiled at each other.

Leila eyed the saddlebag and bit her lip. "Bartholomew will tend Lord Gaston on his return, and you may have labor to do for Lady Ysmaine. I would not see the prize untended."

"And we will not be able to take it to the hall for the evening meal without arousing suspicion of its contents," Radegunde agreed. "Will you take custody of it as before?"

"Gladly," Leila agreed and claimed the bag. A quick rap at the portal and Bartholomew opened it for her. She hastened down the stairs, keeping her head bowed so few would note her features.

"Mind you return in the morning to finish the task!" Radegunde called after the apparent squire and Bartholomew bit back a smile.

They both then bowed at the sight of Lord Gaston at the foot of the stairs. He was covered with blood, but he was hale, to Radegunde's relief.

"Do not be so quick to be rid of the bath," he said, his manner jovial. "The blood is not mine, Radegunde," he chided. "I took a boar this day." As Bartholomew congratulated him, he dropped his voice. "And Duncan reached my side in time, thanks to your quick thinking."

"My lady sleeps, my lord," Radegunde informed him. "And I will see that new water is brought."

"I can take the second water after my lady. There is no need for such trouble."

"Aye, my lord, there is."

Lord Gaston crossed the threshold to the chamber and blinked, evidently surprised by the smell of dung. He looked at Radegunde, a question in his eyes.

"The squire Laurent aided in the arrangement of the chamber," Radegunde said, uncertain who might overhear her words. "The smell of him was such that I insisted he take the second water."

Lord Gaston's eyes twinkled and his voice dropped low. "Well done, Radegunde. Well done." He surveyed her before he spoke. "You will want to wait in the stables, no doubt, for the return of your lover."

Radegunde was startled. "Did Duncan not return with you?"

"He insisted upon walking his steed back alone," Lord Gaston confessed, then set his belt aside with a grimace. "I hope he arrives in time for the evening meal. Bartholomew, can you speed a bath for me? I am mired beyond belief."

Duncan walked back alone?

What madness was this?

Radegunde seized the opportunity Lord Gaston offered and raced to the gates of the keep to discover the truth. As she hastened down the stairs, her anger mounted. How like Duncan it was to put himself in harm's way to see a matter resolved! He would draw out the man who had attacked him twice and face him alone to see others protected and the threat put to rest. Had he stood before her, she would have granted him a good measure of her thoughts on that choice.

As it was, she might not have the opportunity.

The sun was already sinking low when the hunting party had the boar loaded upon the wagon and began their journey back to the keep. There was much joviality in the party at Gaston's skill and good fortune, and Duncan did not doubt that many saw such a kill as a good portent for his suzerainty of the holding. He noted the open admiration in the eyes of those servants who had accompanied the party and knew that the tale of Gaston's valor would travel quickly.

It would likely also be well embellished.

Duncan himself was shaken by Gaston's near-miss. That knight spoke to the men in his party as if naught had gone awry, but Duncan noticed that Gaston's gaze remained dark—and that he spoke little to Millard. Millard appeared to be sulking and gave only cursory replies to Lord Amaury, who was resolutely cheerful. There was a tension between the noblemen, and Duncan was glad that he would not be in their company much longer.

He let the party pull ahead of him and watched the sun sink lower. He was well aware that someone lurked behind him, someone who clung to the shadows and kept out of sight. He gripped the hilt of his knife and began to walk with Caledon, listening for sounds of pursuit.

"Duncan!" Fergus called, glancing back over the company. "Are you certain you would walk alone?"

"Aye, my steed has run too much this day," Duncan lied, patting the horse. "We have seen to each other's welfare often enough and this day will be no different." He waved at the party. "Do not wait upon me, my lord. The keep is within view and I shall be there shortly after you."

He had seen the shadow cross Fergus' features earlier and took it as a warning. The lad had seen something of Duncan's future. Was it good or ill that Fergus followed his request and rejoined the company, sparing only one more backward glance?

Duncan refused to think upon it. He would not consider that his fate was set, by the stars or even by some divinity. Nay, he believed that a man made his own future, with his choices and his blade. God was good. God created all and God should be worshipped, but God, in Duncan's view, was also too busy to plan the destinies of each and every one beneath his hand.

The party was just out of earshot when Duncan heard a soft step behind him. His pulse quickened, though he gave no outward sign of his awareness that he was not alone.

If Duncan had aught to say about the matter, he would survive this day—and the man who followed him would not.

Ysmaine felt the mattress dip as Gaston joined her abed. She had been dozing until his return, then had slept more deeply while he bathed. She smiled as he drew her into his embrace and she curled against his heat, relief swelling her heart.

She had to tell him the news. Such tidings could not be kept to herself, not when she knew they would give her husband such pleasure.

"How was the hunt?" she asked in a murmur, and he planted a

kiss upon her brow.

"Good, for the prey was a boar and not me."

Ysmaine was abruptly awake. "What is this?"

"Fear not. The peril is passed. You have a prize in that maid, for she ensured I was warned in time." He recounted the tale of the gloves to her, his calm manner failing to completely dismiss her dismay and subsequent relief. He drew her against his side and Ysmaine welcomed his heat. He kissed her temple. "And we shall have a fine feast, in addition to my survival."

"I have a fondness for boar."

"As do I." Gaston nodded, but when he continued, she realized it was not the taste of the feast that gave him satisfaction. "To have taken such a noble beast, a king of the forest, will be seen as an omen for the days ahead, to be sure. I could not have asked for a better hunt. Your father was of great assistance."

"Perhaps it is a divine endorsement of your suzerainty," she said and he chuckled.

"I will take all endorsements, no matter their source."

Ysmaine looked up at him, liking how his damp hair curled dark against his forehead. She pushed it back, basking in the warmth of his smile. His eyes were sparkling blue, like a night sky filled with stars, and she was beyond glad that this knight had found her in Jerusalem in her hour of need.

"What is it?" he asked in a low voice.

"It suits you to be a baron of the realm," she said. "I think you doubted it, but I never did."

"I doubted it because I did not know the value of a good wife and the alliance of her family. I could not have done even this much without you, Ysmaine."

Ysmaine smiled, for they were in perfect agreement. The solar was quiet, though she could hear the distant sound of activity in the kitchens.

"You are tired this day. It is not like you to nap."

"I have good reason, in addition to this having been a long day."

Gaston's eyes lit and he seemed to hold his breath. "Indeed?"

"Indeed." Ysmaine smiled. "I know not whether it is son or

daughter, but if all goes well, we will have a child in the spring."

Gaston laughed and kissed her soundly, then recoiled as if she were wrought of glass. "Are you sufficiently warm? Have you rested enough? Should I sleep in another chamber?"

"Oh, Gaston, do not fuss so." She twined her leg around one of his. "I need you close, now and always."

To her relief, he settled back beside her, but he still touched her with reverence. "When? Do you know?"

"Radegunde guesses it will be May."

"Your *maid* knows of this, yet I did not?"

Ysmaine laughed. "I wager Radegunde knows more of the arrival of children than you do, sir."

He chuckled in his turn. "Aye, that is a fair wager." He frowned. "We cannot go to Scotland, then, for Fergus' nuptials in the spring."

"Gaston, it is very early days, yet. Much may occur, for this is my first conception. We can decide about Scotland closer to the time of the wedding. Indeed, I believe none should hear of it before the Yule."

"Surely you will round by then."

"If all goes well."

Their gazes locked and she saw his pleasure. "A child," Gaston whispered. "Ysmaine, these are fine tidings."

He bent and caught her lips beneath her own, doubtless intending that his kiss should be a gentle one, but Ysmaine did not wish to have only polite embraces for the better part of a year. She slipped her hand around his neck and pulled him closer, opening her mouth to him and inviting his ardor.

Gaston took her invitation, his fingers spearing into her hair as he lifted her to his kiss. She felt the quickening of his pulse and slid her hand down his chest to caress him. He was aroused, as she had guessed, and he caught his breath when she touched him boldly.

"Ysmaine, we should not. The child!"

"There are other pleasures we can pursue, sir." She closed her hand around his strength and felt him inhale sharply. "My mother had a number of suggestions, for just such a situation as this."

"She knew?"

"She hoped," Ysmaine confirmed and caressed him more boldly.

"God in Heaven," Gaston whispered, his fingers sliding into her hair. He fell back against the pillows with a gasp of pleasure that made Ysmaine smile, then surrendered to her touch.

The wind rose when Gaston's party had disappeared from view, ruffling the surface of the river and making the boughs of the trees bend beneath its assault. It was an unnatural wind, one that made the forest sound full of whispering specters, and it drove the clouds across the darkening sky at a brisk pace.

There was a storm coming, unless Duncan missed his guess.

He disliked that he could hear little of his surroundings, for the branches of the trees cracked against each other and creaked in the wind. The leaves rustled. The undergrowth seemed to have come alive. He guessed that small creatures sought cover from the pending storm and marched more quickly toward the village.

Perhaps that was why he did not anticipate the stone.

Duncan saw it from the periphery of his vision, thought it a blowing leaf, then jumped when he realized his error. It struck Caledon square in the rump, hard enough that the steed jumped and snorted.

Duncan looked back but could see little for the wind blew from that direction, its cold fingers stretching out of the north.

The destrier might have steadied, but two more stones were lobbed at him, and the steed would have none of it. Caledon shied and whinnied, snapped the reins from Duncan's hand, and galloped for the village. The gates could barely be discerned at this distance, but Duncan could see the sentry's lantern.

Evidently, Caledon saw it as well. The beast fled directly toward the light.

Duncan heard another steed cantering closer and braced himself for attack. He pivoted and saw the silhouette of the horse drawing near. The wind drove dust and leaves at him, obscuring his vision. He guessed that it was a palfrey with a man bent low in its saddle. The creature fought the bit as it trotted toward him with determination.

"You will not escape me this time, Donnchadh mac Domnall," a man cried in Gaelic, the threat in his words making the hair prickle on Duncan's flesh.

That he should call Duncan by that name made all matters clear.

Duncan's past *had* returned to haunt him, and if this man was the first to assault him, he would not be the last.

But the voice did not come from precisely the right direction. It seemed to emanate from the shadowed forest to the right of the horse. Was it a trick of the wind? The horse bore down upon him, something glinting in the midst of the shadow on its back. A knife? Duncan could not imagine anything else. He held his ground until the beast drew near, then as soon as it was alongside him, stepped back crisply and struck at the rider.

The horse passed him by without stopping. The bundle fell from its saddle, revealing itself to be no more than a cloak wrapped around brush. The pin on the cloak had been what glimmered in the light.

Duncan bent to study it, not truly surprised to see it again. Not now that he had heard the Gaelic words. He reached to claim it, as he surely was expected to do, the wind making his plaid blow around him. He froze when he felt a knife blade at his back.

He smiled, knowing his expression could not be seen, knowing that he was not the only one who proved himself to be predictable.

"I had hoped to take you in the forest of Valeroy," the man behind him declared. "I watched you and your wench. I would have liked to have let you watch me with her."

Duncan's blood went cold, but he was not yet prepared to be provoked. He savored the heat of his fury, biding the time it could be released.

No man would ever violate his Radegunde.

"I doubt you could have pleased her," he said mildly.

The man scoffed, as Duncan expected. "I doubt I should have cared," he said and laughed aloud. "I would have ripped her asunder, Donnchadh, just to see your reaction. Perhaps she would have begged for mercy. Perhaps I would have let you kill her in the end."

His triumphant laugh had only begun when Duncan spun and smashed his fist into the man's nose. The attacker staggered backward, blood flowing copiously from his left nostril. His eyes lit with fury and he lunged at Duncan.

Who ducked, then drove his knife upward. It was only when the blade had sunk into his attacker's belly that Duncan realized his move was like that of Gaston with the boar.

The boar, in Duncan's view, was a more noble adversary.

His attacker gasped and stumbled, but Duncan seized the man's knife out of his grip and cast it into the darkness. It clattered to the ground some distance away and could not be seen. The attacker reached for Duncan's blade, still embedded in his own belly, but Duncan caught the man's head in his hands and slammed it hard against a nearby tree. The man staggered, and Duncan pinned him to the tree with one hand around his throat.

The man struggled and Duncan squeezed until his eyes bulged and he stilled. His face was red, his breath came quickly and his blood flowed like a river.

"Who are you?"

"Does it matter?"

Duncan punched him with his left fist and felt a tooth break free. The man's lip was cracked and bleeding when Duncan repeated his question.

The man sagged in his grip, licked his lips, and glared at Duncan just before he raised his knee. Duncan was prepared for the move, given that glare, and kicked the other man's feet out from beneath him. He seized his knife, pulling it from the wound, and his opponent's blood flowed more freely. When the man might have battled him anew, Duncan touched the blade to that man's throat.

"Your name," he repeated with more patience than he felt.

The other man tried to spit to show his disdain, but the spittle dribbled on his chin. "Murdoch."

"And why did my father send you?"

Murdoch scoffed again, but blood flowed from his mouth. "Why do you think? To make conversation? To see how you fare?" He spat with more success this time, hatred in his eyes.

"Domnall might have been the father I never had. You abandoned him for you did not know his worth. I would have served him better as a son."

"I abandoned him because I knew his worth with great precision," Duncan corrected. "Why now?"

"What makes you think I would betray his trust?"

"I would have expected him to send Adam," Duncan said, referring to his older brother. "Or for Adam to have taken the task himself."

"Adam is dead!" Murdoch declared, emotion getting the better of discretion.

"How? When?"

"If you served your father, you would know!"

"Perhaps I would be dead, as well. Dispatched by my father on some quest that could only fail, in pursuit of a dream best abandoned." Duncan felt remorse that his brother was lost but not surprise. Adam had always believed in their father's folly.

Murdoch's eyes lit with fury. "Domnall is right. You do not deserve to be his son! The blood of kings courses through your veins, but you would cast away all and bend your knee in service to whoever would see your belly filled. You are *vermin*. You are unworthy of your father's name and family legacy."

"And you become tedious," Duncan concluded. "You may tell me what you know and I will see that you have aid. Or you may die now, with my assistance." He moved the knife against Murdoch's throat, letting him feel the cold edge of the blade. He felt Murdoch's heart skip and for a moment hoped that he would not have to do what he would have preferred left undone.

Then Murdoch's eyes narrowed in defiance, and he clearly mustered his spittle for his last declaration.

He never made it. Duncan slit Murdoch's throat cleanly and cast his corpse aside with disgust. How many would die in pursuit of this dream? And even if his father's dream was achieved, how could the victory be held? It was madness, ambition run amok, and could not come to any good end.

He had said as much years before, his last words to his father.

Domnall had despised Gwyneth and would have thought little

of Radegunde. He would not have deemed Radegunde to be any more worthy than Gwyneth, who he'd once said was unworthy of being a whore in his court. Duncan knew the merit of both women better.

An old fury ignited deep within him, and he knew that he would have to see this matter concluded himself.

Duncan wiped his blade upon Murdoch's plaid, disliking what he had done but knowing he had had little choice. He fetched the pin and put it in his purse, not in the least bit glad to see it again. He emptied Murdoch's purse, finding little of value in it, but took what was there. He cast the purse into the forest, as if the mercenary had been robbed by brigands. The cloak was not sufficiently fine to keep, so he cast it into the undergrowth as well.

He looked down at the dead man for a moment, dreading the task, then relieved him of his garments. Duncan fingered every hem and checked every lining, but the man carried naught else that could provide any information about his origins.

That Murdoch thought Duncan's father a worthy man said all, in truth, that Duncan needed to know. He ran a hand through his hair, hating that the past pursued him in this moment, then turned to follow the horses. Even Murdoch's steed had made for the village and was out of view. The wind tugged at Duncan's cloak as he marched onward, sorting through his memories.

One thing was certain: if his father was bent upon murder, then Murdoch was but the first who would be sent to hunt Domnall's second son. For all Duncan knew, there were more such assassins already in pursuit of him. His future would not be secure until he and his father came to terms.

Duncan doubted that would be achieved without bloodshed.

Worse, the root of the matter was that he could not take Radegunde to Scotland until this old feud was resolved.

Duncan's stallion had returned to the village gates, reins trailing, by the time Radegunde arrived there. She peered into the shadows along the road, but could not discern any sign of Duncan himself.

"Vexing man," she muttered, crossing her arms across her chest as if that would keep her concern in check. The porter reminded her that the gates would be locked at sunset, and she spared a glance at the setting sun. It dropped all too rapidly toward the horizon.

The clatter of hooves made her heart jump, but it was another steed with an empty saddle. A palfrey. Smaller and less fine.

Radegunde felt as if a cold hand had locked around her heart. Duncan was not alone.

"They said one warrior meant to walk his horse back," the porter said, his brow furrowed. "Not two." He came to stand beside her, peering down the empty road. He, too, looked between road and sky. "I should not send out a runner, not so late as this," he said to her, his tone apologetic. "We could lose more than one man."

"Is the road so dangerous?"

"Aye, in these times, the forests are thick with brigands, and they, like other predators, hunt at night."

Radegunde nodded understanding. Her pounding heart sounded too loud to her own ears. Her palms were damp. Not Duncan. He could not be taken from her now, not so soon as this.

But the road remained stubbornly empty.

The sun sank ever lower.

The shadows drew long.

When the last glimmer of sunlight dipped below the horizon, the porter shook his head. "I am sorry," he said to Radegunde, then closed the portal against the night. The sound of the key in the lock might have been a death knell, and Radegunde fought against her tears.

What had happened to Duncan?

She examined his steed, making an excuse to linger by the gate. The horse was not injured, merely spooked and already it calmed. She supposed that was a good sign, but wondered what it had witnessed. The other horse was of the ilk that one might buy in a market. It was reasonably healthy and its trap was more adequate than fine. She supposed she would take them both back to the stables.

The porter was yet watching the road from his sentry point and cleared his throat. "Do you know him?" he asked Radegunde, and she flew to his side to peer through the portcullis.

To her relief, a man was striding across the bridge with a grim purpose that was all too familiar. He wore a leather hauberk and his chemise glowed white in the light cast by the lantern atop the gate. He also wore a plaid, wrapped around his hips and belted, with the end cast over his shoulder.

Radegunde bit her lip, for his legs were most fine.

"Aye," she said to the porter. "Aye, it is the lost rider and he is hale!"

"And his name?"

Radegunde told him.

The porter smiled at her and shouted. "Hoy there! Who comes to these gates?"

"Duncan MacDonald I am," he replied, and Radegunde was filled with joy. "And I am a companion of Lord Gaston of Châmont-sur-Maine."

"And welcome you are," the porter said and unlocked the gate.

Duncan thanked the man and hastened through the portal, his expression somber. He looked hale, which was another relief, and his eyes lit with a pleasure that sent heat coursing through her when he spied Radegunde.

"You, sir, must cease this habit of sending your steed home without you," she said, knowing she sounded cross in her relief. "I tire of the trick."

"You were with me last time."

"Still. You must cease this ploy."

Duncan grinned and caught her in his arms, then kissed her quickly. "I had need of a good walk, 'twas no more than that."

She fingered his chemise and discovered the blood on his sleeve to be fresh. "Liar," she charged beneath her breath.

"Not mine," he replied in kind, his tone grim. She knew from the glint in his eyes that the tale was not one to be shared with others.

"I am glad you are returned, even if you cannot control your horse," she teased and the porter chuckled. She laid her head upon Duncan's shoulder with relief. She placed her hand over his heart, savoring its steady rhythm beneath her palm.

Duncan held her tightly, even as he raised his voice to the porter. "I saw that there is a dead mercenary back there, in the shadow of the forest." He turned and indicated a tree that rose about the canopy of the others. "His corpse is behind that large old oak, though it is hard to be certain how long he has been there."

"Perhaps that is his horse," the porter said, indicating the other steed.

"Perhaps. I tell you the location now while I remember the site, in case Lord Gaston wishes to have him collected on the morrow and given a Christian burial."

"I will remember the spot," the porter said. "Though there may be little left of him by morning." He nodded toward the forest and Radegunde heard a wolf howl.

"Like to like," Duncan murmured for her ears alone.

"You are certain you know naught of his demise?" the porter asked.

Duncan shook his head. "He was dead when I spied him. Perhaps there are other villains in these woods."

"Indeed, there are many in these times," the porter agreed. "How curious that his horse arrived after yours, if this is his horse."

"Perhaps it was wandering," Radegunde suggested. "And followed the destrier."

The porter laughed again. "Aye, there is an explanation. It would not be the first mare to follow a stallion, to be sure." Apparently reassured by this explanation, he returned to his task of securing the gates for the night.

Duncan escorted Radegunde to his steed. He lifted her into the saddle with care, then took the reins, his horse nuzzling his hair with affection. "Aye, you want only a brush and some oats from me, you old rogue," he teased the beast and the porter laughed.

"In future, sir, be aware that on the March, we like all portals secured by sunset."

"I thank you for admitting me," Duncan said.

The village porter gestured to Radegunde. "'Twas the maiden, sir. I do not think she would have suffered it to be otherwise. Had she not recognized you and vouched for you, though, you would have spent the night on the other side."

They all laughed together and Duncan led Caledon toward the stables. The gate was audibly locked behind them. "Tell me," he invited, his voice low.

"Leila had a bath in my lady's chamber, and we kept your bag there. She has taken it into her custody and Bartholomew guards the portal. My lord Gaston is there with Lady Ysmaine until the evening meal." She watched him from behind, relieved that he showed no sign of injury.

"A bath. There is a fitting temptation after this day," he replied, then answered her query. "I reached them just as Gaston raised a gloved hand to his lips. Millard declared your warning to be folly, but Lord Amaury claimed the gloves. He means to ask your mother's counsel, but Millard is not pleased."

"Perhaps he will see fit to leave," Radegunde said tartly and Duncan chuckled.

"We should be so fortunate. Clearly, it will take more than this day's events to see him dispatched."

"But all ended well for Lord Gaston, thanks to your swift ride."

"And your quick thinking."

"I am glad," Radegunde admitted. Relief made her aware of her weariness. It had been a long day and one filled with trials. It also made her wish to celebrate Duncan's return in private.

"Would it dismay you if I confessed I had no taste for a meal in the hall this night?" Duncan asked, a teasing tone in his voice that prompted her to study him anew. He cast her a sparkling glance and she wondered whether he had read her thoughts. "I confess, lass, that my appetite follows another path."

"You did say you desired a bath," she teased in return and he chuckled.

"A bath and an evening with you," he confessed. "There is naught like a taste of mortality to make me want reassurance that I yet live, Radegunde."

"I share your view in that, to be sure." Radegunde smiled at him. "And I would reassure myself that you tell the truth in this, Duncan MacDonald."

"How so?"

"I mean to aid in that bath and inspect you thoroughly for injuries. Have you so much as a scratch that you have not mentioned to me, you shall face a reckoning."

He turned to face her with a grin. "I am afeared indeed."

"And so you should be. This could take all the night."

"Not all the night, lass," Duncan murmured so the ostler would not hear. "We shall have other deeds to fill the hours in addition to your inspection."

Radegunde smiled, for she could not wait.

CHAPTER SIXTEEN

o Duncan's relief, there was a chamber set aside for him in the stables. It was smaller even than the one had been in Valeroy, but he was glad of it. Fergus glanced up at their arrival and a smile of relief touched his lips, driving away the concern that had darkened his brow. Duncan hoped that all the darkness the knight had seen in the future was now dispelled.

He assumed that Fergus had arranged for the chamber. Laurent brought Duncan's saddlebag into the room, and it seemed to Duncan that the squire and Radegunde exchanged a conspiratorial glance, but then the portal was closed behind Laurent and Radegunde cast herself into Duncan's arms. She flattened him against the wall and caught his face in her hands, kissing him with an ardor that set him aflame.

When she kissed him like this, showing all her passion, Duncan could not resist her. There was no thought of temperance or of progressing slowly, certainly not of savoring. There was only Radegunde, sweet and hot and vital, her tongue between his teeth and her fingers on his belt buckle. She set his belt aside and he unknotted her girdle, then loosened the laces on her kirtle. She

flung off the garment with an abandon that made him smile, then
returned to kiss him anew.

"Quickly this time, Duncan," she murmured against his lips, her
eyes dancing with the beguiling light that drove him wild. "Hard
and fast."

Duncan could not decline such an invitation. He caught her in
his arms and made for the pallet, dropping to it so she tumbled
atop him. She laughed merrily and he slid his hands beneath her
chemise, then cast it aside. He ran his hands over her when she
was perched atop him in only her stockings. She sat up and
unbraided her hair, taking her time so that he could look upon her
perfection. He reached up and cupped her breasts in his hands,
and she threw back her head with pleasure as he teased her nipples
to tight peaks.

Radegunde moaned, then divested him of his plaid more
quickly than he could have expected. She caught his strength in her
hands, and he was the one who moaned then.

"I have need of a bath, Radegunde."

"As do I, but we will soon have need of another." She sat atop
him, her eyes twinkling as she eased his strength against her slick
heat. "Let us fetch the water once instead of twice," she said.

"Bold wench," he teased. "I have not even shed my chemise."

"And you need not, not this time."

Duncan had no chance to reply for she took him within her in
one bold move that left them both gasping. His hands locked upon
her waist and he tried to slow his racing heart. "Radegunde!"

She rolled her hips, laughing when he groaned. She lay then
upon his chest, still straddling him and holding him fast inside her.
"I believe you have survived this day, Duncan," she teased in a
mischievous whisper.

"Believe?" he echoed. "It seems I must remove all doubt from
your thoughts." Radegunde laughed but then was silenced when
Duncan captured her mouth with his. He rolled her to her back,
loving how she locked her legs around him, savoring the sweet
heat of her as he buried himself inside her.

He moved slowly then, ensuring that he rubbed against the
tender nub of her. She gasped and he kissed her again, lacing his

fingers with hers and holding her hands over her head. He moved with deliberation, driving them both to greater heights, savoring the shivers that ran over her flesh. He watched her flush. He saw her eyes sparkle. He swallowed the sound of her moan of pleasure. She tore her lips from his and whispered his name, the sight of her pleasure redoubling his passion again.

Their gazes locked, their breath coming quickly. She writhed beneath him and whispered his name again, rubbing herself against him, so warm and welcoming that Duncan could think of no finer place to be. He eased his hand between them and caressed her with a roughened fingertip, watching her back arch and feeling her fingernails dig into his shoulders.

He suddenly felt her heat clench around him, drawing him deeper, making a claim of her own, then she cried out with a pleasure that could not be mistaken for anything else. The feel of her drove Duncan to his release, more quickly and more forcibly than he could have expected, and he roared with the fury of it.

Radegunde was his woman.

His mate.

His love.

And he would defend her forever. He would give his own life for her, without hesitation. He would protect her and he would love her and possess her for all the days of his life.

Nay, for all eternity.

Radegunde was a little unsteady on her feet when finally she left the chamber in the stables. She was also a bit more disheveled than was her wont, but filled with such happiness that she could scarce care. Duncan had retied her girdle and braided her hair, ensuring that she had both shoes on her feet before she left their little haven. Her heart was glowing, and the heat in Duncan's eyes had a way of making her want to sing.

If not return immediately to his bed. Thrice they had loved, each time more slowly than the time before. Spent and starving, they abandoned the pleasures of the bed for more practical considerations. Duncan was to gather a bath for them. Radegunde would fetch a meal.

The stables and bailey were quiet, for most had gone to the hall for the evening meal. Leila was yet in the stables and at a glance from Radegunde, she took up a sentry position outside Duncan's chamber. The squire appeared to doze, but Radegunde knew Leila would ensure that Duncan's saddlebag remained untouched. As Radegunde entered the bailey, she could hear music from the hall and guessed that there were minstrels, and that most lingered to enjoy the entertainment.

She smiled at the conviction that she would enjoy her own entertainment in Duncan's small chamber.

It was in the kitchens that Radegunde found the moment she sought.

It was yet busy in that part of the keep, for there was much to be cleaned from preparations for the evening meal and a good measure of gossip to be shared. Even those who did not usually labor in the kitchens were gathered there, and the cook was disgruntled to find them so oft in his way. Radegunde imagined that he had much to see done for the feast two days hence and that the sight of so many lounging while he labored was not welcome. Indeed, the laziest of Lady Azalaïs' maids was leaning against a heavy table, picking at a platter of meat that had evidently been collected from the great hall. She surveyed Radegunde with a smirk that did little to redeem Radegunde's view of her.

Radegunde made her request of the cook, who dispatched a small boy for a pot with a lid. There was a pot of soup over the fire and it smelled very fine. "A clear soup of duck stock," the cook said with a satisfied nod. "I did not think there would be much left of it after this day's hunt, but there is yet plenty." He stirred the steaming broth, ordering the boy to fetch bread for Radegunde. "You and your companion did well this day to warn our new lord, I hear."

"If he was truly in peril and you did not merely seek to turn him against us all," the maid added archly.

"I would never do such a deed," Radegunde said with a mildness she did not feel. "And truly it is better to be cautious."

"I suppose the daughter of a wise woman would know much of poison and its administration," the maid said but Radegunde ignored her.

"Lord Gaston survived so many years in Outremer," the cook said. "That is no mean feat. He is either robust, fortunate, or both."

Radegunde smiled for the cook as she thanked him. "Both, I believe."

"I am glad he is returned," contributed the sauce maker. "He reminds me of the best of his father and his brother, which is a fine combination."

"But he is not, perhaps, so fortunate in his choice of bride," the maid interjected. She plucked a chunk of meat from the sauce in the platter with her fingertips, apparently speaking idly but Radegunde recognized that she was one who liked to make trouble.

"I cannot think what you mean," Radegunde said. "My lady is both lovely and nobly born, and a fitting match for my lord Gaston."

The maid's brows rose. "If inclined to bury her husbands." She wagged that finger at Radegunde, who realized that every soul in the kitchens was listening. "I remember why the oldest daughter of Valeroy departed on pilgrimage. Twice widowed, she was, and in rapid succession. Yet here she is, returned with a new spouse, her third in so many years, perhaps the wealthiest of them all. No sooner does he cross the threshold of his inheritance and claim it for his own, than his life apparently falls into peril." She took a bite of the apple, her gaze knowing. "It does not take a wise man to note the similarity." She raised her brows. "And the daughter of a wise woman is her most intimate servant. I fear our new lady may have a scheme."

Radegunde bit her tongue, for she did not wish to make more enemies in this hall than she already had in seeing the solar properly cleaned. She was striving to think how she might turn the conversation to her advantage and reveal the existence of the book in a casual manner. "You are Lady Azalaïs' maid, are you not? I do not believe I heard your name."

"Benedicta," the maid said tartly. "And before you ask, I have served in this hall since I was ten years old. I remember Lord

Gaston's departure." She ate another piece of meat, then smiled. "And I remember Lady Eudaline well. She would not have approved of this match, to be sure. Doubtless your lady anticipated as much and chose to wed early to prevent any interference from Lord Gaston's kin."

"Doubtless not," Radegunde replied crisply. "I journeyed to Outremer with my lady, and we were beset by thieves." Every soul in the kitchen turned to listen, not troubling to hide their interest. "By the time we reached Jerusalem, I had fallen ill with fever, and we had no coin. My lady went daily to pray, and it was there, in the Church of the Holy Sepulchre, that my lord Gaston first saw her. He gave her a coin, as alms, to take her measure, and was well pleased when she insisted on spending it on a cure from an apothecary for me instead of food for herself. He saw us both fed, with a fine broth, much like this, and having taken the lady's measure, he chose to wed her."

"Indeed," murmured the cook, both he and his helpers clearly enthralled by the tale.

"Indeed," Radegunde said. "And it was Lord Gaston who knew that the holy city would be besieged. He intended to see us safely away, and so he wedded my lady in the chapel of the Templars in Jerusalem. We rode out that very day. He defended us from bandits at Acre, choosing to stand alone while we escaped to the port, and he scarce managed to make the last ship with us. My lady and I are indebted to Lord Gaston many times over for ensuring our welfare and our safe return. We neither of us would see him threatened much less imperiled."

"Such adventures!" the cook exclaimed, then ladled the soup into the pot.

"Aye," Radegunde said with a smile.

"But Lady Eudaline still might have objected to the match," insisted the maid.

Radegunde spared the woman a glance. "Aye, well she might have. That was why my lady dispatched me to visit Lady Eudaline when we were at Valeroy, for she felt it fitting that she send greetings to her husband's mother."

"You visited Lady Eudaline?" Benedicta asked sharply.

"I did."

"How did you find her?"

"Hale and most fierce. I found myself daunted by her, to be sure."

The maid and the sauce maker chuckled in unison. "That would be the lady," he said with evident approval. "There are days I miss her well."

Benedicta's eyes narrowed. "And what message did she send to her new daughter?"

Radegunde smiled. "More than a message—she entrusted me with a gift for Lady Ysmaine. A small book most richly ornamented and wrapped in silk. My lady was most pleased by it and the goodwill it represented, as well as relieved that Lord Gaston's mother approved of her son's match."

"How could she know as much?"

"Lady Eudaline had written the full history of Châmont-sur-Maine in the margins of the book, as well as all the secrets that she deemed it important for my lady to know before she took residence in this hall."

There was a moment of tense silence following this confession.

"Secrets?" Benedicta echoed.

"What does it say?" the cook asked.

"I do not know," Radegunde lied. "I cannot read, but my lady was most enthralled. She remained awake all that first night, reading every line and then again. She has insisted that I secure it in her most doughty trunk that she not lose it."

Radegunde knew she did not imagine the glance that passed around the kitchen.

"I should have thought it would have been her husband who would keep her awake all the night," Benedicta jested, but her expression was sly. "Though I hear they argue overmuch in their chambers this pair, and that he only comes to her to deliver the marital debt that he might have a son with all haste."

Radegunde did not have to feign her blush. "I fear the discord between them is due to my choice. I pledged a handfast to a warrior in the service of my Lord Gaston's companion and Lord Gaston believes it unfitting."

"A handfast?" echoed the cook.

"A pledge of loyalty that endures for a year and a day," Benedicta supplied tartly. "I cannot blame Lord Gaston for finding fault with this pagan ritual. Why do you not exchange vows before a priest?"

"It is the way of Duncan's people."

Benedicta snorted. "And your lady takes your side in this?"

Radegunde straightened. "My lady Ysmaine defends my right to choose. She has been most good to me and would see me happy."

Benedicta's brows rose. "If you sow dissent between herself and her wealthy husband, you might be the next to die in her company."

"That is unseemly," the cook charged. "You cannot speak thus of the lady of the keep!"

Benedicta rose to her feet. "I will not be the sole one to speak thus if there is an untimely death in this hall, upon that you can rely."

As much as Radegunde disliked that notion, she feared there was truth in it. She excused herself and hastened back to the stables with the meal for herself and Duncan.

She had planted the seed and must keep a vigilant eye upon Lady Eudaline's book.

It was all too easy to recall Lord Gaston's conviction that an old lock, like the one upon the door to the solar, could have any number of keys—which meant that no matter how many he and Bartholomew gathered, there might be yet another.

Duncan had fetched several pails of water as well as a lantern by the time Radegunde had returned. He was thinking of the future and the influence of this day's events upon it. That he was hunted had to change his plans, though he did not know how to begin to explain to Radegunde. He had thought his family so irrelevant to his life for so long that it was a shock to learn otherwise.

His own father. Would she believe him?

She entered the chamber and fixed him with a look. "You are thoughtful."

"Aye."

"Because you mean to leave me here and fear to tell me so." She spoke with such confidence that he blinked in surprise.

"We knew all along that I should return home with Fergus while you remained with your lady."

"I had considered leaving my lady's service to accompany you, now that we have a handfast."

"Nay, Radegunde. You cannot do this."

"Whyever not?" Radegunde propped her hands upon her hips, and Duncan knew that look of resolve. "We are bound together by your own tradition…"

"You will be safe here. I cannot guarantee that will be the case if you accompany us to Killairic."

"Safe," Radegunde scoffed. "My mother would laugh that you believe a keep perched on the Breton March to be a safe haven."

Duncan returned to her side, taking her hand in his. "Yet it is safer than where I travel."

"Surely the home of Fergus and his father is well defended."

He saw, though, that she knew that was not his destination. "I mean only to accompany Fergus home, then ask his father to release me from his service. This man's presence was no accident. I am hunted and I must see the matter resolved."

"But you felled your attacker. The matter *is* resolved!"

Duncan shook his head, to her obvious dismay. "He was only the first. Unless I silence the one who sent him, he will not be the last." He frowned even as he caressed her hand. "There will be another to take his place, and another and another, until this matter is laid to rest. It is the way of it."

"What has that matter to do with you?" She gestured to the saddlebag but Duncan shook his head.

"Nay, it is my own past that haunts my footsteps." He eased down to the pallet beside her, holding her close against his side. "Let us eat while I tell you about my family." He frowned. "It is not a noble tale, but it is true. It has that merit, at least."

Radegunde studied him for a moment, then served the soup into a bowl and offered him a piece of bread.

"You first," he said and she smiled at his gallantry as she began to eat. She insisted he take a piece of the bread, which was yet warm, but Duncan had little appetite. "In the realms of England and France, the succession of the throne is preferred to fall to the oldest son of the king, born by his legitimate wife," he began. "But this is only one way of defining the succession. In other corners of the world, the blood is of import, whether a man carries it by dint of his mother or his father. The oldest son may not be the one most fit to rule."

"And marriages may not be made the same way," Radegunde contributed. "I should think that in Scotland, a man could have many children by many women."

"So a man can in many places, but you are right. It is the Gaelic way to give greater consideration to the line of the mother than is commonly done in England and France. We also cannot indulge in the luxury of weak kings or boy kings. When the borders are beset by Vikings and others come to pillage, when chieftains battle against each other, each insisting he should be king of all, the leader of any group of people must be a warrior and a proven one. So it is amongst the Gaels that the best man should be king, not simply the oldest son of the current king."

"This makes good sense."

"More than a hundred years ago, in Scotland, there was a king," Duncan continued. "His name was Mael Coluim, or Malcolm, and he was heralded Malcolm II, King of Scotland, for his lineage drew from Kenneth Alpin, of the oldest line of kings. Though he was a clever man and a good king, he had no sons, but three daughters."

"Now there is a conundrum," Radegunde jested.

"Perhaps not in some times and places, but Malcolm was known for his wits as well as his abilities in battle. He knew that he could not pass the suzerainty of his kingdom to a daughter, or even to the husband of a daughter, not if he wished the kings of England to consider his heir to be fitting. Malcolm saw that the ways of the south would come north, and he was determined to be at the fore of change, the better to be King of all Scotland."

"Then the daughters were a bane to him."

"They might have been to another man, but Malcolm was not one to lose any advantage. He married his daughters to other kings to see his borders more secure. The oldest was wed to the Thane of the Isles, the son and heir of a king to Malcolm's west. The youngest was wed to the Earl of Orkney, a king in the distant north. And the middle daughter was wed to the King of Mormaerdom, a king upon his very borders to the north."

"It seems a sound strategy."

"And because he wished for the son of one of his daughters to ultimately claim his own throne, he gave each daughter a golden pin. These were round in the Roman style, and the cloth was caught with a matching pin shaped like a dagger. Each pin was set with gemstones. The one with garnets was given to the daughter who married into the royal family of the Isles. The one with amber was bestowed upon the daughter who married into the family at Orkney. The one with amethysts was surrendered to the daughter who married into the house of the Mormaer. His notion was that they should pass the token through their family, and that it would signify the king born of their line."

"I expect there were battles over such gems."

"Aye, there were. When Malcolm died, the throne passed to his grandson Duncan, son of the oldest daughter, who was crowned wearing the pin of gold and garnet on his cloak. That was when the dispute began. The first man to challenge Duncan was of the line of Mormaer. His name was Mac Bethad and he killed within his own family to make the gem of amethyst and gold his own. Once it was pinned upon his cloak, he turned his gaze to the throne Malcolm had called his own and his cousin who sat upon it."

Radegunde shuddered.

"He killed his cousin and claimed the throne that he insisted was rightly his own."

"He had two of the pins, then."

"Nay, he did not, for his cousin's wife was a woman of much cunning. She fled to safety in other realms with her sons, taking the garnet and gold pin with her. She placed one son in Orkney and one in the court of the western Isles."

"They must have had kin in those two courts, born of Malcolm's other two daughters," Radegunde said.

"Exactly. In 1057, Duncan's sons were of age. One donned the pin of gold and garnets and killed Mac Bethad, taking vengeance for the murder of his father. Mac Bethad's son, Lulach, donned his pin and took the rulership, but the returned son killed him as well. He was crowned as Malcolm III in his time, the gold and garnet pin upon his cloak."

"It is not only the Bretons who need more names," she teased and Duncan smiled.

"Evidently not."

"The amethyst pin was lost?"

"It was feared to be so, but in truth, it was taken back to Mormaer, where plans were made to make a challenge for the throne again."

"The king with the gold and garnet pin must have suspected this."

"He did. They all did, father and son, one after the other. It was a shadow upon their reign, the possibility that another contender for the throne might appear."

"Or conquer them."

"Aye. The succession from Malcolm II continued through this line to David I, who sought to end the strife and ensure his seat upon the throne. He saw much of merit in the ways of the south and brought more of them to Scotland. In 1130, he faced a challenge from Angus of Mormaer, the bearer of the gold and amethyst pin and defeated him soundly. Angus was killed and the lands of Mormaer were brought under the command of the throne and renamed Moray. The pin, however, evaded capture."

"And what of the amber and gold one?"

"In 1151, King Eystein II of Norway captured the earl appointed by David and demanded he pay fealty to Norway. The pin was surrendered to him, and later when David treated with Eystein, it was given to David as a guarantee of good faith."

"And so only the amethyst and gold pin remained outstanding?" Radegunde asked.

Duncan nodded. "I had thought it would be lost by now, due to my father's folly, but it seems I have been the fool. I underestimated his lust for power."

Radegunde sat up with a frown. "I do not understand."

Duncan produced the pin he had taken from Murdoch and held

it on the flat of his hand. It was round, of the same shape as Malcolm's gift, but without gems.

"That is not gold." Radegunde recoiled from it a bit. "It does not even look like silver."

"It is not. It is merely tin, a replica of the pin itself. It is a taunt, wrought to glimmer and draw my eye so that I might be taken unawares."

Radegunde gasped in outrage. "Who would do such a thing?"

"He who hunts me. I recognized it immediately for what it was and braced myself, which is why I was not killed this night."

"You know this villain well enough to guess his intent," Radegunde whispered.

Duncan nodded and locked his gaze with hers. "My father holds the amethyst and gold pin."

She blinked but said naught.

"I left my home in Moray twenty years ago, Radegunde, because I sickened of the fighting. There was no honor in it and no end in sight. In a hundred and fifty years, claimants to the throne have been bred far and wide. It would take a slaughter to eliminate them all, and I chose instead to walk away, to be merely a man."

"To love your wife," she said gently.

Duncan averted his gaze. "It was too late for that," he admitted quietly.

"Who was this man who stalked you? I thought you did not recognize the man in the woods."

"I did not. He is a man in the service of my father. He told me his name. I did not know it or him. It is of little import. He was sent to kill me, to perpetuate this madness, at my father's behest."

"Why would he need to see you dead if he already holds the pin?"

"I have two brothers," Duncan told her then realized his error. "Nay, that is no longer true. I *had* two brothers, one older, one younger. This scoundrel told me that Adam, the older, is dead." He paused for a moment.

"I am sorry."

"There was no great love between us, Radegunde, for he sipped of the cup of my father's ambition. I do not doubt that he died in some incident of his own making. I regret his death, but truly, the sole surprise is that it took so long for him to find his end."

"And the younger?"

"My father's favored son. Guthred is more than ten years my junior, and this pin tells me that he is my father's choice." He snapped it in half within his hand, then heard his voice harden. "I will not suffer it, Radegunde. I will not live the rest of my life hunted, by one assailant after another."

She folded her arms across her chest and glared at him, clearly unconvinced that she had no role in his quest. "So you will ride for Scotland and put yourself in peril?"

"I have no choice but to do as much." He took her hand in his. "Understand that I leave you behind for your own protection."

She exhaled mightily and he knew this battle was not yet won. "Understand that I am not so convinced that my presence is of such little merit. You might well have need of one to guard your back."

"Not you. I will not risk your welfare." He tried to cajole her, knowing it would not be readily done. "Your lady has need of you. Stay with her until Fergus celebrates his nuptials and they ride north to share his joy."

"They may not ride north, not if he is wedded before May," she said stubbornly. She was disappointed and he knew it. He was disappointed as well, but he could not be responsible for her demise.

He would not be able to bear the guilt and the loss.

"Then I will return for you, but I will not take you into peril, Radegunde." He held her gaze, certain his resolve was clear. "You will not change my thinking on this."

"Wretchedly stubborn man," she said, but he could not take insult when he saw the twinkle light her dark eyes. "When will you leave?" She ladled him a bowl of soup, her expression filled with challenge.

"Not soon, I hope. Bartholomew means to journey north with us, so we cannot depart before he is dubbed and gains his spurs."

"Such an event requires preparation."

"Indeed, it does."

Radegunde sat back, her expression triumphant. "Then it appears, sir, that I have time to try to change your mind."

Duncan could not help but smile. "Indeed."

"Or failing that, to conceive your son."

He sputtered on his soup.

Radegunde was watching him, her eyes shining. "That should bring you back to me with all haste."

"Do you doubt that I will return?"

She did not reply but pursed her lips. "Perhaps it is you who must take advantage of the time allotted to us to convince me of your ardor," she teased, her manner so provocative that Duncan could not resist her. He drained the bowl of soup, for it was cool, and set it aside, then caught the ends of her girdle in his hands and tugged her toward him.

"Come here, Radegunde," he murmured, his lips close to hers. "You have need of a bath and a lesson you will not soon forget."

Claire Delacroix

254

MONDAY, SEPTEMBER 14, 1187

*Feast Day of Saint Cornelius
and Saint Cyprianus*

CHAPTER SEVENTEEN

he next two days passed in uproar. There was so much to be done, and Radegunde caught herself yawning more than once. Indeed, she and Duncan loved late every night and oft again in the morning. There was no doubting his ardor.

There was also no doubting his resolve.

Radegunde did not like the notion of Duncan riding out while his father's men yet hunted him, but she had time to argue the matter. Lord Gaston had resolved upon December the sixth for Bartholomew's knighting, which was months away yet.

Who knew what might transpire in that time?

Her more immediate concern was that Lady Ysmaine was now ill in the mornings. She made a habit of rising early to tend her lady, taking her goat's milk from the kitchens before many were awake. If the cook understood why she did as much, he had the discretion to say naught about it.

On this day, Radegunde saw her lady dressed and escorted her down to the board. She did not trust the lady to herself on the stairs in her condition, and Lord Gaston was in the bailey. Indeed, the hall itself seemed to be empty. She hastened back up the stairs to straighten the bed covers before returning to her lady's side—for Lady Ysmaine might need to take a nap—and unlocked the portal to smell a snuffed candle.

They had burned no candles this morn.

She had locked the door behind them. She had been gone only moments.

But Radegunde already knew what she would discover. She locked the door again then crossed the solar, seeing immediately that the clasp on the largest and finest trunk was not exactly as it had been. She opened the lid, bracing herself for the truth.

She was not truly surprised that the book from Lady Eudaline was gone.

The sole question was who had taken it.

Radegunde sat down for a moment, for her heart had clenched in fear of how they might discover that truth.

TUESDAY, SEPTEMBER 15, 1187

*Feast Day of Saint Nicomedes
and Saint Nicetas*

Claire Delacroix

CHAPTER EIGHTEEN

uncan was troubled, but not by the theft of Lady Eudaline's book.

To his thinking, whoever had stolen it was guilty of a crime he or she believed to be documented within its pages. Lady Eudaline's trap had been well-baited. Her ploy would succeed, and there would be one less villain in the world.

Nay, his concern was with his own future.

Or more specifically, for his future with Radegunde.

Duncan wanted only to ensure her safety, but made no progress in convincing her of the merit of his concern. She was bold, his lady, but that did not change his desire to protect her. He struggled to remain still as she slumbered beside him, not wishing to awaken her with his restlessness.

Of course, he failed.

The light was barely sliding beneath the door of the chamber in the stables they had made their own, when Radegunde rolled over. Duncan lay on his back as he had all the night long, and closed his eyes as if asleep.

He did not want to argue with her.

At the same time, he did not wish to keep silent about his

concern. Perhaps he might find the right words with a little more thought.

Radegunde propped her elbows on his chest and leaned her weight against him. "Do not feign sleep now," she chided, her tone teasing. "It would take a less observant woman than me to be fooled. You have not slept all the night long."

Duncan grimaced, then smiled at her. "I did not wish to deceive you, only to keep from interrupting your sleep."

"What are you fretting about?"

"I am not…"

"Aye, you are, Duncan, and the sooner you confess the truth to me, the sooner we shall see it resolved." When he hesitated, she arched a brow and smiled at him. "Surely you have no more secrets to keep from me?"

Duncan sighed. "It is not a secret, so much as a fear."

"Tell me of it and it may seem less."

"I doubt that." Duncan sat up and pulled her into his lap. Radegunde curled against him, like a contented cat, and he wondered how he would ride away from her, even when he intended to return. He had never been so concerned for perils in his days ahead as he was now, because he did not wish to be parted from Radegunde for a day.

Much less months on end.

She considered him and must have guessed something of his thoughts, for her eyes narrowed. "You mean to leave me."

"You know that I will ride to Scotland with Fergus. We have discussed this."

Radegunde drew back. "There is more. What else have you decided that we have *not* discussed?"

Duncan took warning from her tone but knew he could not withhold his conclusion any longer. "I do not think you should ride north after Lady Ysmaine's babe is born. I would have you remain here, until I return." In a way, it was a relief to say it aloud.

In another, it seemed he had erred in so doing.

Radegunde's eyes flashed and she flung herself from his embrace. She crossed the chamber to the bucket of water he had brought the night before and cast off her chemise. She washed with furious haste and donned her chemise and stockings more quickly than he might have believed possible.

Then she spun to confront him, her displeasure evident. "So you would abandon me. This is the merit of your sworn word and our handfast."

Duncan rose to his feet. "Nay, this is the price of learning that my own father hunts my hide," he retorted. "I will not see you imperiled."

"You will see me alone, instead." Her lips tightened. "When does Fergus mean to depart?"

"After the Yule."

She counted on her fingertips. "Which means that our handfast of a year and a day will endure less than four months before we separate."

"I will return to you by the end of our pledged year and a day."

She flung out a hand. "Why should I not come with you?"

"You have Lady Ysmaine to tend."

"Then I will come to you after the birth."

"It is not safe…"

"Safe! Duncan, I desire adventure and a life lived fully. To be safe, to be left behind, to be without the man I love, that is not *living*. I might as well join a convent." She donned her kirtle and laced the sides with savage gestures. "To think that I meant to suggest to you that I ride to Scotland in the party with Fergus and we begin our life together without delay."

"Nay, you cannot."

She leveled a look at him that might have struck fear into the heart of a lesser man. "Do you mean to instruct me, as if I were a child?"

"Nay, I would protect you!"

"And I would be with you!" She glared at him. "I see that you have made your choice. You will ride north without me, but I *will* accompany Lady Ysmaine and Lord Gaston to Killairic to see Fergus wed in the spring."

Duncan shook his head. "Nay, Radegunde. You must not."

She inhaled sharply and granted him a poisonous glance. "Why not?"

Duncan stepped forward and seized her hand to make his appeal. "You must see that the simplest way to trap me or threaten me would be by putting you at risk. I would do any deed to secure your safety, Radegunde, and any man who knows me at all will guess as much." He pressed her hand between his own. "I beg of you, remain here so I will know that you are well."

Radegunde looked down at her hand captured within his. Duncan could not guess her thoughts or understand why her mood was suddenly so reserved. "Is that the real reason?" she said quietly, and he did not understand her doubt. She lifted her gaze to his, and he saw the tears shimmering in her eyes. "Or is it that your love is still not yours to give?"

Duncan did not understand her meaning for a long moment, and so lost his opportunity to refute her conclusion.

Radegunde pulled her hand from his with impatience. "I knew it!" she declared, seizing her shoes and pushing her feet into them with haste. He saw her tears begin to fall. "Still you love Gwyneth! There is naught left of your heart for me!"

"Radegunde! That is not so!" Duncan cried, but he had no chance to argue his case.

A scream of anguish echoed suddenly through the keep. It was such a horrific sound that silence followed it, as if the blood of every soul within earshot had been turned to ice. A shiver slipped down Duncan's spine, and Radegunde hauled open the portal.

"The book," she murmured, then flung herself out of the chamber.

Duncan was fast behind her, though he feared it was to late to be of aid to the victim.

Radegunde raced across the bailey toward the tower, trying to forget her frustration with Duncan. Wretched man! How could Duncan still love a dead woman, when she was alive and prepared to grant him all she had to give?

She supposed he thought it more noble to tell her the truth sooner rather than later. Fool man!

Radegunde stumbled in the bailey, recalling all too well his words before their handfast.

I admire you. I like how you laugh and that you are stubborn and outspoken. I admire how you savor life, and that you believe you can make matters be as you desire. And I find you more alluring than any woman I have ever known.

Not a word about love.

Not even about affection.

And now he spoke of protection, as if she were a bird requiring a secure cage. Did he know naught of her nature? Did he understand so little of what she desired? She had hoped that Duncan would confess his love in time, that his actions spoke of the truth of his heart.

Gwyneth. He *had* said he loved Gwyneth.

And he still carried that lock of red-gold hair.

A woman he had met, loved, and lost before Radegunde had even been born.

She would grant that he was loyal and true, but with that, her admiration reached its limit. Why could he not love *her*?

She had been so sure that Lady Ysmaine had been mistaken in her view about a handfast and its merit, but now Radegunde's conviction faltered. Had she been foolish to surrender her all to Duncan? The possibility made her stomach knot.

Radegunde flung herself through the portal to the hall and hastened up the stairs. There was already a throng of servants drawn toward the chambers at the summit.

"Azalaïs!" a man roared in apparent despair from above. The company froze, and Radegunde forced her way through their ranks more readily then.

The solar occupied the summit of the tower, but there were chambers below it. Lord Bayard's widow had claimed one of these rooms with her youngest daughter, Rohese, while Lord Millard and Lady Azalaïs occupied the other. Radegunde could see Lady Ysmaine and Lord Gaston at the portal of that chamber. It must have been Lord Millard who had shouted.

Lord Gaston stood in his chemise and hammered on the door. Lady Ysmaine had seized a robe but her feet were bare, and her eyes were wide. She would be cold. Radegunde moved with greater speed. Her lady cast a glance down the stairs and relief touched her features at the sight of her maid. She beckoned and Radegunde reached her side just as the portal was unlocked.

"I heard the crack," Lady Ysmaine whispered.

The crack? Radegunde did not immediately understand.

"She jumped and hit her head on the rocks," Lady Ysmaine added quietly and Radegunde felt ill. She could only imagine how horrifying the sound of impact must have been. She held fast to her lady's hand, better prepared for whatever they would find inside.

The door opened to reveal Lord Millard, who looked haggard. "She leaped from the window," he said with such remorse that Radegunde immediately doubted his sincerity. The company gasped. "I awakened to find her reading, then she jumped up and flung herself to her death before I could stop her." He rubbed his brow and wept. The company murmured in consternation, the tidings being repeated in horrified whispers.

"But why?" Lord Gaston demanded. When Millard did not reply, Lord Gaston strode past him into the chamber. Radegunde and Lady Ysmaine followed.

The bed was unmade and there was a stool by the window. Lady Eudaline's book was on the floor beside it with its pages open. Lord Gaston went to the window and braced his hands on the sill to look out. The window was beneath one in the solar and faced south, over the river and toward Angers.

Lord Gaston crossed himself, then turned back with a grimace, seizing the elbow of his lady wife and guiding her away from the window. "There is naught to be done for her now," he murmured, then summoned a pair of men with a snap of his fingers.

Radegunde slipped around the pair to the window and looked for herself. Far below, she spied the broken body of Lady Azalaïs, motionless on the rocks at the base of the tower and half-submerged in the river. She wore only a chemise, which now clung wetly to her pale body, and her hair was unbound. Radegunde saw red blood flowing from the lady's head. The current of the river swirled around the tower and tugged at the corpse. As Radegunde watched, the body was dislodged from the rock to float briefly then disappear beneath the surface.

She felt slightly sickened by the blood that stained the river water and pivoted to find Duncan amongst those crowded in the portal. His gaze was fixed upon her, and as irked as she was with him, she drew strength from his presence. He looked vexed, and she knew it was because their argument was not completed.

He had more to say and she had to admit that if he wished to defend himself, he could not be without feelings for her.

She wanted to hear him out, too.

Radegunde supposed it was not all bad that he wished to see her protected. Aye, there was truth in his assertion that others might use her presence to attack him.

Perhaps she had been too harsh. Or too quick to judge.

The fact remained that a single confession would set all to rights between them. Radegunde held Duncan's gaze for a long moment, willing him to say those three sweet words. He surveyed her and lifted a brow in silent query. Radegunde realized that he awaited some sign from her that she was hale. She nodded just a little and saw relief touch his features.

Her heart softened at that. There was something to be said for a man so constant that even an argument did not shake his sense of duty to her.

Perhaps his actions did reveal the truth of his heart.

Still, Radegunde wished to hear as much from his own lips.

"You will have to retrieve her downstream," Lord Gaston informed the men. "I would have her returned to the chapel with all haste, that she might be laid to rest here, beside her father."

Lady Ysmaine parted her lips but at a glance from her husband, said naught.

Radegunde understood. If it was true that Azalaïs had killed herself, she could not be buried alongside her father in hallowed ground.

Did Lord Gaston doubt Lord Millard's tale?

"It shall be done," Duncan said, gesturing to several other men.

Radegunde's heart warmed that Duncan volunteered to undertake the unpleasant task. His loyalty and steadfastness were why she loved him, and she yearned anew that he would discern her own merit before his departure.

"Make haste before she journeys too far, if you please," Lord Gaston called after them, whose boots echoed on the stairs. "It is imperative that she be buried with honor here in her home."

Lord Millard, to Radegunde's surprise, did not thank Lord Gaston for this. Instead he surveyed the other knight with narrowed eyes.

What did he know?

"Fear not, Lord Gaston," Duncan declared. "It will be done."

Radegunde saw that Lady Marie and Rohese had arrived, but the younger maiden seemed loath to cross the threshold of the chamber. Had she seen her sister's demise or did she simply anticipate a fearful sight? Lady Marie moved quickly to console Lord Millard, but Rohese stood her ground, pale and trembling. It seemed she could not bring herself to take another step. Radegunde could not blame her for not wanting to see her sister in such a state.

Had the sisters been close? To be sure, Radegunde knew little of them.

"Come, we will pray for her." Lady Ysmaine urged the two noblewomen to leave the chamber, while Lord Gaston ushered the household back to their labor. "Radegunde, please accompany me."

That was when Radegunde noticed that the book was no longer on the floor. She hoped that Lord Gaston had reclaimed it, but could not be certain. It seemed a poor idea to ask him when there were so many who might hear her question.

Who else had been close enough to claim it? She made a list while her observations were fresh. Lord Gaston. Lady Ysmaine. Lord Millard. Lady Marie. Perhaps a servant she had failed to observe while looking out the window.

The three noblewomen descended the stairs together to go to the chapel, the priest awaiting them on the landing far below them. He gave his condolences to Lady Marie and appeared to be quite disconcerted himself.

"This is your fault," Benedicta charged in a whisper, slipping into the company beside Radegunde like a dark shadow. "Do not imagine that I will forget it."

Benedicta. If she had not been in the chamber, she had been close at hand. Radegunde met the other woman's malicious gaze and added her name to the list of those who might have the book.

The wild man of the woods was not an impulsive man. He had learned years before to choose his path with care, for a quick decision could steer a man false.

It might even cost him all he held dear.

But it was time to step forward. It was time to demand justice. The return of Gaston de Châmont-sur-Maine to his family holding, and the support shown to him by Amaury de Valeroy, convinced the wild man of the woods that goodness would again prevail. In truth, he had lost track of the years, for there had been only the rhythm of the seasons in the forest since his parting from Mathilde. He had not realized that so much time had slipped away, not until he had seen his Radegunde fully grown.

He had not been able to think of anything else since leaving her with Duncan at Valeroy. His valiant little Radegunde, a woman.

He was keenly aware now of how much he had lost.

Nay, those years had not been lost. They had been stolen.

He might have chosen to become an exile, but it was less of a choice than a lack of other options. In the end, he had retreated to the forest alone to protect those he loved, but now he saw that he could only protect Mathilde and Radegunde and the boys if the villain responsible for his woes was brought to justice.

That man was at Châmont-sur-Maine, and with Gaston returned, the wild man of the woods dared to hope that his word would be believed this time.

The band of troubadours, a merry company passing through the forest, offered the perfect opportunity to achieve his goal. Indeed, their timely arrival convinced him of the merit of his choice.

The troubadours were not so readily convinced that they should add to their company, but the wild man of the woods confessed that he knew of a baron who would welcome their skills in his hall. It was beyond certain that Gaston would celebrate his own return to his father's keep, and the troubadours were sufficiently glad to wager a place in their ranks for such tidings.

Their leader's sole condition was that their new comrade bathe and change his garb.

The wild man of the woods did better than that. He had them aid in cutting his hair. He borrowed a sharp knife and shaved his beard. He washed and clothed himself in borrowed garb, afterward ensuring his hood shadowed his face.

But he knew he walked taller, with both purpose and justice in his step.

The reckoning had come.

Duncan's party was compelled to ride far downriver to retrieve Lady Azälais, nigh all the way to Angers. Even then, the river did not surrender her readily, for she had become entangled in some branches, which had been driven against rocks in the middle of the river. The Maine was wide and flowed steadily southward, its waters muddy after recent rains. The river was waist-deep, and the surface deceptively smooth. The undercurrent was stronger than one might have expected, and it took them a goodly measure of time to safely retrieve the lady.

In the end, it was Duncan, bound at the end of the rope secured to the steeds on the shore, who freed the lady from the boughs. Her skin had paled to a sickly hue and the bruises from her fall were livid on her flesh. Her features were contorted, a clear indication that she had died in pain, and her eyes were open. She looked so wretched and broken that Duncan not only crossed himself before he touched her but said a silent prayer for her soul. He closed her eyes then, and despite the tug of the river, tried to ease the grimace from her face.

It was hard not to find Lady Eudaline's justice harsh in this case, even if it had been meted correctly.

Yet it was here, in the river as he freed a dead woman from the clutch of dead branches and the whirl of the river, that clarity came to Duncan's thoughts. Lady Azalaïs had arisen this morn, much as any other, and had chosen to read while she awaited the awakening of others. Now she was dead, young and cheated, to Duncan's view.

There was no telling when one faced one's last day.

There was no reason not to savor every moment and every pleasure.

He felt a warmth flood through him. Radegunde was right in her joy, in her fearless embrace of every day's pleasures and torments, in her desire for adventure and experience. Radegunde was right to celebrate whatever happiness could be claimed each day, to greet the dawn with delight, to refuse to worry about any pending doom.

The present should not be set aside, surely not for the potential of unhappiness in the future.

He had been a fool.

He should savor every moment with his Radegunde, and ensure that they both held rich memories of this time together. He knew there was only one way to reassure his lady and earn her forgiveness. He was not a man to speak of his feelings, but he realized that in this instance, he would have to do as much to make amends.

Would she believe him?

He must ensure that she did, one way or the other.

Duncan lifted the corpse free, newly resolved to hasten back to the keep. He carried Lady Azalaïs to the shore with no small effort. He slipped once, but lost neither his burden nor his footing, and was relieved to be free of the river's chill waters. Duncan was glad they had brought a shroud, for it was unseemly that many should see her thus. The other men were silenced by the sight of the noblewoman, all of them wet to the bone and sickened by the task.

When she was wrapped, he saw one of the men in service to the house wipe away a tear. "She was a good woman," that man murmured. "Sweet and kind."

"A sparkling gem."

"Lively and possessed of a musical laugh."

"I never heard her laugh," Duncan said, thinking these traits had little to do with the woman who had seemed as insubstantial as a ghost. Indeed, he had scarce noted her presence in the hall, so quiet had she been. Her garments clung to her body, emphasizing her slender figure. At least, she had not been with child.

On this day, Radegunde would have no babe's passing to mourn.

"She was much changed after her marriage," offered the third, and the first two frowned at him.

"I will not speak ill of the dead," said the first. "God bless her soul."

The prayer was repeated and the lady's slight weight lifted between them. They had not brought a cart, and Duncan thought it unseemly to bind her to a saddle. In the end, a makeshift hammock was slung between two of the steeds and the corpse placed upon it. They did not make great speed, but in a way, Duncan thought it fitting that their return be slow, like that of a funeral procession.

Even if he chafed to be by Radegunde's side.

The villagers turned out to line the road as the party approached, more than one clearly stricken as the procession passed to the bridge. They had heard the tidings then and were aware of the burden that Duncan and the men carried. They were so silent that the horses' hooves seemed uncommonly loud, and even the growl of one man's empty belly carried far.

Duncan and the men carried their burden onto the bridge, moving even more slowly. Duncan saw that the priest stood at the gate to the keep, waiting to welcome the lady home. Lady Ysmaine and Lord Gaston stood behind him, their expressions solemn, then Lord Amaury, Lady Marie, Lord Millard and Rohese.

He wondered then who would prepare her for burial and hoped that Radegunde was not assigned this task.

They were at the midpoint of the bridge when the sentry cried out. "A party arrives!" Duncan turned with the other men to see a small noble company galloping along the shore toward the village, taking the same path their own party had followed just the day before. The standards bore the insignia of Valeroy.

Lord Amaury stepped forward with evident concern. Duncan and his party passed through the gates with their burden and Lord Amaury crossed himself before striding across the bridge to greet the arrivals.

Duncan surrendered the lady's corpse to a pair of waiting

maids. Two of the men from his party continued to carry the slight burden to the church along with the maids. Duncan then glanced back at the arriving party to see that one rider had dismounted.

It was Radegunde's brother, Michel. That man seized the halter of a white palfrey to lead it through the village, his own horse falling behind. Lady Richildis rode the white palfrey, followed by a pair of maids and a woman who Duncan realized was Mathilde. It was her posture that revealed her identity, though he could not discern her expression until the party started across the bridge.

Mathilde met Duncan's gaze, then scanned the keep, clearly concerned. Duncan gave the reins of his steed to a squire, then strode after Lord Amaury, hoping he could relieve Mathilde's fears, whatever they might be.

"What is amiss?" Lord Amaury demanded with quiet heat when he was alongside his lady wife. He took the reins from Michel, who bowed and stepped back.

"Mathilde saw a shadow," Lady Richildis murmured. "A portent of doom."

"And rightly so," Lord Amaury replied. "For Bayard's oldest daughter, Azalaïs, is dead this very morn."

Both lady and wise woman crossed themselves and Michel looked back with dismay, then did the same.

"She had the book," Lord Amaury said quietly.

"Poor girl," Lady Richildis said with a shake of her head. "Then you were right, Mathilde, yet we did not arrive in time."

"The shadow is not banished," Mathilde said with conviction. She gripped Duncan's hand and he anticipated her question.

"Radegunde is hale enough, if vexed with me this morn."

Mathilde smiled. "I have no doubt you will win her regard anew."

"I fully intend to do so."

"I knew there was a reason I liked you, Duncan MacDonald."

"There is another matter upon which I would have your counsel, Mathilde," Lord Amaury said, then quickly recounted the tale of the hunting gloves.

"God in Heaven," Lady Richildis said. "May we be glad that you told such tales to Radegunde, Mathilde! Imagine Ysmaine's repute if she buried a third husband! Though the fault would not be her own, I can fairly hear the tales that would be told of her."

Mathilde's expression was grim. "I would like to examine both book and gloves, if it can be done."

"I laid claim to the gloves," Lord Amaury said, then turned to Duncan, his manner expectant.

"I shall endeavor to retrieve the book, my lord," Duncan said with a bow.

"Surreptitiously, if it can be done, Duncan," Lord Amaury said, his lips barely moving.

Duncan nodded as the party continued to the gates.

"I thought to arrive for a feast not a funeral!" Lady Richildis exclaimed, making a clear attempt to disguise the reason for her arrival. She dismounted when she was in the bailey with her husband's aid, then seized Lady Ysmaine's hands. "My child, what a trial has come to you!"

Duncan spied Radegunde behind her lady and so he saw her joy at the arrival of both her mother and brother. He smiled when she glanced his way, but she averted her gaze.

Fortunately, he had the perfect plan to earn her favor anew.

First, though, he had need of a bath.

CHAPTER NINETEEN

ord Gaston had not taken the book, nor had Lady Ysmaine. Radegunde had asked at the first opportunity, and had considered the possibilities while Duncan had been gone.

Who had laid claim to the book?

Did its disappearance mean there was yet a villain in Lord Gaston's hall? Radegunde feared it to be so.

She was beyond glad to see her mother and brother arrive in the party with Lady Richildis. More assistance with this riddle could only see it solved sooner.

"And so you are vexed with Duncan," Mathilde whispered when mother and daughter first embraced.

Radegunde pulled back to eye her mother. "Did you learn as much in a dream?"

Mathilde smiled. "He told me of it."

"Indeed?" This confession did little to improve Radegunde's mood. "It seems he is less taciturn with you than with me."

"Or that he speaks aright. You are vexed, as you seldom are." Mathilde put her hand through her daughter's elbow and they followed Lady Ysmaine and Lady Richildis to the hall. Radegunde saw her mother's eyes narrow as she studied Lady Ysmaine and she caught her sidelong glance. Radegunde nodded and her mother smiled in understanding. "It is good then that I have come."

"Surely my lady's tidings are not the shadow you glimpsed?" Radegunde whispered.

"I hope not." Mathilde gave Radegunde's arm a little shake. "And do not tell me that it was a portent of you casting aside the love of a fine man."

"There is the nut of the matter. He has *never* said he loved me."

"Because it is clear in all he does."

"Nay, he loves his dead wife."

"Why do you say as much?"

"He would leave me behind when he rides for home!" Radegunde flung out a hand. "He instructs me to remain here until his return."

"He fears for your future," her mother said with surprising caution.

"So he insists." Radegunde sighed. "I would be with him, *Maman*. I understand that he may not return, but I would share every moment possible."

"It is not so foul for a man to wish to protect you."

"*Maman*! I thought you would take my side in this. He has spoken of his love for his dead wife, but said naught of any for me. I would know the inclination of his heart."

"Do you not see it in his deeds? He pledged a handfast to you."

"And he did not wish to continue our relations, for fear that I should conceive a child."

"Truly?" Mathilde nodded approval of this notion. "It is not so bad for a man to defend a woman's future either."

"I refused his inclination," Radegunde said. "You should know it. I declined to take the herb you sent to me."

Mathilde surveyed her daughter. "You take a risk."

"I would willingly bear his child. I love him! There can be no half-measure."

Radegunde was surprised that her mother frowned. "Make no mistake, child, for I do not regret a one of you, but my life would have oft been simpler if your father had either remained with me or abandoned my bed completely. I could not resist him or his touch, but it is no easy path to be a mother without a man at one's side."

"You think I err?"

"I think you know enough of the world to make your own choices," Mathilde said mildly. "And I think that if you are left alone with a babe, it will not be by any choice made willingly by Duncan."

"Because he would do his duty by me."

"Indeed."

Radegunde sighed. "But what if Duncan defends me only out of duty?" she asked. "What if he truly does still love his lost wife?"

Mathilde shook her head with a confidence Radegunde could not share in this one matter. "Love is not thus and you know it. He could love both of you."

"I would have him choose. Or at least love me best."

"And there is your error," Mathilde said crisply. "That is pride and not love. Do not repeat my mistake, Radegunde."

"I do not understand."

"I loved your father. I still do. I was convinced that he loved me, but he kept secrets from me." Mathilde looked thoughtful. "And so in my audacity, I erred. I bade him choose between his secrets and our match." She shook her head. "He did not make the choice I believed to be inevitable. And so, by demanding more of his love, I was left with less. For a while, he came for pleasure, but then no longer." She held Radegunde's gaze steadily. "I cheated myself, for I did not know what burden he carried. It is clear that it was greater than his love for me, and when I insisted that he choose, I lost."

Radegunde was surprised by this confession. She believed that her mother never erred, so was shaken to learn otherwise. "Surely you do not advise *me* on the merit of patience," she said, hoping to make her mother smile.

Mathilde did smile. "I speak of trust, Radegunde. Where there is love, there should be trust."

"I would have him make a sweet confession to me."

"And if you press him overmuch, you may cheat yourself of it.

There is naught amiss with a man being slow to confess what is in his heart. Duncan's deeds speak the truth most loudly."

Radegunde grimaced. "I should still like to hear the words."

Her mother smiled. "And I pray that you will hear them before the Yule." She kissed Radegunde's cheek. "Do not torment the man for his honesty or the honor he does you, and think twice before you compel a choice."

Radegunde could see the merit of that advice. If she forced Duncan to choose, and he was not prepared to confess his love, she would lose even their time together before the Yule. She wanted every day and every moment in his company, for she would cherish each memory after he departed.

She and Mathilde reached the hall where Lady Ysmaine was calling for a restorative cup of mulled wine for her mother.

"It is a bit cold here in the hall," Lady Richildis said with an elaborate shiver. "Could we not sit in the solar?"

Mathilde turned and grasped Radegunde's hands. "I will go with the ladies," she said quickly. "Once Lady Richildis knows what you have confided in me, she will want to be reassured that my portent did not involve Lady Ysmaine's condition."

"But I can tend my lady..."

"Do not let this dispute with Duncan fester, child. It is a disagreement and no more, so does not merit such influence."

"But what should I say to him?"

Mathilde reached into her bag and removed a ball of the rough soap she made each fall. She placed it in Radegunde's hand. "If ever I saw a man desirous of a bath, it is Duncan MacDonald on this day. Surely he deserves some solace for seeing such a grim task completed?" She closed her hands over Radegunde's. "Let him speak and do not fear either his words or his heart."

Radegunde hoped that her mother's conviction was not misplaced. Mother and daughter shared a smile, then Radegunde kissed her mother's cheeks. She gripped the soap and ran into the bailey in search of Duncan.

Duncan feared he would never get the stench of death from his skin and his garb. He could not court Radegunde's favor in such a state, which made it doubly vexing.

He had rolled the great tub into the corner of the stables and brought water to it pail by pail, with help from Laurent and Hamish. He dismissed the squires and stripped down when the tub was half-filled. The water from the well was cold and he shivered as he stepped into it, then closed his eyes and ducked below the surface. He scrubbed himself all over with a rough cloth, but the scent was not readily dispelled.

Duncan began to suspect that the smell was in his memory, but still it sickened him. A young woman, dead too soon. Another needless death. His gut churned as he wondered whether all came awry.

Was his ill fortune the shadow that Fergus saw in the future? Had that fated day arrived? Duncan did not like that he and Radegunde had parted badly. He felt unsettled and agitated as seldom he did. The loss of Gwyneth had been devastating, but Duncan realized that Radegunde had not just claimed his affections but had stolen his heart clean away.

He could not imagine being without her.

He could not even bear a disagreement with her.

She was the very blood of his heart.

Yet he feared that a sweet confession might be ill-timed. If he was to lose his quest to set his past to rest, he wanted Radegunde to fall in love again, to be happy, to marry another. If he confessed his love to her, she might be sufficiently stubborn to hold fast to his memory and cheat herself of what he saw as her due.

Curse his father and his wretched ambitions! Duncan scrubbed, not caring if his skin was left raw.

What was the shadow discerned by Mathilde? The same as the one that haunted Fergus, or another? Duncan shook out his hair and eyed the filthy water, knowing he could not change it himself without treating all the bailey to a view of his nudity.

Or donning his soiled garb again.

And he could not summon the squires. Laurent was truly Leila and Hamish had been summoned to serve Fergus.

Duncan's irritation rose as he washed his face yet again. His annoyance was disturbed by an unfamiliar scent.

Not death.

Not river filth.

Duncan opened his eyes to find a bar of soap held before him.

In a woman's hand. His heart leaped for his throat.

Radegunde smiled when he met her gaze. "I think you will make little progress without it."

Had he been forgiven? How? Why? Duncan found that he did not care. "I thank you, lass. Where were you hiding this marvel?"

"Lass?" Radegunde echoed. She folded her arms across her chest and glared at him but there was a twinkle in the depths of her gaze that gave him much encouragement. "If you are going to speak to me as if I were a stranger, I shall see you drowned in this tub, Duncan MacDonald."

He chuckled despite himself and liked that she smiled in return. "I feared you would do as much if I called you anything else."

"You might try some alternatives." Radegunde's manner turned flirtatious, and though Duncan could not name the reason for her forgiveness, he welcomed it.

And he would not err again.

"Wife," he said. "Partner." She granted him a wary glance, and he let his voice drop low. "Lady mine," he said, reaching for her hand when her expression softened.

"You know I am no lady."

"You are *my* lady, if I am not such a fool as to jeopardize that honor." Duncan took a breath. "You are right, Radegunde, in your passion for savoring every moment. Events of this day have made me realize how uncertain all can be. Understand that I wished only to protect you."

"I do not wish to be protected from you, Duncan."

"Nor I from you." He kissed her fingers. "I cannot fathom why your manner has changed, but I welcome it."

"Perhaps I thought of being without you."

"I certainly considered the future without you and found it lacking."

Radegunde laughed with delight and cast herself at him, then recoiled. "You smell foul, Duncan!"

"I know." He brandished the soap and stole a kiss. "Yet you, as the clever woman I know you to be, have offered the solution."

"My mother makes it. She brought it with her."

"She knew I would fetch a corpse?"

"I do not think so. She always has some, and now we do as well. It is not as fine as the soap Joscelin granted to Lady Ysmaine."

"But it does not smell of roses either." Duncan sniffed it with appreciation. "I like this scent well."

"Then we are allied again?"

"Aye, to my relief. I would not argue with you again, Radegunde."

"Nor I with you." Radegunde plucked the soap from Duncan's hand and cracked it on the rim of the tub to break it in two. She handed the smaller piece back to him. She stood taller, her usual purpose restored, and he found his own mood vastly improved by her cheerful presence. "I am glad you like the scent, for your garb will be washed in it as well. Do you need another bucket of water? I shall bring it if no boy can be found. Laurent can aid me in scrubbing your plaid. With this wind and the last bit of sunshine, it may well be dry by the evening meal."

"I thank you, Radegunde." Duncan felt that the obstacles were less insurmountable with Radegunde at his side, that much was certain.

"I shall demand a payment from you, to be sure."

"And I shall be glad to fulfill your desire."

"There is a promise I will remember." She cast him a wicked smile, then set to work. She grimaced as she gathered up his garments. "Was there ever a river so muddy as this one? The smell!"

"Perhaps you might bring my chausses when you have a chance."

Radegunde spun to face him and her eyes danced with familiar merriment. "I like your plaid better."

"But it will have to dry."

She laughed. "Perhaps I should like to keep you here, nude."

Duncan grinned. "Perhaps I would not find it such an ordeal. We might begin on your list of desires."

"We might, had I not so much labor this day." Radegunde's smile heated Duncan to his toes and he was aware that she could see the effect of her presence upon him. "Perhaps you would wear your chausses only to see that I am not tempted to forget my chores."

"Perhaps it is the only sensible choice," Duncan agreed. "For I am sorely tempted already, simply by the reappearance of your smile, and were you bent on seduction, I should have no ability to resist you."

Her smile broadened, and he knew she was pleased. Duncan felt a wretch for having given her any doubts. "Come here, lady mine," he murmured, beckoning to her with one finger. "I think a kiss is warranted now that we have made amends."

When she cast herself at him this time she did not recoil, but lingered long to savor his kiss. Her response heated his blood and set Duncan ablaze, filling him with a yearning for this woman that he knew would never be sated. He slanted his mouth over hers and kissed her thoroughly, trying to tell her with his caress how much she meant to him.

It was Duncan who put distance between them this time, and his rueful sigh prompted Radegunde's mischievous smile again. "You will get wet and cold," he growled. Her gaze flicked downward and she took evident delight in her influence upon him.

"I vow that I will not test your resolve," she whispered and touched her lips to his again.

"Your very presence tests my resolve," Duncan informed her. "But you are right that we must make the most of each day as it comes."

"And you are right to think of the future," Radegunde ceded. "Since we are both right, there is no reason to be at odds."

"My thoughts exactly." There could only be another sweet kiss after such an agreement, but before she pulled away, Duncan whispered in her ear. "I have a request that I do not know how to fill."

"Aye?"

"Aye. Lord Amaury bade me find the book so your mother can examine it. Do you know who has it?"

Radegunde sobered immediately and shook her head. "It was there, on the floor where she had dropped it. But then I looked out the window and when I turned back, it was gone."

Duncan frowned. "Someone picked it up."

"Aye. It was not Lady Ysmaine or Lord Gaston, for I asked." Before he could ask, Radegunde touched her lips to his ear. "I remember who else was there." She whispered a list of names.

Lady Marie.

Lord Millard.

Possibly the maid Benedicta or another servant.

She leaned back and held his gaze, her own filled with concern. "It is too long a list," she murmured. "We are only two and they are three or four."

"Then we must choose our strongest suspect. I will watch Millard," Duncan said.

"And I the maid." Radegunde nodded. "For I distrust her most."

Duncan nodded. "Use care." He smiled down at her, yet holding fast to her hand, feeling her pulse leap. "I would not lose another moment with you before the Yule."

Radegunde nodded and straightened, her expression filled with familiar determination. "Then we must fill this time with memories, the better to sustain us both when we are parted."

Duncan could find no argument with that.

In fact, he was resolved to give his lady a fine memory this very night. A reconciliation deserved a celebration, to his thinking, and Duncan wished to make a sweet confession to Radegunde with his touch, if not with words.

Radegunde had no time to seek either Benedicta or the book, but in the end, it mattered little.

Benedicta found her.

Radegunde was in great demand for the remainder of that day. Lady Richildis did not wish to impose upon Lady Marie so her maids relied upon Radegunde instead. After cleaning Duncan's plaid and fetching his chausses for him—as well as celebrating the end of their dispute with kisses that left her eager for night to arrive—Radegunde directed them and tended to her lady, and fetched for her own mother as well. The kitchen was bustling and the hall was being prepared for the feast on the morrow.

One of the villagers brought the daily pail of milk from his goats and the cook roared that Radegunde see it dispatched to its destination. Between arranging the evening meal for this night and preparing for the morrow, he appeared to be at his wit's end.

"Take the milk, I beg of you! I have not a finger's breadth of space to spare," he complained. Radegunde seized the bucket and made for the stairs.

"I suppose this is merely the beginning," Benedicta whispered, so close behind Radegunde that she jumped and near spilled the milk.

"Aye, there is much to do before the feast."

Benedicta laughed though the sound was harsh. "I mean the beginning of death at Châmont-sur-Maine," she said. It was clear that the older maid had been crying and Radegunde felt a pang of sympathy for her. She guessed who had prepared the body of Lady Azalaïs, and truly, that was a task no maid desired to perform for her mistress.

Then the other maid leaned forward, malice shining in her eyes, and Radegunde forgot her compassion. "Who will be next?" she hissed. "Lord Millard? Lady Marie? Will your lady cease the killing before they are all dispatched?" Radegunde tried to ignore the spew of venom, but Benedicta followed behind her. "And what was their crime? Knowing Lord Gaston before she? Providing competition in future to any child she might bear?"

Radegunde spun on the stairs to confront the older maid. "You should not be so foolish as to disparage the lady of the keep."

"Perhaps it is not the lady of the keep who is responsible," Benedicta said slyly. "Do you not service her in all other ways? Perhaps you, with your sure understanding of poison and your ability to anticipate where it might be found, are the one who saw my lady dead."

"Me!" Radegunde nearly dropped the bucket. "How dare you utter such an accusation, and with no proof..."

Benedicta chuckled. "Oh, you are too clever to leave proof, are

you not? Who poisoned the book? Was it truly Lady Eudaline?"
She leaned closer and lowered her voice. "Or was it you and your
fiendish mother?"

Radegunde gasped.

"Aye, she knows much of poison, does she not? And long in
service to your lady's family. Perhaps it was not Lady Ysmaine who
ensured the death of her first two husbands, but her *maid*."

"Nay!"

Benedicta smiled. "There is no proof of your innocence,
either."

"And you would call me a liar, as well?"

"You told us of the book. You said you fetched it. It was
poisoned and you knew it. Oh, I see your ploy now, when it is all
too late for my lady." Benedicta's eyes narrowed. "I would wager
that you would like to have it back, that you could ensure none
could prove that it killed my lady."

"I would like to see it secured so no others are injured."

Benedicta scoffed. "For you are compassionate beyond all. Of
course. Just as your man is merely a man-at-arms, who does noble
service for his lord."

"Of course he is!"

"And what of the man found dead beside the old oak tree? The
one who was found the morning after your lover was the last
through the gates." Benedicta spat. "You are killers, both of you,
and I do not care whether you do as much for your lord and lady,
or for your own satisfaction. Mark my words: you will be
discovered and made to pay for your sins."

Benedicta surveyed Radegunde once more, then pivoted and
marched back to the kitchen, her chin held high. Radegunde stared
after her, simmering with anger.

It was only because she had not turned away that she heard the
footfall. The barest slip of leather on stone, a fleeting shadow, and
she was alone again.

Who had listened?

And did that person believe Benedicta's words?

It was clear that Radegunde was distressed when she returned to their chamber that night. Duncan had made preparations for a seduction, but knew with a glimpse that she had much to say first.

"Vexing creature!" she declared when the door was closed behind her. "I have no doubt that she knows much of this matter. Indeed, I expect she enjoys the trouble she makes!"

"Benedicta?" Duncan stirred the coals in the brazier, poured her a cup of wine and coaxed his outraged lady to the pallet. Once there, he tucked her beneath his arm and his cloak and waited.

"Who else?" The tale of Benedicta's venom spilled forth with speed, filling Duncan with anger that anyone should so malign his lady. "Do you think any would believe her?" Radegunde asked by way of conclusion, clearly horrified by the possibility.

"Only a fool would believe a charge to fall from that one's lips," he said with vigor. "You are known by your lady and her family, and you are trusted. The merest acquaintance convinced me of your integrity and but a glance told me the truth of that one's dark nature."

Radegunde smiled a little and turned the cup in her hands.

"I did not tell you yet of our good fortune this night," Duncan said. "The castellan has opened the first of the casks to ensure the wine is good for the morrow. I took the liberty of offering to aid in ensuring its merit."

"I thought it was better than usual." Radegunde took only the barest sip before setting it aside.

"Out with it," Duncan commanded with affection.

Her smile flashed briefly, then she scowled anew. "I am skeptical."

"Of all, or some detail in particular?"

"It is Azalaïs."

"A tragedy," he agreed, taking a more considerable sip of the wine as he watched her. It *was* fine. "Or is it the haste of the funeral that troubles you?"

"Nay, it is Azalaïs herself. It is a long time since I have met a woman so nearly invisible. She was meek and quiet, pale in her coloring and sedate in her dress. I barely noticed her on our arrival, or her younger sister for that matter, yet they are daughters of noble blood raised in a fine estate. They should have been pampered if not indulged, and somewhat demanding. Instead, they are as mice. They are more different than the sisters at Valeroy than I could have imagined possible." She met his gaze. "What would make them so timid?"

"One cannot begin to speculate."

"Aye, but one *can*," Radegunde insisted. "Indeed, one *must* speculate, for it makes no sense that such a woman would have the boldness to steal a book from within a trunk in my lady's chamber, in the very solar!"

Duncan considered this. "A quiet person can do much when provoked."

"Exactly so!" Radegunde agreed, her eyes shining. "But what—or who—provoked her?" She sat back but he could tell that she was still thinking furiously. She shook her head. "I do not think she stole the book. Nay, I believe that Benedicta stole it. Such a theft is more in keeping with *her* nature."

"But she might have done it at her lady's bidding."

Radegunde pursed her lips. "Save that I have yet to hear either of the sisters give a direct command to any of the servants. Nay, their mother or Benedicta commands others on their behalf." She caught her breath and turned to Duncan. "Or Millard," she whispered. "I heard him command a bath for his lady the other morning and he made all the servants hasten."

"Perhaps Benedicta heard you tell of the book, then stole it for her lady to know the truth of what Lady Eudaline had confided in Lady Ysmaine," Duncan suggested. "Was that of her own volition, or was she ordered to do as much?"

"She is lazy," Radegunde said, her tone dismissive. "I do not think she would undertake any task of her own volition. Someone bade her do it, even waited to see the task completed. I am certain of it."

"Why not Azalaïs? If she was so timid, she might want another to do the deed."

"Would she even consider the theft? I would imagine her more likely to ask Lady Ysmaine if she might see it." She grimaced. "In a whisper, when no one else was around."

"And yet, she clearly had the book. I still think Benedicta might

287

have stolen the volume of her own volition, then offered it to her." Duncan shrugged. "Or been caught with it, having taken it out of curiosity or even to vex you, and been compelled to surrender it."

"Compelled to surrender it? To Azalaïs?" Radegunde chuckled. "Oh, Duncan, never was there a noblewoman so dominated by her maid as Azalaïs. Nay, it would have to be a stronger soul who claimed any item from Benedicta. Wretched creature."

Duncan could only agree with that assessment.

"Azalaïs had some boldness, it is clear," he said. "Perhaps you have guessed her character wrong."

"How so?"

"She did leap from the tower when she knew she was poisoned. Such a jump is not for the faint of heart, even if she did wish to shorten her own suffering."

"That is true," Radegunde agreed quietly, and he knew she was recalling the events of the morning.

"It might be a better mark of her nature," Duncan continued. "What if she was quiet only because she and her husband feared Lord Gaston's intent and did not wish to provoke him?"

"Lord Millard suffers from no such concern." Radegunde sipped her wine finally, which encouraged Duncan that she did not intend for it to go to waste, then put it aside. "What if Azalaïs did not jump?"

"What madness is this? Her body was in the river!"

Radegunde leaned closer, eyes shining. "What if she was *cast* from the window?"

Duncan blinked. "But why?"

"Because whoever was with her saw that she had been poisoned and knew she would die."

Duncan did not understand. "But the book was known to have come from Lady Eudaline. Lord Millard was evidently with her, but he could not have been accused of poisoning the pages."

Radegunde frowned. "But what if someone compelled her to read the book aloud, so that she took the risk instead of the person who wished to know the book's contents?"

"Why would Lady Azalaïs do such a thing?"

"Because she was afraid." Radegunde straightened, her lips

setting with resolve. "Fear, Duncan. That is what I saw in Rohese's eyes. I could not understand her reaction fully at the time, but her expression was one of terror."

"Fear of what?"

"Of being next." Radegunde leaped to her feet and began to pace the chamber, her words coming low and fast. "Consider this possibility. Lord Millard is most concerned with his own affluence. He wed Azalaïs in haste after Bayard's death, hoping to become lord of the holding. It is possible that he won her heart with his charm, but it is also possible that he forced his will upon them all."

Duncan found himself obliged to be the devil's advocate. "Three women undefended might have welcomed a knight to their hall."

"And been susceptible to his tales of what their future might be, should they remain undefended. In their vulnerability, Lady Marie accepted his suit for her daughter's hand." Radegunde nodded and Duncan had to agree that it made sense.

"They would not have been certain that Lord Gaston would return, even though Lady Marie wrote to him."

"Indeed. But Lord Gaston *did* return, so any aspirations for the holding had to be dismissed with his arrival. Azalaïs might have lost some or even all of her allure as a wife, for she offered neither title nor fortune, and she had yet to conceive a son. Lord Millard might prefer to find a new wife."

"But first he must become a widower, and she was almost twenty years his junior."

"Nature would have need of assistance, to be sure. Then came the tale of the book. What could Lady Eudaline tell Lord Gaston about the history of his father's abode? Who would care more than the son of Lord Fulk's greatest competitor?"

"Millard, son of Sebastien de Saint-Roux."

Radegunde's eyes lit with triumph. "The competitor who believed Châmont-sur-Maine might have come to *his* hand by the king's grace."

Duncan nodded. "And perhaps there is justification in the book to appeal to the king for that result. Perhaps Lord Gaston's claim upon the holding is not so secure and his mother wished to warn him."

"Precisely! And so, Lord Millard hears of the book. He believes it offers opportunity. He commands Benedicta to steal it. He then orders Lady Azalaïs to read it aloud to him, because he is suspicious. And when she is poisoned, he understands immediately what has happened."

"And casts her out the window to her death, pretending that she has jumped. But why?" Duncan shook his head. "We return to the same issue. She would have died within moments at any rate."

Radegunde sat down with a thump beside Duncan. "He wanted to hide something."

"What?" Duncan did not understand her meaning. "She could not have revealed any secret, not once she was poisoned."

"Nay? Duncan, I am surprised at you. There is one tale her corpse *could* have told, but the fall to the rocks ensured it could not." She spoke grimly, then drained the cup. "If I am right, he is a fiend indeed." She claimed his cup then and drank its contents as well, but did not cast him the smile he anticipated.

Nay, there was a shadow in his beloved's gaze.

And a challenge.

That was the moment that Duncan understood her meaning.

Bruises. Millard might have tried to hide the bruises on his wife's body by ensuring that her corpse was battered by such a fall.

Once he had the thought, the other pieces of the puzzle fell readily into place. No wonder that man had urged a quick burial. No wonder the lady's own maid had been the one to dress her for burial. No wonder the men of the household said her nature had changed upon her marriage. If she had come to fear her husband or his fists, she might well have become more quiet and submissive.

Duncan felt ill.

Had Lord Gaston suspected the truth? Was that why he had insisted that his niece be buried in consecrated ground? Or had his choice been a simple courtesy to his brother's memory? Duncan realized that Radegunde was watching him closely.

"You saw her," she whispered. "Was she bruised?"

"Aye, from head to toe. She was too battered for an old wound to be noted beneath the new. If that was his intent, he succeeded well."

"Blackguard! He should be made to pay!"

"But we have no proof, Radegunde. We cannot make such an accusation against a nobleman without evidence. He will simply refute it. The sole result will be the tarnish of our repute for daring to speak ill of one of our betters without apparent justification."

"Such a man is *not* our better."

Duncan agreed but said naught.

Radegunde's lips set with a determination he knew well. "I do not like it."

"Nor do I." He caught her hand in his. "But even if you are right, the lady is dead. She can suffer no more."

"It is poor solace, Duncan."

"Yet it is the sole one we have." He tucked her against his side and she sighed.

"I need a kiss, Duncan," Radegunde murmured. "A kiss to warm me to my toes and a night in your warm embrace."

Duncan caught her close, only too willing to provide that.

"Will you tell me of Scotland?"

"With pleasure."

But first, he would see to his lady's pleasure.

Claire Delacroix

WEDNESDAY, SEPTEMBER 16, 1187

Feast Day of Saint Euphemia

Claire Delacroix

CHAPTER TWENTY

n the morning of the feast, the entire household rose early. The meal was to begin at midday and would continue through the evening. There were minstrels and jongleurs who would perform and such a quantity of food that Radegunde was astonished. The villagers formed a line across the bridge as soon as the portcullis was lifted and the keep was in uproar.

A company of troubadours arrived and were invited to entertain in the hall. From the look of them, they had slept in the forest the night before—perhaps more than one night—but their leader had a fine clear voice. Two in the company had juggled while their leader recounted their skills to Lord Gaston.

Duncan imagined that man found himself welcoming the notion of song and jest, as well, as the troubadours arrived just after the funeral mass.

Or perhaps he sought to see Lady Ysmaine smile. Radegunde had confessed to Duncan that her mistress was uncomfortable in the mornings with her pregnancy. It was good that Mathilde and Lady Richildis had arrived, for their presence would do as much to ease Lady Ysmaine's concerns as their ministrations.

By the time the meal was served, the hall was filled with merriment, which was no doubt encouraged by the generous flow of wine and ale. The villagers cheered at the sight of the roast boar, which was far larger than Duncan had recalled. The troubadours sang an impromptu ditty to Lord Gaston's valor, which the lord of the manor acknowledged with a smile.

It was not unlikely that the funeral for Lady Azalaïs that very morn had also made those yet living wish to celebrate their fortunate state.

The meal was served and the troubadours began to serenade the company while they enjoyed the repast. Duncan sat at the back of the hall, near the portal, where he could watch the others. On this day, he accepted only one cup of wine and made it last.

Something was going to happen. He could feel it in his bones, and the watchfulness of Fergus only amplified his own impression.

It was natural that any challenge to Lord Gaston's leadership should come to the fore on this day, after all. Would Lord Millard stay or would he go? What would Lady Marie choose to do? Decisions had undoubtedly been made and would be announced at the feast. Duncan wished they would hear from Wulfe, if only to know for certain that Christina was well and that Everard had been brought to justice. But it was early days as yet for that. Wulfe might still be in pursuit of the villain.

When all had sated themselves, Lord Gaston stood and clapped his hands. "I thank you all for joining me in celebration this day, and I hope the fare was sufficiently ample."

The villagers cheered and pounded their cups on the tables.

"I would have you linger and take your ease, perhaps dance with someone who has caught your eye." Lord Gaston grinned at the enthusiastic reaction to that suggestion. He indicated the troubadours. "And here we have a troupe to lead us in merriment. May their songs and tales bring pleasure to you all."

Thunderous applause followed these few remarks and the company of traveling minstrels advanced toward the high table. Duncan watched them and knew he would invite Radegunde to dance soon enough. Her mother Mathilde cast him a warning glance, as if to remind him about her daughter's foot, and Duncan waved in understanding. In that moment, he saw astonishment touch Mathilde's features.

The troubadours were just passing her and she stared at one, all the color draining from her face. Then she dropped her gaze and hastily composed herself. If Duncan had not been looking at her in the very moment of her dismay, he would have missed her reaction.

As it was, he wondered what had caused it. Had she recognized someone in the company? There was one man taller than the rest, a great bear of a man, and Duncan felt there was something familiar about the way he walked.

Then the man stepped forward and raised his voice, and Duncan knew.

It was the wild man of the woods.

Radegunde's eyes widened at the sound of the man's voice, which verified his own conclusion.

Her father had left the forest.

Duncan sat taller to watch and listen. The wild man of the woods looked far more reputable than he had in the forest. He wore garb that had clearly been donated by others, for it did not fit him overly well, but it was clean. His hood was raised and he bent over a lute. That pose hid his features from those seated at the high table, but Duncan had glimpsed his shadowed face. He had trimmed his hair and shaved, and was a finely wrought man.

Radegunde and her brothers had his coloring.

"If my lord will forgive me for being so bold, I deem it too soon after such a generous meal to dance," the leader of the troupe said, his voice easily carrying over the company. "Perhaps a tale would suit the company better first."

There was a roar of assent to this and the leader gestured to the wild man of the woods. "We have a storyteller in our ranks."

Radegunde's father stood, handing the lute to another and folding his hands before himself. He kept his head bowed. "I know only one tale," he continued. "So I hope it finds favor with you."

A chuckle rolled through the company. There was a bustle of activity as cups were filled and people moved to sit more at their ease. Bones were cast to the dogs, who gnawed them contentedly beneath the tables. Radegunde's father nodded at his companion with the lute and that man struck a chord of accompaniment.

"Once there was a man," he began. "More than a man, he was a knight and a lord. The tower of his keep was tall, his horses were magnificent, and his forests abounded with game."

"We know that knight!" cried one of the villagers. "He is Lord Gaston!" The others cheered this notion and Gaston waved the company to silence.

Radegunde's father smiled. "Nay, not Lord Gaston, for this lord had bad fortune in marriage. He loved his wife with all his heart, but she died in the bearing of their first son, then the son died shortly thereafter."

Duncan watched, for he knew his Radegunde would shed a tear at this detail, and she did. His heart clenched at this evidence of her compassion, and he felt honored anew that she had put her hand within his own.

"Nay, not Lord Gaston," that man said and claimed his wife's hand within his own. More than one in the company smiled at his gesture, as did Lady Ysmaine.

"This lord was so bereft by the loss that he declared he would not wed again. It was in his grief that he heard of more sad tidings. He had a lady cousin, not so wealthy as he but possessed of great beauty and wed to an honorable knight. That knight had been killed in battle, around the same time that the lord's wife died in childbirth, and the lord's cousin had been left alone with her infant children. She had twins by the lost knight, a boy and a girl, and sent word to her cousin to ask after some aid in these sorry times. The lord did better than send her some coin—he invited her and the children to live with him. In truth, as he oft said, they gave him the gift for they brought sunlight back into his abode."

Duncan smiled for Radegunde was better pleased with the tale now.

"The children grew and blossomed beneath the lord's care, becoming as dear to him as if they had been his own children. His cousin, though, did not fare so well. She could not face the days and nights without her true love and faded in strength. Two winters after her arrival at her cousin's holding, she took a chill and died. After some consultation with her kin, the lord resolved to raise the twins as his own. He hired tutors for both boy and girl, and ensured the boy was trained to win his spurs. The children grew into fine nobles, the lady as lovely as the dawn and her brother both handsome and filled with valor. The lord knighted the boy with his own blade when that time came, and truly, it could not have been said whether the twins or the lord loved each other most. There were rumors that he meant to make the boy his heir, but neither knight ever spoke of it to others."

Duncan sipped his wine, wondering. Did Radegunde's father share his own tale?

"Because the lord did not wish to lose his cousin's son in war, he insisted that the boy participate only in tournaments, an activity at which the young knight excelled. He won many garlands from maidens and more accolades. His sister loved the pageantry of these events, and so they often traveled together when he was invited to participate. If the location was nearby, the lord went to watch as well, but in his winter years, he was less inclined to travel any distance. And so it was at one such tournament, the sister met a knight who was much smitten with her. Indeed the vigor of his interest in her was only equaled by her disinterest in his suit. They argued, and this knight tried to restrain her, so forcibly that he left bruises upon her wrist."

The company gasped at this. Duncan felt his eyes narrow, for it was too familiar a tale. Radegunde was listening avidly, while Millard looked annoyed. Rohese was pale and staring down at her hands in her lap.

"She showed them to her brother on their journey home, confessing that the knight had declared he meant to wed her and if she did not agree, he would leave her with no choice. She was resolved to not upset their guardian with this matter, though her brother argued that course, and hoped it could be quietly resolved between two knights pledged to honor."

There was a murmur of outrage that a lady and a maiden should be treated so ill.

"And so it was that the brother was resolved to defend his sister from this other knight. He knew the cur's name and his colors. He waited to accept another invitation to tournament until he knew that knight would be there. He had hoped to journey alone, to discuss the matter with the knight and dissuade him, but the sister would hear naught of it. She was resolved to accompany him and see the knight shamed and her honor defended. She could not be swayed, so great was her resolve."

Duncan smiled into his cup, well acquainted with a woman of such determination.

"And so the pair departed together, as they had so many times before. The young knight spoke to the one who wished to court his sister, and the knight laughed the matter away. The young knight thought the matter resolved, and so he entered the lists and won much acclaim that day. It was a triumph, his best day ever, and he could not wait to take the spoils home to the lord and cousin who showed them such good care."

Radegunde's father paused and the company was rapt. "It was only when he was showered with flowers and surrounded by admirers, he realized that his sister was not to be seen."

The teller paused to take a sip of wine. Even the dogs seemed to be awaiting the next part of the tale, so quiet were they.

"The knight left his destrier in the care of his squire and hastened to his sister's tent, pitched beside his own. She was not there, nor was she in his own tent. She was not with the ladies of the court, nor in the hall where they offered refreshment. On impulse, he strode to the tent of the knight who had been so determined to be his sister's suitor. He heard sounds of a struggle from within and charged in with his blade drawn."

The company leaned forward.

"His sister was there, indeed, though not in any state in which he should have seen her. Her wrists were bound and her skirts were around her hips. The knight was atop her, one heavy hand over her mouth, and they struggled mightily as he strove to claim her maidenhead. She drove her knee into him and thrashed beneath his weight, then she saw her brother and froze, an entreaty in her eyes. And he knew that if he did not intervene, her maidenhead would be lost to this man, who could then compel her to wed him. The notion filled the young knight with such fury that he lifted his dagger and he threw it at the man who would so violate his sister.

Those listening to the tale gasped as one.

"But a serpent is wily and sees to its own preservation above all else. The abusive knight had heard the brother's entry, though he pretended otherwise. He saw the sister's expression and guessed what the knight would do. And when the knife was loosed, the knight quickly rolled the lady atop him, so that the flying blade landed in her back instead of his own."

"Oh!" the company cried as one.

Duncan saw Lord Amaury and Lady Richildis exchange a quick glance. Did they know this tale already? Was it truth? Lord Gaston was frowning at the board. Duncan knew that Gaston did not approve of tournaments, of playing at war. He might, though, recall the tale.

More to the point, if the honorable knight was Radegunde's father, what did this mean for her prospects?

The storyteller continued. "The villain cast the maiden aside with disdain as the blood seeped out of her. 'She is of no value to me now,' he declared. Then he looked at the knight and he smiled. 'And you will not win at joust any longer, not with this stain upon your honor.' The brother did not understand the words and in truth he did not care. The knight left and the brother fell to his knees beside his sister. He saw immediately that her wound was deep. The knife was buried to the hilt in her back and surely had pierced her heart. He gathered her into his arms, weeping and gnashing his teeth. She forgave him and kissed his brow, their tears mingling as she died in his embrace."

More than one in the hall wiped away a tear, including Radegunde.

"It was only after the sister had breathed her last and the knight had closed her eyes that he realized he was no longer alone. The baron who had hosted the tournament stood in the opening of the tent, all the guests gathered behind him. 'She would have seduced me,' the wicked knight declared. 'I meant to wed her on the morrow and treat her with all honor and dignity, but her brother claimed he would not allow the match. I fear he would not permit her to be happy.' The knight was incredulous but many believed this tale, uttered with such conviction, and faced with the truth of his own knife in his sister's back, he could not think of any tale that would excuse him, even the truth."

"Poor lamb," one of the women from the village murmured and her husband offered her a napkin to blow her nose.

"The knight was relieved of all he had won that day, dishonored as the other knight had declared he would be. He took his sister home to be buried and learned that the tale had been delivered swiftly to the lord who had taken them in. That man was furious and felt that the young knight had acted rashly at great expense. Such was his anger that the knight never told him the truth. He abandoned his armor and weapons, his horse and all his belongings, and he left his life behind. Disheartened, he went into the forest, determined to die there alone as penance for his own folly."

So it *was* his tale. Radegunde's father was a nobleman, Duncan had reached too high in taking her hand in his. The realization made the wine churn in his belly.

"There is a tale to dispel the most festive mood," muttered one man.

"But that is not the end of it," the storyteller said, raising a finger. "For he quickly learned that he was not alone in the forest. Not only were there many creatures sharing the woods with him, but there was a beautiful young woman who came to forage for plants. He became aware of her first because she sang softly under her breath, and the sound drew him like a moth to a flame. He found himself fascinated by her, following her, awaiting her return, but never daring to speak to her. He feared that he would lose the solace of beauty in his life again and so he remained silent."

"Perhaps she saw the truth of his heart, but knew she had to speak first," Mathilde said into the silence of the hall.

Duncan smiled at the reaction of the company, for they had not guessed until this moment that the tale was rooted in truth. They chattered to each other and looked between the storyteller and Mathilde—who had eyes only for each other.

"And so he was blessed with her companionship, because she was bolder than he," Radegunde's father said.

"Perhaps she simply did not know what was at risk," Mathilde replied.

"Perhaps it was best that way," Radegunde's father said, his voice hardening. "For tidings came to his ears one day some years later that the knight who had killed his sister was actively seeking the brother. It seemed he wished the truth to be silenced forever, and the brother had no doubt that this knight would do injury wherever was necessary to see his end achieved. And so the brother left the beautiful woman, though he loved her in truth, though she had borne him a strong son and a daughter every measure as beautiful as herself."

"He left only because he feared they would be injured by the villain, as his sister had been," Mathilde provided.

Radegunde's father bowed his head. "No man could bear the weight of such a crime laid unjustly at his door. Not twice in one life." His words were thick and his voice husky. Then he raised a hand. "But such was the hold this woman held over the brother's heart, that he could not forget her or even stay away forever. He returned to her furtively, when he could, stealing moments of pleasure with her at intervals that were too far apart. He missed speaking with her and seeking her counsel. He missed the easy confidence that had once been part of their match, but he feared to jeopardize her welfare. He was as a mouse, taking crumbs from the table that would not be missed, not daring to hope for more. He missed the births of his three additional sons, but loved them all dearly just the same."

"Surely one day, the hero of your tale must leave the woods and seek justice," Lord Amaury said, no speculation in his tone.

Radegunde's father bowed. "Surely so, and he does as much this day." He straightened and surveyed the company, pride in his stance and a challenge in his eyes. "He stands before you, and appeals to Lord Gaston and Lord Amaury for justice against the fiend who has stolen all from him."

Mathilde raised her hands to her lips. Radegunde's eyes were wide, but those of her brother Michel were even wider.

"Zounds!" Lord Amaury declared as he rose to his feet.

"Amaury!" Lady Richildis whispered. "Do not speak thus before the company!"

"Whyever not?" Lord Amaury boomed, his face alight. "The fairest knight I have ever met on the field is alive, when all thought he was dead. Thierry de Roussignon! I thought to never see you again!"

"Not even in Heaven, Amaury, with the repute I was given," Radegunde's father jested and Amaury laughed.

"I never believed you guilty of it," he retorted. Amaury left the high table and marched to Radegunde's father, shaking his old comrade's hand heartily, then granting him a hug fit to break his ribs.

"Then the old tale *was* rooted in truth," Gaston said quietly.

Millard, Duncan noted, eased away from the table. Duncan pulled his knife covertly but Fergus rose smoothly to his feet and blocked Millard's path. Fergus leaning against the wall with insouciance and smiled when Millard glared at him.

"But why tell your tale now?" Lord Gaston asked. "Why share it here?"

Radegunde's father straightened, his tone becoming solemn. "First, because you are returned and I heard long ago of your thirst for justice," he said and Lord Gaston inclined his head. "And also because the villain who ensured my sister's demise is here, sir." Thierry lifted a finger and pointed at the head table. "His name is Millard de Saint-Roux."

"What madness is this?" Millard demanded, even as the hall erupted in chatter. "Am I to stand accused by a stranger in the hall of my wife's own kin?"

"Have you a defense?" Lord Gaston asked.

"I have no need of one," Millard retorted. "It is his word against mine, and this tale is such folly that no one can put credence in it." He glared at Gaston. "You were not there."

"Not I," Lord Gaston acknowledged. "Not at a tournament where men play at war. One hears tales, though."

"Gossip," Millard said disparagingly.

"Not gossip, for I *was* at that tournament," Lord Amaury said smoothly. "I remember the death of that maiden and the accusations made against her brother." He placed a hand upon the shoulder of Radegunde's father. "Accusations that no one who knew this knight believed."

"His patron believed them, by his own tale," Millard argued. "Surely that baron knew him better than most."

"Surely that man above all others might have spoken in haste and grief," Lord Amaury countered.

"This is madness," Millard said, as if he could dismiss the accusation with his attitude. He made as if to leave the board, but Fergus did not let him pass. "I will not remain to be so insulted. Is it not sufficient that my wife was laid to her final rest this day?"

Lord Amaury turned to Lord Gaston, his hand open in invitation of a decision. Gaston pursed his lips. "This should be the king's justice," he began to protest, but Radegunde's father spoke in the same moment.

"I will abandon the charge against you," Thierry said to Millard with pride. "If you will allow divine justice to decide the truth."

"What is this?" Lord Gaston asked.

"Mortal combat," Thierry said with grim resolve. "Let God ensure that the innocent man triumphs, for He knows the fullness of the truth as well as we two." He offered his hand, and Millard glared at him for a charged moment.

"The ultimate judge," Lord Amaury murmured.

"Games of war," Lord Gaston said.

"God's will being done," Lord Amaury countered. He placed a hand on Lord Gaston's shoulder. "It might be best."

"Aye, it will be." Millard leaped the high table, marched across the floor and seized his challenger's hand. "Let God support his own," he declared. "I will see this lie silenced."

"We shall see a liar silenced, to be sure," Thierry replied.

Duncan ran a hand over his brow. Would there be a second funeral on this day? Lord Gaston and Lord Amaury conferred, the older man's manner insistent.

Meanwhile, Millard and Thierry strode to the bailey with equal resolve, squires hastening ahead of them to muster armor and weapons. The company rose and flowed toward the bailey with obvious excitement, many refilling their cups before they left the hall. Duncan saw Mathilde grip the shoulder of Lady Richildis' maid, then take a breath and follow the villagers. She kept her gaze downcast and he guessed that she believed this was the shadow she had feared.

He sought Radegunde only to spy her slipping from the hall. Who did she follow? He glanced back at the high table and noted that Lady Ysmaine looked pale, although Lord Gaston attended her. Did Radegunde fetch something from the solar for her lady? Duncan surveyed the company and saw that Lady Marie and her daughter Rohese were missing.

Did they mean to retrieve the book for Millard? Or had they another objective?

Did Radegunde pursue them?

Duncan stepped back into the shadows, letting the company flow past him, as he debated his choices. Should he aid with the preparations for the mortal combat and leave Radegunde to learn what she could? Or should he pursue her, in case she had need of protection? If she meant only to retrieve a token for Lady Ysmaine, his aid would not be needed.

When he saw Benedicta head toward the stairs, his choice was made. That maid's manner was covert, and it was too easy to recall her dislike of Radegunde.

And Radegunde's conviction that she was wicked.

Duncan drew his knife and followed, even more stealthy than his prey.

Could it be true?

Could her father be a noble knight, one discredited by a liar and a rogue?

Radegunde found it easy to believe that matters had been so. She hoped that her father fought better than Millard, and that justice was served this day. She wanted to watch, and also to give support to her mother, but something was afoot.

Why did Lady Marie climb the stairs again?

Why did she fairly drag Rohese with her?

Radegunde would know the truth. She clung to the shadows as

she pursued the pair, straining her ears to hear Lady Marie's words.

"It is as good a moment as any to solve the riddle," she declared to her daughter, almost forcibly urging the maiden up the stairs.

"I would rather watch the battle," Rohese declared. "I want to see him die!"

"He will not die, you fool." Lady Marie's tone was dismissive. "We must find some detail in our favor!"

"Your favor, you mean," Rohese complained. "It is your fault that all has gone awry, and your fault that Azalaïs is dead."

"What is the matter with you? Why have you become defiant on this day of all days?"

"Azalaïs is dead!" Rohese cried. "She did as you bade her but it made no difference. She is dead, and it is your fault, and I will not do as you instruct. I do not want to die!"

A slap echoed in the stairwell. "You will do as you are bidden..."

"I will not!"

A few footsteps sounded on the stairs, as if Rohese would flee, but then Radegunde heard her gasp. She peeked to see that Lady Marie held a fistful of her daughter's hair and had her backed against the wall. "Do not be ridiculous," Lady Marie said in a heated whisper. "We will triumph together or not at all."

"I will flee."

"Who will feed you?" Lady Marie scoffed. "Who will see to your welfare?"

Rohese sneered. "As you do, *Maman*?"

"Bite your tongue and fetch the book."

"I will not marry him."

"You will do as you are told."

Rohese made a little squeak, and Radegunde wondered whether she should intervene. Could she protect the maiden from her own mother? She imagined not, for Lady Marie would simply dismiss her—and Radegunde would never discover what detail Lady Marie sought and why.

She trailed the women up the stairs to the top floor. Did they mean to enter the solar? Radegunde paused when she heard the sound of a scraping stone. She peered over the lip of the steps to see that a stone in the exterior wall outside the door of the solar had been removed. It concealed a space, where evidently Lady Marie had hidden the book because she removed it now. She drew a key from her belt then and urged Rohese to the door of the solar.

"It is no longer your chamber," Rohese protested as her mother unlocked the portal.

"And yet it is the most private room in the keep. None will find us there." Lady Marie gave Rohese a little push into the chamber. "We must learn what Lady Eudaline knew!"

"Surely it will only be rumor."

"She might know of some deficiency in Gaston's claim, or even in that of his father, Fulk. We might find evidence that Millard would welcome."

"You have drawn a web, *Maman*, from which there is no good escape." Rohese gave her mother a look of disdain. "You should never have poisoned Papa."

Radegunde bit back her gasp of surprise, but Rohese was not done.

"I did what had to be done," Lady Marie insisted. "Just as you will do what must be done."

"Did you imagine that your lover would wed you, instead of Azalaïs? Is that why Papa had to die?"

Lover?

"Oh, you are a witless fool, Rohese! What merit is there in having eyes if you refuse to use them?" The daughter made another squeak, then the door to the solar was slammed behind the pair.

Radegunde waited, then took a breath and crept to the door. She crouched before it and peered through the lock. She could see Rohese seated on a stool, the one that Lady Ysmaine used in the morning when Radegunde combed her hair. At her mother's command, Rohese opened the book. "It does not open fully."

"It is no matter. Read the notes in the margin aloud. Here."

"You should command Benedicta or a maid to read it to you."

"Benedicta does not know her letters and I trust no other. Read!"

Had Azalaïs been commanded to read aloud by her mother or by her husband? Radegunde hoped it had been Millard, for then there was a chance that Lady Marie did not know the book was poisoned, and did not deliberately condemn her other daughter.

Or maybe Rohese was defiant because she knew the truth. Radegunde bit her lip and listened. Soon enough, the familiar words came from Rohese's lips.

"I arrived as a new bride in 1153, knowing full well that my predecessor, Rohese, had been buried only six months."

Rohese paused. "Your grandmother," Lady Marie said. "Your father insisted we name you in his mother's honor."

Radegunde blinked at the bitterness in the lady's tone, but Rohese continued to read.

"She and her youngest son had been killed when a boat capsized. Fulk did not believe it an accident. He confessed that he was glad he had taken Bayard with him on that day's ride, for he had chosen to do so in the last moment. He was but six years of age and should have been on that boat with his mother and younger brother. They had planned the excursion weeks before and the boy was disappointed to be denied it in the last moment."

Radegunde could hear Lady Marie pacing. It seemed that her steps were becoming quicker.

"Fulk had suspicions as to who might be the guilty party. Châmont-sur-Maine had only come to his hand in 1142, by grant of Geoffrey of Anjou, as reward for loyal service. Fulk held it against the assault of Elias II in 1151, and the grant was reaffirmed by King Henry. But Fulk was not the sole one who desired such a gift from the king's hand."

"And?" Marie demanded when Rohese fell silent.

"The pages are stuck," her daughter protested and Radegunde peered through the keyhole as the maiden raised her fingertips to her lips.

She could not remain silent.

"Do not lick your fingers!" she cried, bursting into the solar. Both women stared at her in anger and dismay. "The pages are poisoned. That is what killed Lady Azalaïs!"

"A leap from the window killed my daughter," Lady Marie corrected, her voice hard.

Rohese looked between the two of them with obvious alarm,

then let the book fall to the ground. "*Maman*! You could not have known!"

Lady Marie seized the book and handed it to Radegunde. "Read," she commanded. She pointed to her daughter when Radegunde hesitated. "And you, lock the portal. This one will not fly to her mistress to tell tales of me."

"*Maman*," Rohese murmured, a warning in her tone.

"I command her only to read," Lady Marie said and her gaze was hard. "I believe no such whimsy about poisoned pages. If this one is so clever, let her defend herself."

Rohese went to the door and turned the key in the lock. She remained by the door, her eyes wide and her uncertainty clear.

It seemed she learned much of her mother on this day.

Radegunde knew that she could not overpower them both. Indeed, she wanted to learn what Lady Eudaline had written and knew she could foil the trap. She had to believe that some soul would come to her aid before too long, and she also suspected that Lady Marie would destroy the book if its contents condemned her or anyone she would defend.

Under Lady Marie's watchful eye, Radegunde fetched an old cloth and the pitcher of water that she had brought that morning for Lady Ysmaine. It was not yet empty and the water was clean. She donned a pair of gloves that Lady Ysmaine no longer favored and hoped her mistress would not mind the loss. They would have to be burned. Then she wet the edge of the pages, used her knife to coax the next page free, and continued to read Lady Eudaline's confession.

CHAPTER TWENTY-ONE

uncan crept up the stairs, uncertain where Benedicta had gone. Indeed, he could not see Lady Marie, Lady Rohese, or Radegunde either. The keep might have been abandoned. When he climbed to the top floor of the tower, though, he heard Radegunde's voice from inside the chamber.

Was she reading aloud?

"*The mercenary Sebastien de Saint-Roux had also served Geoffrey of Anjou, and believed himself deserving of reward. Fulk said they had argued when Châmont-sur-Maine had been awarded to him. He had no evidence that Sebastien might have been responsible for the subsequent demise of his wife and son, but believed his adversary capable of such violence in pursuit of his own ends. Fulk was vigilant in guarding Bayard and dismissed a number of men from his service because he was uncertain of their alliances. It seemed this was sufficient, for there were no other incidents. I bore Fulk another son, Gaston, which eased his concerns for the future, and the boys were as close as blood brothers. Sebastien's son Millard was forbidden to enter the keep, even when he trained for his spurs at the same time as Gaston.*"

She read from Lady Eudaline's book!

Radegunde could not be licking the pages to part them, not

given what she knew of the poison.

Duncan hastened to the door and put his eye to the keyhole. To his relief, Radegunde wore gloves and he saw that she separated the pages with water and a knife.

His clever lady had found a solution.

He would ensure that both knife and gloves were destroyed.

Lady Marie paced across his view repeatedly, almost unrecognizable in her fury, and he could not see Rohese from his vantage point. Duncan listened, certain more witnesses to the book's contents would be better.

"Let me tell more of Fulk's demise. Fulk rode out to parlay with Sebastien, though he told no one of his intent but me, and he rode out alone. He returned with an injury inflicted by a lance but would not accuse Sebastien. He instructed me to ensure that Gaston left France immediately, for he knew he could not survive the wound. He was convinced that Bayard would be safe so long as Gaston drew breath. I had many questions, but did as bidden and wrote to my son, who was in service to the Templars. I heard soon after of Gaston's departure for Outremer. I retired to the convent after Fulk's death to draw attention from Gaston, my curiosity unabated. I have made inquiries these years and finally have learned that Bayard was safe, not because Gaston drew breath nor even because Sebastien had himself died, but because Sebastien had changed his strategy to claim Châmont-sur-Maine."

There was a pause.

"There is a piece of vellum between the pages," Radegunde said, pulling it loose and frowning at it. "It looks to be a family tree."

"Nay! Give me that!" Lady Marie cried and seized the scrap. Radegunde snatched after it but the lady held it aloft. Duncan tried the door, fearing all went awry.

It was securely locked.

"She *knew*! The witch!" Lady Marie declared and dropped to her knees before the brazier. She tried to strike the flint while defending the vellum from Radegunde.

"You shall not destroy it!" Radegunde fought Lady Marie for custody of the flint. To Duncan's satisfaction, she wrested it from the noblewoman. She cast it out the window and was slapped across the face for her defiance. The blow sent her staggering backward and Duncan tried the door again.

"Who told her?" Lady Marie demanded. "Who betrayed me?"

"Who told her what?" Rohese asked, sounding fearful of her mother's wrath. She must have been standing near the door, out of Duncan's view.

"It is not for you to know," Lady Marie retorted, even as Radegunde tried to claim the vellum again. The women fought over it.

"More secrets!" Rohese cried, as if some barrier had snapped within her. She lunged into view, launching herself at her mother. "Is that not the root of all evil in this place? Let me see!" Lady Marie held the piece of vellum out of reach.

Duncan jumped at the weight of a hand upon his shoulder and realized that Lord Gaston and Lady Ysmaine had arrived, with Bartholomew behind them. He stepped aside, so that Gaston could better view events, though he was reluctant to lose sight of Radegunde.

"Wretch!" Lady Marie cried, then Duncan heard someone's weight fall to the floor. He itched to see, but Gaston frowned and straightened.

"There. No one will know of it now," Lady Marie said with satisfaction.

Lord Gaston murmured to Bartholomew and that man fled down the stairs. Had she flung the vellum out the window? Duncan guessed that Bartholomew had been dispatched to retrieve it before the river washed away whatever was written upon it.

"I shall cast you after it if you do not read the rest," Lady Marie threatened.

Radegunde cleared her throat and began to read again. "*As the enclosed document reveals, Bayard unwittingly wed the bastard spawn of Sebastien. Though Marie had been raised at Roquelle, she was not of that family's blood. They accepted payment from Sebastien to raise his bastard daughter as their own, and it was he who suggested to the lord of the manor that her best match would be with Fulk's son. And so it is that Sebastien might have gained the holding for his kin in the end, if Marie had borne a son to Bayard. When she did not, the scheme was thwarted. When I discovered her lineage, I sent word to Bayard for I had no wish for him to shelter a viper in his own bed.*" There was a rustle as Radegunde parted the pages again. "*He died the day after receiving my missive.*"

"A coincidence," Lady Marie insisted.

"A murder," Rohese corrected. "You killed him. You killed Papa!"

"He meant to cast me out!" Lady Marie cried. "She betrayed me to my own husband!"

"And so you poisoned him, the husband who had treated you with honor and dignity," Rohese charged.

"That is sufficient." Lord Gaston placed his key in the lock and turned it audibly. Though he was composed, the vigor with which he kicked open the door showed his anger. The three women spun to regard him with surprise. "It says much of your nature that you believed the murder of your own spouse to be a fitting solution," he said grimly to Lady Marie.

Her eyes lit with anger. "And who would you defend, if you were compelled to choose between your spouse and your blood? Would you take Ysmaine over Bayard, or the other way around?"

"I thought Millard was your lover," Rohese whispered, her features pale.

"Silence!" Lady Marie snapped.

"The family tree was evidence of your betrayal," Gaston continued. "Did Sebastien have more hidden children?"

Lady Marie glared at them all in defiance. "You will never know."

There was the sound of a footfall from behind them, and Bartholomew knocked at the open door, his breathing quick. He bowed and presented a damp piece of vellum to Gaston. "I caught it as soon as I could, my lord."

"Nay!" Lady Marie whispered, but it was too late. Lord Gaston scanned the document, then handed it to his wife.

"It is true. Millard *is* your brother," she said. "Yet you wedded him to his own niece!"

"Half-brother," Lady Marie corrected tersely.

Lady Ysmaine frowned at the piece of vellum. "But you were raised as the daughter of the house of Roquelle."

"They were paid and paid well to shelter me and hide my truth.

314

I owe them naught."

"And so Sebastien's quest to hold Châmont-sur-Maine was pursued by his spawn," Gaston said. "Save that you did not bear a son."

"Azalaïs would have done so, if you had not come home so quickly," Lady Marie insisted. "Or Rohese in her stead."

"Wedded by force to my uncle!" Rohese whispered in horror. "It is unholy."

"And yet you wrote to me," Lord Gaston mused. "Summoning me home."

Lady Marie exhaled in vexation. "I had no choice. The bishop arrived and asked if you had been notified. I had said I had no means to see that any missive reached you in Outremer, but he offered to ensure its delivery." Her lips tightened. "I thought you would be dead, or that by the time you returned, Azalaïs would have delivered an heir. I believed my brother could defend what should be our own." Her eyes narrowed. "Indeed, I prayed mightily for your demise."

"And the futility of your prayers is evidence of divine judgment upon you." Lady Ysmaine stepped forward, putting her hand on her husband's elbow. "For my lord husband found allies on his quick journey home."

Lady Marie glared at them both, her displeasure clear.

"You would have wedded me to him, as well," Rohese repeated, her tone bitter. "And he would have beaten me, as he beat Azalaïs. You are no mother, but a viper who cares for no one."

"Bite your tongue!"

"Nay, I will tell the truth, and I will confess all of it to Uncle Gaston, for he is a man of honor like *Papa*. Millard will die in that duel, by God's grace, and rightly so, for he is a fiend from Hell. Azalaïs knew it well." Rohese's tongue was loosed. "I thought he was the one who had the gloves poisoned for Uncle Gaston, but he is not that clever, is he, *Maman*? It was you, was it not? Are you not the one who knows so much of poison in this keep?"

"She knows as much as me," Lady Marie said, pointing to Radegunde.

"But she saved me from your plot with the gloves," Lord Gaston said with resolve. "The truth of Radegunde's nature is revealed by her deeds, just as your truth is shown by yours." Lady Marie's lips tightened. "You will spend this night in the dungeon, though I regret that it is necessary to treat my brother's widow thus."

"That she is Bayard's murderer absolves you of any such compassion," Lady Ysmaine said and Lord Gaston nodded agreement.

At his gesture, Duncan strode to the lady and bound her wrists behind her back. Her fury was palpable. "You will regret this, Gaston. I will guarantee it."

"I fear you will be the one to regret your choices," Gaston said. "The king does not look kindly upon murderers."

"You will not dispatch me to his court!"

"Indeed, I will, for I could not be said to be impartial in this instance." Lady Marie seethed, but Lord Gaston smiled at his niece. "And you will choose your own course, Rohese. You may remain in my household."

"I would like to share my mother's truth with the people who I have known as my grandparents," the maiden said. "They are owed as much, though they will not welcome it." She squared her shoulders. "They are good people and cannot have known of my mother's scheme."

That they had taken payment from this Sebastien to raise his bastard daughter was a dubious credit, in Duncan's view, but perhaps they had been deceived by that man. Doubtless they had also been deceived by their adopted daughter.

Lady Ysmaine smiled. "And in assuming this task, you show your own nature, Rohese. We will ensure that you journey there safely." She drew the younger woman to her side, and Rohese seemed to welcome the attention though still she looked shaken.

"Steal my home and my child," Lady Marie muttered as Bartholomew urged her from the portal. "I have been cheated well and truly this day." With that, she marched down the stairs.

"I cannot rest in this chamber, Gaston," Lady Ysmaine said. "Not now."

"I will ensure that there is wine for you at the board," Lord Gaston said, then offered one elbow to his wife and the other to his niece. He surrendered the key to Duncan.

When they departed, Duncan crossed the chamber and lit the brazier, ensuring that the flames leaped high. He claimed the knife from Radegunde's grip and cast it into the flames. Lady Eudaline's book and the piece of vellum were wrapped and placed in a satchel to be sent to the king, then Radegunde cast the tainted gloves into the fire as well.

"God in Heaven, it is done," she whispered, then fell into his arms. "I never suspected her. Did you?"

"I knew her too little to guess." Duncan had naught good to say about a woman who would sacrifice her own daughter for her ends. Indeed, he was so relieved that Radegunde was hale that he found he had no ability to speak at all. He pulled her into his embrace and held her tightly. She kissed his throat and sagged against him just as the fanfare sounded from the bailey below.

"My father," she whispered.

"I suspect he will fight well," Duncan said, hoping to reassure her.

"I must see."

Radegunde gripped Duncan's hand tightly as he led her out of the chamber, though, and he hoped that he was right.

Radegunde was glad that they missed the beginning of the battle, for the men fought so hard that she could scarcely bear to look. This was no jest at war. One of them would die. By the time Duncan found her a vantage point in the bailey, Thierry was backing Millard against the packed earth with powerful strokes. Both men sported wounds and had smears of fresh blood on their armor, but Millard appeared to be tiring.

Or perhaps he had been distressed by the sight of Lady Marie being taken to the dungeon.

Radegunde wondered whether her father's vigil in the forest was serving him well, for that interval could not have been a life of ease. In contrast, Millard had been savoring the pleasures of Châmont-sur-Maine these past months and might have neglected his practice.

She hoped it were so, and that her father would triumph soon.

They had a mace and a sword each, and both knights held the mace in their right hand. Thierry swung the mace, but Millard suddenly leaped forward. He brought down his own mace with such vigor that his exhaustion must have been feigned. Their proximity gave Thierry little chance to evade the blow and the mace landed hard upon his wrist. Radegunde gasped. She was sure she heard a bone crack. Thierry dropped his own mace, his pain obvious, and Millard kicked it away. The balance shifted and Millard began to back Thierry across the bailey.

She clutched at Duncan, terrified for her father's fate.

Millard swung his mace as Thierry thrust with his sword. The blade was swept away with a clatter, though her father dove after it. Millard pursued him, the mace swinging high, but Thierry twisted and kicked at Millard's feet. Millard stumbled. Thierry stood up quickly and Millard froze when the point of Thierry's recovered blade was against his throat. There was a gap there, between hauberk and coif, and the point of the blade had found skin.

Millard dropped the mace.

He dropped the sword.

"To the death," Thierry reminded him. The company caught their breath and waited for Thierry to strike the killing blow.

But nay. He lifted the sword away and stepped back. There was a prick of blood at Millard's throat and no more. Thierry removed his helmet and turned to face Gaston. His hair was damp and his face was pale. Radegunde guessed that his wrist was broken.

"Has there not been enough death in this hall of late?" Thierry asked, his voice a low rumble of reason and Radegunde adored her father all over again.

The company smiled as one.

Then they gasped aloud, for Millard leaped after his opponent. He landed on Thierry's back with such force that the other man staggered. The company cried out in outrage, but Millard had pulled his knife and placed it against Thierry's bare throat. Mathilde paled. Radegunde could not bear to blink.

"Marie and I shall walk out of this keep, with Rohese," Millard declared.

"You know I cannot allow as much," Gaston said softly.

Millard made to move the knife.

Thierry slumped in defeat.

Millard smiled.

In a heartbeat, Thierry spun in Millard's grip. He kicked Millard's feet out from beneath him, flung that man on his back, and kicked him in the groin. When Millard moaned, Thierry seized his opponent's blade and held it beneath his chin.

"There will not be another death in this keep on this day," Lord Gaston said with authority. "Millard may keep his life, on the condition that he beg the forgiveness of Thierry de Roussignon on his knees before us all."

"And then I will walk free," Millard said.

Gaston shook his head. "And then you will savor the hospitality of my dungeon, with your sister." Many in the company gasped at this revelation. "On the morrow, you will be escorted to the king's court to stand trial for your crimes."

Millard sneered. "I will kiss no man's boot."

"So be it." Gaston gestured.

Two of the Templars who had accompanied their party from Paris stepped forward and bound Millard's wrists behind his back. He was urged across the bailey, even as he yelled in protest, then disappeared into the hall where the entrance to the dungeon was located.

Lord Gaston visibly took a deep breath. "Thierry, I will send a missive to your former patron, explaining all we have learned this day. If you would visit him to reconcile, I would entrust that letter to you."

"I would be honored to deliver it, Lord Gaston." Thierry bowed low. He turned and offered his hand to Mathilde who hastened toward him with obvious joy. He caught her in his arms and swung her around. Radegunde was not the sole one pleased to see her mother so well rewarded.

Of course, Mathilde was quick to examine Thierry's wrist and to lead him aside so she could tend it. Thierry did not look inclined to protest any of her attentions. Lady Richildis smiled at the reunited pair with pleasure. Michel looked awed and pleased, and Radegunde's own heart was thumping that justice had been served.

"And you should take your son as your companion," Lord Amaury declared. "For you have known little of each other these years, and I would spare him from my service for such a quest."

There were more formalities and polite responses exchanged before Radegunde herself was embraced by her father. Congratulations and good wishes rang out in the bailey, then Lord Gaston's call for dancing in the hall was greeted with enthusiasm.

Duncan held fast to Radegunde's hand, and they returned to the hall as the minstrels struck a merry tune. The tables were pushed back and the entire company took to the floor to dance. It would be late before their merrymaking eased, and if Marie and Millard railed against their situation, not a soul heard their protest.

Or cared for their discomfort.

FRIDAY, DECEMBER 25, 1187

Feast Day of the Nativity of Jesus Christ

Claire Delacroix

CHAPTER TWENTY-TWO

adegunde tried to enjoy the festivities of the season, but could not forget that Duncan would soon be departing. Much had occurred in the months since Lord Gaston's feast and homecoming. Lady Marie and Lord Millard had been discovered to be missing from the dungeon on the morning after their incarceration. It had become clear that Benedicta had aided in their escape for that maid had disappeared at the same time. Rohese had been gone, as well, though none believed she had accompanied her mother willingly.

Lady Ysmaine commented that Lord Gaston had been too generous with the wine the night before, for it seemed all had slept too well. Radegunde's father had undertaken the quest for justice and ridden in pursuit of the pair. It had been thought that they would seek out the family who had raised Lady Marie and seek refuge there. Lord Gaston had written a missive to Roquelle to advise them of the truth, as well as another to the king. The book and piece of vellum had been secured in the treasury.

In November, Thierry and Michel had returned with a courier from the king and Millard's blood on Thierry's blade. The villain was dead, the king held Marie in captivity awaiting his justice, and

Rohese enjoyed the pleasures of the king's court. Radegunde hoped she found a suitor there. Two of the Templars had escorted the courier to the king's court, two had returned to the Paris Temple and the final two of the six who had escorted the party from Paris were to journey with Fergus to his home in Scotland.

Radegunde's father, Thierry, had indeed been made heir of the holding of his former guardian, and Mathilde had left her hut at Valeroy to become lady of that holding. Michel remained at Valeroy, though now Lord Amaury trained him for his spurs. Her other brothers were with their parents, and she did not doubt they savored the change in their circumstances. Radegunde had been invited, as well, but chose to remain with Lady Ysmaine, who had been most ill with her pregnancy. It was right and good that she would remain in Lady Ysmaine's service until her child was born.

Surely Duncan would return to her soon after that. The closer his departure, the more Radegunde worried about his fate.

Bartholomew had been knighted earlier in December and looked most fine in his new raiment. To the surprise of Radegunde's lord and lady, he was determined to ride north with Fergus after the Yule. Radegunde did not fully understand his purpose, but Duncan said Bartholomew was intent upon a particular route through England and that Fergus saw no reason to challenge it, though it made the route home longer.

She wondered what future Fergus saw.

Radegunde had given Leila a gift this Yule, for they had become friends and she knew that Leila would remain with Fergus. A kirtle of green wool and a simple black belt, both women's garb, had been offered in secret and welcomed by Leila most heartily. Radegunde wished she could have summoned word from Leila's cousin in Outremer, but there was no way that might be done. Instead, she listened to Leila's memories and consoled her when she missed what she had left behind.

Wulfe and Christina had arrived for Bartholomew's knighting and brought tidings that Everard had been defeated—but more surprisingly, Wulfe had left the Templars and been named his father's heir. Christina had been restored to her noble family, then courted by Wulfe. Her name proved to be Juliana in truth, and his to be Sir Ulric von Altesburg, but Radegunde had frequently called both by the names she knew better. Juliana was with child.

Radegunde, to her disappointment, was not.

She rose that morning with a heavy heart, knowing that Lord Fergus would ride out soon. There was blood on her thighs, which meant both that she did not bear Duncan's son and that they would not be intimate when they were so close to parting.

It seemed most unfair.

She felt Duncan's gaze upon her as she dressed, but could not bring herself to look at him. She did not want to weep during their last days together, and knew he faced uncertainty. Despite her hope for the future, it felt like his departure would mark the end of all they had shared.

Duncan caught her shoulders in his hands and kissed her nape, before he turned her to face him. His gaze was solemn, and Radegunde suspected that he could read her thoughts.

"It will be a merry meal this day," he said, as if trying to coax her to smile. "There will be venison aplenty, which should please you."

"Aye, it does." Radegunde tried to smile and failed. "Summer seems so distant!"

Duncan frowned and his grip tightened on her shoulders. "I am not convinced I will see you even then," he admitted, and she realized what had been troubling him.

"Do not insist that I wait here for you, Duncan. Lady Ysmaine and Lord Gaston will ride north for the wedding, to be sure. I will find a nursemaid for the babe and..."

"I fear that Fergus will not wed his betrothed."

Radegunde was astonished. "But he loves her so! He has bought so many gifts for Lady Isobel."

Duncan frowned. "Yet I was never certain his regard was returned." He held her gaze. "I think Fergus dreads his reception as well."

"Then what shall we do?"

"I will return Fergus to Killairic as promised, and request release from his father's service. I will ride north then and end my father's quest to have me killed."

"I could aid you," she began but Duncan's finger fell across her lips to silence her.

"I will not put you in such peril and you know it well. Trust me, Radegunde. I will return to you by the last day of our handfast if I am alive to do so."

She sighed, knowing his decision was made. "You know his plans, do you not?" He nodded. "When do you depart?"

"At first light on the morrow."

Radegunde caught her breath.

"I wanted us to have this Yuletide together, without fears for the future."

"How can there be no fears for the future?" she demanded and once she began, Radegunde could not halt. "You will leave and I may never see you again! I may never even know your fate, if it is dire!" She caught her breath, then gestured to her own thighs. "And I will not even have your child to comfort me." Her voice faltered. "Oh, Duncan."

He caught her close and kissed her temple. "It might be better thus," he reminded her gently.

Radegunde tears rose and she did not try to stop them. "I love you, Duncan. I wish that I would bear your child."

"And I love you, sweet Radegunde."

She caught her breath and met his gaze. "You have never made that confession."

"Did my deeds not tell you the truth?"

That his words echoed the assurances of her mother made Radegunde feel that she had been blind. "I feared you loved only Gwyneth."

"Nay!" He gripped her shoulders more tightly and held her gaze, his resolve bearing down on her. "I did love Gwyneth and still I honor her memory. She died in the bearing of my son, and I can never forget that." The corner of his mouth lifted and he surveyed her with wonder. "But you, my Radegunde, are a joy beyond all expectation. It is you who have taught me to hope again, you who have claimed my heart for your own."

"Oh, Duncan." She was going to cry after all. Radegunde sniffled.

He caught her chin in his hand then and tipped her face upward, surveying her with such love in his eyes that her heart raced. "It will test me truly to leave you behind, though I know 'tis my duty," he whispered, his gaze intent. "I loved Gwyneth but that love was a faint shadow of what I feel for you. You are the blood of my heart, Radegunde. Never doubt otherwise."

Before she could reply, he kissed her with a sweet fervor that reassured her completely. She wrapped her arms around his neck and surrendered to his touch, welcoming him with all she had to give. Duncan broke their kiss with such obvious reluctance that she prayed anew that he would return quickly.

"And now your gift this Yule," he said, his tone teasing.

"I have no gift for you!"

"Do not be so certain of that. I have a gift for you and would request one from you in return."

Radegunde eyed him, uncertain what he schemed. There was a glint in his eyes that she liked well, though.

Duncan turned away then, to his saddlebag, which she saw he had packed while she slept. He pulled a familiar red silk bag from its depths and her heart clenched. He no longer carried the token within his chemise or even his purse, but he yet had the braided plait of Gwyneth's hair.

Radegunde said naught but trusted and waited.

Duncan rekindled the fire in the brazier and when the flames were leaping, he removed the braid of red-gold hair. "The past is as ash, my Radegunde, and I will prove it to you," he said softly. "I would leave you in no doubt of your claim upon me." He dropped the hair into the fire and let it burn, the last token of his dead wife.

He straightened and watched it burn to naught, his manner solemn. "There are those who say the Yule is the darkest night of the year, and thus the beginning of our journey toward light again. It can be a time for rebirth and for renewal." He cast the bag into the flames after it, and the silk smoked as it was devoured. When he turned, her heart thundered. "And so I would begin anew, Radegunde, with my heart securely in your possession."

"Just as mine is securely in yours," she said, blinking rapidly to dismiss her tears.

"Will you give me a braid of your hair, blood of my heart?" he asked, his gaze filled with love and his voice husky.

"But the bag is gone."

Duncan smiled and offered his hand. "I would wear it around my wrist, if you will bind it there."

Radegunde did weep then, happy tears that did not obstruct her ability to surrender the gift he requested. She pulled three of her own hairs and braided them as Duncan held the end. It took a few moments, for her hair was long, but she felt cherished as he watched her. When she had wrapped it around his wrist and bound the ends, he kissed her once more.

She felt the tension in him when he lifted his head and drew back to survey him. "What is it? Is there something you have not told me?"

Duncan winced. His fingers tangled in the hair at her nape, his touch making her tingle.

"Do not protect me from the truth, Duncan!"

"The man I killed all those years ago," he admitted. "The man who had spoken first for Gwyneth, was both my friend and my father's most loyal warrior. My father, as chieftain, pardoned me, but there were those who said he showed favor to his son, that had I been the son of another, I would have been condemned. My younger brother Guthred was of that company."

"So you can not rely upon Guthred for mercy, even if your father was inclined to grant it."

"I cannot."

"How can it be that your father pardoned you then but hunts you now?"

Duncan grimaced. "Perhaps he thought to gain my loyalty to his cause by showing me mercy." His gaze locked with hers. "Perhaps he is not truly the one who hunts me."

Radegunde caught her breath.

He frowned. "I must claim the amethyst pin to see this matter put to rest, Radegunde. I may be compelled to kill my brother to see that end achieved." He held her gaze. "I may not succeed."

"You will," she said with vigor. "Justice will prevail, as it did with my father and Millard."

Duncan smiled then, his fingertips slipping over her cheek and his eyes glowing. "Then we shall triumph, as well, and build the future we desire above all else."

"Aye, we shall," she vowed and believed it with all her heart.

Even before Duncan kissed her once again.

Claire Delacroix

SATURDAY, MAY 1, 1188

*Feast Day of the apostles
Saint Philip and
Saint James the Less*

Claire Delacroix

CHAPTER TWENTY-THREE

omething was amiss.

Radegunde saw it in Lord Gaston's thoughtful manner. He had a new habit of standing on the ramparts of Châmont-sur-Maine and watching the land in all directions. It would have taken a less observant person than Radegunde to fail to note that correspondence between Lord Amaury and Lord Gaston was exchanged more frequently, often daily. Once or twice there had been smoke on the horizon, and Lord Gaston had been pensive when he came to the solar. Just the day before, a missive had been delivered from Paris by a Templar, though Lord Gaston had not spoken of it.

Radegunde did not think he had confided in Lady Ysmaine, for she struggled more with her pregnancy as she neared her time. Indeed, Lady Ysmaine had not been blessed with an easy pregnancy, but she was resolute and strong. The babe kicked with increasing frequency and though her lady was tired, Radegunde hoped all would end well.

Lord Gaston was considerate of his wife and constantly tried to ensure her comfort. For this reason as much as any words she had overheard, Radegunde suspected that he hid his concerns about other matters from his lady wife.

Radegunde was lonely without Duncan's presence, although she savored the tidings that Bartholomew had brought on his return the previous month to be invested with his holding in England. Even he had a wife, which made Radegunde feel even more alone. She asked him repeatedly for every detail about Duncan but he had been indulgent.

Perhaps Bartholomew had learned the yearning of love.

She counted the days until the anniversary of her handfast with Duncan. It seemed an eternity away. There was, as yet, no invitation to nuptials in Scotland, which made her believe Duncan had been right about Lady Isobel.

Radegunde was both relieved and filled with trepidation when Lady Ysmaine faltered on the stairs that night. She was retiring early, at Lord Gaston's insistence, for she had been uncomfortable all the day long and had slept poorly the night before. Radegunde accompanied her, and Lady Ysmaine clutched at her hand. Radegunde felt her shaking and saw the ripple of the first convulsion.

"Radegunde! It is time!"

"Aye, my lady," Radegunde said with brisk confidence. "Time 'tis and soon all will be done. I doubt it will be as quickly done as you might prefer, for this is merely the beginning." She smiled and took her lady's elbow, urging her to the solar. Lady Ysmaine visibly took reassurance from her maid's confident mood, and Radegunde shouted that Lord Gaston be summoned.

In a trice, Lady Ysmaine was sitting on the side of the great bed, wearing only her shift, her hair unpinned. The shutters had been drawn, the candles and brazier lit, and the drapes on the great bed drawn on the other sides that she might be warmer. Radegunde meant to comb her hair and braid it into a plait, for the attention might calm her. The lady bared her teeth as another contraction rolled through her body, and was breathing quickly when Lord Gaston crossed the threshold.

Two contractions so quickly in succession and so early. Radegunde was surprised and a little fearful at the import of that.

Lord Gaston claimed his wife's hand and she clutched at him

until the contraction passed. Radegunde wiped Lady Ysmaine's brow as she smiled for her concerned spouse.

"So, will you take this moment to tell me what troubles you?" Lady Ysmaine asked lightly and Radegunde saw that Lord Gaston was startled by the request. "Oh, Gaston, I know you ponder some course of action, and while I appreciate that you do not wish to trouble me with worldly concerns, I would welcome the distraction in this moment."

"I should send for Mathilde," he said instead.

"I suspect there will not be time," Radegunde informed him, keeping her voice calm with an effort. "My mother intended to come for the middle of the month, as did Lady Richildis, but it seems that this babe means to arrive early. It is rare for a firstborn to be so determined to leave the womb."

"He has not his father's patience, then," Lady Ysmaine jested.

But Lord Gaston eyed Radegunde. "Should I send for the midwife in the village?"

"There is no need," Lady Ysmaine said. "I have Radegunde and you, and all will be well." She caught her breath and paled, clearly feeling another contraction. Radegunde was astonished and a little concerned that the child arrived with such haste.

Surely it would not be stillborn? This labor showed the vigor of a miscarriage and she feared the result.

But the babe had kicked only that afternoon.

There was naught to be done but to attend her lady herself. Mathilde could not be fetched in less than a day and a night, and Radegunde believed this babe would arrive—one way or the other—by the dawn. Indeed, it might arrive sooner than that.

Radegunde swiftly finished the plait of her lady's hair and bound the end. When Lady Ysmaine nodded that she was at ease, Radegunde left her side that the couple might confer. Still, she could hear their words.

Lord Gaston murmured to his wife. "It is Richard's doings that concern me," he confided.

"He has taken the cross. You told me this." Lady Ysmaine was very intent upon her husband's words.

"Before the Yule, at Tours, as soon as the tidings from

Outremer were widely known."

"So, he *will* depart on crusade."

"As will his father. You know that Henry took the cross in January at Gisors, when tidings of Jerusalem's surrender to Saladin were received."

"Aye, so he told us when he was here to grant Haynesdale to Bartholomew. What will happen to Aquitaine in Richard's absence?"

"I believe Queen Eleanor will rule it again, in lieu of her preferred son, although the king would prefer to grant it to their younger son, John. The Angevin will not relinquish Queen Eleanor's dowry readily, to be sure."

"Can Henry take it from one son and give it to another?"

"Not if Richard will not relinquish the holding. And truly, Henry's demand that he do as much has created a rift between them. Richard paid homage to Philip II of France before the Yule, as well, for while the divide between father and son is grown wider, it is not new. He and Philip will undoubtedly join forces against Henry."

Radegunde straightened at that.

"There will be war?" Lady Ysmaine asked, clearly hoping that would not be the case.

"There will, at the very least, be battles for supremacy, and for control of Anjou, Normandy, and Aquitaine."

"And you defend the Breton March," Lady Ysmaine said.

"Aye." Lord Gaston grimaced.

"Will we be attacked?"

Lord Gaston kissed his wife's hand. "Not if I can steer a course between these kings and their desires. This is the matter that concerns me most."

"If any man can do as much, Gaston, it will be you."

"I thank you, lady mine, but I have one concern."

"Will you ride to Outremer again, Gaston?"

"Nay, Ysmaine. Such journeys are behind me, but we may undertake a smaller journey." Lord Gaston turned to Radegunde, and she flushed to have been caught listening so openly. She curtseyed and would have apologized, but Lord Gaston made a gesture of impatience. "I would not speak in your presence, Radegunde, without the expectation that you would hear my words. I know full well that you will not repeat them."

"Thank you, my lord."

"What has Duncan told you of Killairic?"

"That it is fair, but not as fair as Mormaer, where he was born."

Lord Gaston smiled at this.

"That it lies upon the western coast of Scotland and is stoutly defended." Radegunde frowned, striving to recall more. "That Fergus and his father are men of good repute and that justice is maintained at Killairic. I have the impression of it being a fine and prosperous estate."

"And its enemies?"

"He told me of none, sir, although it seems all holdings have some opponents." Did Lord Gaston mean to ride to Scotland? Did he know more of the wedding plans of Fergus and Isobel?

And what of Duncan?

Lord Gaston looked thoughtful. "Indeed, though I do not believe it stands upon the March."

"Nay, my lord, nor do I." Radegunde took a breath and decided to ask what she desired most to know. "Lady Isobel, the betrothed of Lord Fergus, is from a neighboring family, but Duncan feared her affections might have changed while Lord Fergus was gone."

"He was right," Lord Gaston said flatly and her heart sank. "I had a missive from Fergus, advising me that there would be no nuptials celebrated at Killairic this spring. Lady Isobel wed another and already has borne her spouse a son."

Then they would not ride to Scotland and she would not see Duncan soon. Radegunde spun to hide her reaction and busied herself with folding her lady's chemise.

What if Duncan did not return? What if he could not? Radegunde had never wanted to consider the possibility of being without him.

"While he was so loyal to her!" Lady Ysmaine declared. "How outrageous! After he bought so many gifts for her? Never have I seen a man so smitten as he."

"Never?" Lord Gaston asked, clearly seeking her smile, and

Lady Ysmaine laughed.

"Seldom," she corrected, her eyes sparkling. "She is not worthy of him, to be sure!"

Lady Ysmaine gasped suddenly again, her grip tightening on Lord Gaston's hand. This contraction was longer and more vigorous, adding to Radegunde's concern for the babe's health.

She realized that Lord Gaston watched her closely and imagined that he saw her fears. She smiled for Lady Ysmaine, though, knowing that it could be fatal for the mother to lose hope. "Perhaps you will sleep better this night, my lady, with your labor behind you," she said cheerfully.

"God in Heaven, I did not know a child could come so quickly."

"Impatient to see the world, it is clear," Radegunde said briskly. "Fear not, for we are prepared." She called for more maids then, summoning both hot water and the birthing chair that had been prepared for her mistress.

"Would you rather I stayed or left?" Lord Gaston asked his wife.

Lady Ysmaine clutched his hand. "Stay, Gaston, for I will not fear my fate when you are here."

He kissed her hand again, then Radegunde gestured to both of them. "I would have you walk a little, my lady."

"Tell me more, Gaston," Lady Ysmaine entreated when she was on her feet. "You spoke of a journey. When and to where?"

But Lord Gaston had no chance to reply. Another contraction bore down upon the lady and she tipped her head back as she shook from head to toe. Her water broke and the dark fluid spread across the floor.

Lord Gaston lifted his gaze to meet Radegunde's and she forced a smile. "Where did this one come by such impatience?" she asked lightly, though she knew that Lord Gaston understood her concern well enough.

As Radegunde helped Lady Ysmaine to the birthing chair and looked between her thighs, she prayed that all would be well and the babe would be hale.

338

Torvean, south of Inverness, Scotland

There would be no Beltane fires on this night.

Indeed, it seemed to Duncan that there was little left to burn in the lands he remembered as verdant and lush with heather. The ground was scorched and blackened, the few trees lifeless, and he fancied he could still smell smoke in the air. On his ride north, he had heard of the devastation the previous summer, the pillaging and the slaughter, but naught could have given him sufficient warning for the sight.

This was his father's achievement: the land ravaged and barren; the people scattered and doubtless terrified. Scavengers dogged his steps, wolves so close behind that his stallion was disquieted. Dark shadows circled overhead, birds of prey awaiting their opportunity. Wolves howled at close proximity. Duncan guessed they were at least four. Caledon nickered and flicked his ears, more than glad to run a little faster.

The devastation made Duncan want to weep for all that had been lost.

The only good thing was that he had not brought Radegunde with him. She was safe, as no one could be in his homeland at this time. It was rife with rebels and outlaws, men who would sell their souls for a penny and were more than willing to take what was not their due.

Duncan might have despaired, if he had not such confidence in the merit of his countrymen. They had need of a leader upon whom they could rely. Perhaps the King of Scotland would provide that governor.

Fergus' father had been more than willing to release Duncan from his service, once his beloved son was safely returned home. The lady Isobel had not been at Killairic to meet her betrothed, and a shadow had touched the older man's brow at Fergus' question about her welfare. Duncan was not surprised that she had wed another, for he had long thought her fickle, but could not guess the fullness of any suspicions Fergus might have had. He might have lingered, but the younger man had insisted Duncan leave the hall, in search of his own fate, the better that he might keep his word to Radegunde.

One of them should be happy in love, Fergus had said.

There had been tidings at Killairic about Scotland and war, battles that had taken place since their departure for Outremer and boundaries that had shifted. Of greatest import to Duncan was the decisive battle in Galloway that had brought those lands beneath the hand of King William of Scotland. He was not surprised that own kin still battled for Moray. The assassin Murdoch had spoken of Adam's death, but Duncan had sought more detail.

In the fall of 1186, the earl of Atholl was said to have massacred a band of outlaws at Coupar Angus, not so far north of Perth and the Firth of Tay. Some sixty men had come raiding out of the north, led by one known as Adam, and finally taken refuge in a church. The earl of Atholl had not respected the law of sanctuary, probably because of the violence of their deeds, and had burned the church to the ground with the villains locked within it.

Had it been Duncan's older brother or another rebel? Duncan wished he could be certain. That the raid had been so far south indicated to Duncan that his father had not abandoned the notion of claiming the Scottish crown for his own—or for one of his sons.

But kingship should not be earned in violence and destruction. A crown won in such a way could not be held. Duncan had seen it time and again. His father desired power but not responsibility. His disregard for all the people whose homes had been destroyed and whose kin had been slaughtered filled Duncan with outrage.

He had ridden north with vigor, following rumor of his father toward Inverness, the ancient seat of the Picts and later the Mormaer. As soon as he passed Urquhart in the Great Glen, he saw the damage. North he rode, ever north, needing to know his father's location and intent, needing to find a haven for himself and Radegunde.

It might well be at Killairic.

Or Châmont-sur-Maine.

He wanted it to be here, in the land he loved best.

The light was fading when Duncan heard the predators draw nearer, emboldened by the darkness. Ahead was the silhouette of the keep on the hill at Inverness. The river Ness flowed beside him, better than any compass in guiding his path. Immediately before him was a new stone cairn, high and long.

He had intended to ride for the Precious Well, Fuaran Priseag, at Clacknaharry, for he felt in need of Saint Kessock's protection. A silver penny was a small price to pay to be guarded from curses and to dispel evil. Duncan was not superstitious, but he felt the presence of evil keenly in his homeland and anticipated a closer encounter with it when he found his father. But his progress had been slower than hoped. He would never reach that well and find shelter before night fell, not on this day.

The gates of the city of Inverness would be closed soon, if they were not so already. He touched his heels to Caledon's flanks, determined to make the walls. Truly, he was uncertain that he would find a welcome there, but there were few other choices.

Only a fool would sleep out of doors in this wasteland.

Caledon cantered alongside the cairn while Duncan surveyed it. There was something about it that captured his attention. Its size, perhaps. How newly built it was. Aye, there was not a blackened stone to be found in its construction. He had a sense that it marked a great battle, and that many warriors slept forever beneath it.

Then a wolf howled close behind him, so close that Caledon nearly reared.

Another wolf added its voice to the haunting cry, then another and another. Duncan could see their silhouettes, their heads down as they moved rapidly toward the ones that howled. It might have been a summons. The cry grew in volume, unceasing, making the hair stand on the back of his neck. Caledon fought the bit in his fear, but the wolves did not target Duncan.

Nay, they converged on a point far ahead and to the left. Duncan urged his steed onward, hoping he would see what drew them. A fallen animal? If so, they were best left to their meal, and their focus upon it might give him time to reach the gates.

"For the love of God!" a man roared in Norman French. "Scatter, you fiends!"

Duncan heard the man shout a battle cry. *Montjoie.* Aye, he had heard that invocation before.

The wolves barked in a frenzy and he knew the man ahead fought for his survival. Duncan did not care for the man's alliance. He could not stand by while one more warrior met his end unjustly.

Duncan turned Caledon hard and galloped in the direction of the man's voice. He soon spied the warrior, on foot and surrounded by snapping wolves, their eyes glowing in the darkness. The cornered knight wore a chain mail hauberk and heavy boots and gloves. His head was bare and his hair was dark. His tabard was mired, but Duncan could see the insignia of William II, the red lion rampart, on the front. As soon as the warrior swung his blade at one, that wolf jumped back, but the others moved closer.

They surrounded him and would wear him down, then fall upon him when he was too exhausted to defend himself.

He would be eaten alive.

It was no way for a man to die.

Duncan loaded the crossbow that Fergus' father had given to him, a most elegant gift that the older man believed would be of use to the warrior. And so, on this day, it would be. He shot one wolf in the back of the head and the creature dropped, to move no more.

Two more he killed with bolts to their chests, then the pack divided, half of them turning upon him with snarls. He spoke to Caledon with low insistence, hoping the steed's fear would not make him unpredictable.

Another wolf was felled with a bolt from the crossbow, then Duncan saw a shadow gaining behind him. He had not yet reloaded the bow, so pulled his knife. When the wolf leaped at Caledon's haunches and bared its teeth, Duncan buried the blade in the beast's throat.

The wolf fell to the ground, uttering one last growl before it was silenced forever.

The knight had rallied and killed two wolves with his sword. Another, perhaps the largest of the pack, made to attack the warrior from behind, but Duncan felled the beast with his crossbow. Several of the wolves backed away then, their manner appearing to be wary as they sidled away from the men.

The warrior dropped to sit on the ground, as if his legs would no longer support him. He held his blade aloft and breathed heavily as he watched Duncan's approach.

Duncan rode to the other warrior's side and immediately saw that his thigh was bleeding. The wound had been bound at some earlier point, but the bleeding had not stopped. The trail of fresh blood would have drawn the wolves.

"Out of the fat and into the fire," the man said in Norman French with a grimace, looking Duncan up and down, his gaze lingering on Duncan's plaid. He spat at the ground, then glared at Duncan, perhaps thinking he would not be understood.

Duncan dismounted. "You should ride," he said, replying in Norman French. "I am due for a walk."

The man was surprised, but not quick to accept Duncan's offer. "Because you would rather kill me yourself?" he asked with suspicion.

"Because we have a better chance of making the city gates that way."

"Forgive my suspicions. I have not seen much mercy from your kind."

"I am just returned from Outremer," Duncan said flatly. "And I have seen sufficient death for all the rest of my days and nights." The man did not look convinced, so Duncan retrieved his knife from the dead wolf, holding fast to Caledon's reins. The steed stamped, unsettled by the scent of blood, and Duncan led him quickly back to the knight.

The man still watched him. His face was pale, Duncan noted now. How much blood had he lost? How badly wounded was he? Why was he on the hills alone? His wariness, though, made Duncan certain that his questions would be unwelcome.

"And so I would ask you to choose. Will you accept my aid, or remain to die here this night?" Duncan asked. He gestured to the eyes glowing in the shadows, for the wolves had not retreated fully. "They will return to finish what they have begun. They do not forget."

"Aye. Wretched beasts. They seek only their own advantage."

The warrior's eyes narrowed. "Why were you in Outremer?"

"To serve a knight who joined the Templars." Duncan eyed the darkening sky and gestured to the saddle. "Will you ride or not? I bid you choose, for I do not mean to feed the wolves myself this night."

The man almost smiled. "Gruff and practical, effective in battle. I could use a man like you." He stood with an effort and hobbled to Caledon's side, stroking the horse before he reached for the saddle. Again, he granted Duncan an appraising look. "A fine destrier for one so humbly attired."

Duncan snapped the reins out of the man's hand. "There was a time when men in these parts shared their names readily and believed the best of those strangers they met, particularly those who had saved their lives."

"You have been away, to be sure," the man retorted. "There was also a time when Gaels did not slaughter Normans." He gestured to the cairn. "Three hundred warriors are there, but it was not enough to stem the hatred. Still they rise against us. I did not jest that you might have saved me to end my life yourself."

"And I do not jest that I have no such intention. I would not save a man to kill him with my own blade. Indeed, I would rather that I never again take the life of another."

"Why are you here?"

"I thought to come home, no more and no less."

"Have you a name?"

"I was called Duncan when I lived here." Duncan deliberately chose to confess no more.

His companion smiled then. "And I am Fitzpatrick, Captain of the Guard of the king's keep at Inverness."

Duncan lifted a brow. "Yet you have neither steed nor company."

The knight winced, then pulled himself into the saddle with an effort. "We rode out this morn to hunt the outlaws who have been harassing the city borders. They are the last of that rabble beneath the cairn. In the fight, my horse was injured and I was dismounted. I awakened alone, so they must have thought me dead."

Duncan could think of other possibilities, but he chose not to speak them aloud. He seized the reins of Caledon and began to walk briskly toward Inverness.

"It is quicker if you take that path to the right," Fitzpatrick informed him. "The gates are yet a goodly distance away but there are several houses on this route. They keep dogs and light fires to repel the wolves."

As if aware that they were being discussed, the wolves howled once more. Duncan looked back to see their shadowy shapes and their eyes drawing close once again. Would they devour their own kind? It would depend upon their hunger. They were bold to attack a man outright, to be sure, and he would wager that there was little for them to eat in such a devastated land.

Caledon nickered and tossed his head, impatient to continue. Duncan began to trot alongside the horse as he wished to reach sanctuary soon. The destrier was only too glad to match his pace.

They passed a cottage, just as Fitzpatrick had predicted, with a blazing fire before it and smoke rising from the roof. Duncan could see the bonfire before a second hut, not too far ahead. Were they Beltane fires after all? He thought not, for no one celebrated with dance and laughter. The fires burned while the people locked themselves away.

He hated that his homeland had become a place of fear.

By the time they passed the fourth cottage, Duncan could neither hear nor see the wolves. Caledon appeared to be less agitated, but Duncan knew that neither of them would rest easy before the gates of Inverness closed behind them.

Would he be admitted? Or turned aside? His companion's attitude did little to feed his expectations.

The gates rose before them, the light of their torches illuminating the road. "Who comes here?" cried a sentry, again speaking in Norman French. Duncan was well aware that his garb would earn him few friends in this place.

"And so I must vouch for you, Duncan," his companion said softly.

"Do you mean to do as much?" Duncan asked, noting that the crossbows were loaded and pointed at him.

"You have saved my life. What else could a man of honor do?"

Duncan turned to look at the knight, uncertain how to interpret his tone.

Fitzpatrick smiled thinly. "See that you do not betray my trust."

Duncan surveyed the wall, bristling with warriors, then looked back at his companion. "If you offer me sanctuary, I would advise you not to betray mine either," he said with quiet heat.

"Spoken like a man whose word is his bond," Fitzpatrick said. "Welcome to Inverness, Duncan." He raised his voice. "It is Fitzpatrick, Captain of the Guard, returned. I demand safe passage and shelter for this man, one Duncan, for he has saved my life."

To Duncan's relief, the crossbows were lowered and the gates were opened.

It was only as he passed beneath the shadow of the gates that he wondered if he was the one who leaped from the fat to the fire.

The babe was perfect.

Washed and swathed in soft cloth, the little girl kicked with as much force as she had within her mother's womb. She had an abundance of black hair, a legacy of her father, and surely was possessed of more determination than most babes. Radegunde cuddled her, imagining that she would show her force of will in more ways than the speed of her arrival.

Lady Ysmaine was clean and garbed in a fresh chemise, the bed linens changed and all set to rights in the solar. Radegunde passed the little girl into her father's embrace, liking how he smiled with pleasure at his daughter.

Her own mother had said that one could never anticipate a man's reaction to a daughter, but it was clear that Lord Gaston was delighted with his first child.

He sat on the side of the great bed where Lady Ysmaine reclined, and they both admired the marvel who had entered their lives with such gusto.

With her labor done for this night, Radegunde made to leave the solar. No doubt the babe would awaken early and Lady Ysmaine might sleep late. Until she found a wet nurse, Radegunde would take responsibility for most of the little one's care.

"You have not evaded the tale, Gaston," Lady Ysmaine said,

covering her mouth as she yawned. "Where would you journey, if not to Outremer?"

"Radegunde, I would ask you to remain for a moment," Lord Gaston said. "And close the portal, if you please."

"Aye, my lord." In truth, Radegunde wished to know this detail as well as her lady.

Lord Gaston gestured and Radegunde drew up a stool alongside the bed. The babe gurgled a little and seemed to drift off to sleep as her father rocked her.

"There is concern in Paris about the safety of a certain item we have defended," Lord Gaston said quietly. "Although it seemed wise to entrust it to Fergus at the Yule, I have been requested to see it hidden."

"Hidden?" Lady Ysmaine echoed. "Not secured in a treasury for worship?"

"It is of great value, and there is much doubt about the future. Richard's battles have left many uneasy about his plans, and it is clear that his father nears the end of his own life. I have heard rumors that Philip means to attack some of Henry's keeps on the border, while Henry is in England collecting tithes for the coming crusade. Richard will doubtless aid him in creating trouble. It is thus feared that any known safehold will be revealed in the turbulent times that many see ahead." He frowned. "I am instructed to secret it, with as few people knowing the truth as possible."

"But when and how will it be retrieved?" Lady Ysmaine asked.

"It may never be," her spouse replied. "It is seen to be preferable to hide it forever than for it to fall into the hands of those who would not revere it."

"But it is at Killairic," Lady Ysmaine said.

"That it is. And any number of records document the names of those who led our party from Jerusalem. It would be simple to seek the prize in the holding of myself, Wulfe, Fergus, or even Bartholomew."

"Then where shall it be safely secured?" Lady Ysmaine asked.

"I have an idea." Lord Gaston traced a map on the coverlet with a fingertip. "We will take a short journey this summer and leave Châmont-sur-Maine under the vigilant care of your father. We shall visit Fergus and meet his father. Then we shall ride east and south, to Northumberland, that we might see the holding Bartholomew has claimed." He slanted a glance at Radegunde. "And of course, we shall take Radegunde with us."

"Northumberland is on the Scottish border," Lady Ysmaine said.

Lord Gaston smiled. "Indeed. Unless I miss the guess, the name of one warrior in our party was not noted by many, and truly, there is someone in our household most desirous of seeing him again."

Radegunde gasped with delight that Lord Gaston should accommodate her thus. "But I do not know where Duncan is."

"Nor do I, but I am certain he can be found," Lord Gaston said. "Indeed, I will ensure that he is, for since he has left you with child, it is only honorable that he wed you in truth before a priest." He kissed Lady Ysmaine's hand. "My lady and I will argue noisily about her maid's state, and I will vow to ensure that the man responsible treat her with honor. We shall then sail to Inverness to begin our hunt for the culprit."

Radegunde clasped her hands together with delight.

Lady Ysmaine frowned, looking between her husband and her maid. "But Radegunde is not with child."

"And who knows of that but you?" Lord Gaston asked. "Nay, I think Radegunde must be with child, as you were, my lady, at the Saint Bernard Pass."

"Oh!" the two women declared in unison, understanding his scheme.

"Which means, since you must have conceived in December, that we shall ride north in August, when you are so ripe that your state cannot be denied. At Killairic, your burden may become a little heavier."

"You must begin to round," Lady Ysmaine said and Radegunde nodded.

She turned to Lord Gaston. "You would entrust Duncan with the prize?"

"He carried it most of the way from Outremer. I know he will defend it with all his power."

"But," Radegunde protested. "If I remain with him, it will become evident that there is no child. I cannot remain pregnant forever."

Lord Gaston smiled. "Of course not." He rocked his daughter, waiting for the women to discern his ploy. "I had the idea this very night, when I saw how much you feared for my daughter's survival," he added, giving them a hint.

"I will lose the babe," Radegunde whispered.

"No doubt from the strain of the journey," Lady Ysmaine added.

"And it will be buried in a churchyard with a stone to mark the spot," Radegunde concluded.

"Hidden in plain sight," Ysmaine agreed, then cast a glance at Radegunde. "Which means you will need the goodwill of a priest. I would think that you and Duncan will have to exchange nuptial vows after all."

"I would be glad to do as much," Radegunde said.

"And if Duncan has won a home for his bride, I do not doubt that he would agree," Lord Gaston said.

"If not, I shall have much to say of it, to be sure." Lady Ysmaine smiled. "And now that Marie has faced the king's justice, we can leave Châmont-sur-Maine under my father's trusteeship without concern." She reached to kiss her spouse on the cheek. "Your scheme is brilliant, Gaston!"

He smiled, well pleased with the reception to his plan. "And so we have a plan, as well as a maiden in need of a name." He eyed his sleeping daughter and then his wife. "I think there can be only one choice, lady mine."

Lady Ysmaine smiled up at him, then caressed her daughter's cheek. "Welcome, Euphemia," she whispered and the babe cooed happily.

Radegunde smiled, for truly, there could not have been a better choice.

And she was going to Scotland!

Soon, she and Duncan would be together again.

ॐ

Duncan had anticipated a challenge, and he did not have to wait long for it. He was brushing down Caledon in the last stall of the stables, well aware that the knights and squires regarded him with suspicion.

He felt the presence of the man at the end of the stall before he heard his words. "Is this a ploy to gain admission to the keep?" a man demanded in Norman French, his voice a low growl. "If so, it is a poorly contrived one. Had you garbed yourself like one of us, your ruse might not have been so readily discerned."

"It is no ruse," Duncan replied calmly. He turned to face the other man. That knight was almost of an age with Duncan, his face lined and his eyes narrowed with suspicion. "I saw a man in peril and I aided him. Surely that has some merit."

The knight snorted, his eyes bright. "You have a fine horse and speak French well. How can you look like the outlaws who assault our borders yet speak like us?"

"Perhaps I would defy your expectation in other ways, as well."

"Aye, that is the root of my concern." The knight stepped into the stall. "Whose steed did you steal?"

"Caledon has been with me all the way to Outremer and back."

"So you say. What is your objective in coming to Inverness?"

"On this night, to find shelter that the wolves might not attack my destrier or myself."

"And beyond that?"

"I seek my family. I have been abroad many years."

"Wife? Child?"

"Father. Brother."

The knight's jaw set. "There are hundreds of your ilk beneath that cairn at Torvean, as well as too many of my own men. The river Ness ran red with blood for days." His tone was bitter. "My own father, governor of Inverness, rode out against Donald MacWilliam, who led this rabble, and slaughtered him before he was killed himself."

Duncan stiffened, though truly he could not mourn his father's loss. Of course, the knight would not use the Gaelic version of his father's name. "What of Donald's son, Adam?" he asked, curious whether this man could confirm Murdoch's tale that Adam was dead.

"Dead at Coupar Angus, declined sanctuary for his crimes and slaughtered in a church, with all his followers."

So, it *had* been Adam.

They were both dead.

Duncan felt a surge of relief, then recalled his younger brother.

The knight's gaze brightened when Duncan did not speak. "Father. Brother." he mused, and Duncan knew he understood. "You resemble him. I see it in your profile." He spat in the straw. "I had a good look at your father's head before sending it to King William's court. Should you wish to see it, I suggest you ride back to Edinburgh." He turned then to walk away. "You will leave this keep in the morning."

Duncan had to ask. "What of Guthred?"

The knight looked back. "There is another son?"

"Three sons," Duncan supplied. "The eldest dead at Coupar Angus, as you say. The middle son abroad for many years, estranged from his father."

"And now returned," supplied the knight.

"The youngest groomed by his father to continue the battle to regain the crown."

The knight frowned in displeasure.

"Where is the brooch?" Duncan asked.

The knight eyed him with uncertainty. "What brooch?"

"The penannular brooch, one of three given to the daughters of Malcolm II, King of Scotland, when he wedded them to neighboring barons. Possession of the pin marks the son of that line with a legitimate claim to the Scottish throne."

The knight's attention sharpened.

Duncan continued. "The gold and garnet one was granted to the daughter who wed into the family of the King of the Isles. Malcolm III was crowned with that pin upon his cloak."

The knight took a step closer, his interest clear.

Duncan continued. "The gold and amber one was granted to the daughter who wed the Earl of Orkney, and was surrendered to King David of Scotland by King Eystein of Norway some thirty years ago."

The knight folded his arms across his chest. "And the third?"

"The gold and amethyst brooch was granted to the daughter who wed into the house of Mormaer."

"The stewards of Moray."

"My father wore that brooch when last I saw him. Was it not upon his cloak?"

The knight shook his head. "It was not at Coupar Angus either."

"Then my brother Guthred claimed it, to be sure," Duncan said returning to the brushing of his steed.

"They follow whosoever wears the pin?"

"Of course, for that is the man with the claim to the throne through the Mormaer line."

"Is this why you came? To claim the pin yourself?"

"Nay. I came because my father sent a man to kill me and I would challenge him over that choice."

"You are too late."

"So it seems."

"And now?"

"And now, I have a choice. Or I might have a choice, if you would deem it fitting. Understand that the Scotsmen who plague your northern borders will follow the warrior who wears that pin, and that my younger brother has sipped from my father's cup of bitterness all his life."

"But not you?"

Duncan smiled and shook his head. "Not me. I have seen enough bloodshed and devastation to sate me. I have spent the last years in Outremer."

"Is it true that Jerusalem has fallen?"

Duncan nodded. "The kings will ride to crusade."

"And you?"

"I would live in peace. I would find a home for my lady, swear fealty to a man of honor I might serve well, and die an old man before my own hearth."

The knight took a step closer, his eyes bright. "If you would hunt your brother Guthred and claim that amethyst and gold pin, I would grant you that, and more." He switched to Gaelic.

"Fitzpatrick said you were named Duncan, which by this tale would make you Donnchada meic Domnall meic Uilliem."

Duncan straightened, for he had not heard his name in Gael for a long while. "It would indeed," he acknowledged and his throat was tight.

"And I am Alexander Comyn, son of the Governor of Inverness and now governor in my own right." He offered his hand. "Reclaim the pin and take leadership of your kin, pledge fealty to King William and I shall see you in command of a holding upon the March." He smiled slightly. "I would have peace, Donnchada meic Domnall meic Uilliem."

"As would I," Duncan agreed and shook hands with Alexander. He would not have fought to possess the birthright of his lineage, but he would fight for peace, for prosperity, and for a sanctuary for Radegunde.

Claire Delacroix

FRIDAY, AUGUST 13, 1188

*Feast Day of Saint Hippolytus
and Saint Radegund*

Claire Delacroix

Greetings to you, Bartholomew, Baron of Haynesdale, and also to your lady wife, Anna—

I trust that all is well in your abode and that the keep has been rebuilt to your satisfaction.

Though it has been long since we have spoken or corresponded, I hope that I may ask of you a favor. I have ridden south this month to swear my fealty to King William of Scotland at his court in Edinburgh, and here have found a knight bound to London to carry my missive to you. The turmoil in the north settles, and I am glad to confess that I have contributed to that happy state. I have claimed my father's legacy from my brother Guthred, but entered an alliance with the crown rather than rising in rebellion against it. It is time for the Mormaer to join the kingdom and I am glad to lead my people in this endeavor.

As reward for my service and my fealty, the king has seen fit to grant me a holding in the Great Glen, the better that I might aid in the defense of the northern borders of his domain. I dare not leave it undefended, for it is key to our success that I claim Morcreig and defend it soon. Aye, I am now Laird of Morcreig and hold that keep as my own.

The sole disappointment is that this assignment from the king means that I cannot journey to Châmont-sur-Maine before the year and a day of my handfast to Radegunde comes to its end. This vexes me beyond all, for she is—I believe you know—the blood of my heart and the sole reason I have undertaken these responsibilities. I would build a home for her, but it will take a little longer to see it secured.

I hope that you correspond with Lord Gaston, or will see fit to do so in the near future. If so, I would ask your assistance in sending word to Radegunde. I will ride south by the Yule to take her hand in mine forever and would ask her to exchange our vows this time before a priest, as Lady Ysmaine doubtless would find acceptable.

My gratitude to you in anticipation of this courtesy.
Until we meet again,

Duncan MacDonald
Also known as Donnchada meic Domnall meic Uilliem
Laird of Morcreig

TUESDAY, SEPTEMBER 6, 1188

*Feast Day of Saint Bega
and Saint Augustine*

Claire Delacroix

CHAPTER TWENTY-FOUR

weight hung upon Duncan's heart.

It was a year and a day since Radegunde, his merry Radegunde, had put her hands within his and pledged to be his own.

And yet, they were apart.

On this day above all others, Duncan would have been with her, but he was not. He hoped that Bartholomew had been able to send word of his obligations to Lord Gaston, and hoped yet more that Radegunde understood the magnitude of his responsibilities.

Although, such was his yearning for her company that he would welcome a scolding as well as a kiss. She had to be by his side to deliver either, after all.

Morcreig had been an outpost of the Mormaer for centuries, and Duncan was honored to command the keep. It had been razed to the ground in the recent turmoil, but the foundation stones were yet in place. More rocks had been brought from Inverness once the road had been secured and the main tower had been half-rebuilt by the time Duncan returned from Edinburgh. He was awed by what his ally Alexander could achieve when he put resources behind a task, and the Governor of Inverness was resolute that this frontier should be secured.

The wolves had retreated into the forests to the north, as had those few rebels who held Guthred's memory dear. They were men of little merit in Duncan's view, worse than mercenaries. They battled for the joy of violence and not out of any desire to see a reward. No matter where they landed, they would make trouble, but he had forced them to depart the area. He had led men on routing expeditions far to the north and west and believed such men to have fled to Ireland.

Those in favor of peace had flocked to Duncan's banner, and a village had grown quickly around the stone tower. Duncan had himself aided in the building of walls and fences, in the thatching of roofs and the delineation of fields. Alexander had sent gifts of chickens and goats from Inverness and it seemed that each day brought more people to Duncan's gates.

They were his people, the ones he remembered so well, the hardy folk with loyal hearts and strong hands, unafraid to labor to build their desire. He had brought scribes from the royal court to aid in the administration of the king's justice, and he was glad he had watched Gaston so often in such matters of negotiation. Already he had secured alliances with three chieftains whose people lived within proximity and had sent word to the king of these successes.

A priest had accompanied him from Edinburgh as well and word had spread of that. More than one family came to Duncan's gates in search of the sacraments. The chapel was small and humble, but the priest was vigilant in tending his flock. There were few tithes as yet, but the next year would be more affluent after crops were planted and harvested.

Duncan supervised all and was glad of his progress. He knew that Radegunde's skills would be much welcomed, for there was no wise woman. She would be busy and purposeful, a perfect companion to secure their future. He yearned to see her again, to tell her all that had occurred, to show her their home. Alexander had vowed to send a man to govern in Duncan's absence by October, lest all their gains should be lost while he fetched his lady.

Duncan would not be surprised if Guthred took advantage of

his absence to set all awry again. His younger brother had surrendered the pin and sworn that he would follow Duncan, then had fled in the night, doubtless to a haven in Ireland. In truth, Duncan had anticipated his trick and let him do it, for he had no desire to kill his own kin.

Even though the gold and amethyst brooch adorned his own cloak, his brother might well return to challenge him. Duncan did not wish to betray the trust of those who had come to Morcreig for protection. He built a fortress to keep them safe.

The day of the anniversary of his handfast with Radegunde was fine, a crisp wind from the west heralding the approach of winter. Yet again, Duncan wished for Alexander's man to arrive soon, for he was impatient to ride south to France and collect his beloved.

Had Radegunde waited for him? Aye, he knew she would keep her vow, unless compelled to do otherwise. Would Lady Ysmaine compel her to wed another once this day was passed?

It was a troubling thought. Duncan hoped his missive had reached Gaston and hated that there was little more he could do. He was impatient as seldom he was.

He was descending to the court when a cry came from the summit of the tower. "A party arrives from the north!" called the sentry.

Duncan climbed the tower to see for himself, shading his eyes against the light. He was not expecting Alexander Comyn and feared that some unwelcome tidings sent that man to his gates.

"A fair company, sir," the sentry informed him.

Even at this distance, Duncan could see the lead horses were destriers. It was impossible to mistake their size and breadth. The first looked to be Alexander's fine chestnut destrier, but the dapple destrier galloping alongside surprised Duncan. There were few destriers of such a hue locally.

Was it a woman riding on the palfrey alongside them both?

Surely it was not Lord Gaston and Lady Ysmaine who rode with Alexander?

Duncan dared to hope. Indeed, he clutched the parapet, trying to discern more details. The party carried no banners and he wondered that Gaston abandoned his colors.

If it was Lord Gaston.

He spied two more palfreys, both good animals, one on either side of the lead trio. Was the young man with dark hair Radegunde's brother Michel? Did he dare to hope that the dark-haired woman was Radegunde herself?

The man who had to be Alexander gestured and the other men in the party fanned out, forming a protective circle around the company.

Duncan could not tear his gaze away from the dark-haired woman. His heart thundered. Could his wish come true this day? He could not imagine why Lord Gaston would come to Scotland, but the more he looked, the more convinced he became that the dapple destrier was as fine a steed as Fantôme.

Radegunde had come!

And Duncan knew what must be done.

"A wedding!" he cried to the men in the bailey below. "Summon the priest and ring the bell! On this day, we shall have a wedding and a feast. Morcreig will have a lady!"

Duncan glimpsed the sentry's astonished expression, then leaped down the stairs, calling for arrangements even as he hastened to the gates.

His Radegunde had come!

Radegunde had had adventure aplenty this summer.

Their party had ridden to La Rochelle and sailed to England, to Plymouth and then Liverpool, then onward to Annan. From there, they had ridden north to Fergus' abode. Radegunde had immediately become enamored of Duncan's homeland with its wild beauty. It was easy to imagine him walking these hills.

She had been most glad to see Leila looking so well. Lord Fergus, it seemed, was more than happy to surrender the reliquary to Lord Gaston's custody again.

Bartholomew and his wife Anna had met them at Killairic, and escorted them to his holding of Haynesdale. Radegunde liked Anna as much as she had when they had met in the winter, for Anna teased Bartholomew and was most audacious. She also could see that being Baron of Haynesdale suited Bartholomew well. He was most proud to show the holding to Lord Gaston, who made no effort to hide how impressed he was with his former squire's accomplishments.

Lady Ysmaine and Lord Gaston had argued mightily there, as planned, and their party had left Haynesdale with Lord Gaston evidently furious and bent on seeing justice done.

They had journeyed north and east from there to Newcastle, where Lord Gaston had found passage for them on a ship bound to Inverness. He had kept their party small, so that they might not draw notice, and even though both Bartholomew and Fergus had offered to aid in this completion of the quest, Lord Gaston had refused. They were but four: Lady Ysmaine and Lord Gaston, Radegunde, and her brother Michel, who served Lord Gaston as squire on this journey.

This strategy was to ensure that all in the party could be trusted, but Radegunde appreciated Lord Gaston's concern for her mother's peace of mind. With Michel to provide a testimony of how and where Radegunde would be settled, Mathilde would be more at ease. She and Radegunde had spent considerable time together before Radegunde's departure, for it was unclear when their paths would cross again.

The North Sea had been cold and gray, the wind making Radegunde appreciate that the land Duncan loved was both fierce and beautiful. Radegunde was well aware that many cast a disapproving glance at the party, for they thought little good of a noble couple who compelled a maid to journey so far when she was ripe with child—at least until Lord Gaston explained that he would ensure the man responsible treated her with honor.

The reliquary was heavy and oft took the chill of the wind, so that Radegunde was more than prepared to be rid of its burden.

She supposed they had a fifth member to their company, the saint herself, and perhaps that was why winds were in their favor, the weather was comparatively fair, and they suffered no setbacks on their journey.

The Governor of Inverness, one Alexander Comyn and a most handsome knight, made them most welcome upon their arrival at his keep. He already knew Radegunde's name, and had many tales of Duncan's valor to share at the board, which warmed her heart. His admiration of Duncan knew no bounds and she was glad that Duncan had found such an excellent alliance.

She smiled to hear that Duncan wore the gold and amethyst pin and had made alliances to defend the future. He had assumed his birthright to ensure peace, as only he could do.

This was the measure of the man she loved.

The day of their departure from Inverness dawned crisp and clear. The sky was a vivid blue and the wind put a vigor in one's step. They rode out without banners or insignia, a company of warriors guarding their flanks.

The governor escorted their party to Morcreig himself, explaining much about the land to Lord Gaston as they rode. Radegunde knew that Michel listened avidly, the better to share the details with their parents upon his return.

The Great Glen was astonishingly beautiful. Even from Duncan's descriptions, Radegunde had never imagined a place could be so lovely. There was something about the sweep of the land, the emptiness of it, the stone and greenery and the endless sky, that made her heart sing. The tales she had heard by the hearth at Inverness made her fall in love with Duncan's home, for they had a similar richness to the tales she knew from her own home. She wanted to speak the tongue of the Gaels, for she imagined that would only enrich her understanding and her admiration.

They would make a home together at Morcreig.

As they rode ever closer to the stone tower that perched in the midst of the massive valley, Radegunde's heart began to race.

She scarce took note of the long glittering lake alongside the keep, though Lord Gaston admired how the tower perched on a promontory.

"From there, the entire valley can be observed," he noted with satisfaction. "It is a most strategic site." He pointed to the lake. "No matter how it is besieged, there will be water for the occupants." He gestured to the land to the west, even as the governor directed his men to ride out and ensure that all was well. "And I would wager that he means to see much of this tilled. This will be a prosperous holding under Duncan's management, to be sure."

"I am glad to see it," Lady Ysmaine said, sparing Radegunde a smile. "For your father's title means that you should wed a man of some affluence. I am glad that Duncan gained this holding, for now I can endorse the match."

"And you would not endorse a match that makes Radegunde happy?" Lord Gaston teased.

"You know that alliance is of greater import in a match than love," Lady Ysmaine said lightly. "And our match is the proof that love will take root in fertile ground."

"As Radegunde's is proof that the order may be reversed," Lord Gaston replied mildly. He winked at Radegunde. "I have a few years to convince my lady of the merit of such thinking before Euphemia takes a husband."

Radegunde smiled. Already that daughter had proven that she had a will of iron and a strong notion of her own desires. The babe remained with Lady Richildis while they undertook this journey, and Radegunde knew it was a measure of Lady Ysmaine's regard for her that she had been parted from her first child for this interval.

Aye, Lady Ysmaine would see for herself that Radegunde's future would be happy.

Radegunde surveyed the tower, knowing that several men stood at its summit, watching their party approach. Would Duncan welcome her? She was sure of it, but proximity made her fear that something might have changed.

Michel reached over and squeezed her hand, as if he guessed her thoughts. "It suits you, this place," he said beneath his breath. "Both unpredictable and beautiful. No wonder Duncan is so smitten with you." She smiled at her brother, for his thoughts had taken a romantic turn.

"You need not fear, Radegunde," Lady Ysmaine advised her quietly. "If matters have changed and you do not wish to remain, you have only to confide as much in me and we shall escort you back to Châmont-sur-Maine."

"Aye, my lady."

"Do not speak such nonsense, Ysmaine," Lord Gaston chided.

Claire Delacroix

"I never met a man so steady and loyal as Duncan."

"I would witness her happiness myself to be certain of it," Lady Ysmaine protested. "Radegunde and I have endured much together. I could not bear it if she were not as happily wed as I am."

The pair clasped hands for a moment, then, but Radegunde watched the gates ahead. They opened as their party drew near and a man in plaid strode through them, standing in the midst of the road with his hands on his hips. His stance was so familiar—never mind his fine legs—that Radegunde gave a cry of delight.

The Governor of Inverness grinned. "We bring you a guest who I think will be most welcome, Duncan," he shouted.

"Duncan!" Radegunde cried. The sunlight glimmered upon his cloak, illuminating the brooch of gold and amethyst that signified his rank and birthright.

"Blood of my heart!" Duncan roared with such undisguised pleasure that Michel grinned. "I should have known that you would contrive a way for us to renew our vows this day!"

He strode to her palfrey even as the bell of a chapel began to ring most merrily.

"Never was there a woman more enterprising than my own lady," Duncan told the governor, even as he laid his hand upon Radegunde's knee. "And now I have a home to offer that is worthy of her." His eyes fairly glowed as he looked up at her and Radegunde thought her heart might burst with joy. She blinked back tears as he reached to aid her from the saddle, his strong hands locking around her waist, and she saw the braid of her hair yet bound to his wrist.

She touched it with her fingertips and he smiled at her.

"Aye, and she arrives by your side in the nick of time," the governor teased, indicating Radegunde's belly. "Or was that your scheme to ensure she thought only of wedding you?"

Duncan's gaze flicked downward then back to her eyes, a question in his own.

Of course, he knew that it could not be his child.

But he did not spurn her or chastise her. Nay, not Duncan. He awaited her explanation, trusting her.

368

Loving her.

Radegunde smiled, well aware of those who listened and watched. "Just as Lady Ysmaine at the Saint Bernard Pass," she said lightly. "I fear it has become a hazard of this company."

"And a most welcome one indeed." Duncan laughed and lifted her down, then kissed her soundly. "Then you are come in good time," he declared. The way he took her elbow might have been in keeping with the ruse, but the warmth of his welcome was utterly sincere. "Was the journey too much for you?"

"Of course not. Not with such reward as seeing you."

"Blood of my heart," he murmured, his voice husky. They kissed again, and as always, his kiss sent sweet heat through her veins.

When Duncan lifted his head, Radegunde leaned against his chest, more than content. She laid her hand over the thunder of his heart, so glad to be with him again. "It is so beautiful," she whispered. "Even your descriptions did not do it justice. Will you teach me Gaelic?"

"Of course!" Duncan held her close as a bell began to ring.

"You have a chapel?" Lady Ysmaine asked.

"And a priest, more than prepared to witness the exchange of our vows." Duncan grinned down at Radegunde. "Shall we go to the chapel first, then celebrate our reunion at the board?" he asked, taking a step back. His hands locked around her own. There was such resolve in his gaze, that Radegunde knew herself to be the most fortunate woman in all the world. "I would pledge to you before a priest, Radegunde, for now I have more to offer my lady wife."

"Aye, for I love you, Duncan."

"And I love you, my Radegunde." He smiled. "A year and a day is not sufficient to be sworn to each other. I would pledge to you for all the days and nights of my life."

She smiled at him, "Aye, Duncan. Let our adventure begin." She stretched to her toes and kissed him soundly, smiling as the surrounding company erupted in cheers.

It was here that Saint Euphemia would be secured, and Radegunde had no doubt that lady would bring good fortune to them for all time.

AUTHOR'S NOTE

lthough many of the events in this series and this book did actually occur, I did take one liberty with Scottish history in Duncan's story. Although it is true that Malcolm II had three daughters and married them strategically, much as described here by Duncan, he did not create three pins to give to those daughters. The brooches are entirely my invention. The inspiration for them was the Huntingdon brooch, a penannular brooch which you can see on the Pinterest page for **The Crusader's Handfast**.

Donald MacWilliam was an historical figure who led rebellions by the Mormaer and was descended from one of Malcolm II's daughters. The historical Donald had two sons, Adam and Guthred, both of whom participated in his efforts to claim the Scottish crown. I gave Donald a third son, a middle son named Duncan, who is entirely fictional. Donald and Adam died as described in this book, while Guthred retreated to Ireland after his father's death. He led an unsuccessful uprising in 1204 and died then, which brought the MacWilliam line of the Mormaer to an end.

Some of you may have thought the name Mac Bethad sounded familiar and you'd be right—Shakespeare's play *Macbeth* uses some of the details of Mac Bethad's challenge to Malcolm II's son King Duncan, but there are many discrepancies between the play and the historical record.

ABOUT THE AUTHOR

Bestselling and award-winning author Deborah Cooke has published over fifty novels and novellas, including historical romances, fantasy romances, fantasy novels with romantic elements, paranormal romances, contemporary romances, urban fantasy romances, time travel romances and paranormal young adult novels. She writes as herself, Deborah Cooke, as Claire Delacroix, and has written as Claire Cross. Her Claire Delacroix medieval romance, *The Beauty*, was her first book to land on the New York Times List of Bestselling Books.

Deborah was the writer-in-residence at the Toronto Public Library in 2009, the first time TPL hosted a residency focused on the romance genre, and she was honored to receive the Romance Writers of America PRO Mentor of the Year Award in 2012. She's a member of Romance Writers of America, and is on the RWA Honor Roll. She lives in Canada with her family.

To learn more about Deborah's books, please visit her websites at:
http://deborahcooke.com
http://www.delacroix.net

Lightning Source UK Ltd.
Milton Keynes UK
UKHW011824200820
368549UK00003B/431/J